Broken Chains
by
Emiliya Ahmadova

'Broken Chains by Emiliya Ahmadova is a touching story that will appeal to a wide audience because of the sensitive, not-so-often discussed questions it raises. In the heart of this story is the important question: What does it take to live with a deep sense of inner freedom? The author opens her narrative with a fortuitous encounter between the parents of the protagonist and moves on to show how this encounter leads to a brief affair that culminates in an unwanted pregnancy. Esmira, the mother of the protagonist, raises her daughter alone, under difficult conditions. Now an adult, Silvana has to face the challenges of growing up and the horrors of abusive relationships. How she deals with her abusive Christian partner is what will blow readers' minds. This is a page-turning tale of one woman's struggle to avoid the same fate that befell her mother, a story of suffering, inhumanity, and redemption.

Silvana is a compelling and well-developed character who will not only interest readers but will be a powerful example of a warrior for freedom and human rights.'

Reviewed By Divine Zape for Readers' Favorite (5 stars)

'A few month ago I have translated Broken Chains into the Russian language. I must say Broken Chains is a fascinating novel, the primary merits, and strengths of Broken Chains are its sincerity and originality. The author is a woman who was raised in a Muslim multinational setting, thereby becoming acquainted with the customs, traditions, peculiarities of life in different countries and even different continents. In addition, she has had the unique opportunity to communicate with a wide spectrum of people from varying cultural backgrounds and outlooks on life. All this has culminated in her relating in fictional form (throughout riveting pages) her multifaceted life experiences and a wealth of knowledge.

In her novel the story line seems so natural, including engaging dialogue. Ahmadova describes her characters so vividly and clearly that readers will not view them as uniform and unipolar. Each elicits sympathy or antipathy in a natural manner. Before encountering the protagonist, readers will learn the dramatic story of her mother's life, followed by that of her grandmother. Such an opening permits readers not only to trace the relationships among generations but also to assess the influence of parental conduct on the lives of the descendants.

Nonetheless, the chain of "hereditary damage" is derailed by the protagonist's faith and hope in God in reaching out for salvation. The main character, Silvana, finds inner strength to change the trajectory of her life. In turn, transforms the lives of many around her suffering alone and in silence, also feeling shackled, chained down by paralyzing fear and hopeless despair enveloping their human condition. In this way, Silvana becomes a role model for all of them, living proof that fundamental human happiness is in their own hands and can make all the difference, together with not only hard work and unquestionable faith in God but also an insatiable desire to make a difference on this earth.'

Ekaterina Staub

'Broken Chains introduces three generations of women trapped in an abusive reactionary lifestyle. The author's ability to reach out to her readers through her main character, 'Silvana', a heroine in many cases, is not only intuitive and empathetic but also very effective.

As you read each word, you will be drawn deeper into Silvana's life. You will take on a deep sense of her fears and loneliness of the many abusive generational relationships she faces to the point that they will become your own. You will feel Silvana's confusion as she struggles with her religious beliefs, seeking strength, guidance that will free her from a roller-coaster of abusive relationships. Her innate behavior to protect her children which provides her with an inner strength to break free from the chains of abuse are commendable and heroic, hence the word 'Heroine', being used earlier in this review.

Silvana's story is truly a voice of strength, promise and hope that a victim can walk away and move past a life of abuse. Broken Chains is a compelling and heartfelt story, written with not only the author's heart and soul but also her need to educate others who may be victims of abuse. In itself, this book can be used as a very resourceful hindsight for all victims of abuse.

The initial focus throughout this book indirectly deals with the dynamics and scars of abuse. This story sends several very strong and encouraging messages to victims of abuse and to those who are amidst its struggles.

1. It is NOT your fault,
2. Abuse of any form is unacceptable,
3. You have the right to walk away,
4. You can forgive in order to move forward.

Womensselfesteem.com: highly recommends Broken Chains for all victims of abuse. As much as it is an emotional and horrific journey, reading Broken Chains most definitely promises positive messages of hope and freedom from abuse. It is one of the most motivational stories I have read to date.'

Dorothyl Lafrinere

'Broken Chains is another moving story pointing out domestic violence. Some people may say these are just common stories. Are they? I don't think so. The fact that too many women live a life of oppression, injustice, and abuse, be it verbal or physical, doesn't mean these life-stories are "ordinary". It should not be considered normal when people, especially women, are treated like slaves, trash, and "second class humans"

Broken Chains is an awesome book. I love it. The plot is rich, unique and really gripping. I couldn't put it down until I finished reading the last chapters at 5 o'clock in the morning. Emiliya Ahmadova writes in her very own fascinating style. Authentic and honest. It's a very touching story of 5 generations of Azeri women. Mariya, Sadaget, Esmira, Silvana and Silvana's daughters. Each of them tries to prepare the next generation for a better life. In vain? Is there a way to escape fate and traditions, break up with unwritten rules and change the future for good?

The author shaped colorful and very believable and likable characters. These women have a lot in common and are so different at the same time. The story seems very real. Indeed it is, because, unfortunately always today, myriads of women deal every day with domestic abuse.

There are never too many stories narrated, too many books written, too many songs sung or too many people raising their voices against abuse, violence, and humiliation. Whoever argue that this is only one more ordinary story never lived it and should hold his tongue. For the rest of us, this book is very inspiring and full of lessons and hope. Hope for a better life for all of us. For a new world, where justice and human rights reign instead of hate and indignity.

This book will find its way to many readers across the world. It is beautifully written, stirring, and full of suspense. The story is filled with drama but also a lot of hope for a better future. I truly want to believe it. Congratulations to Emiliya Ahmadova who created this inspiring story with passion, love, and hard work. Women, get the words out! Each story is important and helps to raise awareness, and finally, shape a new future for all of us.'

Author Christiane Agricola

Broken Chains falls into the genre of women's fiction, and the characters are fictional. Any similarity of the characters to living or dead persons is purely coincidental. Nonetheless, the problems treated in the novel not only plague every part of the world, but have been endured by men and women alike, and are not isolated to any single person.

Scriptures quoted from King James Bible. The NKJV was commissioned in 1975 by Thomas Nelson Publishers.

Copyright ©2016 Emiliya Ahmadova
Cover Copyright © Emiliya Ahmadova
Library of Congress Control Number: 2017902593
Editors: Kathy Ree, Brian Harvey
ISBN-10: 0998686700
ISBN-13: 978-0998686707
Website: www.emiliyaahmadova.com
Printed in U.S.A

Dedication

My novel entitled Broken Chains, is dedicated to every soul who has experienced hardship, abuse, fear, manipulation, exploitation, and pain, and who have cried in silence for rescue yet no one seems to hear. Today I am here to let you know that your voice has been heard. It is time to raise your voices against abuse and simply say, "No!" and "Stop!" Close the old chapter of your life and open a new one, where you can heal, discover happiness, and be at peace surrounded by God's grace and love. My message for all abuse victims is direct. "Get the hell out of the source of your abuse and stand up for your rights!" My protagonist, Silvana, was able to take this step. Now it is your turn, my readers. You can do it!

Table Of Contents

Chapter 1: Esmira Meets Samed....................................1

Chapter 2: Unexpected Pregnancy 24

Chapter 3: The Shocking Discovery............................52

Chapter 4: Silvana Comes Into The Cruel World 69

Chapter 5: Jailed.. 84

Chapter 6: School Life.. 98

Chapter 7: Relocation To A New Apartment 110

Chapter 8: Existence Led By Fear Of Gossip............... 123

Chapter 9: Silvana Meets An Englishman....................141

Chapter 10: The Wedding Day 163

Chapter 11: Dirty Secrets Surfaced 185

Chapter 12: Cry Of The Soul 194

Chapter 13: Unexpected Changes 224

Chapter 14: Enduring Abuse 257

Chapter 15: Broken Chains.......................................277

Acknowledgement 342

Autobiography 343

Glossary...344

"[1]Blessed is the man that endureth temptation: for when he is tried, he shall receive the crown of life, which the Lord hath promised to them that love him."

---

[1]James 1:12 King James Version

Chapter 1: Esmira Meets Samed

On a hot summer day in Baku in 1973, Esmira met a young man in the bookshop that she managed. While speaking to a friend over the phone, her eye caught the mysterious stranger entering the store. Esmira glanced at him. Her gaze was caught by his striking looks: broad-shouldered with hazel eyes and an olive complexion. Esmira's assistant saleswoman, Sveta, approached him with a broad smile on her face.

"Sir, how can I help you?" She tossed a paper fan back and forth in front of her doll-like face.

He shared the smile. "War and Peace by Leo Tolstoy, please."

Sveta located a copy of the classic, after which he paid for his purchase and departed. Her eyes lingered on him as he exited the shop. She sighed audibly.

A week passed, and this elusive male customer returned. When he came into the bookshop, Esmira was standing by the cash register scribbling sales inventory in a notebook. Sveta had abandoned the sales counter to take a nap in the store-room in the back, leaving Esmira as the only other person in the front of the shop. With a broad smile, the man greeted her and asked for a book by Nasradin Nuris. Esmira mounted a stool to retrieve the item. She began to search among the bookshelves. As she found the section where Nasradin's books were located, she noticed out of the corner of her eye that the man was ogling her figure.

Noticeable warmth coursed through the man's body. His heart pounded impatiently. As Samed licked his bottom lip, he pondered her lithe body, beautiful legs, and firm round bottom. The stinging sensations shot through his hands, which were fidgeting nervously. Because of his penchant for curvy women, he clearly aimed to possess her right there, without any regard whatsoever for her own intentions.

Finally, Esmira located the book and came down from the stool. Her long brown hair fell on her round face. He peered into her brown eyes, which were fringed with long eyelashes. Looking down at her plump rosy lips, he suddenly desired to kiss her on the spot.

"How much do I owe you, beautiful?"

"Three rubles."

"Khanum, what is your name?"

The blood gushed into his brain like lightning, making him sweat. She glanced at his hazel eyes and felt her cheeks flush. Smiling shyly, she answered, "Esmira."

"Your name is as enticing as you are." Her admirer grinned, showing his white teeth, and undid the first button of his blue shirt.

She blushed and looked downward, feeling shy. Her eyes blinked like the fluttering wings of a dove.

"Thank you."

Unable to stop looking at her rosy lips, he continued, "My name is Samed. I'm from Zardob."

Beads of sweat dripped down from his temple. He felt an electric shock pass through his body and an ardent desire to peck her on more than just her cheek.

She tore her eyes away from his gaze.

"What are you doing in Baku?"

"I'm finishing my degree at Hazer University."

He stared at her, sighing with the urge. "You possess the most beautiful eyes in the world."

A burning sensation inflamed her cheeks, deepening her blush and rendering her speechless. He paid for his book and left the shop as she stood in shock.

After meeting Esmira, Samed Abdulaev purposely came to the shop and bought books regularly. As a predator of the opposite sex, he enticed too many women, using them merely for sex, then jettisoning and discarding his broken-hearted paramours like debris. However, this time it was different; it was difficult for him to determine his real intentions toward her.

Within a month, they started dating. Esmira was clearly happy with the attention from a man of his good looks. Every day after work, they went out either to the cinema or to Boulevard Park.

One evening while sitting in the film theater, Samed held Esmira's hand gently, patting it as she leaned her head on his shoulder. However, she felt uncomfortable, noticing his evident arousal. To her shock, her boyfriend put his hand on her leg and started caressing it, drawing his fingers up her skirt. Esmira's body tensed, and she purposely dropped her handbag on the floor. She stood, pretending to look for it, then sat back down, hoping not to be touched inappropriately again.

Soon thereafter, she told her mother about dating Samed. Sadaget stared at Esmira thoughtfully for a brief time, and then exclaimed, "I can't imagine you finally have a boyfriend! I hope he is not one of those jerks who are only after sex."

Esmira's lips tightened, turning down at the ends. Her forehead furrowed. "Mother, he is not an idiot, but a good man. Why are you always so negative?"

"I'm trying to protect you. You don't know anything about him. How can you say your boyfriend is a good man? First, ask about his parents, his friends, and livelihood. Please don't jump into a relationship without checking into his background."

Disappointment crawled into Esmira's heart. "Mother, why are you always worrying unnecessarily? When you meet him, ask as many questions as you wish."

On a cold, windy Sunday, Esmira invited Samed to meet her mom. He brought a big bouquet of roses to the shop. Together they went to the apartment she shared with her mother. When they reached their destination, Sadaget opened the door.

"Good day, Sadaget Khanum." He grinned, flashing his perfect white teeth. His left eyelid twitched nervously.

"Hello, young man." Sadaget gave him a cold look. She knitted her eyebrows suspiciously but invited him inside nonetheless.

In the living room, he peeked at her. Cold chills passed down his spine.

"Mother, this is Samed Abdulaev." Esmira looked at her boyfriend gently, giving him a warm smile.

Sadaget again observed him without blinking. "Nice to meet you, young man."

"Pleasure to meet you as well. These are the most beautiful roses I could find, for a wonderful mother like you." He smirked and handed her the bouquet of roses.

She took them forcing a smile. "Thank you very much for the flowers. Please have a seat and make yourself at home."

After putting the roses in a crystal vase, Sadaget offered him tea with a piece of Napoleon cake. They sat down with their cups. As they enjoyed the brew, she asked him questions, all the while staring at his face with a blank expression.

"Young man, what do you do for a living?" Sadaget bit a candy.

"I'm not working right now, just a student at the University."

"What do you study?" Sadaget kept staring at him, her brown eyes trying to catch him lying.

"I'm getting trained in physical education."

Sadaget's staring made him agitated. He began to squirm. His palms started to sweat. The urge to smoke overtook him. He put a hand in his pocket and touched his lighter.

Sadaget calmly sipped her tea.

"Where do your parents live?"

"They live in Zardob." With shaking fingers, he buttoned the top button of his red shirt.

Sadaget put her empty mug on the coffee table. Then she stared into his eyes without blinking.

"What are your intentions toward my daughter?"

Hearing this unexpected question, Samed almost choked on his tea coughing uncontrollably. He didn't know what to say at first. Then Samed muttered, "I like your daughter. I hope that we will have a future together."

A smile of approval flickered on Sadaget's face.

"But it is too early to tell right now, since we met only recently." He wiped his face with a handkerchief, feeling as if he was under interrogation.

The smile on Sadaget's face faded. Displeased with his answer, she sat up straight staring at him without batting an eye.

He looked aside and crossed his legs, feeling an urge to bite his fingernails. He felt baffled as to why this woman persisted in asking so many questions in rapid machine-gun fire. Samed answered politely, giving assurances, not only that he indeed liked her daughter, but also that his intentions were good.

After spending an hour at Esmira's apartment, he left feeling relieved. Esmira's boyfriend was content that he did not have to respond to any further questions from her mother, nor be subjected any longer to her piercing glare.

As soon as he left, Sadaget crossed her arms. "He is a handsome and well-mannered man, but something about him is not right. If I were in your place, I wouldn't trust him."

Hearing her mother's words, Esmira's heart sank. She grimaced.

"Mother, I'm not surprised. You will never approve of any male, in my life or otherwise. It is no wonder you don't have a man in your own."

Sadaget gazed at her daughter silently for a second. "The only reason I rid myself of men revolves around my fear of you getting abused. Do you understand me?" She wagged a finger at Esmira.

Esmira's body tensed as she looked down.

Sadaget scratched her ear. "Did you not witness his body language when I asked about his intentions toward you? He was certainly nervous, leading me to conclude that you should not date him."

Distressed with her mother's negativity, Esmira shook her head slowly. Her eyebrows moved closer together. "Mother, I don't understand you. You can't judge someone without getting to know them better."

"Esi, I am not judging, but I got the feeling that he may make inappropriate advances toward you. I don't know where this idea came from. When I picture him in my mind, it fills me with concern. I feel a weight and tension in my chest. Just be careful."

"Okay, Mother I will not see him anymore," she lied. She knew that, given her mother's character, it would be difficult to meet anyone of whom she would approve.

One day, as winter approached, the roads became covered with a soft white rug of snow. By the afternoon, plenty of snow had fallen, making the roads icy. The ice on the ground caused traffic congestion, but it didn't prevent Samed from seeing Esmira.

With a bundle of pink and red roses under his arm, he walked on the icy asphalt with long strides. Yet Samed was not impervious to the cold; as he approached the bookshop, gazing at the roofs of the two-story brick houses encased in snow, he sensed his blood becoming frigid, while his fingers ached as if someone had pricked them with needles. His body shook slightly. His teeth chattered.

Samed tried to keep one hand in his pocket while holding the roses in the other.

A yellow cab drove up close to him.

"It is cold outside. Let me drop you off where you need to go." The driver rubbed his freezing hands together.

"Thank you, but I am almost there."

As soon as the taxi drove away, Samed felt something hard hit his head. His gray winter hat was knocked to the ground. He turned around and stared at a small trio of children nearby, each holding a snowball. A short fat boy picked up another snowball and threw it at Samed, striking him squarely in the face.

"Hey, you! I'll get you!" he said, shouting angrily at the boy through a mouthful of snow. Samed put his flowers on the ground and made a huge, hard snowball. Then he threw it at the child, but his aim was not as good. The snowball fell harmlessly into the snow some feet away. Embarrassed, Samed retrieved his hat and the flowers. He stomped away, trying to ignore the laughter at his back.

He walked into the bookshop, armed with his beautiful bouquet of roses, and gave them to Esmira.

"When I saw these beautiful roses, they reminded me of your beauty. I couldn't resist buying them for you."

A smile of satisfaction lit up her round face. She took a deep breath while sniffing the roses. I could smell them all day, she thought to herself.

"You are so kind to me." She gratefully caressed his cheek with her left hand.

He took her hand. His eyes bored into hers, making her blink.

"I got up early this morning and cooked a dinner for us. Will you please agree to dine with me in my apartment?"

As he waited for an answer, he looked at Esmira without blinking. At first, she didn't know what to say. She knew that going to his apartment wasn't a good idea. However, as she fell under the spell of his alluring eyes, she acquiesced.

She closed the bookshop. They walked to the train station, which was full of people trying to escape the cold. Some wore long coats with scarves over their heads, whereas others sported short coats. People were shoving each other in the rush to board the train.

After a series of connections, the young couple got off. They walked the rest of the way to his apartment in silence. Esmira's body felt edgy as she debated within herself whether she should refuse and retreat. However, she continued following him.

They walked between five-story buildings that were in disrepair and needed a fresh coat of paint. Esmira noticed a few small grocery shops attached to the buildings. Russian-made cars sat in front, covered with snow. A few children threw snowballs at each other as parents sat alone on nearby benches. She glanced at the road noticing that a portion of it was unpaved and covered with snow mixed with mud.

If someone sees me entering his apartment, neighbors will spread gossip in all directions, she thought.

Meanwhile, his eyes skimmed her body as she walked. He licked his lips. His whole body felt aroused.

They approached a nine-story building. They climbed slowly to the fifth floor, gasping for air at the exertion. Esmira's heart beat increasingly faster at every step. She put her hand over her heart to calm herself for a second.

Why is my heart ready to explode?

He opened the door and guided her into his dining room. Beautifully decorated, the walls had marvelous light-green wallpaper. On one wall was a painting of a beautiful woman. The room had long cream-colored curtains at the windows, a stereo, a small TV on a stand, and a table with matching chairs. He indeed had good taste.

He invited her to sit at the table. She eyed it and saw a couple of wine glasses, a bottle of red wine, roses, candles, and white plates. Her eyes grew wider.

"Wow! I'm struck by your hosting. You even laid out candles."

"I'm a man who knows how to make a woman happy. Please sit at the table. I will be back."

He left the living room and returned with a trolley, laden with their dinner. He removed the dishes of dolma, pilov, potato salad, black caviar from the cart, put them on the table, and lit the candles. Then he poured some wine into the goblets and handed one to her.

Esmira had never drunk alcohol before. She hesitated at first, merely holding her wine, and watched his every move. She breathed heavily as her muscles tightened in an uneasy cautiousness.

He lifted his glass of wine. "Let's drink to our future and new love." At that point, he drank half of his wine glass.

Following his lead, Esmira emptied her glass in a single gulp. They ate dinner, both feeling tense. After completing their meal, he removed all the dishes from the table, put on a soothing, soft song, and invited her to dance. She rose bashfully, looked down, and moved closer to him. Samed gently put his arm around her waist, cradled her. He rocked her back and forth to the music.

Feeling his body pressed to hers made Esmira feel overheated and giddy. The young woman wasn't sure if it was because of the wine or because she was so close to him. He smelled nice. His skin was soft. As she rested her head on his shoulder while dancing, Esmira felt the urge to kiss him.

The music stopped. She sat down in her chair. She gazed around nervously and twirled her hair around her finger. Esmira's whole body burned, especially her hands.

What is happening to my body?

He left the room, only to come back with a bottle of clear liquid and two small glasses. He poured some vodka for both of them. Samed passed her a glass.

"Esi, try this."

She shrank back, looking at her drink. "What is it?"

His left eyelid jumped involuntarily. "Lemon vodka."

She put the glass on the table. "But Samed, I don't drink alcohol.

Samed gazed at his girlfriend with slightly narrowed eyes. His lips pursed together. She felt flushed and loosened her blouse.

"We are not killing, hurting, or stealing from anyone. Just taste it. If you don't like it, then leave it."

She took a few sips.

"Wow, I can taste the lemon!" She drank all the vodka at once.

After drinking two glasses, Esmira felt increasingly giddy and jolly. She was filled with the desire to sing and dance.

I feel so relaxed.

Samed poured another glass of vodka for her, but she tried to decline. He gazed at her with a kind, loving face, smiling widely.

"Let's drink this to our future together."

Esmira changed her mind. One more glass won't do any harm, she thought. How could she resist his charming smile and begging, hazel eyes?

After a while, she made jokes laughing aloud. Esmira tried to get up from the sofa, but fell back, lightheaded. The whole room spun around her. She leaned back and bit her lips as she gazed at him. She felt an urge to get up and kiss him on the lips.

Seeing Esmira drunk, Samed made his move. He sat next to her and kissed her neck. She tried to push him away, all the while giggling.

"Stop, please!" She was confused, trying to understand what was happening.

He continued kissing her neck. "Esmira, you are so beautiful and untouched."

She felt giddy and relaxed, and a warm flow of energy passed through her body as his warm lips touched her neck. Keeping her eyes closed, Esmira enjoyed the sensation of him kissing her. As he attempted to unbutton her blouse, she sought once again to push him away. When he started kissing her lips, she couldn't control her emotions anymore. In fact, she realized that she wanted to make love to the man before her.

"To hell with society," she whispered to herself, barely audibly.

She grabbed him tightly and passionately kissed his lips.

He grasped her hand, took her into his bedroom, undressed her, and then removed his clothing. She lay down on the bed, gazing at his naked, athletic body. He was so perfect and sexy that she could no longer resist her ardent desire. Breathing heavily and burning within, her whole body thirsted for his kisses. As she lay on his bed, she allowed Samed to kiss her lips again, and then her whole body. This made her more aroused. She liked the sensation and didn't want him to stop.

After enjoying his touch on her body for some time, they had sex. Afterward, with both of them intoxicated, they fell asleep.

In the morning, she woke up with a massive headache in Samed's bed. Seeing herself naked, and in his bed, she realized that she had done something shameful and sinful. Esmira sat up slowly, feeling weak. She covered her face with her hands.

Oh, Allah, I have sinned against you and brought shame to myself.

Horrified, Esmira shook her head in disbelief. What have I done?

She went into the bathroom to take a shower. Once dressed, she returned to the bedroom. She sat in the corner of the room, with her head against her knees, and started to cry.

Hearing her, Samed got up, half-naked. He looked over at her with concern.

"What is wrong, Esmira? Why are you crying?" He started putting on his clothes.

Esmira's cries got louder. "I have committed a sin by sleeping with you. I shouldn't have drunk vodka at all. Because of the alcohol, I was not cognizant of my actions. No one will want to marry me because I lost my virginity to you. My mother will kill me!" she declared as she shook her head in disbelief.

He came up closer to her. "Stop crying unnecessary tears, and look at me please."

She lifted her head up and gazed at him, her eyes full of tears.

"You know that I love you. I will marry you." While he spoke, she noticed that his eyes darted from side to side. His eyebrows drew upward toward the middle of his forehead. Short lines across the skin of his forehead formed as he knitted his brow.

"Really?" Naive Esmira looked into his eyes, with a smile on her troubled face.

He forced a smile. "Yes, my dear, I will. But only after completing my degree."

After talking for a while, she left his apartment and walked toward the metro station. On the way, she came across a phone booth. She stopped beside it thinking about her mistake as she gazed around.

If only I had declined to go to his apartment, none of this would have happened.

Then she thought about what she would say to her mother about her night's absence. She decided to tell Sadaget that she had spent the night at her friend Sabina's place.

Esmira went into the booth. She dialed her friend's phone number. Sabina answered the phone.

"Hi, Sabina."

"Hello! It's been a long time since I've heard from you," answered Sabina.

"Look, I can't talk for long right now. Can you please do a favor for me?" Esmira gritted her teeth.

Sabina paused. "What kind of favor?"

"If my mother calls you, just tell her that I stayed the night at your place."

"But where did you spend the night?" Sabina was all ears.

Esmira peeped around and tried to keep her voice down. "There are people around, so I can't talk right now. I promise to call you later, but in the meantime, do as I ask."

"Don't worry. I will tell her whatever you wish me to say."

Esmira felt as if a heavy weight had fallen off her shoulders. "Thank you so much. Talk to you later." Dizzy and light in her chest, Esmira hung up the phone.

She got off at the Narimanov station and took the Number 266 bus, which stopped not far from her apartment. She strolled toward it with her heart beating quickly, while snowflakes fell into the neckline of her white coat. She climbed to the third floor, the tension in her chest making it hard to breathe. She was shaking slightly.

She is going to give me a rough time. Allah, please help me.

She stood by the door for a while rummaging through her bag.

I should not have misplaced my key. Now I have to face her.

She then knocked on the door, her heart throbbing and pounding with a thunderous boom. Sadaget opened it without saying anything, but after the door closed, she crossed her arms and yelled at her daughter.

"Where have you been, whore? I have been worried sick trying to reach you. Did you spend the night with Samed?"

Esmira could only stare at her, wide-eyed. Sadaget's face was furious, her eyebrows scrunched together. She shook as she shouted at her daughter. Frightened, Esmira didn't know what to say at first. Her eyes became wide, and her eyebrows slanted upward. Her breathing was labored as if there wasn't enough air in the room.

"No, I spent the night at Sabina's. She was alone at home and asked me if I could stay with her."

Esmira felt awkward for lying. She knew that fibbing was wrong and a sin, but she was afraid to tell the truth.

"Why didn't you call me? You could have at least called and let me know that you were staying with Sabina." Sadaget sounded like a police investigator trying to get the truth from the criminal.

Esmira continued to fib, avoiding her mother's eyes. "I didn't know that I was going to stay with her. She asked me after I went to visit her. I was going to call you, but her house phone wasn't working."

Sadaget came up closer to Esmira. She pointed a finger at her. "Listen to me carefully. If this happens again, I will throw you out!"

"I won't do it again, Mother."

Esmira slowly walked away. A slight smile pulled on her upper lip. The rest of the day she stayed at home, forced to listen to Sadaget's complaints.

On Monday, she went back to work, relieved to get away from her mother. She sank into her soft chair, closed her eyes, and breathed deeply, enjoying the calmness around her. At least she can't nag me while I'm here.

However, every night after work for the entire week, Sadaget bothered her about her night's absence. While she sat at the table and quietly bore her mother's nagging, she held her head with both hands biting her lip. When will she stop nagging me about the same thing? I can't take it any longer!

Sadaget used to quarrel with Esmira about petty nonsense. She called her a whore for just looking at somebody or for smiling back at a man in the street. However, in reality, Sadaget was not a mean-spirited woman. A difficult beginning in life had given her rough edges. She was born in 1939 in the village of Guba, the daughter of a Russian mother, Mariya, and an Azeri father, Rza. At the age of 16, Sadaget met a teacher named Ali. He was four years older than her and came from a rich family. One day he took Sadaget to his house and had sex with her, promising marriage. However, after a few days, he backed off from his promise and asked Sadaget not to tell anyone about what had happened between them. Nonetheless,

Sadaget told her mother everything. Enraged, Mariya forced Ali to marry her daughter and take her to his house.

Ali's mother was a principal of the high school. She was unhappy that her son had married a poor girl, whose mother was a Russian alcoholic who had spent a year in jail. She wanted her son to marry an upright Azeri Muslim woman whom she would select. Therefore, every day she was bothering Sadaget by saying, "What are you doing in my house? Go back to your shed!" She tried every trick in the book to force them to divorce. She would tell her son lies about her daughter-in-law by stating that Sadaget had treated her brusquely, thereby not demonstrating any respect. Ali believed his mother's complaints and quarreled with Sadaget about her conduct toward his mother.

After a year of marriage, Sadaget miscarried her first pregnancy when lifting a heavy sack of potatoes. Later she got pregnant again and had Esmira. After living for three years in her mother-in-law's house, Sadaget decided to leave her husband. She could not withstand not only her mother-in-law's lies, but also her husband's frigidity and drinking habits. She took her daughter and went back to her mother's house. After some time asked for a divorce. As soon as Sadaget got divorced, she moved to Baku, the beautiful capital of Azerbaijan, with her four-year-old daughter.

In Baku, Sadaget started working in a factory. While she was on the job, Esmira was in a nursery. Sadaget was an industrious, committed, decent woman. She liked to earn her own money and was happy to be independent. Along with that, she had a strong sense of pride and would never accept help from anyone. While employed at the factory, she rented her own apartment and applied for a government one.

Although Sadaget was protective of her daughter, she would never kiss her or say that she loved her. Thus, Esmira grew up feeling unloved. Sadaget was afraid that Esmira would allow a man to ruin her life. Thereby she tried hard to keep Esmira from making the mistakes that she had made by marrying the wrong man, Ali.

Knowing her mother's personality, Esmira tried not to talk back or argue. Instead, she got up, picked up a plate full of cookies. Esmira went back to her bedroom, perplexed.

All of my friends have supportive, loving mothers, but I have a cold-hearted one. Does she take after her Russian mother? No wonder Russian women beat their men.

For the entire week after sleeping with her boyfriend, Esmira hoped that he would come to the shop, yet he didn't show up. Every time Esmira saw a man entering the bookshop, she would look to see if he was Samed. She called him at least six times in two weeks, but he didn't answer.

Why did I fall in love with him? I thought he was different, but he used me to please himself. I should have listened to Mother.

As she waited for him, he was dating Tatyana, who had moved to Azerbaijan from Russia. Tatyana was ten years older than him. She had a fifteen-year-old daughter from a man with whom she had slept only once. Samed heard that she had other failed relationships before. People didn't respect her because of this, but at the age of twenty-five, Samed didn't give a toss. In his mind, if he could possess a woman with readily-available cash reserves and who had an apartment he could move into, he would serpentine his way into her life. This would save him from having to rent an apartment while engaged in his studies.

Tatyana was happy to have a young, handsome man in her life such as Samed. She would spend her money on him. In return, he would iron for her, wash her clothes, and make love to her. Despite his impressionable age, he was a skilled lover who could please any woman in bed.

At the end of March, he went to her apartment again. When he arrived, she gave him money and sent him to the grocery store. After he left, she noticed that Samed had left his backpack on the floor. Tatyana had a curious nature. So, what does a man like Samed carry with him from place to place?

She giggled to herself, then locked the door, quickly picked it up, and looked inside. The top of the backpack's contents was uninteresting- some gym clothes, a pair of shower shoes, a bottle of cologne. However, hidden below those somewhat innocent items she found his address book, a white envelope, and a camera. She looked at every page of his phone book, noticing many female names in it. Then she opened the envelope with trembling hands. Tatyana read a letter written on a small piece of paper:

'Samed, I have repeatedly tried to reach you by phone, but you keep avoiding my calls. Can you please either call me at my office or visit me. I need to talk to you about our night in your apartment. Love you, Esmira.'

Tatyana became enraged reading the letter. She squeezed the plastic cup that she had been holding and threw it at the wall.

"This bastard has been cheating on me! When he returns, I will show him what he deserves!"

Tatyana squeezed her right hand into a fist. Then she picked up a pen. Samed's lover wrote down Esmira's name and phone number.

She removed the pictures from the envelope and looked at them. Some depicted young girls seated at a table, while others featured a blond girl lying on a bed.

Did he take these photos in his bedroom?

Suddenly, her heart filled with more anger, making her chest and head feel heavy. She breathed faster and narrowed her eyes. Then she tore up the letter with the photos, and put the torn pieces back in the envelope. In a rage, she smashed his camera against the wall. "Bastard! Liar! Do you think you can fool me?" she screamed.

Meanwhile, Samed continued shopping, oblivious to what awaited him when he returned. As he picked up a can of creamed corn from one of the store shelves, his roaming eyes fell on a pair of young Azeri women. The taller one noticed him and gave him a shy smile. He winked in return.

He paid for the groceries and walked back to Tatyana's apartment. The grocery store was not far from her place, so it didn't take long for him to reach it.

The rain had begun to fall, making the buildings look gray. People rushed inside, trying to stay dry. The deluge didn't bother the neighborhood children; ignoring the rainy weather, a few children played in a small park across the street.

He climbed the stairs and knocked on the door. Tatyana opened it and let him in, trying to look calm. As he put the bags on the kitchen counter and took off his raincoat, she suddenly shouted. Tatyana shoved his broken camera in his face.

"All this time you have been cheating on me! You said that I was the only woman in your life! Who are these whores in your pictures?" Tatyana's voice echoed like thunder, irritating his ears.

At first, he didn't know what to say. He gazed around the room. His palms sweated. It didn't take long, though, for the liar to come up with an excuse. He came up closer to his mistress, trying to kiss her, but she pushed him away.

"Why do you doubt me? Some of the girls are studying with me. We only study together. You are the one in my heart." His legs trembled, while at the same time he tried to look as innocent as a lamb.

"Why did you take their photos then?"

"I did not. My friend asked me to pick up his photos from the studio. That's what I did." Samed could usually fool anyone with his lies and innocent look, and he was banking on that talent now. "They are just meaningless pictures."

He eyed his lover. Once again, Samed tried to take Tatyana in his arms, but she pushed him away.

"Tatyana, you are the only woman in my life. You must believe me!" His eyes became watery.

"Oh, I must?" She crossed her arms. Tatyana's eyes burned with a deep, unending fury. "Who is Esmira?"

This was Samed's last chance for redemption and honesty.

"She is my neighbor."

She stared into his eyes without blinking. "What is your neighbor doing in your apartment at night?"

Samed rubbed his nose and put his hand by his mouth. Seeing his body movements, Tatyana knew that Samed was lying. She had given him far too many chances. However, he had thrown them all away.

"Well?"

"Nothing. She just came to borrow some salt." His voice squeaked like that of a mouse.

His final lie was pathetic, and he knew it. No longer was his tone that of the cocky, arrogant young man. He now sounded like a lost, forlorn child.

Shaking her head slowly, Tatyana walked to the door and opened it. "I'm not a fool like the other women who were used by you. Just leave my apartment! Go away!"

Feeling as if a heavy rock had fallen on his head, Samed left. He headed toward the metro station.

Having not heard from Samed for several weeks, Esmira despaired of ever seeing him again. As the days and weeks went by, she became convinced that he had used her for his insatiability. Frustrated by her lack of foresight and judgment, Esmira could neither concentrate on her work nor sleep soundly. She regretted having ever agreed to go to his apartment in the first place. She trudged on, remaining isolated and shunning her friends. Esmira spent her days at the main desk, keeping her head down and trying to stay occupied.

One day, Esmira sat in her office, feeling forsaken. To try to take her mind off her misery, she was trying to calculate total weekly sales at the bookshop. After pressing the incorrect numbers on the calculator one too many times, she shoved it aside in frustration. She kneaded her forehead, feeling a stabbing pain above her eyes. Pursing her lips, she clenched her teeth and closed her eyes.

Why did I go to his apartment? How could I have been so stupid as to let such a man get the better of me?

Thoughts about the sinful night spent with Samed made her feel increasingly weaker and exacerbated her migraine. She stopped rubbing her forehead and rummaged through her handbag for an aspirin, her body shivering.

On a wet day, as she talked to a customer over the phone, she saw Samed enter the bookstore. She accidentally dropped the phone in her surprise. He folded his umbrella. Then left it by the door, while Esmira gazed blankly through the glass pane of the office window. The rain beat down unrelentingly. Her widened eyes bored through him. Her heart seemed to burst out of her small frame. Every muscle in her body tightened. Why has this liar come back, if not to torment me?

Esmira felt the urge to slap his face for his insensitive games. Instead, she chose to remain calm and patiently wait for him to approach her.

Soaked from the rain, he walked up to the salesperson. "Good morning, Sveta. Is Esmira in today?"

"Yes, she is. However, she is not in a mood to talk to anyone." Sveta fixed her blouse and breathed heavily. She opened her mouth slightly looking into his eyes.

"Did you cut your hair?"

He eyed her with a sultry glance toward her voluptuous breasts. Then he looked into her eyes and smiled widely. "Yes, I did."

She leaned closer to him over the counter, exposing her breasts. "I love it. Would you like to go out for lunch today?" She hoped that the answer would be yes.

He grinned, staring at her breasts. "No, Sveta, but thank you for the invitation."

His response erased the smile from her face. Her eyes became cold.

"Humph."

As he talked to Sveta, Esmira came out from her office and addressed her salesperson directly without any regard for him.

"Sveta, one of our customers called questioning about Mikhail Bulgakov's novel, The Master and Margarita. Do we have a spare copy in stock?"

"Yes, we have three copies left." Sveta's eyes ran from Samed to her manager.

"Please call Gulnara Kasimova. Let her know that she can pick up the book at any time before six o'clock," ordered Esmira.

Samed patiently waited for Esmira to stop talking to Sveta. When she had finished giving instructions, Esmira turned a stern face to him. Her black brows hooded over her eyes and her lips tightened.

"Hello, Samed."

"Hi, Esmira. May I speak to you, please?" Samed looked pleadingly at his former girlfriend.

"I can't talk to you right now." She felt an emptiness in her heart, mixed with anger.

Sveta stared at the two of them wistfully. Then she dialed the customer's number as directed.

"Esmira, would you at least give me five minutes of your time, please?" Samed tried to grab her hand, but Esmira pulled it away.

"I'm busy right now, but you can come back at six o'clock." She decided to stay deadpan, instead of yelling or slapping him right across his face.

She returned to her office, leaving him slack-jawed. Although she was secretly happy to see him, at the same time she was furious that he had ignored her for weeks.

Samed peered at his watch. After that, he left the bookshop, visibly brooding. The rain had stopped falling. Samed walked to Boulevard Park, which was near the shore of the Caspian Sea. He gazed around, noticing a few boats floating on the water and seagulls in the air. The benches in the park were empty. Some children rode bumper cars on a nearby ride.

He entered a café where a few young couples sat at tables. He ordered tea with lemon, and stayed there for about two hours to ponder what excuses he might tell Esmira concerning his absence. His slacks had become slightly wet, but were starting to dry as he sat in contemplation. After a while, he looked at his watch. It was 5.35 p.m. Overcome by despondency, he paid his bill. Esmira's suitor walked back to the shop.

As he arrived, Esmira was locking the door. Seeing her erased his earlier despondency, and replaced it with his typical predatory arrogance.

Samed approached her with a wolfish grin.

"Hello, Esmira. I'm back."

"I can see that. What do you need now?" Esmira snapped, annoyed.

"I missed you, so I came to see you." Samed decided to play the innocent lamb that had lost its owner.

"If you missed me, you would have contacted me or returned my phone calls." Her voice was sullen, her face chagrined.

Like a serpent, Samed edged stealthily toward Esmira. He went for her hand, but she pulled it back, repulsed.

"After our last date, my sister called, informing me of my father's illness. She thought he was dying, so she asked me to come back home."

He looked at Esmira's haunted expression, which betrayed that she believed his lies. He gave her a radiant smile.

"When I heard my father was ill, I left Baku in a hurry. That is why you couldn't reach me, my dear. I spent three horrific, hellish weeks in Zardob, minding my physically-challenged father. The whole time, I thought of nothing but you. Thanks to Preserver of all things, he is recovering. I came back only last night."

As he spoke, she looked at him with pity. Samed's dishonesty fooled the young woman yet again.

This poor man was looking after his sick father, and I doubted him. How could I be so wrong? Ashamed for judging him unfairly, and as naïve as she was, Esmira believed his every word feeling sorry for him.

She took his hand. "You probably got scared thinking that your father might die. I'm happy that he is feeling better now."

She glanced at the sky and then looked at her watch. "It is late, I must rush back home before my mother gets irritated. Come back tomorrow, in the morning."

Esmira left abruptly. She wanted to tell him how she felt, but she needed to go home to avoid angering her mother.

Why is my mom so miserable? Because of her, I'm unable to spend time with him.

"Tomorrow!" she called back toward him, as her walk turned into a run.

Seeing her walking away, Samed shook his head in disbelief. Usually, he was the one who left women behind, but today this one had left him. The young man felt so downtrodden that he didn't care to do anything but go straight home. He took a shower, watched a Nasimi film. After having dinner, Samed fell asleep.

On Monday morning, he awoke at 7 a.m., brushed his teeth, took a shower. Samed sprayed himself with expensive cologne. He shoveled down breakfast and left his apartment.

He decided to drop by his university campus before visiting Esmira. As he walked to the university, he noticed that small buds had appeared on the bare and naked trees. Some people walked by in thick fur coats, while others wore light raincoats. Winter had passed, with springtime budding forth. However, there still was a frigid, piercing breeze, as if the prior season refused to give up its hold.

The university was housed in a four-story building. The grounds were landscaped to look like a huge yard. Wooden benches were placed under trees and in other convenient places.

Samed spent three hours on campus, then left before his classes were over.

On his way to Esmira's bookshop, he stopped to buy a bouquet of pink, red, and yellow roses. At the beginning of their relationship, he had consistently bought flowers for her. This was a new behavior on his part; usually, he would not spend even a cent on a woman-- rather, they would spend money on him.

On that same day, Esmira reached the bookstore earlier than usual. She tried to keep her head down, busy with work, so as not to think about Samed. She made a few calls and worked on an inventory list, all the while possessed by thoughts of him.

He is coming today. Should I go with him for a date or refuse? This time, I am not going to his apartment at all.

She suddenly noticed that she had accidentally written his name on her inventory list. Staring at it wide eyed and with a gaping mouth, she thought, I need to stop thinking about him.

No matter how hard she tried, however, Esmira was unable to stop thinking about the night she had spent with Samed. Having thoughts about that evening made her cheeks burn and blush. She was ignited and afire, but also thankful that her mother had no idea of what had happened.

When 11 a.m. came not seeing Samed, she began to feel uneasy. Why hadn't he dropped by yet?

At noon, to her surprise, he appeared, clutching roses in his hand. He came up to Sveta. "Hi. Is Esmira around?" he asked.

Without a word to him, she went into Esmira's office to let her know that he was here.

Esmira's eyes glowed. Her heart raced as she quickly applied red lipstick, fixed her black skirt. She rushed onto the main floor.

He looked at her with a sultry glance and wolf-whistled.

"Wow, you look so stunning in that outfit."

"Thank you." She grinned bashfully, her cheeks flushed. "I have been waiting for you."

Sveta stood nearby, filled with envy. She bit her upper lip, realizing that her feelings about them would amount to naught.

21

Samed's eyes sparkled. His blood became warmer as he stood next to Esmira. "Please accept my apologies for being tardy. I went to university today. From there came directly here."

He gave the roses to her. Esmira's face shone with joy. She inhaled them deeply. "They are so beautiful. Thank you so much!"

She turned toward her employee. "Sveta, please put them in a vase," she said handing the roses to her. Sveta took the roses to the kitchen. She sniffed them, with closed eyes and a longing in her heart.

"So, what are your plans for today?" Samed impatiently waited for her answer.

"I was planning to take a lunch break."

"I know a lovely cafe not far from here. We can have not only lunch and tea there, but also a delicious piece of zebra cake," her boyfriend suggested.

Esmira retrieved her black handbag and put on a white leather jacket. They set off toward his suggested destination, the Zeynab Cafe.

As they strolled along, she gazed at the trees. Her heart beamed with joy and eyes sparkled like diamonds. She felt so light and peaceful that, if she'd had wings, she would have flown away like a bird freed from a cage.

Esmira took a deep breath. "I love the spring. It's a time when everything is blooming."

Samed rubbed his hands, feeling cold. "It's still freezing. I love summer time, when it is warm and sunny."

In the small café, he ordered kebab, zebra cake, as well as tea for both of them. The waiter brought two small saucers with armudu, pear-shaped glasses, as well as a teapot, a small plate with lemon, and sugar cubes. He placed everything on the table. Samed put lemon into both glasses and poured tea into them.

While sipping her drink, Esmira looked around noticing four elderly men seated at another table. They wore hats, had mustaches, and played a nard. One of them smoked a cigar pipe and another held a black tasbeeh in his hand.

The waiter came back with the food. While they were eating, Samed talked about his father's health, feigning worry. She looked into his reddened eyes with a sympathetic gaze and gave him a faint smile. Then she reached over for his hand and caressed it.

"Stop worrying. I'm convinced that your father will be on the mend soon."

Her nearness made him feel aroused. Samed's hands burned, and his muscles stiffened. They spent forty minutes chatting. Then the couple set out on foot back to the bookshop. On the way, he kept staring at her figure, filled with desire.

"When can I see you again?" He visualized her naked, taking a shower.

"Come back tomorrow at the same time." She could still scarcely believe that he had returned to her.

When they approached the shop, he gave her a peck on the cheek, and left after saying farewell. In a daze, she kept herself busy until 6 p.m. After closing the shop, she took the bus straight home, thinking of him all the while.

Chapter 2: *Unexpected Pregnancy*

Three months had passed since Esmira had slept with Samed. She noted that her period was late. Esmira thought it was a result of too much stress at work. She had been feeling nauseous, had gained a little bit of weight, but she didn't pay much attention to these warning signs.

At the end of May, when the weather became warmer, her friend Sabina dropped by the bookshop. Sabina was a tall, beautiful twenty-seven-year-old Uzbek woman with long, dark, curly, hair, black Asiatic eyes, a long and narrow face. Esmira's friend took off her jacket. Then she hung it on the back of her seat grinning at Esmira's astonished expression. Esmira was staring openly at her, hardly believing the change that had come over her friend since the last time they'd seen each other.

"Look at you!" Esmira gasped out. "When we last met, you were so huge, but now you are so much thinner and gorgeous! How did you manage to lose so much weight?"

Sabina smiled proudly. "When you have a loving gentleman in your life, he can motivate you toward positive changes." She put three fingers together and kissed them.

Sabina sank deeply into her soft chair, put one leg on top of the other. She lit a cigarette. "Did you hear from Samed?"

"We started dating again." A smile of joy lit up Esmira's face.

Sabina sat up dropping the cigarette. "Are you kidding? He dumped you and you took him back?"

"He didn't dump me. He had some family problems."

Her expression became worried. "In any event, I have other things to worry about. I have not had my period for three months. I never had issues with it before." Esmira got butterflies in her stomach just thinking about it.

Sabina picked up her cigarette and gazed at Esmira with a vacant look, slowly drawing smoke into her mouth. She then leaned forward toward her.

"Did you sleep with him?"

At this unexpected question, Esmira's eyes bugged out. At first, she felt bashful. Her eyes roamed around. Esmira's face burned. She looked away shyly.

"Yes, I did."

Sabina froze for a moment.

"Did he use a condom?"

Esmira frowned, not understanding the question. "What is a condom?"

Sabina grimaced. "Are you kidding? It is a rubber prophylactic that men wear on their penis to protect them from disease and to prevent pregnancy."

Esmira's cheeks started to ignite. She gazed downward. "We are not taught these lessons, nor are we allowed to talk about sex. Where would I learn all of this?"

Sabina inhaled some smoke deeply and coughed. She gazed at Esmira with tearful eyes. "I can't believe that you had unprotected sex without first marrying the man. What were you thinking?"

Esmira nervously played with her jacket button. "It wasn't my fault alone."

"I remember you called me, asking me to lie to your mother. So, I guess that's when it happened."

Esmira then told Sabina everything about the night that she had spent with Samed.

"You are probably pregnant. You need to take a pregnancy test. If it is positive, then you should get an abortion before it is too late. Or, ask him to marry you as soon as possible. Otherwise, you are going to have a real mess on your hands. Everyone will soon know you are pregnant. You know how our people immediately jump to conclusions and pass judgment on others. Also, you are acquainted with our culture. No bastard children!"

Sabina's words sounded like a sentence of death, giving Esmira a sudden stomach pain. Baffled, Esmira got up from her seat, visibly shaken. "I hope you are wrong."

Sabina looked over at Esmira, seeing the frustration on her face, and felt sorry for her. "You are probably pregnant. You never had a bump in your belly before, but I can see it is growing and bulging right now."

Esmira put her hand on her stomach. "No, I always had it."

However, upon hearing Sabina's words, Esmira suddenly felt weak. She sat back down in her chair. She felt like a wounded bird trapped in a cage, unable to get out.

Dumbfounded, she stared at Sabina. "Why do you always have to suggest the worst?"

"I live in the real world instead of daydreaming. I look at the facts. You have a bump in your belly and a late menstruation cycle. These are the signs of pregnancy." Sabina dragged on her Marlboro and exhaled the smoke at Esmira.

Esmira coughed fanning the air in front of her face. "When will you stop smoking?"

Sabina frowned. "Don't worry about me, please. Your pregnancy is a much bigger problem to worry about; one you had better resolve right away!"

Esmira's hands trembled. "What am I going to do if my mother finds out?" she exclaimed.

Sabina blew smoke out of her mouth, and flicked the ash from her cigarette into an ashtray. "As long as you get an abortion, she will never find out." Then she went on to recommend getting a pregnancy test from the pharmacy.

Esmira went immediately to the drug store, leaving Sabina in her office.

Sabina closed her eyes, trying to relax. She leaned her head back against the chair, and thought about her friend's problem. This girl always trusts everyone. Such an innocent! No wonder she ended up in this mess!

After ten minutes, Esmira came back with two pregnancy test strips.

Sabina sat up. "Go into the bathroom. Take the test!"

"All right, I'm going."

Esmira went into the bathroom, feeling nervous about the possible outcome. With trembling hands, she performed the test, then waited for three minutes for the strip to show lines. As she waited for the result, she pleaded silently, Allah, please let this test come out negative.

Esmira looked at the test strip and felt thunderstruck at seeing two lines. Chagrined and feeling dizzy, she slowly slid down to the floor, dropping the test strip. Esmira put her head on her knees, feeling as if she was being swallowed by a huge, dark hole. She broke down in tears.

My life is ruined. Everyone will start gossiping. My mother will kill me.

After spending fifteen minutes in the bathroom, Esmira went back to her office, dragging her feet. As she came through the door, she gave Sabina a sad look. Her eyes were bloodshot and her face ashen.

Sabina jumped up from her seat, stubbed out the cigarette in the nearby ashtray. She rushed toward Esmira. "You look like someone died. From your downcast eyes, I can tell that you're pregnant."

She helped Esmira to make it to her seat. Esmira sat in her chair trying to smile. "Yes, I am," she whispered, "but don't talk so loudly. Sveta might hear."

"What are you planning to do?"

"I don't know." Esmira's eyes narrowed as she bit her lip, feeling anxious.

"You need to see a good gynecologist to terminate the pregnancy. I have the phone number for Doctor Gena Petrovskiy. He is trustworthy and a good Russian gynecologist."

Sabina searched for his number. Then she wrote it down for Esmira.

Esmira's thoughts wandered all over the place. *What am I going to do? Why did this happen to me?*

"Thanks for the number, Sabina. I will talk to Samed first and then seek medical attention."

"Okay, just don't wait too long. Know what has to be done, and soon."

Sabina glanced down at her watch. "I have to go. Dima is waiting for me. Don't worry, Esmira, you will be okay. Just don't delay. Go to Doctor Petrovskiy before your belly starts getting larger."

Pale, Esmira barely cracked a faint smile. "Bye, Sabina. Thanks for the advice."

Esmira spent the rest of the day quietly thinking about what she should do with this pregnancy. She sat in her chair gazing vacantly at the wall. *If I terminate the pregnancy, God will punish me for killing a fetus. It is a sin. How could I kill an embryo without giving him or her a chance to live? Nevertheless, having a bastard* child will destroy my life. She leaned over the desk with her elbows on it, put her face in her hands. All-Knowing Allah, please show me a way. I don't know what to do, but you know what is best for me.

Esmira left the bookshop at the usual time. Once home, she ate her dinner and went straight to bed without saying so much as a word to her mother. Sadaget observed that she was far too quiet and pale, but did not ask for an explanation.

Once in bed, Esmira considered again whether she should go for an abortion at all. She recalled her neighbor Sevda, who had had a child outside of marriage. Some of her neighbors had laughed gossiping behind that poor girl's back. They had remarked tauntingly, "Look at that promiscuous woman! She couldn't wait until she wedded before sleeping with a man." They even stopped talking to her.

Thinking about Sevda's negative experience with having a bastard child troubled Esmira. She covered herself with a blanket, then stared blankly at the ceiling for what seemed hours. She tossed and turned, trying to fall asleep, while tears of desperation wet her pillow. Why do people always judge gossiping about others? Do they not fear Allah will punish them?

Esmira was afraid that they would gossip behind her back as well. She felt as if she was in quicksand, from which she would be unable to extricate herself. Oh, Allah, I'm so confused and scared about this pregnancy. I know you don't approve of abortion, but I don't wish to bring shame to myself.

The next day at 8 a.m. she was already at work going through invoices and helping Sveta shelve books. She checked the total number of books from their latest delivery. Esmira made sure that the correct ones had been shipped.

While helping Esmira, Sveta gazed at her belly, frowning. Esmira noticed, and felt awkward. Her cheeks flushed as she turned away. Why does she keep looking at my belly? Does it look so large?

To distract Sveta, Esmira sent her into a storage room to pack the rest of the books. After finishing with the new stock, she went into her office. Esmira waited for Samed, wondering what he would say or do when he heard the news.

Samed finally arrived at noon; they left the bookshop and walked toward Boulevard Park. As they strolled, he noticed that

Esmira was unnaturally quiet. He wondered if she was still annoyed with him for not calling her previously.

Once in the park, they went into the Qunel Café. They ordered shish kebab and lavash.

She looked directly into his eyes, her face stern. "I have something to tell you."

"Yes?" Samed didn't like the look on her face, and became worried.

"Do you remember our dinner at your place?"

"Um..." His heart sank. He didn't like where this conversation was going.

"I'm pregnant!" Tears filled her eyes. Esmira's lips trembled. "I don't know what to do."

Samed dropped his fork and froze. He stared at his girlfriend, light-headed and wide-eyed.

"What?"

"I'am expecting your child."

"No, that can't be," exclaimed Samed in a shocked tone shaking his head. He got up from his seat, paced in circles, keeping his hands clasped behind his back.

He sat back in his seat. Samed stared at her belly, rubbing his brow.

"My period has been late, so yesterday I performed a test and it was positive."

He got up from his seat again and rushed to her side of the table. He took her hands and gazed into her eyes. "Are you sure you are pregnant from me?"

Taken aback by his rude question, Esmira pushed him away. "You were the only man with whom I have had sex. How could you suggest that I may have slept with someone else?"

He approached her again and held her hands. "Esmira, please listen to me. You should terminate this pregnancy as soon as possible. I will take you to the gynecologist. I'm a young man, unemployed, and still a student. To have a child is an enormous responsibility. I'm not ready for it. I can't tie myself down with a baby neither marry you."

Esmira was startled to hear his words. Her heart filled with sadness. Her eyes grew sad. Esmira's whole body trembled like a leaf. She didn't expect this kind of reaction from him; she'd believed that if he heard about the pregnancy, he would marry her.

Quietly, she stared at him with regret and pulled her hands away from him. Then she got up. Esmira walked away with a heavy heart, not looking back. Samed did not even try to stop her.

He smoked nervously while thinking about the situation. After a while, he paid for lunch. Then he went back to his apartment, where he spent some time drinking vodka and smoking, trying to forget about Esmira's pregnancy.

As for Esmira, she was so saddened that she could barely hold back her tears.

How could he suggest that the child may not be his?

She returned to the bookshop and continued working, trying not to look anxious or to tear up. When her workday was finished, she went back to her apartment.

Esmira knew that it was difficult to hide anything from Sadaget's watchful eyes. Therefore, she tried to look as calm as possible. She helped Sadaget place dishes of dolma, pilov, fried chicken, and bread on the table. They ate their food as they chatted. Sadaget loved talking a lot. However, hated when somebody interrupted or disagreed with her, so Esmira let her ramble on.

Over her meal, Sadaget talked about travel.

"My co-worker is going to Iran, then to Russia for a week. She asked me to come with her. I'm going to purchase clothing and expensive chocolates. I will sell them at work." Sadaget rubbed her hands together gleefully.

Esmira's eyes sparkled as her heart filled with joy upon hearing the news. Her mother was going to be away! This was an answer to her prayers. She looked at the icons of Mary, Jesus, and St. Matrena, which hung in the corner of the living room. They had been given to them by her Russian granny, Mariya, who had brought Orthodoxy into their lives. As a result, they followed some Muslim beliefs and Christian ones at the same time. Esmira wasn't sure who to thank for this favor, so she settled on her Muslim beliefs.

Thanks, Allah. It will be easier to solve my problem when Mother won't be around.

Her thoughts were abruptly interrupted.

Sadaget glared suspiciously into her daughter's eyes. She asked her, "Esmira, are you still seeing Samed?"

She tried not to move her eyes away. There was a thud in her chest; she knew she couldn't lie. "Yes, Mother, we see each other when he comes to buy books."

"I don't like him, so just be vigilant about him," Sadaget fired back.

"Mother, you never like anyone!" Anger appeared in Esmira's usually calm eyes.

"Just make sure you are not doing anything stupid when I'm away, like Sevda. I don't want you to become pregnant like her," warned Sadaget, her face serious.

At those words, Esmira glanced at her belly. She felt chills passing through her body. Her shoulders moved jerkily. Aggravated at what her mother had said, she snapped, "Why do you always expect the worst from me?"

Sadaget rested her knife with a fork by her plate and gazed calmly at her daughter. "I don't expect the worst from you. I'm trying to protect you from mistakes."

Esmira lost her appetite, put down her fork. She got up from her seat. She shook her head in disbelief and stared into her mother's cold, brown eyes.

"Mother, you are constantly choking me with your overprotective stance. You never give me any space. You read the Bible and the Quran, therefore you should know better how to treat others." Esmira put her hand on her chest, pointing to herself. Her round face turned purple and eyes sparked with fury as she spoke.

Witnessing her daughter distressed, Sadaget decided to back off.

"I will try to give you more space," she said with a grunt, "but remember, don't ever let any man touch you before marriage. A man who would fancy touching you without marrying you does not love you, but instead lusts for sex. Anyhow, having sex out of marriage is a sin."

Her words reminded Esmira of the night she had spent with Samed. Out of anger, she was tempted to blurt out to her, "It's too late. I'm pregnant and a big sinner!"

Instead, she cried out with a pleading voice, "Mother, I wouldn't forget this, because you have been telling me this since I was nine years old! Please, stop telling me the same thing repeatedly. I'm not a child. I need my freedom and some peace of mind."

Aggravated with her mother's negativity, Esmira stopped talking to her. Instead, she removed everything from the table, as was her usual routine. Then she went back to her bedroom. As soon as she put on her pajamas, she settled down in bed, trying to rid herself of the rage that caused her chest muscles to constrict and gave her a headache. She is always expecting the worst, attracting negativity to herself and me. Why is my life a total failure?

Two weeks had passed since she found out about her pregnancy. During this time she lost track of Samed; he seemed to have disappeared without a trace. A few times Esmira tried to make an appointment with a gynecologist, but as soon as she dialed the number, she would put down the phone and stand silently next to it, feeling the need to cry.

In the middle of June, Esmira decided to call again to make an appointment with the gynecologist. She rang up Doctor Petrovskiy's office and asked when she could see him. The receptionist told Esmira that the doctor would be available at 1.30 p.m.

After making an appointment, Esmira tried not to think about the pregnancy for a while by remaining occupied at work. At noon, she looked at herself in the mirror. Esmira put on some bright red lipstick to match her scarlet dress. Then she left the bookshop and took a train to the Sahil station. From there, Esmira walked through Icheri Sheher for about half an hour in search of the clinic. She took her time, since she was in no real hurry to meet with the doctor.

As she passed near Gyz Galasy, she stopped to read about its history. This building was a cylindrical eight-story tower that stood 29 meters tall and was built from stone. The legend said that, a long time ago, the daughter of the Khan jumped from the top of this tower into the Caspian Sea. Esmira couldn't help but wish that she could do the same thing.

She walked near the Palace of the Shirvanshahs-a two story stone building, and admired its structure. Then she spent some time gazing at Boulevard Park, which was located across the highway from the Palace of the Shirvanshahs.

She approached the clinic's two-story building, her heart pounding.

I hope nobody from our neighborhood sees me in there.

She climbed to the second floor. Esmira entered the lobby area, where she slowly approached the secretary. After she gave her name, she was told that the doctor would see her in 20 minutes. While sitting in the clinic, to her surprise Esmira saw her neighbor's daughter, Elvira. She was a 20-year-old, tall, thin woman who talked too much. As soon as Elvira entered the lobby, she saw Esmira.

"Hi, Esmira! It has been a long time."

"Hello, Elvira!" The two women hugged one another. "You know how it is with work." Esmira shrugged. "It keeps one too busy."

What is this gossiper doing here? thought Esmira.

Then an unsavory answer struck her. She wondered if it could possibly be true. She had to know.

"Elvira, what are you doing here?"

Elvira smiled with a sparkle in her eyes. "I have been employed here for four months, working as a doctor's assistant."

"I didn't know that." A muscle twitched at the corner of Esmira's right lip.

"Why are you here?" Elvira asked, eyeing Esmira suspiciously.

"I just came for a check-up," Esmira tried not to look at Elvira's eyes. A fiery, burning sensation of embarrassment covered her cheeks and ears.

"Oh, okay." Elvira turned away. "I have to go back to work. Talk to you later." She picked up a patient's card from the desk and left.

As Elvira departed, Esmira breathed a sigh of relief, though she still felt anxious.

What should I do now? If Elvira finds out about my pregnancy, every neighbor will know. I can't see Doctor Petrovskiy now.

She was about to leave, but just then Elvira came up to her again. She asked Esmira to follow her. Esmira's neighbor showed her to the doctor's room and left.

"Good afternoon, Doctor Petrovskiy," announced Esmira when she entered the examination room.

"Good day, Esmira Khanum, please sit down. How can I assist you?"

Esmira sat on the chair. She put her handbag on her lap, trying to hide her belly. She stared into the doctor's deep black eyes, not knowing what to say, and suddenly started coughing.

Doctor Petrovskiy put down the pen he had been using before she entered the room.

"Esmira Khanum, are you okay?" uttered the doctor in a concerned tone.

"Yes, I am," said Esmira breathlessly.

The doctor leaned forward over the desk. "What brought you here?"

Esmira felt beads of sweat rolling down her neck. "For the past four months, my period has been heavy. I was cramped more than usual," she uttered.

Should I tell him about my pregnancy? she wondered briefly. No, it's better to keep quiet.

"Do you have any other symptoms?"

"No, I don't." Her breathing became rapid. She felt the pulse pounding in her temples.

"This is common. Such a change happens to many women, due to stress, hormonal imbalances, thyroid problems, or some other medical conditions. Have you been experiencing any stress recently or taking any medications?"

She stared at her belly playing nervously with her handbag's handle. Then she looked directly at the doctor. "Yes, the last few months have been stressful for me."

"Your problem could be due to stress, but to confirm my suggestion you should take a blood test. You will need to take Ibuprofen and Naproxen to reduce heavy bleeding and stop the pain. I would like to examine you."

He gestured toward a closed door. "Please go to the next room. Remove your pants."

She got up and slowly walked toward the examination room.

He is going to find out that I'm pregnant, she thought nervously, trying not to quiver uncontrollably.

When she approached the examination room, Esmira stopped and turned to the doctor. "I'm getting heavy bleeding right now. I feel nauseous. Can we perform the ultrasound when my period is over?" Esmira asked with a faint smile.

"No problem. You can come back next week," replied the doctor reassuringly.

She sat back down in her seat, shaking slightly, while he wrote a prescription as well as referrals to check her hormone level and to get a thyroid blood test. He handed both scripts to her.

"I would like to see you as soon as you get your test results," said Dr. Petrovskiy as he passed them to her.

Esmira took the slips from the doctor and got up. "Thank you, Doctor! As soon as I get my results, I will be back in touch. Bye!"

She then exited his office in a big hurry. Esmira left the medical center. She walked back to the bookshop, feeling lighter. Esmira was glad that she had seen Elvira before saying anything to the doctor about her pregnancy.

I feel like a stone has fallen off my shoulders. If I had known she was in there, I would never have gone in. What should I do now? Apparently, I need to find another gynecologist, she thought.

After sitting down in her chair, she called Sabina to relate what had occurred at the gynecologist's office.

"Did you see Doctor Gena Petrovskiy?" Sabina asked with curiosity.

"Yes, I did, but I met my neighbor, who works there. Because of her, I hid the actual cause of my visit." Esmira moved from side to side in the swivel chair.

"You have to go back to him for an abortion."

"No, I can't go back. If she finds out that I'm pregnant, everyone will know," exclaimed Esmira anxiously, rolling her eyes.

Sabina promised to get the name of another gynecologist. Hearing this eased some of Esmira's fears.

Later, when Esmira reached home, her mother was anxiously waiting for her. Sadaget eyed her sternly with a pinched and knitted brow.

Suddenly she demanded, "For heaven's sake, Esmira, why did you visit a gynecologist?"

At first, Esmira paused, tongue-tied. Her eyes roamed about the room while she thought of an excuse. Finally, she told her, "For a few months, I have been cramping and getting heavy periods."

She hated lying. Therefore, barely looked at her mother's eyes, knowing that lying is wrong.

Sadaget sat on the sofa and stared at Esmira's face. "What did the doctor say?"

"He asked me to take a blood test to find out the cause." Esmira felt every beat of her heart, while fear crawled through her veins like a spider.

"Let me know the results." Sadaget eyed Esmira suspiciously from head to toe.

"Okay, I will. I'm going to change now," her daughter said, with a sigh of relief.

Esmira went to her bedroom and changed out of her work clothes. That evening they managed to have a peaceful dinner. Sadaget mentioned that her travel plans had been postponed, which was hardly good news for Esmira. She had hoped that when her mother was away she would be able to arrange for the abortion without her knowledge.

They spent an hour talking. Then around 11 p.m., they retreated to their bedrooms to go to sleep.

***

As the days passed quickly one after the other, Esmira neither visited the office of a gynecologist nor heard from Samed. Her unexpected pregnancy continued to dog her conscience. Adding to her frustration, Esmira's belly started swelling. She would start each morning by standing in front of a mirror in only a black bra and panties. Esmira was dismayed to see her belly grow day by day. All she could do was rub it.

Oh, it is growing! I need to act before people notice it.

Esmira knew that time was of the essence and feared that soon Sadaget would detect her pregnancy. It was plain that soon she would have no time left to think about what to do.

One morning, without having breakfast, she left her apartment. In her bookshop office, she tried to get an appointment with a different gynecologist, but the doctor there was away from the office. Failing to get another appointment, she put down the phone.

She felt as if she was drowning in a deep sea, unable to escape. She sat in her office chair and put her head on the table. For some time, she stayed in that position, feeling despondent.

Why is it so difficult to find a gynecologist? What will happen if I can't find one?

Esmira was disturbed that Samed didn't yearn for a child. He'd simply discarded her, like taking out the trash. She lifted her head and looked at down at her belly.

Why did I fall in love with him? Why didn't I listen to my mother; after all, she was right!

Suddenly nauseous, she stood up. Esmira rushed to the bathroom, where she leaned over the toilet bowl and vomited. Her stomach emptied, she rinsed her mouth. After she returned to her office. She spent a long time sitting in her chair without doing anything, staring vacantly at the ceiling.

As her belly continued to grow, she hid her pregnancy by wrapping it tightly with a scarf and wearing a loose blouse over it. Sometimes, she squeezed her stomach so tightly that it made her feel like vomiting. For five months of her pregnancy, she had been able to conceal it without detection.

Her co-workers thought that she was just gaining some weight. However, Sveta suspected that Esmira was pregnant, but she kept her mouth shut so as not to lose her job.

Unfortunately, as July approached, her pregnancy became more than apparent. One morning she got up early, craving pickles. She was thinking that Sadaget was still in bed. Esmira headed for the kitchen without wrapping herself, wearing only a bra and undies, leaving her big round belly exposed.

When Esmira entered the kitchen, she stopped short and abruptly, right in front of Sadaget, her big belly in full view. Sadaget had been unable to sleep; she had come into the kitchen to have some tea and read the newspaper. Hearing Esmira's steps, Sadaget lifted her head.

Seeing her mother, Esmira froze, aghast. Her whole body suddenly felt weak. She felt like she was going to black out. Esmira held onto the table to keep from falling, her heart beating fast.

Allah, have mercy on me!

Sadaget saw Esmira's belly, and her jaw suddenly dropped.

Her mother's facial expression made Esmira agitated. Her knees began to shake.

"Are you pregnant?" Sadaget screeched, wide-eyed. She stared, disbelieving, at her daughter's belly.

Esmira didn't know what to say, so she kept silent, her eyes downcast, trying to avoid facing her mother's gaze.

"Answer me! Are you pregnant?" exclaimed Sadaget, shaking with rage.

"Yes, I am," answered Esmira in a hushed voice, shaking slightly and trying not to look directly at her mother.

Sadaget got up, dropping her newspaper. She looked into Esmira's sad eyes. "Who did you sleep with?" she demanded.

Esmira remained silent.

"What happened? Have you swallowed your tongue?"

"I'm ashamed," answered Esmira in a low voice.

Sadaget picked up the newspaper. She threw it at her daughter. It hit her belly and fell onto the floor. Esmira moved two steps back.

"You should have shame, jumping into a man's bed without marriage!" yelled Sadaget. She shook her head and, approaching Esmira, she spat on her. Next, she slapped her face.

"Whore! Was it Samed?"

Esmira turned her face to the left and shut her eyes tightly.

"Talk to me!" Sadaget held her fist in front of her daughter's face. Her demanding voice echoed in Esmira's aching ears.

"Yes, it was him," replied Esmira meekly, recoiling from Sadaget.

"You opened your big mouth. Demanded that you needed space when I advised you about him. I gave you space. Look at the result now!" exclaimed her mother, pointing at her belly and shaking her head in disbelief.

She peered down at her daughter's belly. "How far along are you in the pregnancy?"

Esmira wished that she could become invisible; instead, she stood helplessly in front of her mother. "Six months, I think, but I'm not sure."

Sadaget sat down and started tapping her fingers on the table.

Lastly, she raged, "How could you do this to me? Did I not tell you repeatedly not to let anyone touch you before marriage? You really cannot wait until a man marries you! You are indeed a whore!"

Upon hearing that word, Esmira stared at her mother angrily. The weakness that she felt flushed out of her body and her chest constricted.

"Mother, stop yelling; the neighbors will hear you. You have been calling me a whore for no reason ever since I was a teenager. Yes, I made a mistake, but I'm not a whore! He got me drunk. After that, we had sex. I wasn't aware of my behavior."

She came up closer to her mother, pointing a finger at her. "Don't call me a whore. I don't like it!" Her legs ached from standing, so she sat down, breathing hard.

"I cautioned you that he was no good, but you didn't listen to me. Why do children never listen to their parents? If you had listened to my advice, none of this would have happened."

Sadaget got up and poured another cup of tea, then sat back down. "You have made a huge mistake. Do you know that people will be pointing their fingers at you? Does that scoundrel know about your pregnancy?" Sadaget was getting over the initial shock. She was calming down a little

"Yes, I told him about it." She started suddenly, feeling movement in her belly.

"What is he planning to do about it?"

"He does not care for a child or marriage," Esmira answered in a shaky voice.

"If this bastard thinks that he can make you pregnant and get away with it, he is making a huge mistake. I'm going to call him and make sure that he marries you!" Sadaget yelled, waving her fist in the air. She slammed her tea mug down on the table so hard that some of the tea spilled.

"What will happen if he refuses?" implored Esmira.

Sadaget got up from her seat. "He won't have a choice other than to marry you; otherwise, he has to go to court for raping you! Go back to your room. Don't go to work tomorrow."

Esmira got up from her seat, relieved. She breathed lightly and closed her eyes for a second.

Good, I don't have to sit next to her with my belly wrapped any longer.

Her mother interrupted her thoughts. "However, this is not only his fault; you allowed this to happen to yourself. Nobody pushed alcohol down your throat. Why did you allow yourself to get drunk?"

Esmira didn't have an answer to her mother's question. She merely stood stone still, silently listening to her mother's burning words.

"Anyway, just get his phone number for me," demanded her mother.

She went into her room, copied down Samed's phone number, and gave it to her. Esmira's mother went into her bedroom. Sadaget pondered whether she should call him now or early in the morning. She decided to wait until morning, then settled down in bed. She tried to fall asleep.

I did everything to protect her from male predators, worrying she would become a single mother like me, thereby facing condemnation from society. After all, what sort of Muslim man would want to marry a fornicator, ending up with a bastard child on her hands?

Sadaget was disappointed with Esmira. She herself had purposely stayed without a man after the divorce to protect her daughter, but still, Esmira had done what Sadaget was afraid she would do.

The younger generation should listen to their elders, who have lived long enough to gain the wisdom and knowledge that the younger generation lack, thought Sadaget, barely keeping her eyes open.

Restless, Esmira could not fall asleep, pondering what Samed would do after Sadaget talked to him.

Will he agree to marry me or try to get out? I hope Mother won't go too far. She tends to over-stir the pot and make too much noise.

She looked at the clock hanging on the wall. Oh, time is passing so fast. I need to get some sleep.

Even though she was worried, she somehow managed to fall asleep. Esmira slept for about four hours.

Early in the day light, Sadaget called Samed. He was getting dressed when the phone rang. Samed wondered who was calling him at this early time. He looked at the number, but not recognizing it at first, he ignored the call. However, his phone continued ringing. Samed became infuriated.

Finally, he punched the answer button and practically shouted, "Yes?!"

"Good morning, may I speak to Samed, please?"

"Er...good morning. This is Samed."

"I'm Esmira's mother. I would like to talk to you, face to face." Sadaget tried to stay calm. "Can you come to my apartment, please?"

Samed's head suddenly started to pound; he sensed danger and knew that he was unable to get away. The game was up. He was in deep trouble. "Sadaget Khanum, I'm busy these days and won't be able to come."

"Listen to me, bastard." Her voice was still calm, but underneath was a brewing fury. "Were you busy when you impregnated my daughter?"

The storm hit. "You had better make time, before I report you to the police for raping her!" shouted Sadaget.

"I didn't rape her. She willingly slept with me!" Samed blurted.

Sadaget squeezed the phone tightly, and rage rose from her chest to her cheeks. "You made her purposely drunk and used her drunkenness to your advantage. You had better come or I will go myself to the police."

Hearing Sadaget's threat made him uneasy. He removed a handkerchief from his pocket and wiped his face.

"Please calm down, Sadaget Khanum. There is no need for the police. We can solve the problem in a civilized manner. When would you like me to come?" asked the coward in a gruff voice. Beads of sweat rolled down his temples.

"You can come at three o'clock. Don't delay!" she yelled, and slammed the phone down.

Talking to Samed made Sadaget even more furious. I'm going to put this man in his place!

After Sadaget's call, Samed felt at a loss as to what to do. His head hurt and his heart raced.

He sat on the sofa, pondering what he should do or say when he went to see her. Samed decided to spend some time at Boulevard Park with a friend. From there go by Sadaget's apartment.

When he reached Boulevard Park, it was not as busy as usual. A strong wind blew, swaying the palm trees from side to side and making the waves crash into the rocks.

Samed walked toward Zeynab Café. There he met his long-time friend, Imran. His friend was a rotund, short man with black eyes and short black hair. He loved eating a lot. Subsequently had a big belly that appeared even larger when he was sitting.

Samed met him as he was drinking tea and having his breakfast. He stared at his friend's stomach with surprise.

"Good morning, Imran."

Imran got up. He slowly approached his friend. "Hello, my friend. It's been a long time since I've seen you," said Imran, hugging Samed.

"I have been busy with my studies."

"Are you sure you haven't been occupied picking up women?" Imran winked jokingly, knowing his friend's proclivity for the opposite sex.

Samed smirked, rubbing his nose. "Yes, I suppose you're right!"

Samed ordered tea with lemon and sugar. While sitting and sipping tea, they talked about their good times together, women, and plans for the future.

Imran bit into a big piece of cake, leaving crumbs on his lips. Samed gazed at him with wide eyes.

"Kishi, I can't believe you are having cake for breakfast. You are putting on pounds. In a few months, you'll look like an elephant! You'd better get some of that weight off before you start having health issues.

Two deep wrinkles appeared on Imran's forehead. Peeved, he wiped his lips with a napkin. "Leave my weight alone," he demanded. Imran moved his hands as he talked. "I have tried many times to lose weight, but I gave up."

Samed lit a Marlboro and inhaled, then settled down comfortably in his chair. "To lose weight, cut down on sugar and carbohydrates. Use less oil. Also, eat a lot of vegetables, fruits, and drink plenty of water. To succeed overall when dieting, you ought to exercise. Remain mobile as much as possible, rather than being stationary."

Imran looked at his belly. He gave a snort of disgust. "You think it is so easy to stop eating all of this garbage? Sometimes stress and anxiety drive me to overeat. It helps to calm down my nerves. In fact, a friend of the same weight as me finds it bothersome to exercise on a daily basis."

Samed grimaced inwardly. This man has no willpower. A bit of a dim bulb too, and has no will whatsoever to better himself.

Imran got tired of hearing comments about his weight. He gazed at Samed with a frown and suddenly coughed. "I really can't understand you. You are giving me a lecture on losing weight, but you have this nasty habit of smoking. You are not only infecting your lungs, but the health of those around you."

"Leave my smoking alone, please," retorted Samed.

Imran decided to change the subject. "How are things going between you and Tatyana?"

"We had a fight. I have not seen her since."

Imran grinned winking. "You didn't lose anything. She was too old for you. I don't understand what a man like you found in her," Imran said. He took a sip of his tea.

Samed put the butt of his cigarette out in an ashtray. He smiled cockily. "When I came to Baku, I didn't know anyone. She was the first woman I met. I had a good time with her."

Imran winked again. "Not only did you have fun with her, but she dated others while seeing you. Doesn't that bother you?"

Samed grinned widely as he sank further into his chair. "Not really. I wasn't planning to marry her anyway. She was just a woman I slept with."

"Samed, you use women for your benefit. Then you dump them. God will surely punish you one day."

Imran's warning irritated Samed. "Again, you are starting with your preaching. Please, not today."

Samed got up suddenly. "Imran, please accept my apologies, but I have to be somewhere."

Imran gazed into his friend's eyes, grinning mockingly. "As usual, you are running away when someone points out your mistakes."

"Imran, I'm not running away. I have a meeting to attend."

Samed caught the waitress's attention. "Khanum, can you bring my bill, please?" asked Samed with a wink.

After paying his bill, he promptly left. Samed decided to go to the cinema and watch an Azeri film before going to Sadaget's apartment, who he didn't wish to face. He bought a ticket for a Runway movie. After buying some sandwiches at the concession stand, he went into the film theater. Samed found a comfortable seat for himself, directly before the giant screen.

As Samed was watching the movie, Sadaget cleaned the apartment, thinking about what she should do about her daughter's pregnancy. She knew that if she didn't do something soon, her daughter would end up having a bastard child. She decided to insist that Samed marry her as quickly as possible.

Esmira stayed in her room, trying to avoid her mother's stern scolding. She patiently waited for Samed, looking at her watch repeatedly. It seemed as though the clock ticked too slowly.

Glancing at her watch once again, she saw that it was midday. Three more hours and he will be here. Will he agree to marry me or will he make up excuses?

Samed enjoyed the film, as well as his two sandwiches. Watching the film helped him forget his earlier conversation with Sadaget and their upcoming meeting. However, the film ended. It was time to leave the cinema. Samed walked to the bus stop. He took a bus that went straight to the street where Esmira lived. The bus was full of people standing close to each other. Samed didn't even have space in which to move. He became furious when someone accidentally stepped on his foot.

"Hey, watch where you're putting your feet!"

"I'm sorry," said the passenger, backing off and looking shocked.

It took twenty minutes for the bus to reach Nasperin Street. He paid one ruble and got off the bus.

After a ten-minute walk, he ended up in front of the tall building that housed Sadaget's apartment. Children rode bicycles around him. A few Volga and Zill vehicles lined the street in front of the building. Samed looked up and perceived clothes hung on the balconies. A few plants peeked over the edges. In some places, the asphalt in front of the building was cracked and filled with dried mud. The wind blew, raising dust into the air.

"Potato, tomato, onion, come and buy it!" shouted a middle-aged man as he passed Samed. There was a big sack on his back.

"Fresh farm milk!" said a young man pulling a cart. A few women with covered heads, long skirts rushed to him, their big glass jars in hand to buy fresh milk.

Samed entered Block Five and climbed the stairs. His heart raced so fast that he could feel every beat. Thoughts of facing Sadaget scared him. From conversations with Esmira, he knew that she was a strict, tough woman. He rang the bell twice. His heart skipped a beat as Sadaget opened the door.

"Good afternoon, Sadaget Khanum," he mumbled nervously.

"Come in, young man! We have been waiting for you." Sadaget bared her yellow teeth in a grimace.

He slowly entered and walked into the living room. There he saw Esmira sitting in an armchair, drinking tea.

"Hi... Esmira," Samed greeted her, a frown on his face.

A few wrinkles appeared on her forehead as she looked at him. "Hello."

He sat on a brown leather sofa near Esmira staring at her big belly.

"Samed, would you like a cup of tea?" inquired Sadaget.

"Yes, please," answered Samed. Watching her made him nervous. She went into the kitchen, and he relaxed a little.

He looked at Esmira, forcing a smile. "How are you doing?"

"I must be doing great, now that you have impregnated and dumped me," said Esmira sarcastically, tossing her head from side to side.

"I didn't force you to have sex with me."

Esmira got up from her seat. She came toward him. Her finger jabbed at his chest. "You might not have forced me to have sex with you. Nonetheless, you knew that I was drunk and you still poured vodka for me. If it wasn't for that vodka, I would never have agreed to sleep with you."

Sadaget came back with two cups of tea and gave one to Samed. Seeing Esmira standing near him, her eyebrows crunched together like two vehicles in a crash.

"Esmira, is everything okay?"

"Yes, Mother, just getting something off my chest." A grimace crossed Esmira's serious face. She moved away from Samed.

Sadaget sank into the sofa right next to him. Her narrowed eyes observed him closely. Uncomfortable, Samed moved away from her.

"Young man, we have an enormous problem here. We have to solve it right now! My daughter is expecting. This pregnancy will bring shame on our family. You made her pregnant, and you alone have the responsibility to solve this dilemma."

The frown on Sadaget's face deepened. Samed sank deeper into the sofa. His muscles tensed as his left eyelid twitched.

"What do you want me to do?" he asked nervously.

"You are going to marry my daughter as soon as possible. If you refuse, I will file a rape report with the police. You will end up in jail!"

He bowed his head and rubbed it, kneading his brow with both hands for a while. "I can't marry Esmira. I'm already married. I have two small children in Zardob," Samed told them. It was the best lie he could think of.

Sadaget glared into his eyes. "Are you trying to trick us with your lies? You never told Esmira that you had a wife."

Samed got up, took out a passport from his pocket. He gave it to Sadaget. "Please, look at the passport; it shows that I'm married with two children."

His hands shook. He hoped that his lies would work. Samed had pilfered the passport from a university student. The poor fellow had had to get a new one. Before the renewal could be sent to him, Samed had used the one he had stolen numerous times, to avoid marrying the innocent prey that he had lured into his bedroom.

Sadaget took his passport and went through the pages. On page thirteen, she saw the names of two children. Sadaget shook her head slowly in disbelief, appalled at his behavior. She was so angry at his lies that she could barely keep herself from slapping him. Instead, she got up and tossed the passport in his face.

"You are a dirty man who chases every skirt you can find. All this time, even though you are married, you still dated my daughter! Just to sleep with her."

Samed retrieved the passport and put it away.

"The fact that you are married does not change anything. You are going to marry my daughter under religious law," insisted Sadaget firmly, pointing her finger at him.

Samed stood up and took a few steps back. "My father wouldn't agree to this marriage. He believes that a man should have one wife. I can't go against his will. He will stop paying for my studies."

"I don't care what your father will do or what he won't! You slept with my daughter, got her pregnant. Now you ought to pay the consequences. Don't force me to call the police and report a rape!"

Samed stood silently, looking at the ground. He felt a strong urge to urinate. His legs shook.

"I...," he mumbled. His face turned pale. Samed felt a stabbing pain behind his eyes as if someone had thrust a knife into his head multiple times.

"I'm sure you would spend a few years in jail. With your good looks, big men will rape you. Do you want that to happen to you?" threatened Sadaget.

Samed paced around the room nervously, keeping his hands behind his back.

"All right, I will marry Esmira. However, I wouldn't be able to take her with me because of my first wife. I'll move into your apartment, but I will be going to Zardob to spend time with my children and wife. Please do not contact any members of my family. Once I finish my studies, then I will tell my father about this marriage," Samed said, knowing full well that he would never do such a thing.

"How many more years do you need to complete your studies?"

"Two years."

As they talked, Esmira bit her nails, nervously listening to their conversation. She felt relieved when Samed agreed to marry her. Esmira was afraid that Sadaget would not be able to control her temper, and either hit him or, worse, kill him.

Sadaget got up from her seat. She stood behind Esmira's armchair, resting her hands on it. "Tomorrow, I'm going to meet Imam to organize the marriage ceremony. I will let you know the date. Just make sure that you are ready! For two years, I will keep my mouth shut. After that, I will let your family know about this marriage."

She stared into his eyes sternly pointing a finger at him. "You can leave now! Just make sure that you don't try to vanish without a trace!" she warned him.

Samed got up and walked quickly to the door. He was getting a headache from the conversation with her. When he reached his apartment, he took two aspirin tablets.

The next day, Sadaget called her childhood friend, Imam Nasir. Over the phone, Sadaget let him know that she needed to talk to him about something important, face-to-face. Imam Nasir agreed to meet Sadaget at 1 p.m. in his mosque.

At midday, she left the apartment. Sadaget went to see Imam Nasir. He greeted her with a big smile and invited her to his small office beside the mosque. As they sat together, Imam Nasir said, "I have not seen you in our mosque, nor heard from you, in a long while."

"I have been busy these past few months. Now I have a big problem weighing on my shoulders. I'm trying to resolve it," Sadaget replied.

Imam folded his hands in front of himself and frowned. "Sister, no matter how busy we are, we should always remember our Creator. You know He wants to see us in His house. I have not seen you in here for a long time."

"You are right, Imam. We shouldn't forget to give Allah what is due to Him, but I really couldn't make it." Feeling guilty, Sadaget did not dare to raise her eyes.

"May He forgive you, Sister. Please find time to come and pray in His house. When we think that something is significant to us, we always find time for it."

"You are right, Imam Nasir. I will try to change and build a stronger relationship with Him," agreed Sadaget.

"Good. We can't enter into Paradise unless we establish a good relationship with Him. We have to pray daily, demonstrate kindness, love to others, and stay away from wrongdoings," continued Imam Nasir.

He leaned over the desk toward her. "Sister, you mentioned that you have a significant problem. What is it?"

Sadaget's eyes ran across the room. She was nervous, and her eyelid kept twitching.

"Imam Nasir, this topic is so delicate that I don't know where to start. I feel ashamed to talk about it. My daughter was dating a young man. He invited her to dinner and got her drunk. Well, what one would expect transpired between them. She ended up pregnant. All this time, she has been hiding her pregnancy from me. I only found out about it recently by chance."

Sadaget noticed a frown on the Imam's face. A few deep wrinkles appeared on his forehead. He got up from his seat. "How many months pregnant is she?"

"Six months." Sadaget's face flushed red. She stared at her hands.

Imam shook his head in disbelief.

"A woman's belly at six months is obvious. How were you not able to see anything?" asked the stunned Imam.

Sadaget put her hand to her forehead. "She has been wrapping her belly and wearing loose clothes."

"Sister, this is an enormous sin and shame. In Europe, it is acceptable for a woman to have a relationship with a man without marriage, but not in our society. Decent women shouldn't sleep with men without benefit of marriage, but because she was intoxicated, I can't blame her alone. He purposely made her drunk, but she shouldn't have gone to his house in the first place."

Sadaget began to feel dizzy and ashamed.

"Do you know him, Sister? Who are his parents?" questioned the Imam.

"I don't know his parents, but they live in Zardob. He came to Baku to study at university. I met him only twice." Sadaget removed a tissue from her pocket and wiped her face.

"Did you talk to him about the pregnancy?"

"Yes, I did ask him to marry my daughter. But to my surprise, I found out that he is already married with two young children," Sadaget replied. Her hands trembled slightly.

"Hmmm," said the Imam, touching his chin. "The fact that he has a wife makes things worse, Sister. What are you planning to do?"

Sadaget pulled herself upright."Doesn't Muslim law allow a man to have four wives?" she asked.

"Yes, a man can have up to four wives."

"Then Samed can marry my daughter," posited Sadaget, beaming a smile.

Imam nodded. "Yes, he can."

"Are you in a position to perform a nikah ceremony as soon as possible?" asked Sadaget.

"I understand your situation, Sister. I will do my best to help you. Bring them on Friday at 10 a.m."

Sadaget gazed gratefully at the Imam with a relieved smile. "Thank you, Imam Nasir."

She got up from her seat, feeling light. "I have to go now, but will be back on Friday."

"Go with peace, Sister."

While Sadaget was visiting Imam Nasir, Esmira remained busy with her work. In the morning, she called her friend Sabina, relating to her everything that had happened the day before. Esmira let her know that Sadaget had discovered her pregnancy. Sabina was bewildered that it had taken so long for Sadaget to notice.

"If you had listened to me and gone for the abortion, none of this would have happened. When a problem arises, you have to solve it without delay before it takes on a life of its own," said Sabina.

"Abortion is killing a life, and is a sin in our religion, so I simply couldn't do it."

Sabina was happy to hear that Samed had agreed to marry Esmira, but she warned her that he might change his mind and could not be trusted.

"He wouldn't. My mother threatened him with jail."

Sabina chuckled. "As for your mom, I wouldn't fancy being in his place, since she will undoubtedly 'fix' him."

When Sadaget reached home, she called Samed and told him about the arrangements with the Imam. "Don't be a fool and try to escape from your responsibilities. One more lie or trick. I will travel to Zardob to meet your father personally," threatened Sadaget.

Cold chills shook and shuddered through Samed's body. He did not like the threat at all. "I will marry Esmira. There's no need to threaten me."

They agreed that on Friday, Samed would come to Sadaget's apartment, and from there all of them would go to the Imam. Samed was not happy with any of this, but he knew that he couldn't get away this time. Suddenly, he realized that because he was using a false identity, his marriage would not be legal. His heart eased and he decided to just go ahead with this marriage, and somehow extricate himself from the mess at a later time.

Chapter 3: The Shocking Discovery

The night was windy and full of lightning fireworks. The flares lit up Esmira's room, illuminating the tiger pattern on the wallpaper. Thoughts of a Nikah ceremony kept Esmira awake. In even her worst nightmares, she had never fathomed this type of engineered marriage. Esmira had always fantasized about a big wedding ceremony, with a resplendent reception and live music. She had imagined herself wearing a beautiful white dress, and surrounded by her friends, relatives. Now she despaired that tomorrow none of her relatives would be there. Neither would there be any music, nor a celebration after a formal and dignified ceremony. Nonetheless, she was pleased that her mother had forced Samed into marriage with her, which would prevent malicious rumors from spreading.

Very early in the morning, she got up and took a shower. Esmira decided to set off to work and open the bookstore, but after that, she would return home promptly. She left the apartment at 7 a.m. and took the bus to the bookshop.

That same morning, Samed got up with a heavy heart. As he brushed his teeth, he wondered, "Why did she get pregnant? I've slept with others and no one got pregnant, so why her?"

A Russian song played in the background on the radio:

"You are the man of my dreams. I crave to make love with you. Come, darling, to my bed. Let me feel you inside of me."

He stood in front of the mirror naked, proud of his strong, wide shoulders, athletic body, and six-pack abs. Foreign women adored them. He loved to show them off as he strolled along the beach during the summer in Moscow. As he admired himself in the mirror, he beamed with pride. Then he took a shower and left the apartment, setting off to Sadaget's place.

Sadaget also awoke early, feeling distracted. She stayed in bed for a while, preoccupied with Esmira's future. She felt disappointed as she thought about the proper weddings of the daughters of her friends, with grooms bringing jewelry, gift baskets, and the bride arriving at the wedding in a decorated car amid joyous music. On the contrary, her daughter would have none of these niceties and embellishments. Esmira's mother couldn't understand why young people didn't think before making careless mistakes. If they stopped to think, they would not end up in unfortunate situations.

Sadaget recalled the stigma that she encountered when people all around her spoke ill of divorced single mothers, even suspecting them of having secret lovers. Her mother, Mariya, used to say, "Everyone has a husband, yet you have nobody in your life, so don't even try to raise your head up high and walk forth proudly." She sighed at the memory.

After staying in bed for some time, she got up. She collected herself and prepared her mind and body in order to be able to enter the mosque.

Esmira reached home at 8.45 a.m. She shed her work clothing and put on an attractive long-sleeved brown dress. She heard the doorbell, and mother's voice as Sadaget opened the door to let Samed in.

He entered with a fake smile on his face. "Good morning, Sadaget Khanum."

"Good morning, young man." Sadaget glared at him with a riveting stare. He slunk into the living room, feeling awkward.

In the lounge, Sadaget stood with her face close to his. "Esmira is my only child. This is not the kind of marriage ceremony I had planned for her. Your appearance in her life ruined everything. As it stands, I will no longer tolerate any more of your games or lies."

Samed backed away and sat down quietly. His eyes roamed all over the room as if looking for a means to escape.

"I called a cab. As soon as it comes, we will head off to the mosque and settle this problem."

She stepped away from Samed. He exhaled audibly, regaining his composure feeling more at ease.

"While waiting, would you like a cup of tea?" she asked him grudgingly.

"No, thank you."

The phone rang. Sadaget picked it up. The call was from the cab company.

"Yes, we are ready, but please give us about ten minutes."

She put the phone down and called to her daughter, "Esmira, the cab is here. Are you ready?"

"Yes, I am," Esmira called down. She felt nervous and trembled slightly.

"Hurry up then! Don't forget to cover your head."

Sadaget picked her handbag up from the sofa.

Esmira emerged from her bedroom with a veil over her head. They all headed outside.

Sadaget gave the taxi driver the name of and directions to the mosque. Along the way, the driver passed other cars on the bumpy road, driving far too close to the other vehicles. The entire cab shook, causing the passengers to toss back and forth like the ingredients of a salad. At one point, the driver stuck his hand outside.

"Son of a bitch, drive your car properly!" he screamed.

Sadaget hung onto the half-broken grip above her, "Please don't drive so fast and recklessly," she demanded.

"If I don't pass other cars, it will take about an hour to reach our destination." The driver looked at her crossly in the rear-view mirror.

Sadaget raised her voice. "I don't care about the time! Our lives are more important!"

The driver slowed down. He refrained from passing other cars. In an hour, the cab stopped in front of an enormous green mosque.The passengers climbed out. They walked toward the mosque and entered Imam Nasir's small, light-green office.

"Good morning," said Sadaget as she entered.

"Hello," answered Imam.

Samed looked around, taking in the simplicity of the décor. The Imam's office had a small white wooden desk with a simple wooden white chair. There was a green carpet beneath them.

Imam gazed with curiosity at Esmira and Samed. "It is indeed nice to see a young couple like you. Are you ready to tie the knot?"

"Yes," answered both of them, glancing at each other.

"Do you know that marriage is a big responsibility and a long-term commitment?" Imam met Samed's gaze.

"Yes," answered the groom.

"It should be based on mutual understanding, respect, trust, and love," continued Imam Nasir. He gazed at them, his lips stretched broadly in a smile.

"I hope your marriage will have all these qualities. It will be the happiest you can imagine and hope for," he continued.

The Imam's phone rang.

"My apologies." He excused himself and picked up the phone. "Yes? Everyone is here. Are the sisters, Sevinch and Afet, in the mosque? If so, send them to my office, please," he said into the receiver, and then hung up.

After a few minutes, two middle-aged women entered the Imam's office, breathing heavily, as if they had rushed over.

"Good morning," they said.

"Good morning," everyone answered.

Imam gestured toward the ladies. "Sadaget Khanum, these are Sevinch and Afet Khanum. They are here to witness the marriage ceremony."

Sadaget gazed at them. Sevinch was a short plump woman, while Afet was tall and lithe.

"Did you bring your birth certificates or passports?" asked Imam.

Sadaget took out Esmira's birth certificate from her handbag and handed it to the Imam.

"What about you, Samed?" asked Imam.

Samed glanced at him. A muscle twitched in his lip. "I forgot," he fibbed.

Imam's eyes narrowed. "How could you forget it? Before starting a marriage ceremony, I need to see a passport or a birth certificate."

He noticed the panicked look on Sadaget's face, and sighed in resignation. "Just the same, I will proceed without them, but you need to produce it later on. Since this marriage is unexpected, I'm not going to follow exact procedures. May Almighty, Allah, forgive me."

He checked Esmira's birth certificate and then looked at Samed again. "What is your surname?"

"Abdulaev," lied Samed. A faint smile played on his lips. His eyes tried to avoid Imam's gaze.

After taking his notes, Imam got up from his seat. "Please follow me."

He left his office and headed toward the mosque, followed by the others. Everyone removed their shoes. They entered the large building.

Imam pulled a copy of the Quran from a shelf. Standing by a wooden minbar, a sort of altar, he invited everyone to draw closer to him. He read a piece from the Quran, then stopped.

"Samed Abdulaev, do you agree to take Esmira Babaeva as your wife?"

"Yes," Samed muttered.

"Sister Sadaget, is your daughter willing to marry Samed Abdulaev?" continued the Imam.

Sadaget gazed at Esmira. "Yes, she is."

Imam proceeded to talk about the importance of marriage. Then he read another passage from the Quran. When the marriage ceremony was over, Imam asked the witnesses, the bride, and the groom to sign a marriage certificate.

After they had finished signing the document, he announced, "You are now husband and wife."

A pleased smile formed on Sadaget's lips. She felt light as a feather. "Thank you, Imam Nasir, for helping us out. May Allah bless you with good health and a long life."

"You are welcome, Sister."

He looked at his watch. "Oh, it is late! I have to visit someone who is sick. My apologies, but I must leave now. Please go in peace," said Imam Nasir, flashing some of his gold teeth. He stole a glance at Esmira's protruding belly.

I fail to understand how such a woman could fornicate and produce a child out of wedlock and sin. Hasn't she read the Quran? Imam mused while walking away.

Sadaget spoke with the two witnesses and thanked them. "It's time for us to leave as well."

The trio left the mosque, as did the witnesses. The building was quiet once again.

***

Esmira felt blissful after the marriage ceremony, thinking that Samed was legally bound to her. However, the thought of his invisible alleged wife plagued her.

Why does religious law allow men to have more than one wife? He will be sleeping with this mystery woman, and then come back to my bed. Why should I share him with someone else? At least no one will call my child a bastard, nor will they dare call me promiscuous, or speak ill of me for jumping into his bed unmarried.

Samed soon packed all of his personal effects and relocated to his wife's apartment, which had two bedrooms and one living room. Sadaget's new son-in-law was happy to move to her apartment, since it saved him the money that he would have used to pay rent otherwise. While living with Esmira, he was so stingy that he did not contribute his money to buy groceries. Sadaget spent her money buying him Marlboro cigarettes and razor blades. Although she did not like spending her money on him, they got along well. Samed helped her to clean, cook, and even washed his clothes. Esmira's husband knew how to secure people's trust and love by pleasing them.

He had been reading many books on building relationships with people and influencing them. Every technique that he learned from these books, he used on everyone he met, especially women. His life of lying and not fearing punishment on judgment day puzzled his best friend, Tarhan. Once, while they were sitting on an old wooden bench in a park playing dominos, Tarhan remarked, "Friend, I'm genuinely astonished by your sinful and reckless lifestyle. You lead your life carelessly and hurt women. This is not the Muslim notion or tradition of living a chaste lifestyle. How did you adopt this destructive pattern of misconduct? Aren't you concerned and fearful that Allah will punish you?"

This line of conversation was annoying to Samed. He lit a cigarette and inhaled. He then leaned back, glared at Tarhan. Samed blew smoke into his friend's face.

"Who has appointed you the judge of me? Live your life on the tried, true, and right path but leave mine alone," said Samed in an infuriated tone, staring vacantly at his friend.

He crossed his left leg on top of his right. Samed inhaled and repeated his childish action. Tarhan coughed as his eyes welled up. Irritated he glared at his friend. He pursed his lips together into a thin line. "I'm not judging you, but there are always consequences of sinful and evil actions. Since you are my friend, I worry about your transgressions."

Samed twisted his lips. He rolled eyes and grimaced. "You are pointing out my mistakes. Thus standing in judgment of me."

Tarhan shook his head. "Do you know the difference between judging and just pointing out mistakes? If I had said, Samed, that you are a dishonest, lying womanizer who sleeps around, hurting women without a second thought, then I would be judging you, which would not please our Maker. However, if someone does something wrong and it affects him or others negatively, I can't turn a blind eye. If I do, I will become a callous, unfeeling man. Allah may punish me too." Tarhan coughed and fanned his face, trying to chase away the smoke.

Samed ignored his friend's actions and continued to blow smoke at him. "Tarhan, you are always 'blah, blah, blah', about things that don't concern me. Can you speak about something else, please?"

"Would you please stop this annoying habit of blowing smoke into my face?" objected Tarhan. He rose from the bench, irritated by his friend's boldness. Tarhan looked as if he was going to throw a punch at Samed.

"As I said earlier, I'm not judging you, but trying to lay bare your mistakes to prevent you from facing the negative consequences."

"That's my problem, not yours," retorted Samed, crossing his arms and raising his chin into the air. He gave Tarhan a self-satisfied smile.

"You're right," Tarhan acquiesced. "However, you are my friend. I'm trying to help you to find the right path."

"Did I tell you that I needed your help? You can only help people if they ask for help," objected Samed. The smile disappeared from his face, and wrinkles darted across his brow.

"Sometimes people are afraid or ashamed to ask for help. Some don't know that they need help. Therefore, I don't wait for them to ask me. Allah also expects us to love each other, but we can only show our love by virtue of our good deeds and our care for one another."

Fed up with Tarhan's preaching, Samed rose from his seat, unable to hide the scowl on his face. "Every time we meet, you are preaching. I'm fed up hearing it. Talk to you later."
With that, Samed turned on his heel and left.

***

Samed's lies about having another wife allowed him to spend a few days with Tatyana. It didn't take him too long to convince her to accept him back after the last break-up. This time he told her about Esmira and his false marriage arrangements. With his lies, he made Tatyana think that Sadaget had forced him to live with Esmira.

"What did you say to them?" Tatyana asked anxiously.

Samed leaned back and cupped his hands behind his head.

"I showed them my friend's passport but made sure that I had glued my picture on top of his. We have the same name but different surnames. My friend is married and has two children. I made sure that Sadaget saw all that information in the passport," he said. He held his chin up proudly.

Tatyana leaned toward him. "Did it stop the marriage?"

"To a certain extent, yes, but because of Esmira's pregnancy, Sadaget was insistent about this, so the Imam joined us in marriage. However, because I used a false surname, my marriage is not legal." Samed beamed, content with himself.

Tatyana's face became vacant for a second. Then a grimace ran across her face as she processed this information- that he was not in a legal marriage.

"So, Esmira thinks that you are her legal husband."

Her eyes widened at a sudden realization. "Wait, is Esmira carrying your baby? I almost missed that part."

"Yes, she is." Samed shook his head. I should have used a damn condom, he thought.

"How did it happen?" asked Tatyana, jealous that Esmira was going to produce his child. Her facial expression soured as she bit her lip.

"Tatyana, just leave the matter be. You ask too many questions," Samed objected angrily.

"Where did you meet her?"

"She works as a manager at the Sabayil Bookshop."

"Oh, I know that shop because I used to buy books there. When are you planning to tell them the truth?"

"I don't know."

Samed was getting frustrated; everywhere he went, people kept preaching at him and judging him. He suddenly stood up and exclaimed, "I'm leaving!"

Without allowing Tatyana to ask any further questions, he stormed downstairs, outraged by her questioning.

After a few days of thinking about Samed's false marriage, Tatyana's jealousy grew to a point where she could no longer contain her rage. She decided to visit Esmira and expose the nasty truth. On Tuesday morning, she deliberately put on a short red skirt and black, tight blouse, just to annoy Esmira. She was not as young as Esmira, but at thirty-five, she still looked sexy-the reason twenty-five-year-old Samed kept going back to her.

Another reason Samed kept returning to her was her lack of morals, which coincided with his own views. At age twenty, she had given birth to a daughter. When the girl reached school age, Tatyana sent her to a boarding school. The poor girl saw her mother only once a month.

It was 10 a.m., when Tatyana left her apartment. As she sat on the bus, she thought about how Esmira would react to the news. At the same time, however, she wanted to ensure that Samed would leave Esmira for good. When the bus stopped opposite Boulevard Park, Tatyana got off and walked through Torgovaya Street, a large pedestrian shopping center. Three-story buildings that housed clothing shops, chayhana, restaurants and a hairdresser salon surrounded the street.

As soon as she came into the shop, Tatyana asked for Esmira. Sveta directed her into Esmira's small office. When she arrived inside, Esmira was writing something in her notebook.

"Hello, Esmira."

The other woman peered at Tatyana, curious. "How do you know my name?"

"I'm Tatyana, Samed's girlfriend."

Esmira dropped her pen. "Pardon me?"

She got up and picked up the pen. Esmira gazed at Tatyana's face. Her eyes narrowed, and she tilted her head toward Tatyana.

"Did you mean ex-girlfriend? Are you aware that we are married? I'm carrying his child!" Esmira said sternly. However, she couldn't hide her shock.

Tatyana stretched her shoulders back and stood up more erect. "Ha, ha, ha! What marriage are you speaking of?" A wide, cold grin appeared on her face. "He fooled you. You are not married at all."

"Yes, we are," Esmira answered defensively. She narrowed her eyes at Tatyana, and her right eyelid moving involuntarily. Who is this woman? Who gave her the right to come here and spread lies?

She got to her feet, swayed dizzily walked to the door. With a scowl, she opened it and turned toward her unwanted visitor. "Tatyana, I don't know what you are trying to achieve. I would appreciate it if you left my office right now!"

"Esmira, please let me finish. It is for your sake," Tatyana snapped. She walked briskly toward the door and, standing tall, glared into Esmira's eyes.

"He has never been married and does not have any children. He tried to avoid marrying you."

Esmira closed the door. She walked back to her desk, growing weak and quivering. Her eyes dropped, and her voice became belligerent.

"This is not true. His passport shows that he has a wife and children."

Tatyana snapped back, "Esmira, how could you be so naïve? He used his friend's passport and glued his picture on it."

Tatyana sat down in a chair, crossed one leg over the other, and continued talking. "Instead of going to his non-existent wife, he visited me. We had sex many times." Tatyana grinned broadly and stared directly into Esmira's eyes.

Tatyana's words made Esmira lightheaded. Everything spun around her. She slowly sat down in her chair, and placed her hands on her belly. In a soft voice, she pleaded, "Tatyana, please go away before I call the security guard."

Tatyana sneered at seeing Esmira's condition. She felt victorious and on top of the world. "There is no need for a security guard. My job is done. I'm leaving now."

If this naïve girl thinks she can keep him away from me, she had better think twice, thought Tatyana.

She left Esmira's office content, leaving a thwarted Esmira behind.

Esmira felt sick and developed pains below her abdomen. She tried to get up from the chair but couldn't.

"Could this be true?" she asked herself. She began to cry.

"What am I going to do now? If he leaves now, neighbors will certainly assume I have been living with a lover."

Growing up in a Muslim world, Esmira had witnessed how national cultures and beliefs infected their judgments of poor women who had made unfortunate choices, were raped, wore modern clothes, or even simply smiled while talking to a male. She was afraid that her name would be sullied and her dignity thereby polluted.

After sitting silently for a few minutes, she called Sabina and related everything to her.

"Esmira, stop crying. It won't help you. You need to stick to the plan of terminating the pregnancy. Leave the child in the hospital. Forget about that idiot. You don't need a man like him."

Esmira rested her head on her left palm. Her tears fell onto the desk. "I'm not sure if I should induce an early labor and give away the child."

"You have to do it," advised Sabina.

She leaned back in her seat, her shoulders drooping. "How can I give away my child to a stranger? It could be abused or mistreated."

"Are you prepared to deal with the judgments our community will pass on you? Don't be silly, Esmira. You know how tough it is to bring up a bastard child in Azerbaijan," directed Sabina.

"All right, Sabina. I will think about this option, but I need to discuss this with my mother first."

"Okay, talk to her and let me know when you are ready. I will take you to a woman gynecologist in the hospital."

"I'm so distraught by Samed's lies," Esmira said, frustrated.

"That's just how some men are. They will lie to get you in bed, and once they get what they want out of you, they dump you. I don't understand what you found in a man like him. Yes, he is good-looking, but inside he is rotten to the core. You should select a man not according to his appearance, but because of his inner beauty.

My Dima is not attractive, but he makes me feel like a woman and treats me like a queen. He is a real gentleman, with a good heart and mind." Sabina smiled.

"You're right. Make sure you hold him tightly. Don't let go." Esmira sighed. "I'm so confused now. How in the world am I going to break this news to my mother?" She rubbed her temple.

"Just tell her the truth and go with the flow," advised Sabina. "Anyway, be calm. Don't panic. Things will work themselves out."

Sabina looked at her watch. "Esmira, I have a date with Dima. I have to go now. We'll talk later."

"No problem," answered Esmira. She hung up the phone and tried to concentrate on her work.

That day, Esmira closed the bookshop an hour early. She needed time to herself, to think about how she would approach Sadaget with the news. Esmira knew that her mother wouldn't accept it well. She might fight with Samed. At the same time, she was curious to know if he was aware of Tatyana's visit.

She walked to the train station and boarded a train. At around 6 p.m. she reached home. Samed was in the lounge, watching a football match. Her mother was in the kitchen, fixing dinner.

"Good evening, Samed." A look of disgust covered her face as she wanted to shout, Get the hell out of my life, you liar and womanizer!

However, she kept quiet. In her heart, she felt a heaviness brought about by profound disappointment.

How could I have been so naïve? She exhaled a sad sigh.

"Hi, Esi," answered Samed, without turning from the TV. It was a football match between USSR and Italy.

She continued staring at him with displeasure in her eyes, which he didn't bother noticing. Before opening her mouth to blurt out everything, she decided to change her work clothes, and then speak to both of them.

"Mother, I'm home," declared Esmira, calling out to Sadaget.

"How was your day at work?" asked Sadaget from the kitchen.

"It was okay. I'm going to my room." She trudged into her bedroom, feeling as if the earth was collapsing under her feet.

"Samed, please put plates with cutlery on the table. Don't forget napkins," shouted Sadaget.

Irritated, Samed waved his hand in the air as if he was swatting a fly. *Why does she always have to disturb me when I am watching football on television?* He got up from the sofa and followed Sadaget's instructions. Then he helped her to set the dinner on the table, agitated that he was missing the match.

"Esmira, dinner is ready," said Sadaget loudly.

"I'll be there in a minute."

She came out of her bedroom wearing a long blue dress. They sat at the table. After thanking God for the meal, they started eating. As they ate, Esmira gazed at her husband with narrowed eyes and a furrowed brow.

How could I have been so blind as to not to see his true nature? Look at him. He looks like an innocent angel, but within he's a big liar. She gave a long, deep breath.

Sadaget glanced at her daughter's pale face. "Esmira, is anything wrong? Your face is pale and you are quiet."

"I had a bad day." Her mouth twisted into an ironic smile.

Sadaget started cutting dolma. "What happened?"

Esmira stared at her husband. "Samed's lover visited me. I found out that he again fooled us."

"What?!" asked Sadaget, raising her eyebrows. She shot a piercing glance at Samed.

Samed dropped his fork and tried to get up.

"Sit down!" commanded Sadaget.

He dropped back into his chair.

Her eyes went to Esmira. "What did he do this time?"

"His trash said that he has never had another wife or children, and used a false surname to marry me."

Samed tried to get up again but Sadaget was faster. She got up, stepped over to him, put her hands on his shoulders. His wife's mother looked directly into his eyes. Deep wrinkles crossed her forehead and her eyebrows joined.

"Sit down!" she hissed. "This conversation is not over. Did that whore tell the truth?"

He wished that he could become invisible. "Yes," he mumbled, avoiding Sadaget's stare.

Sadaget grabbed Samed's shirt and gave him one hard slap across the face, making him shake. "Listen to me, you bastard. I have allowed you to reside in my house and have accepted you as a son, but all this time you have been fooling us."

"Please, forgive me, Sadaget Khanum," mumbled a frightened Samed. His whole body tensed, expecting the next slap. He held his hands over his face.

Sadaget stabbed her finger into his chest. "Again, you tried to get away from marrying my daughter with your lies. Since you are not married to the other woman, you will marry my daughter or I will choke you with my bare hands for dishonoring my child."

"Sadaget Khanum, please calm down. Stop poking me. All of this happened so fast that I was confused and made mistakes," postured Samed, sweating and shuddering slightly.

She stopped poking his chest but continued standing very close to him. "Stop playing the innocent lamb. You knew well what you were doing. Just make sure there are no more mistakes or lies this time around."

Sadaget moved away from him. Silence followed, with no one moving. Finally, Samed threw his napkin on the table.

"I lost my appetite, so I am going for a walk." He hoped that he wouldn't be stopped. His mother-in-law stared at him, her left eye twitching.

"Just make sure you come back," she demanded.

He walked toward the door and exited the apartment. Samed needed to get some fresh air. He realized that this time he could not get away.

Esmira lost her appetite as well. Hoping to avoid Sadaget, she went back to her bedroom. She lay on her bed, crying and rubbing her belly. After a while, she spoke to her child within.

"Mommy is sad today because your father lied again. It might turn out that you won't even have a father. I'll have to put you up for adoption, but I didn't want this to happen." She sobbed uncontrollably. After a short time, she fell asleep.

Samed came back late to avoid Sadaget. It was midnight. Esmira was sleeping. He looked at her for a while, then went to the bathroom and brushed his teeth. Then, without making any noise, he lay down next to Esmira, hoping that she wouldn't wake up. He stared at her, feeling guilty but determined to leave.

Before sunrise Samed rose, packed most of his clothes, and left. He decided to move in with Tatyana. Therefore, he hoped she would take him in. By the time he reached Tatyana's apartment, daylight had emerged. He climbed the stairs and rang the bell. He heard Tatyana's voice, angrily demanding, "Who is ringing my bell so early?"

She peeked through the peephole, saw Samed, and opened the door. She rubbed her eyes yawning loudly. "What are you doing in here so early and with bags?"

Dropping them by the door, he stormed into Tatyana's living room and announced, "I left Esmira because you messed up everything with your visit to the bookshop. You shouldn't have talked to her at all." He looked at her coldly.

Tatyana was radiant with joy. "I only tried to help you."

"However, you made things worse. Her mother almost choked me!" screamed Samed at the top of his voice.

"I wanted her to leave you alone," replied Tatyana. She tried to take hold of his hand, but Samed pushed her away.

He nodded his head, frowning. "Now they are pushing me to marry. I can't extricate myself any longer."

Tatyana sat on the sofa, her half-open nightdress exposing her legs. "If they can't find you, they can't force you to marry."

Samed's eyes fell to Tatyana's enormous breasts. Seeing him peering at her, she purposely played with them. She winked and sent him a kiss.

"I agree, but Esmira knows where my university is and has a phone number for my relatives. If she and her mother can't find me, they will either look for me at the university or call my relatives. If my father finds out about this mess, he will cut my financial support or may demand that I marry Esmira. He has a responsible and influential position in Zardob. He won't be pleased if I stain his reputation."

"What are you planning to do then?" asked Tatyana, biting her lower lip.

"I will stay with you and decide what to do later on."

At the same time that Samed was talking with his mistress, Esmira was getting up. Not seeing him or his clothes, she realized that he had left. She rushed into Sadaget's bedroom, distraught.

"Mother, Samed took his clothes and gone!"

Sadaget got out of bed. "Are you certain?"

"I am," she answered, quivering.

"Esmira, get his friend's phone number for me, please."

Esmira left her mother's bedroom and searched for the phone number.

"Here it is."

Sadaget came out of her bedroom. She picked the phone up. "Please read it off to me."

Esmira recited the phone number. Sadaget dialed it a few times, but the phone just rang.

"He is not answering," Sadaget snarled, holding the phone firmly.

"What do we do now?" Esmira was distraught.

"Go get ready for work. Tomorrow I will go to Samed's university," instructed her mother.

"Mother, leave him alone. I'm tired of his lies," said Esmira in a high-pitched voice.

"If I allow him to shun his responsibility, your child will be a bastard and fatherless. Do you want that for your child?"

"No," answered Esmira in a gruff voice, "but I can't make him love me, or marry me against his will. I don't know if I will ever be able to trust him."

"You don't have a choice; he has to marry you," stated Sadaget bluntly.

Esmira decided not to argue with her mother, but rather to follow her advice.

For two weeks, Sadaget tried to locate Samed, but to no avail. Not being able to find him, she got dismayed and advised Esmira to abandon the unborn child once it was born. "Leave the child in the hospital and forget Samed."

Knowing that Samed had dumped her, Esmira lost interest in everything. After he left, she took a few days off from work. Sadaget's daughter spent her time sitting on a bench in Boulevard Park gazing at other couples.

They are so happy and in love. Why couldn't I have met a decent, loving man instead of a womanizer and liar? she thought, sighing deeply as the tears welled up.

She stood up from the bench and walked toward the boats. As she walked, she suddenly felt an urge to empty her bladder, so she walked quickly toward the public bathroom.

As she entered, to her surprise she heard a moaning sound and a familiar male voice talking in broken English. She locked the door of her stall. She stood gazing through the space between the door and the frame, trying to see the man.

However, she could only see his back. He had his pants pulled down. The woman continued making noises, keeping her eyes closed. At the same time, she said something in a foreign language, while passing her hands over the man's back. Esmira's cheeks burned, as she realized she was seeing a couple having sex.

How can they have sex in a public bathroom? Well, it doesn't surprise me in the least. Some western tramps even have sex in automobiles.

The man lifted the woman's blouse up and sucked her breasts. As Esmira watched them, she felt a burning sensation throughout her body. Overcome by the scene, she purposely coughed loudly, hoping that the sound would make the couple go away.

Hearing that, the man stopped sucking the woman's breasts. He pulled up his pants and turned around. The woman looked worriedly in Esmira's direction, then she picked up her bag from the sink and rushed out.

"Oh, it's Samed!" Esmira exclaimed in a hushed voice, bewildered.

Her whole body grew weaker. She saw lights flying in front of her eyes. She sat down on the toilet slowly, shaken to her core. She began to feel nauseated and wanted to vomit, stunned by his reprehensible conduct.

This bastard has no shame whatsoever. I can only scorn him and hope he never returns.

She threw up right on the ground, barely missing her shoes. After the couple left, she slowly unlocked the door, holding onto her cramped belly. Then she washed her hands and mouth. She left the ladies' restroom. Slowly Esmira walked toward the metro station.

Chapter 4: Silvana Comes Into The Cruel World

During a rainy September night, as thunder roared, Sadaget hailed a cab. Together with her mother, Esmira headed off to Narimanov Hospital in order to have labor induced and to give away her child. On arrival, they spoke to the registrar to get the paperwork started in order to give up the child for adoption. After she was admitted to the hospital, Esmira signed the adoption papers, agreeing that she would leave the child in the hospital after it was born.

The nurse guided Esmira to her room, where Esmira saw a new mother breastfeeding her newborn baby. After greeting her roommate, Esmira sat on her own bed to await further instructions.

The nurse gave her Pitocin to induce labor and told Sadaget that she could go home for now. Once she had departed, Esmira put on a blue sleeping gown with tiny buttons down the front. She spoke for a while with the other mother. After a short time, she fell asleep.

She had a dream of Jesus Christ lying in a coffin and wearing a long white robe. Many women encircled Him, praying and pleading for His assistance and intervention. He eventually opened his eyes. "Your prayers are heard. I will help you," he said.

Sadaget came back the next day at lunchtime. As she was entering the hospital, Esmira developed painful contractions. Her water broke.

Esmira grabbed her lower abdomen, grimacing with pain. "I need a pain killer! My back and belly hurt unbearably."

"Let me look at your cervix to see what is going on," said her doctor.

Sadaget entered the room just as the doctor was checking Esmira's cervix, and was met with a closed privacy curtain. She could hear the conversation from within.

"It's time to take Esmira to the delivery room. Her cervix is dilated. She is going to deliver soon," said the doctor to the nurse standing next to her.

When the doctor stepped out from behind the privacy curtain, Sadaget approached her.

"Good afternoon."

The doctor turned her head toward Sadaget. "Good afternoon. Are you Esmira's mother?"

"Yes, I am." Sadaget was all smiles.

"It's a pleasure to meet you. I'm Doctor Vusala Kasimova. We have to take your daughter to the delivery room. However, before doing this, I would like to clarify some issues. Are you aware that as soon as the child is born, she or he will be taken away from your daughter?"

Sadaget placed her palm on her face and bowed her head. "Yes, we are aware of this. That was our arrangement."

"What about the child's father? Is he aware of this agreement?"

A few wrinkles ran across Sadaget's forehead. "He left my daughter and didn't want anything to do with this child."

"I wanted to ensure that everything is clear. If you change your mind, it is your right to keep the child," advised the doctor.

"Thank you, doctor, for your concern, but we are not going to change our minds," reiterated Sadaget.

"Excellent! Esmira, we have to move you to the delivery room." She turned to the nurse. "We need a wheelchair to move the patient."

The nurse left the room and came back with a wheelchair. She helped Esmira sit down, then pushed it out of the room.

"Mother, come with me. Oh, it hurts!" wailed Esmira. She held her hands against her belly, shutting her eyes briefly. There was a sheen of sweat covering her skin.

"May I come into the delivery room, as well?" asked Sadaget, gazing at Esmira with a worried expression.

"Hmm, usually we don't allow visitors into the delivery room other than the child's father, but I will make an exception this time. Please follow me," said Doctor Vusala.

When they entered the delivery room, Esmira moved painfully to the bed.

Doctor Vusala picked up the phone and made a call. "I'm in the delivery room. I need a pediatrician right now." She hung up the phone, washed her hands, and put on medical gloves.

Esmira squirmed on the bed, the painful cramps increasing. "May I please have a pain killer? I can't take the pain anymore!" she pleaded, grabbing her stomach.

Doctor Vusala approached Esmira. "I can't give you a painkiller right now. Start pushing, and it will be over soon."

Esmira bit her lip, grabbed onto her sheet tightly, and tried pushing a few times, but the pain made her stop. Beads of sweat cascaded down her face. She grimaced in pain. "I can't push anymore; it hurts too much!"

"If you want the pain to go away, you have to push," said the nurse, dampening Esmira's head with a compress.

"Breathe deeply and push," said the doctor in a firm voice.

Esmira pushed again, putting her lips together and blowing. Deep wrinkles appeared on her face, as a crash of thunder from outside echoed throughout the room.

She looked at the dark sky through the window. Lightning brightened up the heavens while raindrops landed on the window. She closed her eyes, fighting the urge to cry, and continued pushing as Sadaget held her hand.

The doctor looked at her cervix. "Esmira, it's going to be over soon. The baby is coming out!"

A female pediatrician entered the room.

"Esmira, you are doing well. Keep pushing," encouraged the nurse, caressing Esmira's head.

Esmira continued pushing.

"The baby is out," announced the doctor and she cut the umbilical cord. She picked up the crying baby. "It's a girl!"

She gave the baby to the pediatrician, who wiped the baby with a towel, put a stethoscope on the baby's ribs to check her lungs, heartbeat, and took her weight. After that, she wrapped her in a blanket.

"The girl is healthy. Her weight is six pounds," she announced. She then gave the baby to her mother.

Holding her tiny daughter in her hands, Esmira realized that she could not give away her little angel. Her heart filled with love for her child. She smiled blissfully and kissed the baby's forehead.

"Mother, I'm going to keep my daughter." Esmira gently rocked the newborn.

Startled Sadaget gazed at Esmira, wide-eyed. "Are you sure you want to keep her?"

"Mother, look at her face. My baby looks just like an angel. How can I give her away? She is my blood." All in smiles, Esmira glanced at her child, filled with joy.

Sadaget picked up her grandchild and held her in her arms, gazing at her face. The child resembled Esmira. She had her mother's lips, nose, and ears. A tiny smile appeared on the baby's face.

"Oh, she is so adorable. You are right; we can't give her away," said Sadaget. Her heart softened as she radiated with bliss. She turned to the medical staff.

"Doctor Vusala, we are going to take this child home with us," said the grandmother.

Gynecologist nodded her head, unable to repress her smile of satisfaction.

"I'm happy that you've changed your mind. Every child deserves to be loved, cared for by her mother. There are many women unable to conceive, but God gave you this blessing. Keep this child and cherish her."

The doctor caressed the child's head. "What name did you choose for her?"

Esmira glanced at her mother. "We never really thought about the name," she answered.

Sadaget shrugged, unable to answer this unexpected question.

Esmira gazed at the baby, trying to choose a name. She was so tired. It was almost too hard to think. Finally, though, her face brightened.

"Her name is Silvana."

"That is a beautiful name," said Doctor Vusala.

"We have to take you back to your room now," said the nurse. She helped Esmira to get up. Esmira sat in the wheelchair, the baby in her arms. She was taken back to her room. Sadaget followed them.

In the room, Esmira put the baby in the crib and lay down on the bed. Sadaget picked Silvana up again with an affectionate smile on her face.

"Esmira, she looks just like you." There were tears in her eyes, which surprised Esmira. In her entire life, she had never seen tenderness in her mother's face.

Sadaget's eyes widened as she was struck with a sudden realization, and she exclaimed, "I didn't buy anything for her. I'm going to go buy some clothes and cloth diapers." She placed her granddaughter in the crib.

As soon as Sadaget put Silvana back in the crib, the baby started crying.

"She is probably hungry," Sadaget suggested, picking her up again. She handed the child over to Esmira. "You need to breastfeed her."

Esmira unbuttoned her nightgown and put the baby to her breast.

"I have to leave before the shops close. I will come back in a few hours."

Esmira held her child gently in her arms, beaming with radiant happiness, as Sadaget left.

"You are my baby. You came into my life unexpectedly. You are my sunshine. I love you, my baby. You are an angel and my joy," she sang to Silvana.

She kissed Silvana's forehead gently as she wondered about Samed and her future. Although she knew that others would judge her for sleeping with him outside of marriage. It was too late to do anything about her predicament.

Why should I care what people say about me? I didn't prostitute myself, kill someone, or injure anyone, nor did I jettison my fundamental human values or ethical morals. In any event, my life and happiness don't depend on these people.

Looking at her new baby, Esmira realized that if she were to continue to fear public opinion and judgment against herself, she would neither lead her life to the fullest nor remain happy. She had faced the consequences of her weakness and her oversight. She was determined to keep her head up high. She realized that the past could not be altered. Esmira decided to move forward and take steps, not only to establish a happier, fulfilling life for her daughter but also to find her own happiness in doing so. She understood that it did not make sense to dwell on her past mistakes, which would result in a negative frame of mind. Instead, she would concentrate on building a stable future for her and Silvana.

I'm going to fight for myself and my child's happy future together. I won't let anyone deter us or affect us adversely.

***

The doctor ordered that the mother remains with her child in the hospital for a few days. The pediatrician wanted to ensure not only that the baby could breathe on her own, but also that all her vital organs were functioning properly.

While Esmira was in the hospital, Sadaget bought some clothes for her grandchild, along with a small bassinet. She again tried to reach Samed by phone, but after vain attempts, Sadaget set off to his university. Once there, she met his friend Namik, a twenty-five-year-old Azeri student with an olive complexion. In contrast to Sadaget's dwarfed height of only five feet, he looked like a giant. It was difficult to talk to him; she had to crane her head to look into his face. Namik gave Sadaget Tatyana's phone number. He told her that Samed was staying with her. Before leaving the university, Sadaget remarked to Namik, "I may not be able to find Samed. If you see him, please tell him that my daughter gave birth to his child."

Namik's eyes opened wide as he covered his mouth. "He has a child? No way!"

Sadaget crossed her arms, frowning. "He left my daughter right when she became pregnant with his daughter."

Namik shook his head in disapproval. "I have known him since he came to Baku, but he never told me anything about your daughter. He has broken many hearts. I'm stupefied that this time he left a woman with his child. I hope he will accept his responsibility and do right by her."

"Thank you for your concern, young man."

Namik gazed at the students climbing the stairs. "I have to go to my next lecture."

"Bye. Thank you again," said Sadaget, heading off.

"Bye-bye," answered Namik.

I thought Samed was cautious. How did he manage to impregnate her? Namik pondered this while going to his classroom.

After staying in the hospital for three days, Esmira went home with her daughter. The neighbors were stunned to see the new addition to Sadaget's family. Because Esmira had made every effort to conceal her pregnancy, as well as her false marriage, her neighbors did not suspect that she was pregnant and living with a man. When they saw her with the child, they wondered who the child's father was. Some stood outside watching the family enter their apartment. A few neighbors started to gossip about Esmira.

"Can you believe Sadaget's daughter had a bastard child? What a shame!"

"How did she manage to hide the pregnancy?"

"Do you know who the father is?"

"I saw a young man staying with them. Maybe he is the father."

"I thought he was Sadaget's nephew."

Inevitably, when they would leave their house, the neighbors would start gossiping maliciously behind their backs. Sadaget was unable to comprehend the reasons and motivations for these evil, vicious conversations, as they swirled around her and her loved ones. Those she had thought to be at least friendly toward them turned out to be the most vicious.

Instead of going back to work, Esmira took three months of maternity leave to look after her child. However, "looking after" the child soon became the responsibility of the grandmother. Esmira became lazy when it came to her responsibilities, so Sadaget had to take care of the baby much of the time.

The young mother didn't even bother to get up at nights to feed her child. Sadaget had to interrupt her own sleep to bottle-feed the crying baby.

Instead of washing Silvana's clothes and cloth diapers, Esmira left them to soak in water for days. Sadaget couldn't bear this carelessness; when she saw clothes and diapers soaking in the water, she would wash them while quarreling with Esmira.

Finally, she became fed up with her daughter's habits. While Esmira was breastfeeding her daughter one afternoon, Sadaget brought over a bucket full of water and dirty diapers.

"Why are you soaking soiled diapers for so many days in a bucket? Smell this water. It smells bad. It may have worms too." Sadaget put the bucket close to Esmira's face.

Esmira got irritated. She pushed the bucket away. "I'm feeding the child. You can't just come and push that mess into my face. Throw them away."

Sadaget put the bucket next to Esmira. "I'm not going to throw away anything. I paid good money for these. After feeding Silvana, you will get up and wash them." She left the room without allowing Esmira to say a word.

To avoid Sadaget's nagging, after feeding her daughter, Esmira did as she was directed. She washed the clothes and diapers.

Months passed after Silvana's birth. They didn't hear from Samed. Gossip about Esmira's bastard child continued to spread, even reaching Sadaget's workplace. Her friends asked Sadaget about the child's father. This maddened her, and on occasion she said, "Mind your own business. Leave my daughter alone. She is not your concern."

***

Samed continued living with Tatyana, until the night he caught her flirting with another man. He had gotten up at midnight, needing the bathroom. Tatyana was not in bed so, curious as to her whereabouts, he left the bedroom. He found her sitting on the sofa in the living room talking on the phone.

His lips twisted. Who is she talking to so late?

Samed tiptoed quietly back to the bedroom. He lifted the other phone, put it to his ear. Samed heard a male voice talking to Tatyana in Russian. He had picked up the receiver right at the beginning of the coy and lewd phone repartee. The Russian suitor addressed Tatyana in vulgar, graphic sexual terms, ones that Samed thought only he had the privilege to use. Samed was glad that he had learned her language, but it enraged him that this was what he was hearing. His muscles tensed, his heart filled with anger. Samed clenched his teeth together tightly.

This whore is having sex over the phone with some jerk. Sleeping with men isn't enough; now she has turned to phone sex. Such a nasty woman!

Then the man suddenly changed the topic. "Why did you change the color of your hair?" he asked. "You looked so sexy when I saw you last time with your blonde hair."

From his post, Samed could see his girlfriend's actions in the living room. Tatyana touched her hair stretching her lithe legs. "I'm tired of looking the same all the time. Do you not like how I look now?"

"Babe, you look great in every way, but I'm accustomed to your blonde hair," said the Russian. His tone of voice left no question as to his meaning.

"Okay, Koliya, I will change the color back to blonde just to make you happy," said Tatyana in a soft voice, twirling the locks of her black hair.

"I will be happy when you stop fooling around with different men. When are you going to dump that Azeri idiot?"

"Whenever the time is right. You didn't have a problem when I was dating an Englishman. Why are you jealous now?" asked Tatyana with a giggle. She glanced around to make sure Samed wasn't there.

"This has nothing to do with jealousy. As you know, I have myself been sleeping around with women. You and I have been having wild sex. I love it."

He paused, and his voice turned serious. "However, something happened to me after going to the Orthodox Church. I met a good priest. That man has shown me my mistakes and my sinful nature," explained Koliya.

"So that's why I didn't hear from you for some time. Usually, you call me to satisfy your dirty desires." She pursed her lips, grimacing.

"Tatyana, that was in the past, but let me finish, please," pleaded Koliya, becoming angry with Tatyana's playful giggling.

"Okay, go ahead," said Tatyana, purposely yawning loudly.

"After talking to the priest, I became closer to God. I understood that if I don't change, I will end up in Hell."

"Since when do you worry about your soul?" Tatyana asked mockingly. She rolled her eyes raising her brows.

Koliya inhaled deeply, sounding disappointed. "Tatyana, can you be serious once in your life, please? We humans satisfy our sexual needs just like wild animals, without thinking about the consequences of our actions. It is wrong. We should be making love not for the sake of enjoyment, but because we love someone. Sex out of marriage is a sin."

Tatyana couldn't believe her ears. "Oh, my Jesus, that priest has brainwashed you."

"He didn't. He merely opened my eyes to my wrongdoings."

Tatyana sat up and crossed her legs. "Koliya, I honestly don't understand men like you. At the beginning of our conversation, you were horny and tried to arouse me with your dirty talk. Why are you now playing the role of a saint?"

Why can't she shut up and hang up the phone? thought Samed, tired of listening to their repulsive conversation. Why did I leave Esmira for such rubbish?

He snorted softly; he already knew the answer to that. If it weren't for my insatiable sex appetite, I would have married Esmira. However, my problem is that I can never seem to commit to only one woman.

Koliya was explaining himself to Tatyana. "I'm a human being with emotions and desires. I'm not perfect, so when you called me, I couldn't control my desire for you. Consequently, I allowed myself to go too far."

Samed sat down on the bed, trying not to make noise. He continued to listen. He clenched his teeth, pursed his lips, and made a fist.

"You don't love that fool. He is a liar and a wicked man. Why do you need a guy like him?"

Hearing this, Samed squeezed the phone. If Koliya had been nearby, he would have decked him for sure. Indeed, I am a fool for dumping a decent, chaste woman for a complete tramp, who has been around the rodeo and in too many beds.

"He is a good love-maker, cleans my apartment. Samed helps me with the groceries. I have a man at home this way," Tatyana declared. She curled her hair with her fingers, grimacing.

She needed a house cleaner and a sex machine, not a man. So, that's why she chased me, Samed thought. He felt cheated and betrayed.

"Forget what he gives you. Leave him alone. You can't be sleeping around. It is wrong and sinful."

Tatyana paced around the room. "You were making love to me at the same time I had another boyfriend, and while you were dating Irina. Why did you not think about what is sinful and wrong at that time?"

"I'm a new man now. If you don't change, then your soul will pay for it," warned Koliya.

His words irritated Tatyana. "This is my life. I don't need a preacher. As long as that idiot knows how to make me happy by satisfying my needs, I will stay with him," she retorted and slammed down the phone.

Samed hung up the phone quietly. He clenched his fists.

I'm going to choke that whore with my bare hands, he thought angrily. However, after thinking over, he changed his mind.

Don't be a fool. Leave her alone. You always knew that she was dating others. Would you like to end up in jail for taking a life?

He went to use the bathroom. When he was finished, he purposely banged the door open. Tatyana walked into the bedroom, startled.

"I heard a door bang. Is everything okay?" she asked in broken Azeri.

"Yes, everything is fine," said Samed, trying not to expose his anger, forcing a smile. "Why are you up so late?"

"I got up from a horrible nightmare that gave me a headache. I couldn't fall asleep. Thus, I decided to read in the living room," Tatyana lied, looking into his eyes without blinking.

Samed wanted to shout: Liar! I heard all of your conversation but decided to play her game of lies. Instead, he asked, "Did your headache go away?"

She came closer to him and tried to hug him, but he pushed her away.

"Darling, what is wrong?"

"Nothing, I just want to go back to sleep." He walked to the bed.

She lay down next to him. After a while Tatyana fell asleep, dreaming of making love to Koliya under the shower.

***

Later, Samed found out that Esmira had borne a daughter. He wanted to see his child, but was afraid to confront Sadaget. Even though he did not plan to marry Esmira, he decided to take on his

79

responsibility as a father without marrying her. A few months after the birth of his child, he mustered his courage and decided to visit Esmira. Early in the morning, he showed up at her door. She opened it. Upon seeing him, she tried to close it again. However, Samed grabbed the door handle, keeping it open.

"What are you doing here?" demanded Esmira, startled.

"I came to see my daughter."

Esmira scowled. "After all this time?"

"I didn't want to face your mother's nagging. May I come in?"

"Esmira, who is at the door?" asked Sadaget, who was feeding the baby.

"Mother, it's Samed," answered Esmira. She faltered in doubt for a moment, then let him in. Esmira's mom put Silvana back in the bassinet. Sadaget entered the living room.

"Good morning, Sadaget Khanum," mumbled Samed nervously.

Sadaget didn't bother to greet him. Instead, she stared into his eyes.

"You left my child when she was pregnant. Why did you come back now? Go back to your whore!" exclaimed Sadaget.

The tone of her voice made him nervous. Samed wiped his face with a handkerchief and rubbed his head. "Please, let me explain," he mumbled.

He looked at Esmira. "After thinking for some time, I have decided to be part of her life."

"What did you say?" Sadaget demanded, shocked but wary.

He lifted his head and looked straight into her eyes. "I would like to take part in my daughter's life," Samed repeated, louder this time.

"What do you plan to do about Esmira?"

"I will move back, but I wouldn't be able to marry her until my academic program is complete. I can't tell my parents about Esmira and the child as yet. My father will cut me off from financial support."

Sadaget moved closer to him, making his muscles tense. She poked his chest with her finger. "You are selfish, only thinking about yourself. Why didn't you worry about this before you impregnated my daughter?"

A few drops of her saliva landed on Samed's face. He noticed that she was breathing heavily. Therefore, he tried not to irritate her further.

"You have lied to us so many times! How would we know that this is not one of your lies?" screamed Sadaget.

He moved away from her and wiped the saliva from his face with his sleeve. "I came to my senses. I won't make the same mistakes again. Can I see my daughter, please?"

"Go ahead," said Esmira.

He entered Esmira's bedroom and approached the bassinet. As he leaned over and gazed at his child, Samed put his hand gently on her belly, thinking, You are sleeping so peacefully. Looking at you, I feel so guilty. I wish things could be different, but my nature is like a slab of concrete dropped in a riverbed. I tried to stop, but I kept running after women with an unstoppable sexual appetite. It feels like a disease that I cannot control. His eyes filled with tears.

Esmira entered the bedroom. He stood up straight looking at her. "What is her name?" he asked.

"Silvana," replied Esmira.

Samed lifted Silvana, put her close to his chest, and rocked her. She suddenly began to bawl.

"Silvana, stop crying. Daddy is here."

He sat on the bed, put her on his lap, and smiled softly at her. Silvana became quiet.

"Esmira, she has my nose, but mostly looks like you."

He looked up at Silvana's mother, his eyes serious. "I actually want to take part in her life."

Esmira stared at him, expressionless, and shrugged her shoulders. "Do as you wish. I don't care any longer."

After spending about an hour with Esmira, Samed left, promising to come back. Sadaget was not happy knowing that Samed still refused to marry Esmira, but at least he had agreed to live with her and help with the child. People would see that the child had a father.

After a few days, Samed packed all of his clothes. He moved back to Sadaget's apartment. For a few weeks, he tried to stay away from Tatyana, but his yearning for her drew him back into her arms and back into the sack. He helped Esmira look after Silvana, but secretly took her to Tatyana's apartment without Esmira's knowledge.

Tatyana became fond of his daughter. She loved sitting in the rocking chair and holding Silvana against her chest. Rocking her, she sang a lullaby.

"Sleep baby, sleep. Keep your eyes tightly closed. A new day is coming soon. It will give you joy and peace."

She also enjoyed keeping Silvana on her lap and watching her sleeping. Tatyana was blissfully peaceful. Little Silvana resembled her own bastard daughter, whom Tatyana had abandoned many years ago. Her girl had already grown into a teenager. Although Tatyana missed her own offspring, she was accustomed to living alone. In fact, she knew that her 15-year-old girl would not find a place in the chaotic life that Tatyana led.

However, spending time with Silvana brought back Tatyana's maternal instinct in such a way that she asked Samed to come back to live with her and to bring Silvana too. But he refused to move back. The longer he lived with Esmira, the more he realized that he had feelings for her. Samed planned to marry Esmira. However, he was not ready to approach his father with the truth. Therefore, his family in Zardob was not aware of his relationship with Esmira and the existence of his Silvana.

Months passed as Esmira waited for Samed to marry her legally. However, he kept delaying, making excuses while secretly dating Tatyana. He insisted that he was telling the truth when he promised to marry her.

Esmira began to notice strange marks on Samed's body, and lipstick on his undershirt. A few times, she saw red bruises on his neck and scratches on his back when he removed his sweater.

One time, she came closer staring at his back. Seeing her peering at him, Samed faced her and put his undershirt back on.

"Where did you get those scratches from?"

"You are always asking too many questions," he said, annoyed. He waved his hand as if chasing away a fly.

"I'm just curious how scratches and red bruises ended up on your body." Esmira raised an eyebrow. "Were they caused by Tatyana?"

Samed moved closer to the mirror, raised his head up. He looked at the bruises on his neck. "Don't be silly. Did you forget kissing my neck?" He shook his head and gestured at his back. "If your mother kept the windows closed, this damn apartment wouldn't be full of mosquitoes biting me."

He lay down in bed. I should be careful. If Sadaget finds out about Tatyana, she'll send me straight to Hell, he thought.

Chapter 5: Jailed

In her concern that Samed might leave her, Esmira decided the best course of action would be to hurl out more children for him, like cannonballs. After many attempts, she gave birth to two boys, Zaur and Lachin. During this time, she also continued to work in the bookshop.

Silvana remained Samed's favorite child, with whom he played most of the time. He did not feel any sort of warmth toward the boys.

One time, when Zaur was three, he pulled Silvana's hair, making her cry. Samed got so irritated that he bit Zaur's hand. The poor little boy cried, and carried a bloody gash on his hand from his father's teeth for some time.

Even after having these other children by Esmira, Samed continued seeing Tatyana. Although he was sexually attracted to her, he had no feelings otherwise, and certainly had no intention of marrying her. Nonetheless, Tatyana wanted to marry him, to give herself a good reputation, the halo of the upright married woman. At least it would stop the locals from gossiping about her sordid past. She strove to turn Samed against Esmira, but to no avail.

After failing to maneuver her way into Esmira's life to cause divisiveness, Tatyana instead repeatedly frequented her bookshop, hoping to provoke a quarrel with her rival and thereby ignite open warfare. During one of their argumentative exchanges, she revealed that Samed still frequented her apartment, and planned to ditch Esmira once and for all. She firmly implored Esmira to leave Samed alone, but Esmira ignored her, even though she felt betrayed by his cheating.

On a windy day during September, Tatyana came to the bookshop again. She entered Esmira's office and immediately unleashed her poisonous tongue at her.

"When are you going to leave Samed? Don't you see he doesn't love you? He only stays with you because of the children and your mother's insidious threats."

Esmira rose from her chair. She drew closer to Tatyana. She shook her head, annoyed as if Tatyana was merely a gnat circling her head.

"Aren't you tired of running after other women's men? Go back home. Leave me alone. Haven't you already spread enough poison with your smart-ass mouth, hurling salvos ad nauseum?"

Tatyana smiled widely. "Are you such a dumb woman that you don't realize that Samed is going to dump you like rotten rubbish and take Silvana with him? I'm going to be her stepmother!"

Esmira gave Tatyana a firm whack across her face. Tatyana clutched at her cheek and fell back, astonished.

"I'm fed up with your nonsense. Listen to me. Men don't need garbage like you. They are only using you for their sexual appetite. Get out of my office, slut. Don't come back!" Esmira shouted angrily, as she pointed to the door.

Bewildered by Esmira's rage and venom, Tatyana retreated quickly.

Although Tatyana's constant meddling at the shop embarrassed Esmira, she didn't breathe a word to Samed or her mother. This angered Sabina, who failed to understand how Esmira could put up with Samed's cheating.

"Do you seriously need a man in your life who chases other broads and tramps?" Sabina asked during a phone conversation. "Esmira, for goodness' sake, love and respect yourself. Discard him like leftover food from the refrigerator!"

"I don't have a choice. I have to stay because my children need a father," Esmira said in resignation. She bit at her nails, a nervous habit of hers.

"You are misguided, my dear. You always have choices. Out of trepidation, there is a tendency in human nature not to find solutions to problems or to discover exits out of predicaments. People like you have bound themselves in chains of fear, uncertainty, hopelessness, frustration, and society's expectations overall. Instead of leading lives, they seek to please society and merely lead a robotic existence; in fact, afraid of being themselves. Your chains ought to be broken to allow you to breathe, move around at will, and just be yourself. How long do you think you will be able to withstand his lover's trespassing or his constant cheating? Do you think your children will be happy seeing you so miserable? This will eventually affect them emotionally."

"What do you expect me to do?" Esmira asked, as her heart filled with despair.

"You could try to change him. If he admits his weaknesses, faults, then forgive him and begin your lives anew. However, if he can't redeem himself, let him go. You and your children can be perfectly happy without him. Just get rid of your fears and doubts. Believe in yourself, your abilities, thereby breaking the chains and obstacles that prevent you from true happiness," argued Sabina passionately.

"Many thanks for the counsel. I will indeed mull this all over, and eventually decide on an appropriate course of action," agreed Esmira.

Nonetheless, Esmira proved to be a stubborn woman; although she tended to listen to someone's advice, she never followed it. In fact, she ignored Sabina's sound recommendations and stayed with Samed, not wanting to embark on a struggle alone. More than likely, she felt a little bit more secure with Samed in her life. However, she needed to stop being insecure and start believing in herself.

When Silvana reached the age of four, Esmira became pregnant again with Elnara, despite the fact that Samed didn't want any more children. He expressed his concern about Esmira's pregnancy to Tatyana.

"Why don't we pressure Esmira to get an abortion? We ought to force her to go to the clinic," she said.

Samed kissed Tatyana on her forehead. "Tatyana, you are brilliant! I never thought about that. However, before going over there, we must ensure that Sadaget is not at home."

He snapped his fingers as an idea hit him. "Oh! Esmira is going to be at home alone with the children on Tuesday, at which time we can corner and isolate her to go for an abortion on that same day."

He pulled Tatyana closer. "I have to go now."

Samed blissfully smiled. He grabbed Tatyana's bottom and kissed her forcibly on the lips. She put one of her hands on his crotch and caressed it.

"Are you trying to seduce me?" asked an insatiable Samed.

"Let's go into the bedroom," offered Tatyana.

"Leave that adventure for our next meeting." He let go of Tatyana and headed out the door. She watched him leave and smiled.

On Tuesday, Sadaget went to work, leaving Esmira and her son-in-law at home with the children. Samed anxiously waited for his Russian lover to come. He was afraid that Sadaget would disrupt their plans.

During lunchtime, Silvana and her brothers slept as Esmira cleaned the apartment. The doorbell rang.

"Samed, please answer the door," Esmira said.

Samed put the newspaper on the table. He walked toward the door. Seeing Tatyana through the peephole, he opened the door, beaming broadly. "Why did you take so long to come?"

"Who's there?" asked Esmira from the bedroom. Samed didn't answer.

"Hi, handsome," chirped Tatyana, kissing him right on the lips.

He eyed her from head to toe moving his lips. She let go of her long blonde hair. Her purple top showed off her voluptuous breasts. He let Tatyana in and led her to the living room.

Tatyana sat down on the sofa, crossing one leg over the other. She gazed around. "This bitch has good taste."

"Tatyana, knock it off!" whispered Samed, glancing toward the bedroom.

"Did you speak to her about the abortion?" asked Tatyana, annoyed.

"No, I didn't," said Samed meekly.

"Are you sure you will be able to persuade her? We need to rush because the cab is waiting for us. My driver agreed to take us to the clinic." She looked over at the bedroom door.

Hearing a woman's voice, Esmira came out of the bedroom. She was stunned at seeing Tatyana in her living room. She stood motionless as her eyes darted from Samed to Tatyana. She exclaimed, "What is she doing in my apartment?"

"I invited her," answered Samed in a subdued voice, avoiding Esmira's glare.

The blood rushed toward Esmira's temples. "How could you invite your ex-lover into our apartment?"

Tatyana got up from the sofa and moved closer to Samed. She clutched his hand.

"Did I ever tell you that I was his ex-lover? I'm his woman, and we still see each other, as I told you in the bookshop. He does not want another kid from you, and the child probably is not his."

She looked coyly at Samed. "Maybe I'll pop out another kid for him myself!" Tatyana blurted boldly.

Hearing that Tatyana had visited Esmira in the shop and had spoken about their relationship, Samed grew angry. He pulled his hand away from her.

"Stop, Tatyana," ordered Samed. He glared at her.

"You jaunt into my apartment, accusing me of infidelity, when you have slept with so many men that you don't know the father of your own daughter? You slut! You had better go and find out before producing another offspring," taunted Esmira, her voice shrill.

Tatyana launched herself at Esmira, but Samed grabbed her hand tightly. He pulled her back.

"Shut up, bitch," Tatyana said, furious.

Esmira scowled, seeing only the despicable in Tatyana. "Make sure he does not catch HIV from you, or any other disease for that matter."

"Don't you see, Esmira, he has exploited you?" asked Tatyana, ignoring Esmira's final words. She struggled to get away from Samed's firm grip.

"Tatyana, stop! You have said more than enough," said Samed, gripping her hand tightly.

"Let go! You're hurting me!" she yelled.

Samed loosened his grasp. Tatyana was finally able to pull her hand back. She rubbed it with her other hand and moved away from him.

"Samed, don't you know that it is better for her to know the truth rather than leaving her in the dark? Those who can't accept the fact can't see the light; they are living with false hopes and beliefs. Let your lover know that you are living with her because you are under the weight of her mother's threats."

"Shut up, Tatyana." Samed moved closer to her, irritated.

Esmira shook her head in disbelief. Her heart filled with sadness and anger. Her eyelids twitched as pain swelled behind her eyes.

She hissed, "Both of you deserve each other."

Tatyana ignored her words and stared at Samed as she laughed. "Are you afraid to tell her the truth? The truth may hurt, but not as much as the lies. So, haven't we in fact been seeing each other every week?"

Esmira had had enough. She came up to him and slapped him.

"Samed, you are a coward. You didn't have enough courage to talk to me yourself, but brought a whore to speak in your place. I pity you. A man who hides behind a woman's skirt is not a man." Esmira spat in his face.

"What do you know about men? You couldn't even keep your man faithful to you," said Tatyana.

Esmira turned toward Tatyana and stared into her eyes without blinking. "At least I know who the father of my children is."

"Father or fathers?"

"Tatyana, enough," begged Samed.

"I want both of you out of my apartment!" Esmira shouted, pointing to the door. She abhorred both of them.

"Don't worry, Esmira. He will be out of your life soon, and then be only with me."

Esmira approached Tatyana. "I don't need a man like him. You can keep him." In a fury, Esmira slapped Tatyana with all her might.

Not expecting the slap, Tatyana was thunderstruck. She fell back, shaken.

"Listen, tramp! Take Samed and leave my apartment!" screamed Esmira. She raised a clenched fist.

Tatyana managed to get a fistful of Esmira's hair. She yanked it, hard. Then she pushed her to the ground and kicked her.

Esmira got up and tried reaching for the phone. "I'm going to call the police!"

Samed wrested the phone from her hand. He dragged her to the door. "We are taking you to the clinic for an abortion," he told her.

"Leave me alone!" Esmira screamed, trying to kick him away.

"Stop yelling, bitch!" Tatyana shouted.

Esmira pushed Samed away and ran back to the living room. While she tried to dial the police, Samed picked up the nearest thing he could find, a chain from Silvana's bike, and hit her with it. She screamed out in pain.

"Esmira put down the phone. Come with us!" demanded Samed.

"No! Stop! You're hurting me!"

He hit her hand with the chain. She dropped the phone and tried to run back to the door.

"Rashid! Rashid!" Esmira shouted, yelling for the next-door neighbor. Samed caught hold of her. He dragged her back to the living room by her hair.

The screams woke and scared the children. Esmira's sons hid under the bed, but Silvana, curious and alarmed, came out of the bedroom. She screamed when she saw her mother being dragged.

She ran to Samed, grabbed his shirt. She tried to pull him away from Esmira.

"Leave my mother alone!" she shouted kicking him.

Tatyana picked up Silvana and carried her back into the bedroom. Silvana kicked out and tried to get away from Tatyana.

"Put me down!" Silvana shouted, and bit Tatyana's hand.

Tatyana put Silvana down. "Little doggy, you hurt my hand," she murmured, rubbing it. Silvana dashed away from her.

Hearing Esmira's and Silvana's screams, Rashid and another neighbor knocked on the door.

"Esmira, what is going on?" they shouted, as they tried to open the door. Hearing the neighbors, Samed stopped hitting Esmira.

Silvana sprinted to the door and opened it.

"Uncle Rashid, please help! Father is hurting my mother!" Silvana yelled, sobbing.

The neighbors came inside. Seeing Samed with a chain in his hand and Esmira with a bruised face, they attacked him. Rashid pushed him down and hit him as the other neighbor kept Samed pinned to the floor.

"You son of a bitch, how can you raise your hand and strike a woman, the mother of your kids?" shouted Rashid, punching Samed right in the gut.

"Let me go!" yelled Samed, trying to get away.

While the neighbors dealt with Samed, Tatyana managed to leave the apartment.

After hitting him, the friends tied Samed's hands behind his back. They dragged him to the corner of the living room. They spat on him and kicked him a few times.

"You are not a man. A real man neither hits a woman nor cheats on her."

Samed cowered in the corner as blood ran from his nose, staining his shirt. He also spat blood.

"What is happening in here?" asked more neighbors, as they spilled through the doorway.

"They attacked me!" Samed cried.

Esmira wiped the blood from her forehead while a neighbor called the police. When they arrived, they looked at Esmira's wounds, took a statement from both her and the neighbors, and arrested Samed on the spot.

As they pushed Samed against the police car door, he pleaded, his body shuddering, "Please let me go. I didn't commit any crime."

A huge, muscular police officer looked at him and shook his head. "Aren't you aware that hurting or abusing a helpless woman is a crime? Violence is punishable by the rule of law. Shame on you."

At the station, the police proceeded to fingerprint him. After taking a statement from him, they put him in a cell with a fifty-year-old prisoner.

The male detainee eyed him licking his lips. "Hey, handsome. I hope you stay with me for a long while." He winked and grinned broadly.

Samed frowned and moved away from the man. Then he walked around the cell, keeping his hands behind his back. After a while, feeling tired, he sat in a corner next to the wall, bent his legs. Samed rested his head on his knees and started to mumble to himself.

I need to get out. I don't belong here.

He pulled his head up slightly to glance at his fellow detainee. Seeing the man staring at him, he quickly put his head back on his knees. Why does that freak keep staring at me?

His cellmate continued leering at Samed's athletic body, licking his lip.

"Hey handsome, stop mumbling. Sit next to me." The older man pointed to his bed. Samed's heart filled with fear. He sat in the corner without moving.

When Sadaget came home, she couldn't believe that Samed had dared to invite his lover over to their place, and had beat Esmira while Silvana looked on. She was horrified and asked Esmira to make sure that he stayed in jail.

"Esmira, didn't I warn you that he wasn't any good? Yet you refused to hear me. He left you pregnant, again, this time with three children on your hands. What do you intend to do now?"

Esmira was too distraught to answer. She shrugged her shoulders. "I don't know."

"Just make sure he goes to jail," exclaimed her mother.

Esmira was not sure if she should press charges against Samed or let him go free. In the morning, she decided not to press charges against him, but Sadaget insisted that he had to pay for his misconduct. Both of them went to the police station. After Esmira's second statement, Sadaget pressed charges against him. Police charged Samed for assaulting Esmira. Unable to pay for his bail, he was forced to call his father.

"Father, I'm in jail," he mumbled guiltily. His father dropped the phone to the floor.

"Father, are you there?"

His father picked the phone up again and put it to his ear. "How did you end up in jail?"

Samed stumbled for a few seconds, unable to find the words to respond. He scratched his head. "I'm accused of assaulting a woman."

His father could not believe his ears. He slowly sat down in a chair. "Oh, my God, who did you assault and why?"

"I was living with a young woman. We had children, but then she got pregnant again, this time by another man." Again, Samed tried to justify his actions with lies and blamed Esmira.

Shocked and ashamed, Samed's father could not think of what to say. He put the phone down and sat motionless for a few minutes. After what seemed an eternity, he put the phone back to his ear. His fingers shook.

"Son, I'm very disappointed with your irresponsible behavior. How could you raise your hand to the mother of your children and bring bastards into this world? This is not the traditional or accepted Muslim way of living."

He sat on the floor with his knees bent and rubbed his eyes.

"Father I beg you, come. Pay for my bail. They put me in a cell with a homosexual detainee."

The news of the children disturbed his father a lot more than Samed's cellmate. "All this time you have been living with a woman and had children, yet never told us anything. What will people in the village think if they find out my son was arrested for beating a pregnant woman?"

Samed started quivering, ready to cry. His eyes filled with tears. "I will explain everything later. Just... right now, please get me out."

A tall and broad-shouldered police officer approached Samed and took away the receiver from him.

"It's time to go back to your cell."

Samed got up. He started walking, and as he did, the policeman kicked him in the rear.

Samed's father, Barhan, was too distressed to go take care of the bail himself. Instead, he sent his two other sons to Baku. Samed's brothers went to the police station to see him. They gave him a hug as soon as he appeared in the waiting room. He looked thinner, rumpled and unshaven.

"All this time you have been living with a woman. You had children but didn't tell us anything. How could you put yourself in this situation?" appealed one of his brothers, Fakir.

"Father is troubled and frustrated by your careless behavior. Why did you beat that poor woman?" asked a disappointed Timur.

Samed felt ashamed and gazed at the floor. Then he raised his head.

"Brothers, I know that I have disappointed you. Nevertheless, this woman has been cheating on me. She gave me a daughter, but two boys born subsequently are not mine. Apparently, she got pregnant from someone else. I just couldn't take it any longer and tried to make her have an abortion."

Fakir shook his head in disbelief. "I don't know what to say, but the fact is that you are in jail now. We have to do something to get you out of this mess."

"I will try to talk to your woman. She may retract the charges," said Timur.

Samed looked desperately at his brothers. "Please make sure she takes back her charges against me, or raise the funds to pay my bail."

He gave his brothers Esmira's address. They went to see her.

Pain caused by the bicycle chain shuddered through Esmira's body. She took a few days off work and stayed at home, trying to heal. Sadaget also took a week off to help Esmira with the children.

On Saturday morning Sadaget's doorbell rang. She peered through the peephole. Sadaget saw two strange men.

"What do you want?" yelled Sadaget, without opening the door.

"We are Samed's brothers. We would like to talk to you," answered Fakir.

"Go away. I don't want to speak to any of you!" said Sadaget.

"Please just give us twenty minutes," begged Fakir, standing by the door.

Sadaget picked up a broom, then opened the door cautiously. "All right, come in." She had them go into the living room, all the while watching them closely.

"Esmira, these are Samed's brothers."

Esmira was sitting in an armchair reading a book to Silvana and her brothers. At her mother's words, she stopped reading and glanced at them. She noticed that one of the brothers was short, olive-skinned, but the other was slimmer, lighter, and had a mustache.

"Nice to meet you," she said, getting up. The children gazed at their uncles with curiosity.

"Mommy, who are these men?" Lachin asked, hiding behind her dress.

"They are your uncles," answered Esmira.

"So, you are Samed's girlfriend. These are your children," said Timur, as he gazed thoughtfully at the children.

"Yes," answered Esmira.

The brothers continued gazing at Esmira and her children, trying to see if the little ones resembled Samed. Both noticed Esmira's beauty.

"Mommy, but you said that we don't have uncles," Silvana said, staring at them with her wide hazel eyes.

"Silvana, we will talk about it later. Please take your brothers into the bedroom."

Silvana left with her brothers.

"We are here on behalf of Samed. You have filed a complaint against him. Can you please take it back?" asked Timur.

"Do you know that your brother and his whore attacked my daughter?" Sadaget asked angrily.

"Yes, we know, but he didn't have a choice. Your daughter cheated on him," said Fakir.

Sadaget moved closer to them and raised her voice. She pointed her index finger at them. "Listen to me. Don't come to my house accusing my daughter of such garbage. Leave immediately!"

"Please retract your complaint. Otherwise, he will end up serving a few years in jail," stated Fakir.

"That's not our problem. Why didn't he think about incarceration as a consequence when he beat my daughter?" yelled Sadaget.

"He can't go to jail. It will affect our father. Please have a heart," said Fakir, looking at Sadaget with weary eyes.

"Nobody pushed your brother into a life of sin and crime. He willfully hurt my daughter. Now should face the consequences. That is how life works. When you make stupid mistakes, you pay for them. His payment is jail."

Sadaget walked toward the door. She opened it wide. "Just go, and don't come back."

Heartbroken, the brothers left the apartment.

"Look at this bastard. He beat my daughter and expects us to remove the complaint against him," Sadaget snapped furiously.

"Who gave those two idiots the right to come here, in my house? To what end; to accuse my daughter of infidelity?" Sadaget fumed to herself.

Sadaget took too long to decide what she should do with Samed. By the time she decided to forgive him, it was too late. The case went to court. They could not stop it. Found guilty, Samed was sent to Russia to serve his three-year term. While in jail, his last child, Elnara, was born.

After serving his term, he met a Russian woman, married her, and had two girls and one boy with her. When she first found out that he had other children, she warned him not to search for them. Otherwise, she would kick him out of both her house and her life.

Unable to forgive Esmira and her mother for the three years he had been incarcerated, Samed decided to follow his wife's advice by erasing Esmira and her children from his life. In addition, since Samed had deceived both his brothers and his father into thinking that Esmira's offspring were not his own, they essentially obliterated her children from their memories and their own lives, as well. They didn't even mention their existence to the rest of their relatives.

Esmira left her job as a manager and worked as a wedding singer for United Musicians Company. She sang at weddings in different villages in Azerbaijan. This profession changed her entirely. She left her children with her mother and partied a lot or visited her friends. She bought expensive clothes and jewelry for herself. Sadaget wasn't happy with these changes. She didn't approve of Esmira's friends. She made sure Esmira kept them away from her children.

One night when Esmira was away with her singing band, the property owner evicted Sadaget and her grandchildren, so as to allow his newly-wed son to move in with his wife. Sadaget stayed with the children outside with nowhere to go. Since it was night, she couldn't rent another apartment, and didn't want to beg her friends for a place to stay. Therefore, she took her grandchildren to the train station, which was noisy and full of people. They settled down on the cold iron seats and tried to fall asleep. It wasn't easy at first with all the chaos. However, after leaning on each other, the children fell asleep. Sadaget stayed awake to guard her grandchildren and their belongings.

The next day, Sadaget tried to rent an apartment, but to no avail. Instead of staying in the train station again, Sadaget bought a ticket to Georgia. They slept on the train as they traveled to Georgia and then back to Baku. When they returned, Sadaget was able to rent another place in Montina. All of them moved there, where Silvana liked living, and met her best friend Arzu. Together with him, she climbed trees and played outside.

Chapter 6: School Life

Living in Montina brought a negative experience into Sadaget's grandkids' lives, because Sadaget could not provide a safe environment for them. Instead, she kept leaving them unsupervised at home as she went to work. The eldest, Silvana, had to mind her siblings.

On one of those days, five-year-old Zaur was molested. While he was playing outside, a male neighbor snatched him and took him away to his house, promising to give him toys. He molested him, then threatened to beat him if he didn't keep his mouth shut. After leaving the abuser's house, Zaur ran to Silvana, who was playing outside, and revealed what had happened. He pleaded with her not to tattle on him to Granny.

When Silvana was six, someone tried to sexually abuse her when she was alone outside. On that day, Silvana was playing behind a storage area meant as a garage for automobiles. Meanwhile, a young, predatory male on the make for free sex was walking not far from where Silvana was playing. Knowing that a Muslim woman wouldn't agree to have sex with him, he decided to stalk an innocent child to satisfy his licentious sexual appetite.

On a few occasions, he had seen Silvana playing outside, but because other people were crowded around, the predator could not take her, like a wolf would attack an innocent doe. However, this time she was alone. As soon as he detected this change in the situation, a pernicious grin spread across his sinister face.

The young abuser appeared out of nowhere, directly in front of her. After trying to engage her in small talk, he grabbed her hand and pushed her toward the garage wall where nobody could see them.

Silvana became frightened. She wanted to scream out, but felt her throat constrict.

"Don't make a noise or I'll kill you!" he said, putting his hand over her mouth. He was ready to rape her but was suddenly interrupted by a voice. It drew closer, calling Silvana's name. It was the voice of her friend looking for her.

"Silvana, where are you?"

The attacker quickly disappeared around the corner, leaving his intended victim alone. Silvana couldn't understand what he had been planning to do, but knew that he had intended to injure her. When Silvana's friend found her, she didn't tell him anything about it. This experience put fear in Silvana's heart; she stopped trusting men altogether, and was always afraid of getting hurt by them. She started seeing them as sexual predators and molesters.

At age seven, Silvana started going to school. This was short-lived; one day other schoolchildren trapped Silvana in a locker. She was frightened and refused to go back. Sadaget took Silvana out of school and decided to keep her at home.

In September of 1985, Sadaget enrolled her grandchildren in the Internat, placing them in the same Russian class together all but Elnara, who she left with a neighbor instead. The school not only offered an education in both Russian and Azeri, but was also designed for underprivileged children who were parentless or had a single parent in their household. At that time, Silvana was nine years old, Zaur eight, and Lachin seven. Sadaget didn't consider Internat as a good school for her grandchildren, but because of its convenient location, she chose it nonetheless. With the new school, Sadaget didn't need to worry about leaving her grandchildren unsupervised. They could stay overnight at the school.

Poor Silvana didn't want to stay, because she remembered her experience of when she was trapped in a locker. The day that she was left at Internat, and Sadaget left in her brown raincoat and black boots, Silvana ran after her. She begged Sadaget to take her back home.

"Granny, please take me with you!" Teardrops streamed down Silvana's face. She clutched Sadaget's raincoat, raising her head. "Granny, please don't leave me in this school!"

"Go back to school, Silvana! Your brothers are waiting for you there," ordered Sadaget, pushing her toward the building.

Silvana grabbed her hand. "No, Granny. I don't want to stay in that school!"

Sadaget tried to take a step forward, but Silvana kept holding her hand.

"Let go!"

"No, Granny!"

"You know I can't take you home now," said Sadaget firmly, opening Silvana's fingers to remove her hands from her coat. Silvana closed them over the material again.

"Why?" asked a teary-eyed Silvana.

"I have to work. It is too far for me to travel every morning to drop you off at school. When we move to a new apartment, you will stay at home."

At last, she was able to remove Silvana's hands.

"Go back to school, or I will yank your ears!"

Silvana stood for a moment as her granny walked away. Then she followed her, right up to the bus station. She slipped into the bus with Sadaget.

Her granny spotted her before the bus pulled away. She pinched Silvana's hand. Then pushed her out of the bus.

"Go back to school! Now!"

The bus started to move forward, leaving behind a frustrated Silvana.

As a result of Sadaget's pinching, a boil on Silvana's hand burst, causing painful bleeding. She blew air gently on the boil to reduce the pain. The troubled child stood at the bus stop, wiping her wet eyes with her coat sleeve.

Why am I always the one left behind? What did I do?

When Sadaget's bus disappeared from sight, she began to walk back to school, feeling wretched and abandoned. She wiped her tears as she entered the school building. Silvana climbed upstairs to the third floor.

It was quiet because lessons had started. Silvana was late. When she entered the classroom, she saw her brothers standing in the corner. She asked her new teacher, "Why did you put my brothers in a corner? What did they do?"

The teacher eyed her suspiciously. "It is not your business, my dear. First, you came late. Second, you are not allowed to ask questions, other than those relating to your lessons. Now go and stand in the other corner!"

Silvana joined her brothers in punishment. The poor child spent most of the day standing on her feet in the corner, pondering why the teacher had been so harsh to her for no reason. She was barely allowed to go to the bathroom. When class was over, Silvana was relieved to leave her corner and mingle with her new friends. This was her first day at this school, and one she would never forget.

While Silvana and her brothers were going through their first day at school, Sadaget sat on the train on her way to the factory. She thought about her grandchildren and daughter.

She is such a cow, popping out Samed's kids like cannonballs, neglecting them, and leaving them hanging around my neck like a noose! She does not even bother to live with them, and stays God knows where.

Sadaget's heart ached, seeing her grandchildren growing up without their parents' presence in their lives. She mostly worried about Silvana, fearful that without a paternal presence she might end up like her mother. She decided to be firm and disciplined with Silvana, to train her not to allow any man to hurt or abuse her. At the same time, Sadaget wanted to provide her grandchildren with a fundamental education, so they would not struggle as she did. Sadaget was angry that, instead of going on to university, Esmira had ruined her future, first by meeting and dating Samed, and now by choosing exploitative friends.

She disembarked from the train and walked toward work in deep thought.

I was paying for her university fees. Then like a lunkhead she started dating that abusive bastard! Now she sings for a living, and barely spends time at home. She could have not only met a decent, loyal husband like any good woman does, but also could have stayed at home while her man earned money and brought home food. Because of her poor choices, I have to put my grandchildren in a segregated school for children with no parents, as if they had no one in their lives.

Sadaget started coughing as she walked. The road was covered with dust and ruts, desperately needing new pavement. The swirling dust always invaded her lungs. As she wiped her watery eyes, Sadaget glanced over at a group of women at a park across from her. They sat on benches, watching people.

Sadaget sniffed in disdain. These elderly women, in their long skirts and with their heads covered, were hardly the religious women they pretended to be.

These women have nothing better to do than sit outside like lazy cows and gossip for the sake of gossiping.

She recalled Silvana's desperate plea not to abandon her at school, and sighed wearily as she drew near to her destination: a two-story factory.

She had had no real choice in the matter. Zaur had been tearing strips of wallpaper from the walls while Sadaget was at work. Plus, the property owner had begun to complain that her grandchildren were playing too loudly when she was not at home. They have to stay in that school. I work, and I can no longer leave them alone at home, thought Sadaget.

***

The first two years of school were distressing for Silvana because of two venomous teachers, who had an unjustified dislike of both her and her siblings.

Silvana suspected that Bahar Mamedova treated all of them maliciously because of her mother. In the first year of school, Esmira had bought flowers for Mamedova on her birthday. When she gave the carnations to her, the teacher had responded in a repulsive tone.

"You can give these flowers to someone else. I don't need them."

"Well, it looks like I have wasted my time and money buying these flowers for you!" Esmira angrily exclaimed. She threw the flowers in the garbage bin in front of Mamedova. Esmira immediately left without saying goodbye.

After that confrontation, Esmira never went back to the school. The teacher felt offended because Esmira had disrespected her in front of her students. Thus she treated Silvana in a harsh manner.

She put Silvana and her siblings in a corner as punishment. She also gave Silvana bad grades for no good reason. Sadaget didn't like the way Silvana's teacher treated her grandkids, and quarreled with the teacher frequently.

At the end of the first year of school, Mamedova gave Sadaget a referral letter to send her grandchildren to a segregated school. As soon as Sadaget learned that her grandchildren had been referred there, she became enraged and scheduled a meeting with the teacher. Unfortunately, it was during a study time, and the meeting was held in the classroom.

Sadaget tore the letter in front of the teacher's face and tossed it to the floor.

"How could you refer them to a school for mentally challenged children? Do they look retarded to you? They are as intelligent and healthy as your other pupils!"

The teacher sat back, alarmed at the anger in Sadaget's voice.

"Sadaget Khanum, please let me explain. That school specializes in drawing and painting. Your grandchildren are good at drawing; they would be able to further their talents."

"No, they are not going to that school. As far as I am concerned will stay here until the end. Ever since they started here, you have been harassing these children. What is your problem?" Sadaget shouted.

The students in the classroom stopped what they had been doing. Everyone looked at her and the teacher.

"Please calm down, Sadaget Khanum. The children are looking at us." The teacher was worried that other teachers might hear them.

"Don't try to silence me!" yelled Sadaget, raising her voice. "I'm leaving, but if my grandchildren complain of being treated unfairly, I will be back! I will report you to the Ministry of Education."

With that, she stormed out of the room. She banged the door shut and bolted off.

After Sadaget left, Zaur could not concentrate on his studies. He talked to his friends and made jokes, drawing funny cartoons representing Mamedova. For him, making funny jokes, drawing pictures, and talking to his friends were more important than his lessons.

Zaur drew a cartoon of an old man with a long, crooked nose and a big belly. He showed it to a friend. That got them both chuckling.

While writing on the blackboard, the teacher heard the giggling, became infuriated. She turned around to see who was laughing. She narrowed her eyes suspiciously, gazing at the class.

"Who has been laughing?" she asked sternly. Zaur and Elshan became frightened. The boys tried to go unnoticed. They bowed their heads and pretended to read their textbooks.

"Zaur and Elshan were laughing," said Roma, who was sitting in front of them.

"Rotten egg! Why did you tell on us?" whispered Elshan.

"Come to the front of the classroom. Tell us why you giggled!" commanded their teacher.

The friends got up and walked toward the blackboard. They stood silently in front of their classmates.

"I'm waiting," demanded the teacher.

"Zaur drew a funny cartoon," said Elshan, gazing down at the floor.

"Both of you, put your hands on the desk!" exclaimed the teacher. As soon as they did so, she hit their hands with a ruler.

"Don't draw during my lessons! Sit down and don't make any more noise!" shouted Mamedova.

The boys sat down in their seats, rubbing their bruised fingers.

Every day, when school was over, the children were allowed to go to the dormitory, where they changed clothes, took a little nap, and then went outside to play. Late in the afternoon, the children did their homework, and at 6.30 p.m., they went to the cafeteria to eat their dinner. After dinner, they went to their respective rooms to retire for the evening and go to bed.

In the children's minds, 'bedtime' was not a time for sleep. In fact, sleep time was a time for fun. The girls slept in one big room; and the boys, in another. Both groups found ways to enjoy their evenings until someone came to stop them. The girls liked to jump on the beds, and throw pillows at each other.

One night, Silvana decided to trick the teacher. She put her clothes under her blanket, wrapping a shawl around her other clothes to make it look like a head. From the side, it looked as if someone wearing a headscarf was asleep in the bed.

Meanwhile, the girls all continued to raise raucous trouble by making noise and jumping on their beds. Fidan smacked Silvana with a pillow, hitting her directly in the face, before falling to the floor. Laughing, Silvana picked up the pillow. She pelted it at

Aidan's face. Silvana's friend almost fell off the bed. She glared at Silvana angrily.

"You are always throwing everything so hard. You almost made me fall!"

"I didn't do it on purpose."

"Silvana, let's see who can jump higher," suggested another friend, Zeynab.

Silvana tried to leap higher than the others. Her brown hair tossed about in the air. Her hazel eyes brimmed with joy. She spread her hands outward, pretending to be a bird taking flight.

Suddenly, she heard steps approaching the door. Her heart started pounding. She quickly stopped jumping and hid under the bed.

The rest of the girls tried to get back in bed and lie down before the teacher, Galina Ivanova could open the door. Some were not fast enough.

"Girls, didn't I tell you not to jump on the beds?" she snarled, a stick in her hand. "Fidan, get back in bed! Layla, pick up your pillow! Zeynab, clean up the room!"

Zeynab retrieved her clothing from the floor as Fidan laid down in her bed, trying not to move.

From her place under the bed, Silvana gazed at Ivanova, trying not to breathe too heavily. It was interesting for her to see a short, fat woman in a tight nightdress attempting to look severe and slim, but instead looking like an overfed cow long put out to pasture.

Ivanova approached Silvana's bed and stared at it, smiling. "Look at Silvana. She is sleeping, whereas the rest of you are misbehaving. Why can't you behave like her?"

Hearing this, Silvana could barely keep herself from giggling. She had to put her hand on her mouth to try to remain quiet.

Noticing two pillows on the floor, Ivanova pointed at them with the stick. "Why are these pillows still on the ground? Pick them up right now!"

Zeynab got up and put them on an empty bed.

The supervisor turned off the light. "Don't let me catch you playing with your pillows or making noise again!"

As soon as the teacher left, Silvana emerged from under her bed. She removed her clothing from under the blankets and lay down, relieved that Ivanova had not discovered her trick. After a short time, she fell asleep and began to dream. She was in Jerusalem, inside a synagogue. The Rabbi opened the Torah and read to Silvana: "You are a lamb that came into this world to be sacrificed."

Knowing that his words predicted suffering, Silvana's mind filled with alarm. She awoke and sat upright, her heart racing.

Seeing her awake, Zeynab asked, "What happened?"

"I had a strange dream. I was told that I'm a lamb that came into this world to be sacrificed," said Silvana, confused.

"What are you worrying about? It is just a dream."

"Jesus Christ, the Son of God, was a Lamb that was sacrificed for our sins and suffered as a result," explained Silvana. She shook her head. "This dream predicts suffering. I don't want to suffer," she continued in a breathless whisper.

Zeynab came over to sit on Silvana's bed. "Jesus is not the son of Allah. He is a prophet. My uncle said Allah cannot have a son."

Silvana stared angrily at Zeynab. "Your uncle is wrong. God is all-powerful. He can have a Son if he so chooses. My great-granny Mariya stated that He is the Son of God, as recorded in the Bible. I read it myself."

Zeynab's eyes widened. "As a Muslim, you should neither read the Bible, nor believe that Jesus is Allah's son."

Silvana yawned. "I do not see myself as a Muslim. I have faith in my great granny's teachings about Christianity."

She suddenly grasped Zeynab's hand, her voice full of worry. "But I don't want to meet misfortune later in life. My childhood has already been so gloomy and lonely."

Zeynab squeezed Silvana's hand. "You are not going to suffer. My mother says that we must ignore our dreams, because they are merely manifestations and beehives of our worries." Zeynab frowned because she could not understand how Silvana, as a Muslim, could believe that Jesus is the son of Allah.

Silvana lay back down and rested her head on the pillow as she thought.

"Sometimes dreams come from God as a message. I saw other strange visions as well," said Silvana.

"What were they about?" Zeynab was all ears.

"Once I dreamed that Jesus sat at my table. I couldn't see His face, but I saw Him from behind. He wore white clothes and had long hair. He opened the book that was on the table, and angels with bracelets came out of it. Next time, I dreamed about Mary. She said that I would save people from disaster. In my other dream, I stood outside and looked at the sky. I saw a cloud in the form of a man spreading his hands out in front of himself. Suddenly, I heard a voice saying, 'This is Jesus, and He does not come to everyone. Hurry up! Tell Him your wishes.' I quickly made a wish."

"What did you wish for?" asked Zeynab, rubbing her eyes.

"I asked Jesus to send back my father."

Zeynab's eyes started closing. She kept yawning. "Your dreams are strange."

"Yes, but in another dream, I saw many shining stars, each connected to the other with a shiny golden line. Again, the voice declared, 'Stars don't appear this way to everyone. Quickly tell your wishes. They will come true."

"What did you ask for this time?"

"For my father to come back."

"I don't remember any of my dreams. I'm perplexed that you remember all of them," said Zeynab.

"Yes, I remember almost every dream, and some are recurring. I keep seeing myself flying in the sky like a bird. Most times I leave my house but can't find a way back. I'm being chased by a killer."

Zeynab heard steps approaching. She quickly got up from Silvana's bed and ran back to hers.

Silvana yawned. "Anyway, let's go back to sleep," she said.

However, she lay awake in bed for some time, thinking about the meanings of her dreams and her father.

I am so tired of waiting for him. How can he live in peace, not concerned about our whereabouts? If he came back, not only would my life change, but also my mother would stop struggling and cease letting people mistreat her. Instead, she would stay at home with us.

On Saturday morning, Silvana got up at 6 a.m. She picked up a bag of dirty clothes from under her bed and left the bedroom. She walked outside, fearful of being alone so early in the morning. Silvana made her way to the huge iron sink that they used for washing laundry. Silvana ran the water, then dumped her clothes into the sink. She washed and rinsed them, then walked back to the dormitory. Quietly, she hung the clothes in the bedroom on the line that ran across the room.

Later, Sadaget came for her grandkids and took them to the apartment in the city. The children were so happy to be back at home after not seeing Granny for two weeks. They spent the weekend with Sadaget, but it was too short. To their disappointment, early on Monday, they were taken back to school. Downstairs in the school's academic building, Sadaget met Silvana's teacher. She let her know that, as soon as they could move to a new apartment, Sadaget would more than likely remove her grandchildren from school.

Days passed slowly as Silvana anxiously waited for the day when her family would relocate to a new place. In truth, she had started to like her school, but she still disliked the rudeness of the teachers toward her and her siblings.

Mamedova was too strict and whacked the hands of the pupils with a ruler. The others were afraid of her, but not Silvana. She failed to comprehend why the children feared the teacher.

One day, when Mamedova was absent from school, an Armenian teacher, Elona Petrosyan, replaced her. She was a thin, tall, beautiful woman with a long, curved nose.

During class, Silvana asked, "Elona Muallim can I go to the bathroom, please?"

The teacher purposely stepped on Silvana's foot. "No, you can't go."

Silvana's bladder felt full. She could barely keep from wetting her panties. She was dismayed at the teacher's answer, and with the dismay came boldness. She got up from her seat and stared into the teacher's eyes without blinking. "If I wet myself because you didn't allow me to use the bathroom, please don't blame me."

Elona Petrosyan approached Silvana and stared at her for a while. Silvana returned the stare. The teacher finally relented.

"Okay, Silvana, go now but come back quickly!"

When Silvana left the classroom, the teacher said, "That girl has a big mouth, one I will cut short."

Silvana descended the staircase, trying to reach the bathroom in time. On the steps, the principal's assistant grabbed her ponytail and angrily asked, "Why is your hair not braided?"

"I didn't know that my hair was supposed to be."

"Go back to your classroom! You shouldn't walk around during lessons."

"I'm not just walking around. I'm going to the bathroom."

The principal's helper let go of her ponytail. "Okay, go to the toilet. Quit strolling about aimlessly!"

"Why is your hair not braided?" mimicked Silvana under her breath. She twisted her mouth in a grimace as she walked away.

Silvana went to the bathroom, then immediately returned to the classroom.

Chapter 7: Relocation To A New Apartment

The school hired a barber. Silvana and her brothers were sent for haircuts. After shaving her brothers' heads, the barber asked Silvana to sit in the chair. Under the impression that she would get a new hairstyle, Silvana sat in the chair beaming with anticipation. The barber started to cut her hair. Then he simply shaved it all off. When Silvana realized that she was bald, she glared at the barber. She had been completely deceived.

"Why did you shave me bald? Now I'm going to look as ugly as a boy!"

"I was told that you and your siblings had lice," snickered the barber.

Her eyes watered. "We don't have any lice. That's simply not true!"

Silvana left the room with her brothers. Her heart was filled with resentment; once again, she had been treated in a demeaning fashion by a member of the opposite sex.

In the middle of October 1985, Sadaget moved into a four-room apartment. There was a kitchen, bathroom, and two big porches. It was located in Darnaqul, thirty minutes from Internat. For the first time since she had moved to Baku, Sadaget felt calm. As soon as she moved to this new accommodation, she decided to bring her grandchildren home for weekends. Thus, on the third Saturday of October, Sadaget took Elnara with her to get them from school, only to be astonished that her grandchildren were now hairless. Upon seeing their shiny domes, she scolded them in a shocked voice.

"What happened to your hair?"

"They cut all our hair, claiming that we had lice," Silvana answered in an angry tone.

Sadaget shook her head in disbelief. "That teacher has gone too far this time," she thundered.

She went directly to Bahar Mamedova, who was watching over breakfast in the canteen. Sadaget started to quarrel with her. The other students sat at their tables, eating breakfast.

"Why did you cut off all my grandkid's hair?" she demanded, without even greeting the teacher.

"They had lice," replied the teacher, smirking slightly.

"I sent my grandchildren to school with clean heads. So where do you suppose they got lice from?" demanded Sadaget indignantly.

"They probably got it from their classmates." The teacher squirmed as she answered. She looked at the children to ensure that they had not heard anything.

"These children are not orphans. They have me and their mother in their lives," Sadaget said loudly, pounding a fist on her chest. "You don't have the right to touch my grandchildren's hair without getting my permission."

The teacher's eyes wandered around the canteen as her lower lip began to twitch. "Sadaget Khanum, please calm down. You're not setting a good example by bickering in front of these children."

Sadaget ignored her advice; rather, she raised her voice and pointed at Silvana's bald head. "Look at this child! She looks ridiculous with no hair. You could prevent lice without cutting their hair."

"Sadaget Khanum, please accept my apology."

"An apology won't bring their hair back. I hope this won't happen again." Sadaget crossed her arms. "I'm taking them home. I will bring them back to school on Monday."

The teacher stood motionless for a few minutes, keeping her eyes on Sadaget. Her eyes were haughty.

These people abandon their children, dropping them like nooses around our necks, only because they don't want to look after them themselves. Then they wonder why we don't mind them to their standards.

"Let's go," Sadaget said to her grandchildren. As she left the cafeteria, she purposely slammed the door shut.

"Silvana, gather all your dirty clothes, as well as your brothers'," her granny said.

Silvana quickly ran to the dormitory, collected dirty laundry, and gave it to her granny. They all left the school.

Instead of going to the bus stop, Sadaget walked in a different direction.

"Granny, where are we going?" Lachin asked anxiously.

"We are going to our new apartment."

Lachin paused for a minute, his mouth wide open. "Are you kidding, Granny?"

"No, I'm not," she replied.

Sadaget told her grandchildren that she had moved to a new place. They jumped and cheered.

"Yes! Now we can live in our apartment together!" said Lachin, skipping happily.

"Would you allow us to come home every day?" Silvana asked, shining with jubilance.

"I'm taking you home today, but you will end up staying in school for a few more weeks again."

"Why?" Zaur asked, puzzled.

"Since we don't have electricity and gas as yet, our apartment is cold and dark at nights," explained their grandmother.

"But, Granny, we can still stay there," said Silvana, frowning.

"No, there are no beds, chairs, or even a table. However, I promise as soon as we get electricity and I buy all the necessary things, you will come home to a safe place every day."

Sadaget stopped and beamed at them. "I have good news for you! Your great-granny Mariya will visit us soon."

Silvana gazed at her granny. "Is she coming to live with us?" she asked excitedly.

"I am not certain," said Sadaget, resuming her brisk walk, "but I hope she will stay with us for a long time. The fact is that her son-in-law treats her poorly. He doesn't allow her to drink vodka or smoke cigarettes."

"Why?" asked Lachin, as he jumped over a dirty puddle.

They were walking through a neighborhood that was strange to the children. The road was muddy and full of potholes filled with water. Silvana kept looking at the newly-built five-story buildings.

"He says that there is no place for haram such as alcohol in a house, where Quran is kept and prayers are going on."

He is just a grumpy man, thought Sadaget.

"But Great-Granny is not a Muslim. She does not have to follow his rules," said Silvana innocently, shading her hazel eyes from the sun's glare.

"Are we Muslims?" asked Zaur, holding his granny's hand and pulling her forward.

"Stop pulling me!" commanded Sadaget, stopping to take a breath. She gazed warily at some stray dogs that were running not far from them.

"Since your parents are Muslim, that makes you a Muslim, as well," she said, patting his head.

Upon hearing her granny's explanation, Silvana frowned. "No, I believe in Jesus."

"I guess you followed your Russian ancestors' path in life," said Sadaget.

They walked on silently, gazing at the people passing by. Silvana was happy that they had gotten a new apartment. It meant that soon she could stay at home after her classes. However, hearing that they had to wait again smothered her excitement somewhat. When they approached their new nine-story building, Silvana noticed another five-story building not far from theirs. She looked around and saw a few vehicles parked in front. Little pine trees stood opposite their building.

As soon as Sadaget's grandchildren entered the apartment, they inspected it. They looked in every huge bedroom, the bathroom, the porches, and the kitchen. The apartment was empty, but had beautiful pink wallpaper with little flowers.

Silvana entered the living room. She noticed two icons hung on the wall. She stood silently, looking at Mary's and Jesus' images. Her eyes bulged and mouth dropped open. Mary was holding the baby Jesus in her arms.

"Wow! So, beautiful."

Then she glanced at the opposite wall. Silvana saw a picture of the Kaaba.

The apartment had a new stove, two sinks, and a bathtub. The children were amazed by the size of the porches and the tall ceilings.

Zaur hopped on one foot from one side of the porch to the next. "Wow, it's so huge!" He stopped by the railing and gazed outside. The sight of a graveyard made his eyes open wide.

He turned to his sister. "Silvana, it's so odd to live near a cemetery."

Silvana rubbed her arms. "Yes, it's creepy. I don't even like seeing a cemetery." Both of them went back indoors, unsettled by what they had seen.

"Where are we going to sleep?" asked Lachin, not seeing any beds.

"I'm going to put a mattress on the floor," answered Sadaget.

"Go outside to play for a while. Just keep in mind that our apartment is located in Block 8 and on the fifth floor. Don't go far or you will get lost!"

After her grandchildren left, Sadaget took out an oil-burning cooker and prepared a big pot of Russian borscht. Two hours later, Silvana came back home with her siblings. They ate soup and spent the rest of the day playing on the porch.

Sadaget's grandchildren stayed at home for two nights, and on Monday they walked back to school. They reached it somewhat early, and when they entered the classroom Bahar Mamedova was sitting at the desk, preoccupied with scribbling notes in her notebook.

"Good morning, Bahar Muallim," said Silvana, putting her backpack under her desk. "I have good news."

The teacher raised her head.

"Yes, Silvana?" she inquired.

Silvana's face expressed her joy. "My granny got a new apartment. Soon we will start going home every day after school."

The teacher removed her spectacles and wiped them with a tissue. "I'm happy for you, but when are you going to leave our school? Your granny indicated that, as soon as you moved to a new apartment, she would put you in a different school."

"I think we are going to stay in this school for another nine years," answered Silvana, flashing her teeth. She knew that the teacher didn't want them there.

"What did you say?" asked Mamedova, taken aback by Silvana's answer.

Silvana's bold eyes met the teacher's. "My granny told us that we don't have any reason to leave this school, so we will continue studying here," Silvana replied.

"Good for you. Go and clean the blackboard," said the teacher, clearly irritated.

Silvana got up from her chair and cleaned the blackboard as the other classmates entered the room.

On the following Friday, Silvana decided not to wait for her granny to walk her home. As soon as her teacher dismissed the class, Silvana with her siblings left school and walked in the direction of their apartment building.

On the way, they encountered a few similar buildings, but they couldn't find theirs. They were lost, but they kept walking on the bumpy and muddy road. The children passed by a small, white-colored shop that had a long, triangular window. There was a big garbage storage container outside of it, filled with trash. Some of the torn garbage bags lay on the ground, with their contents scattered around them.

"Zaur, do you remember which building is ours?" asked Silvana, looking at two identical buildings.

"I don't know. Maybe we should go back to school," he suggested, scratching his head.

"No, we can't go back," said Silvana.

After walking for a bit, Silvana was able to find their building but wasn't sure in which block they ought to enter. She noticed a middle-aged woman walking toward them and approached the woman.

"Aunty, we are looking for our Granny Sadaget. Do you know which block she lives in?"

The woman eyed all of them with curiosity. "My little one, we have a few people with the same name here in the compound. What is her surname?"

"Her surname is Babaeva," answered Silvana.

The woman looked vacant trying to recall where Sadaget lived.

"Oh, she lives in Block 8," she told them and walked away.

Before entering Block 8, Silvana raised her head up to look at the porches. Some of them had clothes hanging on the lines. On one of the porches, she noticed a tall, old woman sitting and smoking. The woman's head was covered by a blue shawl. It was shaking somewhat.

They entered Block 8, climbed to the fifth floor, and gleefully rang the doorbell. Mariya opened the door and was very astounded to see them.

"What are you doing here?" she asked in a startled tone.

"We don't want to sleep or study in that school any longer," said Lachin. He passed Mariya as he went inside. He stared at her, befuddled upon seeing his great-granny.

"Granny Mariya, when did you get here?" asked Zaur, also going in.

The smile on her face showed her yellow teeth, filled with cavities. "A few days ago. All of you are looking thin, as though Sadaget is not feeding you properly. You are lucky I am at home."

Mariya told the children that, earlier, she had been with a neighbor, and had come back right before they'd arrived back home.

"If I weren't at home, you would have to go back to school," scolded Mariya.

"The teachers treat us badly. They're always asking when we'll move to another school," Zaur complained.

"You can't just walk home alone. You have to stay in that school until Sadaget collects you. Do you understand?" Mariya asked firmly.

"Yes, we understand," answered Silvana.

"Come and give your granny a big hug. It has been a long time since I last saw you."

The children hugged her. Then they went into the living room. Mariya returned to the porch to continue smoking.

Silvana followed Mariya and stood quietly gazing at the old woman's wrinkled face. Red patches encircled her blue eyes. Mariya's long fingers had become crooked.

"Why are you here?" asked Silvana.

Mariya stared at her thoughtfully and blew some smoke circles. "I'm not only here to visit you, but I am also fed up living with a control freak. He even hides tea and sugar from me, saying that I am wasting it. He had better learn to show some humility and love." Mariya spat on the floor.

Silvana smiled at hearing Mariya's complaints. She took her hand gently. "Next time when he opens his mouth, tell him to shut up."

Mariya looked at Silvana's eyes. The old woman noticed a deep sadness and pensiveness in them, a trait seen by other people as well. She uttered a sigh of sadness.

I hope this family curse will not pass to Silvana. It must cease somehow, Mariya thought. She realized that three generations of women had found themselves without husbands.

"Silvana, come inside. Granny's here!" shouted Zaur.

Sadaget was startled to see her grandchildren.

"Why are you not at school?" she asked.

Lachin hugged his granny. "Silvana brought us here," he said.

She scolded them for coming home on their own without supervision.

"But we missed you and wanted to see Mama. Where is she?" asked Lachin.

"She is staying with her friend."

"Since we started going to the new school, we have not seen her at all," said Lachin, frowning.

"When is she going to come here?" asked Zaur.

"I don't know. I have to call her. Why are you still in your school clothes? Go change, and I will call her!" Sadaget said.

"Silvana, Granny bought new furniture for the house. Come and see it," said Elnara, yanking Silvana's skirt.

Elnara was Silvana's favorite. Therefore Silvana always looked after her.

Silvana decided to inspect the rooms with Elnara while Zaur and Lachin went into the kitchen. They were all curious to see what Granny had bought. In the dining room, Silvana found a sofa and a table with six chairs. One bedroom had a new closet but no beds.

"Silvana, come and look at our new fridge and the table!" Zaur shouted, surprised. They ran to the kitchen, where Zaur stood in front of the fridge. He opened the door a crack to inspect its contents, but found that it was half-empty.

After running through the rest of the house, the children changed their clothes. They went outside to play. When it started getting dark, all of them went back home.

"Granny, did you call Mama?" asked Silvana.

Sadaget waved her hand as if swatting an annoying insect. "No, I was waiting for you to come back. All of you go to the front porch. I will call her in good time. Do not make any noise, since Mariya is sleeping."

"But I would like to speak to her, too," implored Zaur.

"Zaur, go to the porch! You don't need to talk to her now. You will see your mother next week," Sadaget said crossly, pushing him toward the porch.

After the grandchildren went out, Sadaget picked up the phone and dialed Esmira's number.

"Allo," said Esmira.

"Esmira, it's your mother. When are you planning to visit your children? They are asking after you."

Esmira's sigh was a mixture of annoyance and exhaustion. "I will drop by next week."

"Since these poor children started going to Internat, you haven't even bothered to visit them. You haven't bought any food, or even clothes. What kind of mother are you? Even dogs don't leave their pups, but you have left them around my neck like a noose," scolded Sadaget in a raised voice.

Esmira's body tensed and her heart started to race. "Mother, I didn't leave them. I can't keep them with me because I travel often. I can't live with you because you always nag me. I can't take it!" snapped her daughter.

"If you hadn't brought this shame into my life by sleeping with Samed, I would never have started to nag you." Sadaget squeezed the phone tightly and felt her throat constrict, leaving it parched. She wanted to say so much to her daughter, but she decided not to.

"You never loved me, but always tried to find fault in me," Esmira accused in a sad voice.

"I never loved you? Who brought you up? Not me? Who looks after your children?" Sadaget demanded loudly.

Esmira put her hand over her left eye. She had developed a stabbing pain behind it. "Mother, please don't get distressed," she pleaded. "I will bring groceries and money next week."

Sadaget ignored Esmira's words.

"You shouldn't have jumped into Samed's bed, giving him offspring, if you didn't want to mind them. You only embarrassed yourself and me." She hit the phone stand with her fist while talking.

Esmira's face was inflamed with pain. "How many times have you told me the same thing over and over again?"

The impact of Esmira's mistakes on her life filled Sadaget's heart with fury. "As soon as you got Samed between your legs, they caught on fire. Therefore, you needed to extinguish the flames. Did you not think that sleeping with a man outside of marriage would lead you to Hell and thereby bring shame on your head?"

"Mother, stop. Please." Esmira shook as she tried to light a cigarette.

"Don't try to shut me up! Do you hear me? If you had put a lock between your legs, none of this would have happened. You brought them into this world, so come and look after them!" shouted Sadaget over the phone.

"All right! I already told you that I will come next week. I have to go now," Esmira said with annoyance. She hung up the phone without letting Sadaget say anything more.

Sadaget put the phone down and went to the front porch.

"Granny, did you call Mama?" asked Elnara.

"Yes, I called her."

"When is she going to come back?" asked Lachin.

"She will come next week. Now it is time for dinner."

"Why can't she come tomorrow?" asked Elnara, saddened.

"She does not care about you, that's why," sniped Sadaget.

"That is not true, Granny. She loves us," said Silvana, as her eyes became teary.

"Yes, but who looks after you? Who is here for you when you are sick? Who stands up for you when people are calling you fatherless?"

"You are," said Zaur.

"Now you know who cares more about you. Let's eat, and cease any further talk of your mother."

Without another word on the subject, she gave them borscht, a Russian soup. Then she spread mattresses on the ground and sent them off to sleep.

Not long after, Silvana started having a nightmare. A long, black demon with red eyes and big horns on his head was chasing her. She kept running and shouting.

"Babushka!"

As the demon grabbed her she woke up in a sweat. She screamed out, "Babushka!" Her voice echoed through the bedroom, reverberating and ricocheting off the walls.

Mariya came into the bedroom, dressed in a long pink nightdress, with her gray hair uncovered. "Silvana, why are you screaming?"

Shaking, Silvana sobbed, "A demon was chasing me in my dream. This is not the first time that I've seen him."

Mariya sat on Silvana's mattress and took her hand. "It is just a dream. Lie down and sleep."

"No, I'm afraid."

Mariya took a crucifix on a chain from around her neck and put it in Silvana's hand. "Put this under your pillow and say 'Jesus Christ, cover me with Your precious blood.' The devil will not come to you any longer."

Silvana looked at the golden crucifix curiously and put it under the pillow.

Then she lay back. "Jesus Christ, cover me with Your precious blood."

Mariya patted Silvana's head. "Now close your eyes. I will stay here until you fall asleep.

Feeling peaceful, Silvana shut her eyes. After a while, she fell asleep.

Silvana's great-granny sat on Silvana's bed. She pondered both her past life and her great-grandchildren's future.

"I hope their opportunities and choices will be vaster than those of my generation," she thought to herself.

Then she recalled the day when she had first arrived in Azerbaijan. In 1934, Mariya traveled from Russia to Azerbaijan to visit her Russian aunt, never to return. There, Sadaget's mother met her future spouse, got married, and had four girls by him.

At one point, Mariya's Russian relatives had been wealthy. In particular, her father had been a well-respected priest in Russia. However, when the Bolsheviks took control, they had seized her family's property and had displaced them to another city.

During World War II, Mariya heard that her parents and brothers had been killed; the Nazis threw a bomb at their house while they were still in it. Mariya never returned to search for her family. She assumed that all of them had died from the explosion. In 1941, Mariya's spouse was posted to a war zone. In 1943, she received a letter from the government stating that her husband had vanished without a trace. After her partner's disappearance, Mariya remained alone with four children on her hands and started drinking vodka on almost a daily basis.

Realizing that she was drinking too much and therefore unable to care for her girls, local social services took them away and put the girls in an orphanage. To get her kids back, Mariya landed a job as a security guard in the local school and stopped drinking for a while. Fortunately, social services returned three of her girls; however, they took away her eldest daughter. After getting her girls back, she started drinking again.

While working the night shift, Mariya used to put her kids to sleep, leave them at home alone, and then leave the house for her job as a security guard. Mariya's older daughter used to mind her two sisters while Mariya was at work.

When Mariya was not drunk, she remained strict with her girls. She would talk to them firmly and strike them if they disobeyed her instructions. The poor girls never got any hugs from her, just licks and whacks.

They were growing up without any other relatives around. Mariya's husband had sisters, but they did not want anything to do with Mariya, especially after their brother's disappearance. In those days, the mentality of most Azeri people was severe and old-fashioned. They would never respect a Russian woman who was a single mother and an alcoholic.

One fateful night, Mariya went to work in a drunken state. She fell asleep during her night shift. While she was sleeping, someone broke into the school, burglarized the principal's office, and stole some money. Since the locks on the doors appeared not to have been tampered with, Mariya was accused of stealing the money. She was sent to jail for a year.

During that year, Sadaget's oldest sister, Tamara, cared for the girls by cleaning other people's houses. She would take her two sisters to work with her. It was a trying and arduous time for them. However, after a year Mariya has been released from jail to mind her girls.

The memory of her detention in jail plagued her, so Mariya stopped mulling over her past life. She gently covered Silvana with a blanket and stood up.

"Jesus Christ, please fill Silvana's life with abounding joy and everlasting happiness. Give her that happy ending that we never grew up with." Mariya sighed heavily as she left her great-granddaughter's bedroom.

At around 3 a.m. Silvana woke up, feeling a touch on her hand. She opened her eyes, yawning, and saw tiny Elnara. Her black eyes were teary.

"Why are you crying?"

"My belly is hurting. Can you please rub it?" Elnara pointed at her belly.

Silvana sat up and put her pillow on her legs. "Come and lay down here."

Elnara rested her head on the pillow. Silvana moved her legs from side to side, rocking her sibling. At the same time, she gently rubbed Elnara's belly. After her sibling fell asleep, Silvana rested her head on the mattress and closed her eyes.

Chapter 8: Existence Led By Fear Of Gossip

As the years flew by, Silvana's school life became more fascinating. More responsibilities fell on her shoulders, especially after Elnara started school. Silvana's little sister was miserable. She refused to go to school unless Silvana carried her school bag. So, along with her own books, Silvana used to carry Elnara's school bag while holding her hand.

It was Silvana's responsibility to take her siblings to school. She earned considerable respect from anyone who knew her, and was viewed as a strong, intelligent girl who could stand up for herself. Silvana loved going to school so much that she wouldn't dare miss a day, even during the times when she had bronchitis.

As snow and ice covered the roads, and classrooms became colder, thirteen-year-old Silvana came down with bronchitis.

Every year, during the winter, Silvana coughed for a month because her grandmother wouldn't take her to a doctor or give her modern medicine. Sadaget preferred to use traditional medicine. She would say that doctors and modern medicine only made people sick and landed them in the grave.

One morning, Sadaget left early and went to the factory. Silvana got up and ironed her siblings' clothes, coughing the whole time. She made breakfast for them, took a shower, and put on her brown long-sleeved school dress and white apron. Then she woke her siblings up and gave them breakfast.

When everyone was ready, Silvana picked up Elnara's bag pack and walked with them to the school.

During her lessons, Silvana coughed constantly, irritating her teacher.

"Silvana, leave the classroom and come back when you stop coughing! You are disturbing my lessons!"

"Bahar Muallim, I'm not coughing on purpose. If I were to leave the classroom, my cough wouldn't go away." Her eyes became teary and her throat burned, making Silvana to cough harder. Her chest was congested with mucus.

"Then stay at home until you get better."

"I don't want to miss my lessons."

Silvana stayed in the classroom, trying not to cough and swallowing her mucus so as not to have to step out. When school was over, she complained to her granny about her cough.

She asked Granny to take her to the doctor. Sadaget just kept giving Silvana traditional medicine. Eventually, she recovered, but it was largely due to her strong physical constitution.

On a Friday, when the snow started to melt, Silvana took six of her girlfriends for a short trip, a bus ride to Rasina. When the girls got off the bus, they walked through the city, gazing at the speeding cars, buses and visiting different shops.

Most of the girls didn't have money to buy anything, but they loved gazing at the beautiful objects for sale in the malls. While they walked, Silvana made sure that her friends were safe and did not get lost in the city.

During the trip, Fidan bought a small Christmas tree. The next day she took it to her classroom and placed it on her desk. Unfortunately, a substitute teacher removed it.

When Silvana heard the news the next morning, she couldn't comprehend how someone could seize property that didn't belong to them. She decided to approach the teacher directly. She went into the classroom while lessons were going on. The teacher was writing something on the blackboard. She turned around as Silvana came in.

"Good morning," said Silvana, smiling.

"Hello, Silvana," answered the teacher, Elona Petrosyan. She stared blankly at the girl.

"May I please have the Christmas tree that you took away from Fidan?" demanded Silvana.

"No, you can't have it. I put it in the classroom for decoration."

"The tree doesn't belong to you. You can't take what is not yours." Silvana stared into the teacher's eyes without blinking.

Elona drew closer to Silvana as her students perched on the seats of their desks. They stared at Silvana with their mouths wide open. They were afraid of their teacher and couldn't believe that Silvana was brave enough to talk to her in such a manner.

"It is on the shelf, so take it," the teacher barked, shaking somewhat. Silvana took the tree and returned it to Fidan.

Later in the afternoon, Bahar Mamedova asked Silvana and Zeynab to check the other students' work. She left them behind in the classroom while she went to a meeting, locking the door behind her.

By 5.30 p.m. the girls started to wonder why the teacher hadn't returned.

"Zeynab, it is getting darker. We need to go home."

Silvana glanced outside, worried. A cluster of gray clouds moved in the dark sky. A few students walked from the canteen to another building, as the snow melted and soaked the ground.

Zeynab tried the door. "We can't leave. The door is locked!"

Silvana opened the window and noticed a classmate, Samir, who was walking toward another building. He was gazing at the blackbirds sitting on an electric wire.

"Samir!" she shouted.

He turned around to see who was calling him.

"Over here. Look at the window!" she said, waving her hand.

"Hey, Silvana, what are you doing in there?" he asked with a smile.

"Samir, we are stuck in the classroom! Please go to the director's office and ask for the key!" yelled Silvana.

After ten minutes, Samir came back with the key and unlocked the door.

"Thank you, Samir. You are our savior!" Zeynab cried.

"Please lock the door and give the key back to Bahar Mamedova. We have to run home," said Silvana.

The friends were afraid to be outside alone in the dark. They ran, churning the wet soil under their feet, all the way home before total darkness overtook them. As they ran, Silvana constantly looked around to make certain that no one followed them.

***

A few years had passed since Sadaget had moved to Darnaqul, and many changes had occurred.

Sadaget's favorite grandchild grew up and became more independent. She was now a beautiful fifteen-year-old teenager. When she was younger, Silvana went outside to play with her friends or siblings. Anytime when she played with her brothers, she played with their buddies as well. Throughout her childhood, she had been a tomboy, who enjoyed fighting, climbing trees and walls. In school, during physical education lessons, she played soccer with the boys. She was so good that the boys called her 'Fever.'

As soon as Silvana reached the age of fifteen, however, she stopped playing with boys and acted more like a girl. She became conscious of everything around her, and stopped going outside to play with her friends. Suddenly she was painfully conscious of a birthmark under her eye, which looked like a blue bruise and spent most of her day at home because of it.

People thought that someone had hit her or that she had had a fight. Until the age of twelve, her birthmark had not worried her a great deal, because at the time she had sported short hair and loved wearing pants. Owing to her short haircut, some people thought she was a boy.

When Silvana entered her teenage years, however, boys her age started to bother her about it. One afternoon while walking home from school, some bigger boys began following her. One of them approached her from behind.

"Hey, Silvana, who put a hickey on your beautiful face? Show me the one who hurt you."

Silvana turned and looked at the boys. She bit her lip and curled her hand into a fist, ready to hit them.

Another boy spat on the ground and spoke. "Why are you always coming to school with bruises? Who beats you?"

Silvana was frustrated and fed up, wishing that she could stay alone where no one would bother her anymore. She crossed her arms angrily.

"Idiot! Every day you see me in school, and my birthmark does not go away. Doesn't this prove that it's not a bruise? Leave me alone before I kick your bottom!"

The boys looked at her silently. Then they walked away.

Silvana thought, Why can't people leave me alone? I wish I could go away where no one would find me!

Silvana preferred to stay at home instead of hearing hurtful comments about her birthmark. She was a beautiful girl with hazel eyes and long, thick brown hair. People always used to look at her because of her beauty. However, if anyone stared at her, she always thought that the individual was peering at her birthmark. It made her feel as if something was wrong with her. She shunned people; instead of taking the bus to school, she preferred to walk on a route less populated. When her friends invited her to play outside, Silvana remained indoors. She was bothered so much by their remarks about her birthmark that she couldn't forgive Esmira for not doing anything about it.

Other children have single working mothers, but their mothers find time for them. Why is mine so careless? She has the money. Why can't she take me to the surgeon to get rid of my birthmark?

Meanwhile, Esmira continued living in the city, visiting her children once a week. During these visits, Silvana and her siblings never received any affection whatsoever from her. She never bothered to celebrate their birthdays or buy them gifts. Esmira made good money as a wedding singer but wasted most of her earnings on expensive clothes, taxi rides, jewelry, makeup, and food. Because her birthday was never celebrated as a child, she did not consider it important to celebrate the birthdays of her own children.

Most times, when her children heard the sound of a car stopping in front of their building, they ran to the front porch to see if she had arrived. Not seeing their mother saddened them, because they missed her and wanted to be near her as much as possible. Every time Esmira was at home, the children gathered around, following her into any room she entered.

One particular Saturday, the doorbell rang. Sadaget was in the kitchen seasoning meat, while Silvana sat at the table doing homework.

"Zaur, check who is at the door!" shouted Sadaget.

He stopped playing his game and ran to the door. The boy peeked through the hole but could not determine who was knocking. "Who is there?"

"Zaur, open the door. This is Mama."

Hearing his mother's voice, Zaur immediately opened the door. Upon seeing Esmira, his heart filled with joy.

"Elnara, Lachin, Silvana, Mama's here!"

Esmira entered carrying two large bags in her hands. Silvana got up from her seat and ran to meet her mother. She reached for the bags, trying to help Esmira bring them into the kitchen.

Everyone crowded in, and Esmira placed the bags on the floor.

"Hello, Mother. I brought groceries for the children. You can now cook whatever they want."

Sadaget put aside the bowl of chicken, washed her hands, and looked at the bags. "I'm not starving your children. With or without your groceries, they still get nourishment."

Esmira did not bother to respond and left the kitchen. She went into her bedroom and sat on the edge of the bed. Her children perched right next to her.

"Mother, I've been ill. Why didn't you come last week?" asked Silvana.

"I was in the village with my wedding band."

Zaur held his mother's hand, while Elnara leaned her head on her mother's shoulder.

Silvana looked sadly at her mother. "You are always absent, and barely spend time with us. We have grown up mostly without you."

"If I spend time with you, who will make money to buy food and clothes for you?" questioned Esmira. She removed a cigarette from her pocket, lit it up, and put it in her mouth. She inhaled, then blew out a plume of smoke.

"Mother, without feeling loved in my life, clothes and food cannot and do not make me happy in the least."

Silvana silently gazed at her mother for a while. Poor Mother never rested, trying to make money for us, and took the rubbish hurled at her from false friends--allowing them to exploit her kindnesses. I hope one day I will be able to give her a better life.

Silvana coughed. "Mother, can you please smoke on the porch?"

"It's cold outside. I'm going to smoke in here. All of you leave the room if you don't like it. When I finish, you can come back."

Silvana and her siblings left their mother alone. The disappointed girl entered the kitchen. Sadaget stood by the stove, frying onions with garlic.

"What is your mom doing?"

"She is smoking," replied Silvana.

Sadaget removed the pan from the fire. "Didn't I tell this woman not to smoke in my house?"

She went into Esmira's bedroom and opened the porch door.

"Why are you opening the door in this cold weather?" asked Esmira.

Sadaget approached Esmira, breathing heavily. She waved her hand, trying to chase away the smoke.

"Why are you smoking in my house? You are poisoning the air. I don't know where you picked up this nasty habit."

Esmira got up from the bed, feeling tension in her forehead, and threw her cigarette outside. "Mother, leave me alone. Every time I come here, you pick a fight."

Esmira went into the living room, followed by her children. Seeing her mother's distressed face, Silvana felt sorry for her.

She sat next to Esmira and gave her a hug. "Mother, don't pay any attention to Granny's words. You know she always likes to quarrel."

Esmira smiled, patting her daughter's head. "Don't worry. I'm all right."

She spent a few hours with her children and then left. Esmira's work as a wedding singer meant traveling to different cities. During weddings, Esmira sang Turkish or Azeri songs, and drank alcohol with her musical group. By the time she arrived home, it was midnight and she was drunk.

A few times, Silvana stayed for a few days with her mother, but after meeting Esmira's friends, she decided to go back to living with her granny.

One winter night a yellow cab stopped in front of Sadaget's building. Esmira slowly got out, enveloped by the smell of alcohol. Staggering from side to side, she climbed upstairs. Esmira could barely drag her legs from one step to the next, and made only slow steps as she held onto the rails. She took out the key to the front door, but couldn't insert it into the lock. Irritated, she rang the bell.

Sadaget opened the door. Esmira passed her without a word and walked slowly into her bedroom. She took off her coat and boots, leaving them on the floor. Spreading herself out on the bed like a flag, she moaned for a while, then finally raised herself up and vomited on the floor, messing up her boots.

Sadaget came into the bedroom at the sound of vomiting. She stood for a while, silently glaring at Esmira. Her face reddened at the smell of alcohol.

"Did I ever get drunk like you and vomit on the ground? You are embarrassing the children and me. Nasty woman, you better get up and clean up your mess!"

"Why are you shouting? All our neighbors are going to know that I came home drunk," Esmira mumbled, barely keeping her eyes open.

"The neighbors are already talking about your adventure with Samed. I don't need any more gossip than is already swirling around you!"

Esmira picked up her bag from the floor. She pulled out a penknife and put it around her neck.

"Please stop talking, or I will kill myself."

Sadaget ignored her. "Don't come here so late, and drunk! You had better stay in the city if you're going to be this way!"

"Leave me alone," Esmira said, enraged. She clasped her hands to her ears.

She got up from her bed and exited the bedroom, leaving Sadaget behind. She went into the living room and locked the door.

This made Sadaget even more furious. She approached the door and banged on it, shouting, "Open the door, you little whore! This is my house! Don't lock doors in my house! If it weren't for me, you would be on the streets with all of your children."

Esmira opened the door. Sadaget pushed her aside. Esmira then picked up a cigarette from a table and tried to light it a few times, but her hands shook. After vain tries to light the cigarette, she tossed it onto the table.

"It's midnight, Mother. You're going to wake up our neighbors."

Sadaget again ignored her words and continued talking. "Haven't you embarrassed your children enough? I feel sorry, not for you, but for your kids. Do you know that people call them bastards and ask their children not to play with them? They also call them fatherless and orphans. How much more can these children take?"

Esmira remained quiet as Sadaget fumed. A headache rapidly developed, and she suddenly grabbed her head.

"I have bickered with neighbors because they offended your children," Sadaget continued. "Because of you, I stopped talking to some of my friends. They are now my enemies. Do you know why? Because they bad-talked you behind your back."

Esmira rubbed her head with both hands, frustrated. "Mother, please go back to your bedroom or I will leave."

"Go ahead, but you can't come here drunk and then puke on my floors. If the neighbors see you in this condition, what do you think they will say about you then?" yelled Sadaget.

Without saying a word, Esmira exited the apartment.

Why does she hate me? She has never supported me. Other parents praise their children, but she always puts me down, thought Esmira, distraught.

She walked in darkness to the bus stop, all the while trying to hail a cab. When one stopped for her, she took it to the Neftchiler metro station, and headed back to her own apartment.

Sadaget always found a reason to argue with Esmira or make her feel poorly about herself. Esmira's mistakes affected Sadaget's and her children's life. Sadaget felt ashamed of this sort of daughter. When Sadaget gave advice to other people, they would reply, "Why don't you give advice to your own daughter?"

People whom Sadaget thought were her friends in fact laughed behind her back. Many people who knew Sadaget from her work also resided in apartments in the same building. As soon as these people settled in the new building, they proliferated gossip about Sadaget and her daughter. These people knew the whole story about Esmira's fake marriage to Samed and her bastard children. Sadaget couldn't comprehend why people didn't mind their own business and keep their mouths shut.

Silvana overheard portions of the old women's mindless and malicious gossip about the absence of a father figure in her life. She regretted that her mother had slept with their father without marrying him. People kept asking Silvana questions, wanting to know where her father was. In fact, she felt so embarrassed about not having a father in her life that, when the electrician came to change electrical wires, she told the neighbors that he was her father.

Another time, when Esmira came back home in a private cab, Silvana told her friends that the driver was her father. Seeing her friends walking around with their fathers, aunts, and uncles filled her heart with despair, so she concocted these stories to make herself feel better.

Everyone I know has two parents, cousins, aunts, and uncles, yet I have none. If my father were to return, I would find all of these relatives, she thought, staring at them with sadness in her heart.

One thunderous night, Silvana had been sleeping peacefully until she dreamed about her father. She saw herself walking along a dark street looking for him. She found him walking on the street without even noticing her.

Silvana shouted, "Samed, I'm your daughter!" Her father stopped and gazed at her.

"Child, I'm not your father." He ran away, leaving Silvana behind.

Silvana ran after him, shouting, "Father, please wait!"

He vanished down a dark street. Silvana awoke, distraught and crying. She lay in bed and prayed, "God, everyone has a father, but I have none. I don't want to be fatherless any longer. I want to have a united family, living under the same roof with me. Please send him back home."

Silvana wiped her tears and turned on her side. She lay that way for a while, staring vacantly into the dark, and then fell asleep.

When Sadaget started getting a stabbing pain in her heart and shoulder, Silvana feared that she would be losing her granny. The poor girl was worried that, while she slept, her granny might have a heart attack and die. Silvana would get up at nights and check on Sadaget to ensure that she hadn't died. She would pray to Jesus before going to sleep: Please do not take away my granny. We do not have anyone, other than her and Mother.

On the afternoon of a cold winter day, Esmira brought home two girlfriends. Sadaget opened the door and let them in.

"Good afternoon, Sadaget Khanum."

"Good afternoon," answered Sadaget, flashing her yellow teeth. "Don't stand by the door. Come into the living room."

Sadaget offered them tea. They sat at the table, drinking tea and smoking.

Sadaget coughed when she inhaled the smoke, but she didn't say anything. The talk turned to men.

"Aliya, do you have a fiancé?" asked Sadaget, smiling broadly.

The female quest let out a heavy sigh. "With my weight, it's not easy to find a man."

Sadaget leaned closer to her. "Don't worry, you are a beautiful woman. You will meet a man soon."

Esmira sat silently, observing her mother's conduct, and was amazed to see Sadaget's friendly side.

However, that changed when her friends left. Once they were gone, Sadaget blurted out, "Didn't I tell you not to bring your friends to my house? I don't need such trash in my house!"

"Mother, did my friends do anything bad to you?" Esmira asked, irritated. She tried to light a cigarette, but her nerves left her shaking.

Sadaget marched over to Esmira. She picked up her pack of cigarettes from the table and threw it in the garbage.

"Why did you throw away my cigarettes?"

"Put that thing out or go smoke on the porch," Sadaget growled.

Esmira stopped lighting the cigarette and looked at her mother, shaking her head in disbelief. "You are always talking about God, and consider yourself a holy woman, but look how you treat people. You only judge them. God does not approve of judging others."

Unbeknownst to the two women, Silvana was listening to their conversation.

Sadaget went up to Esmira, and waved her fist in front of her face. "I judge people by whether they laugh behind my back over your promiscuous behavior with Samed. After all, they haven't allowed their children to play with yours, which is an attitude that affected you negatively, whether you admit it or not."

Esmira got up from her seat and tossed her cigarette into the garbage. "Mother, stop talking or I'll leave," she said with annoyance in her voice.

"Look at you. You didn't use to smoke, wear makeup, or drink. As soon as these so-called friends appeared in your life, you adopted their filthy habits."

Sadaget suddenly noticed the young eavesdropper.

"Silvana, why are you still here? Go to your bedroom," said Sadaget.

Sadaget was protective of Silvana, fearing that she would end up like her mother. Therefore, she went to great lengths to protect

Silvana by not allowing male relatives to come to her apartment. She would always say, "I have a girl in my house. There is no place for a man."

She did not approve of any of Esmira's friends because of their lifestyles. Most of them were wedding singers, actors, and musicians who liked drinking, partying and smoking. She did not want Esmira to bring friends home and would usually put up a fight if Esmira invited them.

"Mother, why don't you speak about your friends?" Esmira asked suddenly, moving away from Sadaget. She knew that this question would anger her.

"They are using you. You gave your monthly pension to Sevda. So far she hasn't bothered to pay you back, even knowing that you have four grandchildren to support. Yet, when it comes to me, you can't even give me one ruble."

Sadaget burst out in anger. She hit the table with her left hand and looked straight into Esmira's eyes.

"Leave my friends alone! I can do whatever I want with my money!" she shouted loudly.

She left the living room, slamming the door, and spent the rest of the day in her bedroom.

After this argument, Esmira rarely came to Darnaqul. Every time she visited home, her belly got bigger. Sadaget suspected that Esmira was pregnant.

She confronted Esmira in front of Silvana. "Are you expecting again?"

"Yes, I am," Esmira answered, irritated.

"Who is the father?"

Silvana looked at her mother's burgeoning belly in shock.

Why does she always have to embarrass us? Now the neighbors are going to say that my mother is promiscuous. Who will marry a girl whose mother drinks excessively, comes home intoxicated, and gets pregnant by anyone?

"What's the difference?" Esmira's hands trembled as she shouted at her mother.

"Listen to me! You already brought shame into my life by bringing into this world these four unhappy children. You couldn't look after them. What, yet another one? Go for an abortion and get rid of the child."

Esmira quietly went into her bedroom, followed by Silvana.

"Mother, I could look after the child," the young girl suggested, "but neighbors will say that you have slept with a man without marriage. Please give it away." Silvana feared the shame of her mother's most recent mistake.

A few months later, Esmira hired a midwife and gave birth to a girl in her girlfriend's house. Esmira's friend adopted her child, whom she named Arzu. With this arrangement, Esmira was able to hide the existence of this fifth child.

After finding that her sister had been given away, Silvana's heart sank. Nevertheless, what could she do at that time? She had been a child, and then a teenager, who was under her granny's, and Islamic society's, influence.

Sadaget would always tell Silvana not to go anywhere with her friends. Once, while drinking tea together, Sadaget said, "Silvana, friends are dishonest and tend to stick around only if they need something. Beware of the disingenuous pattern of users. They take incessantly but never bother to reciprocate. Therefore, you must be careful in whom you place your trust because most times people tend to betray it."

"Granny, how can I live my life without trusting people and with no friends? Most of my childhood I have been alone. I don't want to be alone anymore," Silvana answered her.

Sadaget looked into her grandchild's eyes and saw her despondency. "Your best friend is our Allah, who never betrays you. You will make friends, but you need to make certain that they are your real friends."

"How will I know who is my faithful friend?"

"You will recognize your true friends by their actions toward you. They will be there for you when you need their support. Real friends will find time to listen to what worries you, support you emotionally, and always have kind words for you. However, at the same time, you have to be a good friend as well."

Silvana scratched her head and considered her granny's words.

"Granny, I think you're right. It's like Zeynab. She is my best friend. We always walk to school and back home together. I always help Zeynab with her lessons and protect her from bullies. However, when I ask her to help me with chemistry or algebra, she says that she is busy."

"Then she is not your true friend, but a mean girl who exploits your kindness," answered Sadaget.

She poured tea into her mug and continued.

"Silvana, life is full of disappointments. In fact, people wear masks, smiling broadly to your face but gossiping about you behind your back. Therefore, you can only rely on God. Not having Him in your life is like not having a soul. He alone gives you the strength and ability to endure experiences and to make the right steps. Be kind and loving toward others, always help the poor, and God will bless you with Paradise."

Sadaget knew that the world was cruel. She wanted to protect her grandchildren. In this manner, she tried to teach them everything she knew. But she overdid it with her teachings.

Silvana followed all of her granny's teachings, augmenting it with her own rules and restrictions. She became judgmental of and strict with herself, just like Granny.

Later in life, Silvana understood that her granny's attitude toward Esmira's friends and life was misguided. She realized that, before judging, one must walk in another person's shoes, and to live the life that he has lived.

Esmira's friends were normal people like everyone else. Silvana felt bad, recalling her conduct toward them, and felt guilty about asking Esmira to give away her baby. She knew that her little sister lived somewhere near and that Esmira was in her life without telling her the truth.

Slowly, Silvana's attitude toward people changed. Before judging peoples' actions, she thought about the cause that made them act in a certain way. Still, she never justified any wrongdoing. She developed love and compassion for others, mostly toward those rejected by society, which brought them flowing to her.

***

Close to the end of the eighth grade, Silvana learned that the school board had decreed that all classes would be conducted in the Azeri language, not Russian, from now on. Those who preferred to study in Russian were offered two options: either to transfer to the

Azeri classes or to relocate to a Russian school in another district. Not wanting to be taught in the Azeri language, Silvana knew that she would have to move to a new school for Russians. Disappointed, Silvana realized that she was going to lose all her friends.

In the warmth of the springtime, when the buds began to appear on the trees, Silvana climbed upstairs to attend her math class. She met the principal on the steps.

"Good morning, Ramiz Hachiev."

"Good morning, Silvana. What is that under your eye?" asked Hachiev, his eyes fixed on her birthmark.

"It's just a birthmark. For heaven's sake, you've asked me about it six times already."

"I'm sorry. I forgot." He smiled at her. "You are an excellent student and a well-behaved girl. All the teachers always praise you. Indeed, I'm sorry that we are losing a student like you."

"Ramiz Muallim, if I'm an outstanding student, why are you terminating my class? I don't want to move to another school."

"The Ministry of Education has made this ruling. I can't do anything about it."

At that point, the bell rang. "I have to go to my classroom," Silvana said.

She ran upstairs, annoyed with the principal's question about her birthmark.

The last term of the school year finished on May 26th. On that day, Silvana's classmates wrote notes on each other's school aprons. The girls hugged one another and exchanged gifts. Everyone knew that, in the new term, the students would be in separate schools.

In June, Silvana took her documents from Internat and applied to 145 High School.

In early September, when the rain started falling, Silvana began attending a new school. At first, it was somewhat difficult for her to adjust to not only new classmates and teachers but also an alien academic environment. In her old school, she had been a leader for eight years, and boys had tended to fear her. In the new school, she was just an ordinary student, a face in the scholastic crowd.

It took a year to adjust and adapt to a new school. Good luck had it that her best friend Zeynab moved to the same school. Even in this new location, Silvana had to continue to defend Zeynab when other girls mocked and bullied her. However, Zeynab turned around and forged a friendship with a girl from another class, leaving Silvana feeling betrayed.

Three years passed, and in May, at the age of nineteen, Silvana graduated from 145 High School with stellar grades. Now she anxiously awaited her prom party. She had been dreaming about attending it in a beautiful dress. Long before prom day, Silvana had asked her mother to buy a dress, but Esmira had decided to delay its purchase.

Two weeks before the prom, Esmira broke her leg and ended up in the hospital without getting a chance to buy a dress for Silvana. Not having a dress, Silvana missed her prom. For her, it was a disaster. For a few nights, she cried herself to sleep, thinking about the lost opportunity.

Esmira stayed in the hospital one month without even being able to get out of bed. She lay in bed, sobbing at night and worrying about her children and mother. A year before, Sadaget had quit her job and embarked in later life as a pensioner. In the meantime, Esmira was increasingly involved in her children's lives, always ensuring that they had clothes to wear and food to eat.

That month was the worst in Silvana's life. Since Esmira couldn't sing at weddings while in the hospital, she wasn't able to make money to support her children. Therefore, her children and Sadaget were left without any sort of personal finances to sustain themselves.

As her grandkids searched for a job, Sadaget left the apartment at 9 a.m. every morning to sell plastic bags. Wearing a long black skirt, a cream-colored long-sleeved blouse, and a scarf over her head, she stood outside and hawked her wares. She was feeling increasingly tired. Her feet swelled and ached.

"Beautiful and fashionable bags! Come and buy one!" she shouted, holding them out with an extended hand.

While standing there one day, she talked to a beggar and made jokes. A police officer came. He chased both of them away twice, but when he left they returned.

She gave some of the bags to people for free and donated her first profits to an old beggar woman. She returned home late in the evening, after making just enough money to buy bread.

Silvana felt sorry for her granny, knowing that the poor woman had stood outside all day just to make sufficient money for them, instead of relaxing at home.

Within a few days, Sadaget got sick and stayed at home. For three days, she prepared some soup by using only water with flour. This had to suffice until she was healthy enough to return to her bag-selling.

At the same time Esmira was released from the hospital, Silvana was accepted to San-Marto University. To her disappointment, Esmira wouldn't allow Silvana to study there because the university was located in a different city.

"You can't go there alone," her mother told her. "There are many evil men who might take advantage of you."

Esmira shook her head. "That isn't the entire truth. The fact is that I do not have sufficient funds to pay for your tuition."

"I will be careful."

"You're so fearful of leaving the house alone. How will you be able to live in a strange city, at liberty to move around on your own? Seriously, you can't go."

Hearing her mother's words, Silvana felt as if she had died within herself. Matriculating at the university had been one of her biggest dreams, which now had to be abandoned.

She looked at her mother silently and regretted not being wealthy.

If you have money or social status, you are a queen and people are attracted to you like bees to a hive of honey. If you have neither, even doctors may let you die. Money is like a drug to which some are addicted. I need this drug to get my education and solve my other problems, thought Silvana.

She walked away from her mother, barely holding back her tears. She nodded her head, sighing deeply.

In September, as she saw other students entering universities, Silvana wished that she were in their place. She couldn't shake her disappointment. Mother always finds money for my siblings, but when it comes to me, she has none, thought Silvana. It felt like her mother had robbed her of her dream to get her degree.

After completing high school, Silvana took a few courses to learn the English language. As soon as she finished her courses, she looked for a job.

After a long and wide search, Silvana landed an assistant manager's position at the Baku Recruitment Company. She enjoyed her new job and the company of her co-workers and customers. As part of her responsibilities, Silvana visited different companies to find suitable employment for registered candidates.

However, after working for six months, Silvana realized that her earnings were not sufficient. Most of her salary was spent on her trips to different companies. At times she barely mustered enough money for transportation to and from her workplace. Silvana decided to leave the job and search for a better one.

On a very wet day, she arrived early to work and went into her manager's office. Mr. Mamedzade sat at the desk, writing. Seeing his bald head, Silvana smiled.

"Good morning, Ahmed Bey."

He lifted his head slowly. With an equally broad smile on his face, he answered, "Good morning!"

Her expression got serious. "I'm sorry to have to tell you this, but this is my final week here. I'm leaving my job."

Silvana's words erased the smile from Mamedzade's face. He looked puzzled. Her boss leaned over the desk, his brow wrinkled.

"Why are you leaving? You have been working industriously. I like how you communicate with our clients."

"Ahmed Bey, thank you for the kind words, but I have to leave because of personal circumstances," Silvana replied.

He leaned back in his brown chair and then got up. "I can't keep you here against your will." He smiled, flashing his stained and yellow teeth. "Good luck in your future endeavors. It has been a pleasure to have you here."

"Thank you," said Silvana. She went back to her office to review a contract with a client company, one of her last projects for the company.

Chapter 9: Silvana Meets An Englishman

Silvana had never wanted to marry the sort of male who might restrict her freedom and keep her at home, making her wear hijab. Silvana had grandiose dreams; she wanted to become financially independent, to travel, and to become an educated human being.

Growing up, she had read not only many literary classics, but also her mother's romance novels and books about foreign countries. In reading them, she developed a dream of meeting her modern Prince Charming, a man who would appear from far away and rescue her from her loneliness.

While waiting for this "Prince Charming", Silvana met Mark, who was in Baku working for an oil company as an engineer. Mark was a tall thirty-five-year-old English man who had been raised in an orphanage. He had two children from another marriage, his ex-wife had left him for another man, and had taken their two boys with her. The divorce proceedings and his wife's cheating proved gruesome and wrenching for Mark, causing him many sleepless nights.

Right after the divorce, Mark was posted to Baku for a three-year contract. He was relieved to depart England and forget about his divorce. However, moving to Azerbaijan was a substantial challenge for him, because of both the language barrier and the drastically different culture. It took a long time for Mark to figure out how to get around, either by train or by bus, in a non-English-speaking country. While living in Baku, he learned a great deal about Azeri culture. For instance, in March, the nation celebrated Novruz bayrami, the approach of spring. During that festive time of the season, people baked pastries. They placed ornate sweets, nuts, and colored eggs on trays for everyone to eat.

Traditionally, in the middle of this tray of treats, townsfolk place a plate with a particular type of wheat seed that sprouts green grass upward toward the sky. Around the grass, locals tie a red ribbon. The children run from door to door, collecting sweets. At night, the kids jump over a campfire and have a lot of fun doing so.

He also learned that some men did not allow their wives to work, keeping them at home as homemakers. They tend to think that the place of the woman is at home as a mother and a wife.

Grandmothers play a substantial role in the lives of their grandchildren, sometimes replacing their mothers.

Mark liked the hospitality of the Azeri people, in that no matter how poor people were, they were always happy to receive guests at their home. He found that he was able to visit his Azeri friends at any time, and was always met by healthful food and tea, together with a selection of sweets. Their hospitality and delicious food amazed him. In England, he would never allow himself to visit his friends without invitation; however, in Baku, it was accepted as the norm. He loved such Azeri dishes as dolma, pilov, kebab, and cakes.

Nonetheless, he still felt somewhat lonely. Because of their cultural constraints and religion, his Azeri female co-workers refused to date him. While employed in the capital city, Mark had decided not to date anyone until he met Silvana.

During the spring, his company hired the twenty-three-year-old Silvana as an assistant manager. She was a hard-working young woman who was shy and didn't talk to or interact with many male co-workers.

As soon as Mark saw Silvana, he fell head-over-heels in love with her. He tried to approach her a few times but didn't know how to do so. He heard from others that Silvana was a home-girl sort, and was not only a righteous woman but a virgin as well.

One day, when spring was over, Mark gained the courage to approach Silvana as she sat at her desk.

"Good morning, Miss."

Silvana raised her head and looked directly at him.

"Good morning," she answered shyly, smiling.

"My name is Mark. I was told that you have papers for me to sign," he stated.

"What is your surname?"

"Jonson," answered Mark, as he gazed into her beautiful hazel eyes.

"Oh yes, Mr. Stephen left the documents for you," stated Silvana. She removed some papers from a folder and passed them to Mark.

When Mark took them from her, his hand touched hers. They both felt a warm shock pass through their bodies. Mark signed the papers and gave them back to Silvana.

She looked at him with interest. "Where are you from?"

"England," he replied.

"Please sit down," said Silvana, offering him a chair. Mark sat opposite her.

"How long have you been working in Baku?" asked Silvana, looking deeply into his blue eyes.

"I have been working here for a year," he replied.

"Do you like living here?"

"Yes, but there are challenges that I am trying to overcome." A smile crossed his face.

She leaned over her desk. "What challenges?"

"Most people here in Baku don't speak English. At times I find it difficult even to shop because I can't explain to salespeople what I need exactly."

She leaned back in her seat. "Why don't you learn Azeri language?"

These foreigners enter our country and live comfortably, yet do not bother to learn our language, Silvana thought.

Mark laughed. "I'm not adept at languages. I have tried to learn some foreign languages, but keep giving up."

Mark's cell phone started ringing. He got up from his seat. "Silvana, it's been very pleasant speaking with you, but I have to leave."

Silvana smiled. "I understand, and look forward to seeing you later."

He left Silvana's office and took the call on his cell phone. She could hear him yelling loudly. "Listen, stop calling me, you idiot!"

Mark seemed to realize that he had been very loud, once he was off the phone. He calmed down and walked away, all the while ruminating about Silvana's hazel eyes and soft voice.

After a period of about six months, Silvana grew accustomed to foreigners as colleagues in her workplace, and her English-language abilities, and skills improved exponentially.

Mark tried to ask Silvana out on a date, but his attempts always proved fruitless. That is, until the birthday celebration of Gulshan, one of their co-workers. On a blustery, snowy day, Gulshan invited her Azerbaijani colleagues and a few foreigners, including Mark, to her birthday party at her home.

Silvana glanced through the window outside, and saw that the ground was layered in diamond-like white snow. It was still cascading down. She would have rather stayed at home than go to a party, but she couldn't miss her friend's birthday. She put on her black dress, red boots, and a black fur coat, but didn't apply any makeup. When she arrived at the party, Mark was already there. As soon as Silvana entered, she was uncomfortably aware of the men leering at her.

"Happy birthday," said Silvana to Gulshan. She gave her an ornate perfume bottle, along with some makeup. The birthday girl took the gift.

"Thank you, Silvana. Give me your coat please."

Silvana took off her coat and passed it to her friend. Gulshan led her to a table resplendent with food and drinks.

"Help yourself. There's plenty to go around," instructed the hostess.

"Thanks."

Gulshan nodded and grinned. Then she turned away from Silvana to put her coat in another room and to greet other friends.

Silvana poured an apple juice. When she turned around, Mark was standing right next to her.

"Wow, Silvana, you look beautiful."

"Thank you, Mark," Silvana said shyly, trying not to look directly at him.

"When will you agree to date me?" Mark asked.

"Maybe never, but who knows? I may change my mind," she replied, winking at him as her cheeks blushed.

"Why won't you date a handsome man like me?"

"Our culture and religion are different, and women here don't date a man unless they plan to marry him," said Silvana, looking at him thoughtfully. "You are not only from a different country, but you are also a Christian. I'm sure we will never marry."

Mark's eyes lingered on her, and then fell on the table where the alcohol was.

I need to wet my parched throat. I haven't had a drink since I moved to this damned country, he thought.

His eyes returned to Silvana.

"How do you already know that we may never marry? If we fall in love with each other, we can marry."

"I don't think this will happen."

"Silvana, life is full of surprises. You may change your mind."

"We will see," Silvana answered, smiling.

Just then, slow music began to play. Some of the guests moved to the floor to dance.

"May I invite you for a dance?" asked Mark.

"Sure," answered Silvana, putting her glass of juice on the table.

They moved to the middle of the room. Mark put his arm around Silvana's waist and pulled her closer to him.

Silvana felt the warmness of his body, and wondered at the strangeness. She had never danced with a man before.

She looked at his clean-shaven face and blue eyes.

Could he be the one I have always waited for? He is a foreigner and attractive. Perhaps I should date him. However, would Granny approve? Silvana thought to herself.

"Are you married?" she asked him.

"No, I'm divorced, but I'm looking for a new love." He winked jokingly as Silvana's cheeks flushed.

"Do you have children?" she continued.

"Yes, I have two boys, but they live with my ex-wife. Are you dating anyone?"

"No, I'm not."

"Why doesn't a beautiful woman like you have a boyfriend?"

Silvana's cheeks got redder. I do not want to marry a local man, ending up in servitude, no better than a house cleaner at home, she thought. But she kept that remark to herself.

"I'm not in a rush, and have not met the man of my dreams." Silvana looked away. She breathed deeply, taking in his scent.

Oh, he smells so good! She leaned her head on his shoulder and wished that she could stay this way longer.

"What kind of qualities must the man of your dreams possess?"

"First, he should be a godly man," she replied.

He's not a jerk like my father. Mother made a big mistake by sleeping with Samed and ruining our lives altogether. Wise people do not make the same mistake twice. Unfortunately, Mother keeps making the same mistakes, she thought, feeling scornful and angry.

"What do you mean by 'godly man'?" inquired Mark.

"A godly man is one who lives according to God's commandments, and fears His punishment."

They stopped dancing and moved to the other side of the room.

"What are the other qualities you expect from a man of your dreams?"

"He ought to be loving, romantic, kind, gentle, respectful, and understanding. He must show his love not in empty words, but by his actions and behavior toward women. This type of man should be my best friend, a passionate lover, and partner all at the same time."

"Shouldn't women possess the same qualities as well?" Mark asked. He stared at Silvana's feet.

"Yes, they should, I agree. For a relationship to work, both parties have to make sacrifices and put an effort into the relationship. They should not only give what they expect to get in return, but also learn to listen, understand, and respect each other. It takes two for a relationship to work," Silvana replied.

The music stopped. Most of the guests returned to their tables and started eating. Silvana and Mark walked toward a table. They sat next to each other and dished out their food. Silvana noticed that the guests were looking at them, but she didn't bother to move away from Mark.

He gazed at the guests forcing a smile. "I just hate being around a bunch of stupid people," he thought, and then looked directly at Silvana.

"I have noticed children begging for money on the streets," he commented to his new friend. "Why are they not in school? Isn't your government making enough money to help the poor?"

Silvana leaned back in her seat and looked firmly into his eyes.

"Our economy is developing. Oil and gas are playing an important role in our country's development. The government also promotes agriculture to decrease the unemployment rate. However, even with these developments, some people are still living in poverty. Parents are forced to send their children to beg instead of going to school."

"It is sad to see children begging on the streets," Mark stated.

"The government does its best to help, but they surely can't help everyone," said Silvana.

"Then what is the solution?" asked Mark. He picked up his wine glass and took a sip.

"Instead of complaining about their situation or waiting for help, people must try to help themselves by first making all the necessary steps. Only after failed attempts should they ask for help."

"Do you think that people shouldn't help others?" asked Mark. In his mind, he was thinking, These stupid beggars all about. I don't know why the police can't lock them up.

"No, people should always help others. Even the Bible asks us to love one another and to be compassionate toward others. We can help the sick, children, and the abused because they can't help themselves. However, there should be limits, because we can't have others depend on us all the time. Otherwise, they won't be able to survive on their own. They won't attempt to make independent steps to bring positive changes," Silvana answered him.

Mark listened attentively, gazing penetratingly at Silvana's oval face, which illuminated a glow and a halo of peace and love.

She is both a beautiful and an intelligent woman.

As Silvana talked, his mind wandered. In general, Muslim women serve as good wives, obeying their husbands without question or doubt. Perhaps I should marry one of them, mused Mark.

Mark's eyes again stopped on Silvana's red leather spiked heels, which looked sexy.

Those boots add to her curves. He found himself almost salivating and had to distract himself by scratching his left ear.

His gaze caused Silvana to become disconcerted. Her cheeks reddened once again.

Why does he keep staring at me, and at my boots? Is something wrong with them?

Her thoughts were interrupted by Mark's answer.

"I agree with you, Silvana. People should act as a change agent and try to help themselves by using all of the tools available. When they can't help themselves, then we can step in. For example, if I help my neighbor to buy school clothes and books for his son, that child will have a chance to go to school. Sometimes people need help to make the first step, and then they will be able to make the second step on their own."

Stupid fools expect a great deal of you. Do they give you back anything whatsoever? However, only uneducaffed people put themselves in deleterious situations and then beg others for help, thought Mark. He agreed with Silvana in words, but only because he didn't want an argument.

"Are there any beggars in England?" questioned Silvana.

"Yes, we have them, but I never came across children asking for money. Our social services make sure that children are not on the streets."

Gulshan came up to the table and put her hand on his shoulder. "Mark, I hope you are enjoying your lunch."

Mark's face shone with joy. "Yes, thank you. I must say it is appetizing." His eyes briefly stopped on her black high-heeled spiked shoes.

"Silvana, may I talk to you privately please?" asked Gulshan.

"Certainly," answered Silvana, getting up. She smiled at Mark. "I'll be right back."

Gulshan led Silvana into another room. When they were alone, she said, "Rovshan has asked me to marry him. I don't know what I should do."

Gulshan smiled faintly. She glanced at Silvana with desperation in her eyes.

"Why? Don't you love him?"

"No, I don't, but he is a good man. He has an apartment, an automobile, disposable income, and a small business. If I were to marry him, I would live like a queen and see the world at the same time."

Silvana stared disapprovingly at her friend and thought, Money motivates people. Indeed, money rules the world. If you have no money, most people pass you by without even saying hello. Is this what you value the most?

"What is the sense of marrying a man who you don't love? If there are no feelings, whatever property he has won't make you happy. Material things don't bring happiness," she replied.

"I know this, but my parents are pushing me to marry him. They worry that I will be an old spinster," remarked Gulshan as her facial expression became gloomy.

While they spoke, Mark sat alone, fidgeting and squirming in his seat. Everyone spoke in Azeri, and some were laughing.

I just hate big crowds. Why is she taking so long to return?

He felt himself perspiring, so he unfastened two buttons around the collar and neck of his dress shirt. He then got up and walked toward the others.

Meanwhile, Silvana was still giving Gulshan advice.

"Gulshan, your future depends on what decisions or steps you make now. Therefore, don't let anyone push you to take measures that you will regret. Let God and your heart's desire be your guide. Without His guidance and blessing, you can make mistakes or even fail. Also remember, before making any decision, consider the pros and cons," said Silvana.

Gulshan's eyes brightened up. "Thank you very much for your advice. You are a true friend."

"You are most welcome."

They returned to the party room. Mark was talking to other guests. Silvana decided to join them.

As she approached, she heard Mark say, "I've done research about Azerbaijan. I'm amazed by your culture and history. Can you believe that during Median and Persian rule, Caucasian Albanians followed Zoroastrianism? They then turned to Christianity, then to the Muslim faith during the Arab rule?"

"We do have a rich history," said one of the guests.

"Mark, did you know that ages ago people from India traveled to Azerbaijan to worship fire?"

"Honestly, I had never heard about it."

Silvana's phone rang.

"Excuse me." She moved away and answered the phone.

"Hello," she said.

"Silvana, when are you coming home? Narmin came and wants to see you before she goes back to her village," said Sadaget.

"I'm going to leave soon."

Mark approached her. "Silvana, is everything okay?"

"Yes, everything is fine, but I have to leave now. My relative from Guba is waiting for me."

"I wish you could stay longer. I have enjoyed talking to you," Mark said pleasantly.

"Me too, but I have a guest at my house waiting for me. See you tomorrow."

"Bye," answered Mark.

Silvana came up to Gulshan, thanked her for the invitation, and left the party. Mark decided to leave too.

***

As the days passed, Silvana and Mark talked with one another every day, either at work or by phone. Once she came to know Mark better over time, she agreed to go out to dinner with him.

Later, when she told her granny that she had a date that night with a Christian foreigner, Sadaget became distraught. As they sat drinking tea together at the table, Sadaget talked about Mark.

"Why do you want to date a foreign man when you could date a nice, upright Azeri man?"

Silvana shrugged her shoulders. "I haven't met an Azeri man whom I admire or like, but Mark won over my heart."

She took a tiny bite out of a piece of candy.

Why does she fail to understand that I neither need nor want a man? Especially one who would restrict and constrain my lifestyle by not allowing me to study, work, wear what I want, and achieve my full potential. Life is meaningless if you cannot live it to the fullest, thought Silvana.

Sadaget poured another cup of tea for herself. "I don't understand what you find worthy of him. Men from that part of the world cheat and drink in excess. Plus, you are a Muslim and he is Christian."

Silvana put her teacup down in its saucer. "Granny, you indeed astonish me! Have you forgotten that your mother is a Russian Orthodox Christian woman? Moreover, your great-grandfather was an Orthodox priest in Russia. Therefore, religious beliefs ought not to matter to you."

"Religion alone is not the issue. He grew up in a different culture," said Sadaget, putting a piece of chocolate into her mouth.

Silvana looked at her elderly granny, and saw her gray hair, wrinkled face, which had the scars of a difficult life, and realized that it was one of endurance. Silvana pitied her. This old woman would never stop trying to protect her from making mistakes.

With a loving expression on her face, Silvana rose and kissed her grandmother's forehead.

"My dear Granny, when it comes to love I don't care about religion or culture. Thus, different religious beliefs and opposing denominations should not concern or trouble you as influencing me in dating, courtship, or eventually marriage.

"Most importantly, he believes in God and is a good man. I always dreamed of meeting a man from far away and then marrying him."

Silvana smiled thoughtfully. He is an intelligent and loving modern man, one with whom I can talk about anything and be myself.

Sadaget nodded her head. "As usual, Silvana, you prove both stubborn and erroneous. Relationships endure when spouses share common belief systems, view culture in cohesive terms, and frequent the same religious institution. The fact remains that Christians do not understand or appreciate Muslims; they look down on us as nothing but mere terrorists. Having different beliefs is apt to provoke discord and dissent in a relationship in every way, shape, and manner. We become unable to nurture ourselves spiritually together or pray as one family. However, the fact is that he may not marry you, my dear."

Silvana would have taken her words into consideration, if not for Sadaget's flat, overbearing, and commanding tone.

"Grandma, I know you are trying to protect me, but I'm not like my mother. I'm not going to jump into bed with him. If he does not marry me, we will simply remain good friends."

"I don't want you to make the same mistakes your mother made by messing up both her life and yours," Sadaget insisted.

Granny's words distressed Silvana because she disliked the comparison to her mother. Esmira was a kind, good woman, but she had made misguided mistakes. Silvana blamed Esmira for her unhappy and lonely childhood, and was unable to forgive her mother for bringing her into this world as a bastard child. Lessons learned, Silvana knew that she would follow neither her mother's sad example nor her path in life. She was convinced that she would become a loving and protective mother. Deep wrinkles appeared on Silvana's solemn face.

"Granny, I will never let any man touch me without marrying me first. By now, you should know that I respect myself too much to let anyone exploit and manipulate me," said Silvana, annoyance in her voice. She was happy that her granny loved her and tried to protect her decisions in life, but sometimes Sadaget's reactions were overwhelming.

Hearing irritation in Silvana's voice, Sadaget softened her tone. She said calmly, "I'm just trying to protect you. When I used to try to advise and discipline your mother, she would also say that she knew what she was doing, yet she still ended up sleeping with your father, and got pregnant with your sister Arzu by still another man."

"Granny, people are different. You can't judge another person because of one person's mistake," Silvana replied with a smile. She approached her granny and gave her a warm hug. "Don't worry. I will be fine."

People wonder why I never follow anyone's advice. The fact is that I have common sense, and no one knows more about what is right for me, after God. Nonetheless, God knows more than I do, thought Silvana.

"You are at liberty to invite him over for lunch." Sadaget sipped her tea.

"I will invite him. Thank you, Granny." Silvana gave her a peck on the cheek. "I have to go now and prepare for dinner."

Silvana went into the bedroom. She looked through her closet. She found a beautiful green dress and immediately decided to wear it.

Right after taking a shower, she dressed and left the apartment. Next to her building, she caught a mini bus. As she expected, the bus was chock-full of people packed together like sardines. Silvana detested taking an overcrowded bus, because some men purposely tried to position themselves closer to women, sometimes groping them.

She looked around for an empty seat. A young man sitting not far from her got up and kindly gave his place to her. Silvana was relieved to be finally off her feet. She looked bashfully at the young man, and as she sat down, said, "Oh, thank you very much!"

Silvana thought about dinner, and felt herself getting nervous. This was the first time in her life that she was going out on a date. A few Azeri guys had wanted to date her, but she had refused, only interested in marrying a foreign man, her "Prince Charming."

The bus drove to the Neftchiler metro station. From there Silvana took a train to the Nasimi station.

Trains in Baku were old and outmoded. However, each subway station was decorated beautifully and looked brand-new. Nasimi station had pictures made of small tiles, representing characters from the writer Nasimi's tales.

From the Nasimi subway station, she walked for fifteen minutes before she reached Baku Restaurant. As Silvana entered, she saw Mark, already seated at a table having a drink. Silvana walked to the table.

"Hello, Mark," she said with a big smile on her face.

"Hello, Silvana." He got up and moved out her chair for her to sit down.

As Silvana thanked him, she asked whether he had been waiting for a long time. He replied that he had just gotten there.

A server approached them to ask if they were ready to order. Silvana asked for an apple juice and Mark, a whiskey.

Silvana frowned slightly at his choice of drink. Does he frequent pubs and get drunk like other non-Muslims do? I hope not. I do not respect people who drink too much and cannot control themselves, behaving like animals.

As they both looked over the menu, they discussed starters, with Silvana choosing Azerbaijani dovga and Mark, kufte. For the main dish, both of them chose pilov and kebab. When the waitress returned, Mark ordered one dovga soup, one kufte soup, and two portions of the pilov with a kebab. He asked for all of the dishes to be brought at once.

Silvana gazed around, admiring the walls of the restaurant, which were colored orange. In the middle, an enormous chandelier shone brightly, its faceted glass beads looking as if they were cascading down from the ceiling. Although the place wasn't large, it was packed with people.

"I have been in here a few times. I've found the cuisine pleasant," said Mark. He looked at the people around him, some of whom were laughing uproariously.

Why are they laughing like gorillas, assaulting my ears? I detest being in places when they're full of people, he thought.

Silvana took a few sips of apple juice, while Mark looked into Silvana's eyes affectionately.

"Silvana, if you had the opportunity to leave Baku, would you?" he asked.

"I'm not sure. It would depend on the reason."

"What if you met a foreign man and fell in love? Would you agree to move to his country?"

Silvana dropped her fork and paused for a second, staring at him.

"If we were to marry, I would move to his native country," answered Silvana, her cheeks burning.

Why is he asking these questions? Is he planning to marry me? I would not mind marrying him. She smiled inwardly. He seems to be a good man, and charming at that.

The waitress came with the trolley. She put the food on the table, then asked if they needed anything else. They told her that they were fine with the dishes they had already ordered. The waitress left, and the couple dove into their soup.

Silvana felt awkward and uncomfortable with Mark's pointed questions. She tried to avoid his gaze. She realized that she had developed affectionate and romantic feelings toward Mark. Silvana enjoyed hearing his masculine and commanding voice. Mark was an intelligent man, one who could speak about any topic at length. Everyone viewed him as Mister Charmer, a crowd pleaser.

"You have a beautiful soul and a warm heart," he said with a smile. She's a virgin, as well. A wife like her would stay at home, cleaning house and minding my children, neither drinking nor smoking.

"Thank you for the compliment," Silvana said shyly.

"I admire your good values, personality, and the purity of your heart," continued Mark. Silvana's ears burned. She decided to change the topic of the conversation.

"I love the soup," she said.

"I've had dovga before, and must agree. It is delicious, yet Azeri cuisine is expensive," Mark replied.

He glanced at the couple sitting not far from them. Why do these dummies keep staring at me as if I am a monkey in a cage? he thought.

Silvana finished eating the dovga and put her bowl aside.

"Would you like the pilov?" asked Mark, to which she answered yes. He picked up the plate of pilov and dished it out for Silvana and himself, then did the same with the kebab.

"Mark, my granny would like to meet you. Will you be able to come to my apartment on Saturday?" Silvana asked.

Mark agreed and asked where they lived. Silvana offered to meet him at Neftchiler metro station, then they would go to the apartment together. They would meet up at 12.30 p.m. at the metro wagon, where Mark would disembark.

The waitress returned to ask if they would like to order dessert, which they declined. Mark asked for the bill. She removed the dirty plates from the table and left. After a while, she came back with the bill, which Mark paid, leaving her a tip.

They exited the restaurant and walked back to the metro station. Mark waited until Silvana boarded a train. Then he went back home.

Early Saturday morning, Silvana cleaned her apartment and helped Sadaget cook. They prepared dushpere, pilov, fried chicken, and spinach with lamb. They even bought whiskey for Mark.

Elnara and Lachin left the apartment to meet their friends in Boulevard Park. At noon, Silvana left the apartment to meet Mark at Neftchiler metro station.

When she arrived, Mark was standing in the station, waiting for her. As he waited for Silvana, he noted that people were staring at him. Although he knew that the local population hadn't acclimatized well to foreigners and would always stare at them, he disliked being the center of attention. As soon as Mark saw Silvana coming down the stairs, he breathed deeply with relief.

She came up to him, her smile shining.

"Hello, Mark. Have you been waiting long?" she asked.

"Not really," he replied.

"Let's go outside. From there we'll take a bus," suggested Silvana as they walked toward the exit.

Silvana's heart started to beat more rapidly as she walked alongside him. She was afraid that people would think poorly of her because she was dating a foreigner.

Near the metro station, they took a mini bus that was full of people. There was no place for them to sit down, so Mark and Silvana squeezed in among the other riders who were standing. The bus took thirty minutes to reach Darnaqul.

They walked to the building, entered Block 8, and then climbed upstairs. She didn't want to look for her key, so Silvana rang the doorbell. Sadaget opened the door, and Mark beheld a face full of wrinkles and a head covered with gray hair, with bald patches on the side. Mark greeted her. Sadaget welcomed him in Russian, with Silvana translating every sentence.

Sadaget then directed them into the living room. She pointed to the sofa, offering the two of them seats. She offered Mark tea, soft drinks, whiskey, and vodka. Mark asked for a whiskey, his poison of choice, as Silvana sat down next to him on the sofa.

Mark looked around at the surroundings. The living room was huge, but had old wallpaper, and the white door needed painting. He commented on how large the apartment seemed. Silvana told him that it had, in fact, four rooms and two big porches.

Zaur entered the living room, and Mark rose from his seat. He approached Mark and gave him a hug. Then he poured vodka into his own glass and sat at the table.

"Where did you find this clown?" asked Zaur in Azeri, looking with curiosity at Mark.

"He works with me."

"Is he Muslim?" asked Zaur.

"No, he is Christian," stated Silvana.

Mark looked at them, wondering what they were talking about.

"I won't allow you to marry a Christian man. He is haram," said Zaur sternly. He cast a firm look at Mark.

"Drinking vodka is not haram for you. In any event, who told you that I'm going to listen to you? You can't even get a job for yourself, but you want to control my life? Drink your vodka and leave the room, please," answered Silvana in an irritated tone.

"Just be careful. He could be a big liar like our father. Image-builders may charm or fool you. They have one goal: to impress you with false images," warned Zaur.

Even now, after all this time, Zaur couldn't forgive their father for leaving him to live an unhappy life. Zaur wanted to make sure that Mark wasn't like Samed.

Irritated with her brother's remarks, Silvana grimaced. Sometimes it is better to play stupid than try to prove something to an ignorant fool, she thought.

Mark then asked if everything was okay. Silvana replied that her brother had needed information from her about something.

Sadaget came into the living room with a plate of dushpere and kebab. She asked her granddaughter to bring the rest of the food. Silvana went into the kitchen, hoping that Zaur wouldn't torture Mark.

Nobody knows 100 percent about everything, and that's why life is a learning experience. I truly don't understand my brother's negativity. Undoubtedly, he picked this up from Granny.

Meanwhile, the conversation continued in the other room.

"Mark, I'm happy to see you here," Sadaget began. "Just remember, Silvana is like a diamond. Make sure that you don't hurt her." She pointed a finger at him.

Mark looked at her helplessly, not understanding anything that she said. He nodded his head and said, "Okay, Granny."

Silvana came back with the rest of the food. She put everything on the table and announced that lunch was ready.

Over their meal, instead of eating, Sadaget spoke a lot and drank vodka. Poor Mark couldn't understand what she was saying. He just gazed at her, and then looked helplessly at Silvana, expecting translation. However, he did enjoy his lunch, and thanked Sadaget.

She nodded to him, then asked him about his religion. He remarked that he was Anglican Christian. Silvana didn't like playing translator, but she continued. Sadaget went on to ask if he had children, to which he replied that he had two boys.

Sadaget turned her head toward her granddaughter. "Silvana, why do you need a man with children when you can get a better man, and without children at that?"

"Granny, I love every child. What's the difference if they are not mine?"

Mark looked from one to the other. Silvana was glad that he didn't understand Azeri.

When Sadaget took the last bite of her meal, she rose to ask Zaur if he had finished eating. Since he was done, they decided to leave Silvana and Mark alone.

After finishing their lunch, Silvana and Mark relaxed on the sofa. Mark commented that Silvana had a nice granny. Silvana told him that her granny had spent most of her life taking care of her and her siblings.

Mark looked at Silvana's downcast eyes. "I've wanted to ask you a question, but always found myself reluctant. Every time we talk, you seem to smile, but I see the sadness in your eyes. Where is it coming from?" he asked.

She breathed deeply, trying to remain in control of her emotions.

"It comes from my unfortunate childhood," said Silvana. Her face became as gloomy as a gray cloud.

She could see that Mark wanted to hear more. She shrugged her shoulders but could feel the tension in her body. "My life wasn't easy at all. My father left me when I was four years old. He married another woman, had children with her, and never bothered to look for us."

"What about your mother?" Mark asked.

"She was busy with making money to support us. For her, it was more important to buy us expensive clothes and food, instead of giving us emotional support. I guess this was her way of showing love," explained Silvana.

Mark continued gazing at her affectionately and saw her eyes getting sadder. He asked if she had any close relatives. Indeed, she had relatives, but had never met them.

"When my mother put my father in prison, they decided to forget about us. In fact, some of them don't even know about our existence. However, on my granny's side, I have many distant relatives. They live in the village of Guba. I rarely see them."

"It is indeed sad," said Mark, feeling sorry for Silvana. He understood her pain, because he had grown up without parents or relatives. While living in the orphanage, he had wondered why his mother had rejected him. What was wrong with him that she had given him away like a piece of garbage?

Talking about her childhood brought despair into Silvana's heart, and she could barely keep herself from crying.

"It was disappointing to see other children have fathers, uncles, aunts, and cousins, all whom I never had," she lamented, tears falling down her face. "I was so lonely, and just wanted someone to hug me and tell me that they loved me. Instead, they called me a fatherless bastard."

Seeing her tears, Mark moved closer to her. He hugged her and said affectionately, "Silvana, I'm here for you. I love you."

Silvana didn't pay attention to his words, so deep was her sorrow.

"Every day, I begged God to have my father come back, but he never returned to us. I wanted to feel a father's love and protection, but I never got what I dreamed," she sobbed.

Mark's heart filled with warmth. He wanted to comfort her. Unbeknownst to the couple, they had an observer. Curious, Zaur stood by the door, peeping inside the living room.

"Silvana, stop crying. You need to forget the past and think about your future. Dwelling on the past won't help you to find a solution, and will not give you the happiness you crave. Replace negative memories with good ones and move on," advised Mark.

Her eyes were red from crying. "Mark, I can't help it. Every time I see couples or watch romantic films, my loneliness surfaces. I just want to feel loved, needed, and appreciated."

"Silvana, you won't be fully happy unless you relinquish your past, and allow your wounds to heal." Mark held her hand and caressed it.

"To heal, I need someone who can give me all the love that I never had." Silvana wiped her tears with a napkin.

"Your happiness shouldn't depend on others. It should come from inside of you. You need to love yourself and do what makes you happy. When it is the right time, love will enter your life like a flower blooming at the beginning of spring. When it does happen, however, love needs to be nurtured and appreciated; otherwise, it can die."

Silvana smiled slightly. "Mark, have you experienced true love?"

"I thought my wife was my true love, but I was wrong. No, I have not experienced it yet with that intensity," said Mark. That stupid woman always bickered with me. I am relieved that she is gone, he thought.

"Do you believe in true love?" asked Silvana, gazing at Mark.

"Yes, I do, but sometimes people lose it because they don't know how to nurture the relationship and the feelings." They are just imbeciles, idiots, and jerks.

"I will devote my life to finding my true love and following God. I will love him with my whole heart and be his best friend, companion, and wife all at the same time."

"Your intentions are good. I hope that one day you will be able to get rid of your sadness," Mark said warmly.

"I tried to get rid of it, but I couldn't. This sadness comes from deep within my heart, which craves love."

Only weak-minded people feel sad, thought Mark.

Aloud, he said, "As soon as sadness enters your heart, chase it away and try to think in positive terms. Spend your time with loved ones, doing something that brings you joy. Most importantly, talk to God and ask Him to fill your heart with His Grace. Only God's Grace can make you genuinely happy."

A smile of hope formed on her face and warmed her eyes. "Thank you for your support and advice."

Right then, Sadaget came into the living room with a zebra cake, and put it on the table. She noticed Silvana's red eyes, and asked if everything was alright. She gestured toward the lunch things, wanting to clear the table.

Silvana got up and removed the dirty dishes. She took them into the kitchen and left them in the sink for her granny to wash. Sadaget always complained if someone washed the dishes in her place. She complained that detergent was wasted or plates were never washed properly.

Silvana came back with smaller plates and forks for the cake. Mark had never had zebra cake, so Silvana cut a piece and offered it to him. However, he was still full from lunch, and didn't want a piece. Sadaget smiled, looked at Mark, and jokingly said, "Translate please, Silvana. If he does not eat my cake, I will put it in his pocket."

"Mark, please, at least have a small piece. My granny said if you don't eat it, she will put it in your pocket." Silvana chuckled.

"Since I don't want any cake in my pocket, I will have a piece, please," Mark said, winking.

In his mind, he was thinking, This fool is stuck to me like a tick trying to suck my blood. I do not want the damned cake!

Silvana gave him the dessert. Sadaget left the living room to wash the dishes, while Mark ate his cake.

"This is good." Mark closed his eyes for a few seconds.

"Our country's cakes are always good," Silvana stated proudly.

"Why are you not eating your piece of cake? It seems as though you want your piece to end up in your pocket," said Mark.

"I will have it with tea. Would you like tea too?"

"No, thanks."

Silvana left for a moment. She came back with a cup of tea. She sat at the table and ate her cake. Mark asked if Sadaget would be joining them.

"She decided to give us space. Most times, she does not approve of my or my mother's friends, but it looks as if she likes you." Silvana blushed, and fluttered her lashes like a butterfly's wings.

"Who wouldn't like a good-looking blue-eyed guy like me?" Mark joked. Silvana's cheeks burned. She knew that Mark was right; many women would like him.

Mark then asked about her plans for the coming week, and Silvana told him that she had two projects to complete, and her boss had given her only two weeks to finish. Mark wondered whether she had plans on Saturday because he was planning to spend that day in Boulevard Park. From there, he intended to go to Movie Town to see "Titanic."

He asked Silvana if she would join him. Silvana said that she would do her best to come with him. However, because Boulevard Park is huge, she wanted to know where they could meet. Mark told her that he would wait for her near Hazar Restaurant at 10 in the morning. Mark checked his watch and remarked that he had to take his leave.

"A bus will take you straight to Neftchiler station. From there you know where to go," said Silvana.

Sadaget entered the living room again, wondering why Mark was rushing off. She wanted him to stay longer since she hadn't had a chance to chat with him.

"Miss Sadaget, I'm grateful for your hospitality. I have enjoyed the delicious Azeri cuisine. Thank you very much, but I must go," said Mark, with Silvana translating for him.

Sadaget then asked Silvana to tell Mark that he could visit them anytime he wished.

Silvana was mystified, then realized that her granny had evidently been charmed by him. Mark thanked Sadaget for her hospitality, indicating that it was time to leave.

Mark walked toward the door, with Sadaget and Silvana following him. They all bid farewell. Silvana and Mark went downstairs. From there they walked to the bus station, where Silvana waited for Mark to board the right bus before walking back home.

When she got back, Sadaget was drinking tea. "He looks like a friendly and solid man. The smile never left his face, but sometimes looks can be deceiving."

"He is truly a good man, and smart as well," said Silvana, unable to suppress a smile of satisfaction.

"Just don't make brash decisions, but get to know him better. Some people only show you false aspects that actually do not exist."

"I agree with you, Grandma," Silvana replied. "Now, if you don't mind, I'm going to go lie down. Today has tired me out."

She went into her bedroom.

Chapter 10: The Wedding Day

Spending time with Mark made Silvana's days exciting. She stopped feeling lonely. Instead she felt inclined to sing, dance, or amuse herself in other ways. On the one hand, she looked forward to every working day, because at the office she could see Mark. On the other, Silvana's mother baffled her. Esmira didn't approve of Silvana's decision to date a foreign man. Mark's visit to Sadaget's apartment without her knowledge upset Esmira, who called Silvana on Monday evening and spoke to her. She could hear the irritation in her mother's voice.

"Silvana, Zaur said that you got a foreign boyfriend and he was by our place. Why didn't you tell me?"

"Mother, most times when I needed your presence in my life, you were never there for me. Where were you when I was applying for university and sat for my exams? Students came with their parents, but I went alone."

Esmira lit a cigarette while holding the phone to her ear. She inhaled, then blew the smoke out. "I was away at that time."

"What about the time when I was sick? Were you away then, as well? I called you and asked you to come, but instead, you chose to take your friend to see a doctor. Your friend was more important than me, but now you question why I didn't tell you about Mark," replied Silvana. She shook her head.

"It happened a long time ago, so there's no sense talking about it now," Esmira said, upset.

"Yes, fine, it did occur some time ago, but it demonstrated that you don't care about me. Did you ever bother to come to my school? Teachers always asked after you. They used to say that they were tired of seeing only Granny all the time."

Esmira's hands shook slightly, since hearing these remarks about her mistakes always overwhelmed her. She had been working hard to make money for Silvana to have food and clothes, which was the reason that she wasn't around. She smoked nervously, and a grimace appeared on her face.

"Mother, other parents had been working as well, but they still were there for their children. I didn't need expensive clothes. I needed a mother."

Esmira admitted that she hadn't been a good mother or role model. However, she cautioned Silvana about having a man in her life, given that most men were liars, snakes, and manipulators.

"At times, a foreign man will pretend that he wants to marry a woman, only to relocate her back to his country and then abandon her to prostitution," said Esmira. She had heard many stories of trafficking, whereby destitute women looking for a better life or marriage ended up thrust into the clutches of sex traders.

Silvana shook her head. "From your experience with Samed, I have learned not to trust men. You don't have any reason to worry about Mark."

Esmira's muscles tensed. Her left eyelid twitched. "My point is, just use your logical mind, not your heart. Do not rush into a relationship you might regret."

Silvana grimaced upon hearing her mother's advice. Why didn't you use your mind upon meeting my father? Silvana wanted to ask her.

Instead, she said, "I always use my logical mind before taking any action, weighing the pros and the cons of any decision. Only a fool jumps into the fire without thinking about the consequences."

"Today I met Arzu. She is beautiful and looks just like you," said Esmira, changing the topic.

"Who is Arzu?" Silvana asked, puzzled.

"She is your thirteen-year-old sister whom I gave away."

"Does she know that you are her mother?"

"No, Arzu's adoptive mother does not want her to know the truth." There was a pause on the line. Then Esmira said, "I regret that I gave her away."

"Yes, we should have kept her," said Silvana, feeling guilty. She recalled asking her mother to give her away, and felt as if something squeezed together in the depths of her heart.

Not able to deal with her feelings any longer, Silvana decided to end the conversation, and quickly.

"I'm cooking now. I can't leave the pot unattended, bye!" she blurted suddenly. She hung up the phone and went into the kitchen.

If she had not given away her child, I would now have another sister, Silvana thought, sighing.

She went into Zaur's bedroom. He was staring intently at a movie.

"Zaur, why did you tell Mother about Mark? Now she is distraught because we didn't invite her."

"It slipped out accidentally," said her brother, keeping his eyes on the TV.

She shook her head. "You never can keep anything a secret, can you?" She rubbed her eyes. "I'm going to sleep early tonight. When the soup gets colder, put it in the fridge, please."

Silvana took her shower and went to bed, feeling worn-out and guilt-ridden.

As the days passed, Mark's feelings for Silvana grew. Within a few months, he managed to meet every member of Silvana's family except Esmira.

Silvana's mother wasn't the least bit happy with Silvana's choice. She was afraid that he would take her daughter far away and mistreat her, or even sell her into prostitution. Esmira wanted Silvana to marry an Azeri Muslim man, but Silvana was stubborn. She never liked following another person's advice. An inexperienced woman saw Mark as fundamentally a good guy, and found not only his affable and approachable manner alluring, but also his personality and winning, charming smile.

However, one day a different and darker side of his behavior stupefied her. When they were in the pharmacy, Mark asked the chemist for eye drops, but because the woman couldn't understand what he wanted, she brought him the wrong remedy.

"God damn it, this blockhead can't even understand simple English. Let's go, Silvana," he said furiously. Both of them left the pharmacy. Silvana was taken aback by Mark's abruptness and rudeness but didn't say anything about it.

***

Mark suddenly found out that he was going to be posted to Kenya. This pressured him to ask Silvana to marry him. On a Saturday, as they walked in Boulevard Park holding each other's hands, Mark said, "I'm going to leave Baku soon, but before leaving I would like to do something."

Silvana's body grew weak when she heard Mark's plans to leave, and she felt as if her legs had lost their strength.

"When are you leaving?" she asked in a low voice.

"I'm leaving somewhere between September 23rd and 26th. However, I would like you to come with me as my wife. Would you marry me?"

Silvana's jaw dropped. She stood in silence, gazing at Mark for a while. Excitement soon replaced the shock, and she almost danced with joy.

"Yes, I will marry you!" she said happily. "But we must have a real wedding. In my country, it is a tradition, and I always dreamed of having a large wedding, inviting all my friends and relatives." Silvana's heart raced.

"I don't have a problem with a wedding. You can ask your mother to organize everything. I will cover the cost," Mark replied.

"Thank you, Mark!" Silvana was so happy that she wanted to jump and scream. Overjoyed, she decided to share the news right away with her mother. As they stood by the shore of the Caspian Sea, Silvana quickly called Esmira.

"Mother, I have good news. Mark asked me to marry him."

"What?" Esmira asked, startled.

"I'm going to marry Mark. We need to arrange the wedding as soon as possible." Silvana could barely keep herself from laughing. "I will talk to you when I come back home."

"Wait," said Esmira, but Silvana hung up the phone.

Silvana couldn't believe that her dream of marrying a foreigner was coming true. She was so overjoyed that she felt dizzy and lightheaded.

Wow! Soon I will be living in a faraway country, and will have the children I'd always dreamed of!

Silvana loved children and could not wait until she would have her own. She felt sure that she would be able to hold onto them tightly and give them the love that she had never had.

They walked toward a bench and sat down. Mark took her hand and caressed it. Silvana heard the wind blowing and the waves crashing. The breeze tossed her hair from side to side. As she looked at him, she felt the urge to kiss him. Other ideas and plans got in the way, though.

"Mark, are you going to invite your relatives?"

"I grew up in an orphanage so I never met any of my relatives. We will just invite your relatives, friends, and our co-workers."

"It looks like we have parallel lives. I have uncles, cousins, and aunties, yet I never met them. It feels as if I never had them," said Silvana. Mark asked if she knew where they lived. Because Silvana did know, he wondered why she hadn't searched for them.

Silvana brushed the hair from her face. "My granny does not allow us to contact them. When we needed them in our lives, they never tried to find us. They have erased us from their lives. Why should we look for them now?"

Seeing Silvana's fight with her hair, Mark smiled. He let go of Silvana's hand and slowly moved her hair from her face, putting it behind her ear. "People make mistakes. We should be able to forgive them and move on."

Deep wrinkles ran across her face. Her eyes became gloomy. She shook her head slowly. "No. I'm not a small child any longer, so who needs uncles and aunts? I have passed that stage already and can lead my life without them. So, let's not talk about them any longer. Talking about them only fills my heart with anger."

Mark sighed deeply. "Since talking about them fills your heart with rage, it shows that you are still living in the past and feeling hurt by being rejected. You are letting your pain from the past affect you in a harmful fashion. You can't even forgive those who hurt you. Do you not know that without forgiving others, you won't find peace or enter Paradise?"

Silvana looked thoughtfully at the waves and listened to their rhythmic sound, sighing deeply. "Peace of mind, that's what I need."

"To find peace, you should learn to forgive others. That way you will be able to get rid of anger and be forgiven by God."

"Mark, I'm trying to forgive them, but it is so difficult to forgive people who hurt you, especially when you remember what they did to you or failed to do. If they hadn't rejected me, I wouldn't have had such a miserable life."

Mark grimaced, thinking, People have miserable lives because they keep making the same senseless mistakes, and spend their time day-dreaming or guided by fear. Some only sit around moaning and complaining about their pitiful plight or blaming others.

He again took her hand and looked at her, feeling gloomy.

"Silvana, let me tell you a secret. Suffering does not go in vain. It gives us needed wisdom and opens our eyes and hearts to many things. Those who turn a blind eye and are devoid of experience cannot see. Therefore, they cannot understand the reason nor see truth and compassion. One learns of life, not from reading books, but through living and experiencing. Because of your enriching experiences, you have learned to understand everyone's suffering. You have built a good relationship with God. Don't you think that your life of endurance and the abandonment by your relatives should be considered a blessing because it made you who you are now?"

He smiled and touched her cheek. "Let's go back to our wedding plans for now. Would your mother be able to organize a wedding on such short notice?"

Silvana's eyes sparkled. She became livelier again. She sat up straight and turned her face toward Mark.

"In my country, once you have money, everything can be done on short notice. It's shameful, but money is power. Without it no one will even want to deal with you."

She shifted in her seat. "I'm tired of sitting. Let's walk to the other end," she suggested.

They got up and continued their walk. Soon they stopped at the edge of the park, which overlooked the Caspian Sea, as a few seagulls flew over the water. A ship stood stationary at anchor not far from the seaside.

"So what exactly is going to happen?" asked Mark.

"First, my mother will locate a restaurant for the wedding, talk to the marriage registrar, and then invite people. You need to get a black suit. I have to buy a wedding dress," Silvana told him.

Mark blew out a breath. "Can we do this tomorrow?"

"Yes. I will ask Zaur to go with you to the store. I will go with my mother to buy a dress," replied Silvana.

After discussing wedding plans, both of them took a boat ride and from there decided to go home. Silvana was excited and wanted to reach home quickly in order to spread the good news. They walked back to the metro station. From there Silvana rode home alone. As soon as she arrived, she told the news to Sadaget and her siblings.

"You don't know him well. Why are you rushing to marry him?" asked Sadaget, as she tried to get a plate from the cupboard.

Silvana watched her five-foot granny. This woman is so short and thin, but packs power behind her words.

"He is leaving Azerbaijan soon, but hopes that we marry before he leaves," Silvana told her.

Sadaget came down from the stool and put the plates on the table. "You need to spend more time with him, study his personality, observe how he treats others. Only then think about marriage. Otherwise, you might not know his tendencies toward cruelty."

"Granny, he is a good man. There is nothing to worry about. When he talks to others, he smiles, makes jokes, and is friendly. He's simply the perfect man for me."

"What if he sells you or treats you badly? You will be there alone with no help," said Zaur, who was having an early dinner at the table. He put long noodles in his mouth, leaving some hanging down his chin.

Irritated, Silvana's temper overflowed. "Zaur, you are talking like your mother! Plus, you are always putting your nose in other people's business, exactly where it does not belong. If you have nothing good to say, please keep your mouth shut. This is my life and my future. Therefore, I decide what I should do or shouldn't do. How long are you going to hang like a noose around your mother's neck? If she dies, who is going to support you? Leave me alone and focus on worrying about getting a job."

She left the living room, leaving her granny and her brother behind. She went into her bedroom.

I'm no longer a child. They can't tell me what to do. It's time for me to be happy, and I won't let anyone ruin my happy future with Mark.

Silvana decided to do what she thought was best for her. She hoped that her decision was right. She prayed to Jesus, asking Him to prevent her from making wrong decisions in her life.

"Jesus, You know everyone's heart and mind. If You consider that Mark is the right man for me, please bless us. If You think he will make me unhappy, please give me a sign."

Once she had finished her prayer, she called her mother and started talking about the wedding plans.

"I don't think you should marry him. He is a Christian, while you are a Muslim. You will move far away from here. If anything happens to you, we won't be able to help you," Esmira told her.

"Mother, nothing is going to happen to me. Please organize the wedding, and talk to the marriage registrar. After that, we can invite everyone." Anxious, Silvana rolled her long brown hair in her fingers.

"You are stubborn, just like me. It looks like you won't change your mind. If you think that he can make you happy, then go ahead with the marriage plans, but if anything goes wrong don't say that we didn't warn you. Tomorrow, I will talk to my friend who has a restaurant. We can have the wedding there."

"Please don't forget that the wedding must be before September 23rd," warned Silvana.

"Don't worry. I will organize everything. But who is going to pay for the wedding?"

"Mark will pay for everything."

Silvana yawned. "I'm sorry, Mother. I am tired, and I'm going to go to sleep."

"Take a rest. We will talk tomorrow," said Esmira as she hung up the phone.

Why is she marrying someone older than her, pondered Esmira. A man with kids, and a Christian at that? Neighbors will only gossip that she married a Christian man.

Silvana lay down on the bed and tried to fall asleep. She tossed from side to side, but her excitement didn't allow her to fall asleep easily. Thinking about her new life and her mother's problems with the gossip swirling all about her, as well as her Granny's constant quarreling, she simply reached the breaking point where she couldn't face it all any longer. She finally fell asleep. She dreamed that she came to her wedding, meant to be under a tent. When she reached that spot, the tent was broken and all the people were gone.

In the morning, Silvana got up and thought about the meaning of her dream. She hoped that it wasn't an ominous prediction about her married life. However, after a few days, she forgot all about it.

During the next four days, Silvana bought a white wedding gown, gloves, a veil, and a wedding ring for Mark. In turn, Mark bought a nice black suit for himself, a wedding ring for Silvana, and an engagement ring with a beautiful necklace. He also purchased two tickets for Dubai and booked a hotel, where he wished to spend his honeymoon with his new wife. Esmira spoke to her friend and booked the wedding date in Sabuhil Restaurant. She not only booked a live singer with musicians; she also invited a famous actor, a comedian, to entertain the guests. Along with this person, she hired a famous dance group and also ordered a limousine to drive the bride and the bridegroom to the restaurant.

Silvana called up all of her distant relatives, neighbors, and friends to invite them to the wedding. "Yes, I'm getting married," she told everyone, putting her hand to her heart.

Because none of Silvana's relatives were aware that she was even dating, they were stunned when they heard that she was getting married, and to a foreigner at that, the Prince Charming for whom she had been waiting for many years. At the same time, they were happy for Silvana and planned to come to the wedding to dance all night. Unfortunately, the day before the wedding, Sadaget's brother-in-law Chafar, who had been sick, died. When Silvana heard about his death, she shed a few tears, knowing that most of her relatives wouldn't come. When a death occurs in a Muslim family, people do not attend weddings, nor any other celebrations, for a year. Such a death can even cause cancellation of one's wedding.

Why did he have to die the day before my wedding day? Silvana asked herself. He always used to tell everyone that we do not have a father, and spoke ill of my mother. Now, besides that, he has chosen to spoil my wedding ceremony.

She wished that she could postpone the wedding and wait until everyone could come, but because of Mark's departure date, she decided to go ahead with the nuptials after all.

***

On the wedding morning, Silvana woke up feeling serene. Her face shone with a smile, and her eyes sparkled with happiness. As soon as she got out of bed, Silvana sang,

"You are the man of my dreams.

When I'm near you, my worries go away.

My heart fills with joy.

My dreams are coming true."

As she sang, she spun around the room and moved her hands about like a bird in flight. Then she stood in front of the mirror. Silvana looked at herself, noticing that her eyes weren't gloomy any longer. Deep dimples appeared on her cheeks.

"I'm so happy that I feel like dancing. Thank you, God, for answering my prayers."

The happy bride looked at her silver watch, and was shocked at the time. Oh, I have to get ready! Mark will be here soon.

Silvana ran to the bathroom and put on an attractive, long-sleeved, green dress. She then went out and waited for Mark.

He arrived at midday and pressed the doorbell. Silvana opened the door. Mark's eyes widened upon seeing her.

"Wow, your whole face is sparkling with joy! What did you do?"

"I didn't do anything. Your love fills my heart with joy."

Mark entered the living room and greeted her siblings, all of whom were sitting on the sofa.

Silvana put a hand on his arm. "Mark, I have to go to the hairstylist with my neighbor. She is outside waiting for me."

He glanced at her siblings. "I don't want to stay in here without you. I don't speak your language. How would I communicate with your family?"

Silvana beamed as she touched his chin. "Don't worry, I will be back soon."

She left the apartment, rushing downstairs to meet her neighbor. Together, they rode to the hairdresser to get her hair and makeup done.

Mark, a nervous wreck, stayed in her apartment, uncomfortable with so many non-English speaking people surrounding him. He put on his black jacket and anxiously waited for Silvana, wiping his face continually with a handkerchief.

Silvana sat in the hair salon, patiently waiting for her hairdresser. The wedding was scheduled to start at 4 p.m., and she needed to reach home in time.

"Ulkar, why are they taking so long to attend to me?" Silvana asked, uneasy.

"They always take longer on busy days," answered Ulkar, who was accustomed to visiting the salon.

At last, the hairdresser approached Silvana and introduced herself as Quzel.

When asked what sort of styling she wanted, Silvana replied that it was her wedding day. The hairdresser congratulated her and asked about the lucky man. Silvana replied that he was British. She removed the white veil from her bag and gave it to Quzel, who touched Silvana's hair and told her that she needed to wash it over at the sink. The stylist put a towel around Silvana's neck and washed her hair with warm water. Afterward, she combed it and then dried it with the blow-dryer. All the while Silvana kept looking nervously at the clock.

Quzel fixed Silvana's long hair in a bun, pinned the veil to it, and put beautiful white flower pins in Silvana's hair. After finishing, she asked about facial makeup. Silvana told her that she wanted her birthmark concealed. The stylist applied foundation and then powder on Silvana's face. After that, she added black liner on her eyes, mascara, and red lipstick. When Quzel finished with her makeup, she turned Silvana towards the mirror.

"Wow! You look like a beautiful doll," said the hairdresser.

Silvana thanked her and went to the mirror to get a closer look. She was hit by a sudden realization, so instead of looking at herself, she glanced at the clock.

I'm going to be late, she thought.

She paid her bill, and was about to leave when Ulkar decided to fix her hair, as well, since Silvana was paying the bill.

"Ulkar, please hurry up. I'm going to be late for my wedding."

"Don't worry; my hair won't take as long as yours," said Ulkar.

The hairdresser fixed Ulkar's hair. They left the salon in a rush. They waited for a cab not far from the salon. A few young men surrounded Silvana.

"Who is the lucky one?" one of them asked her.

"Wow, such a beautiful bride," said another.

Silvana smiled and moved away without saying anything.

As she waited for the taxi, instrumentalists and other people arrived at her apartment. The musicians grew irritated by Silvana's absence. "Where is the bride? Why is she taking so long to come back?" they asked.

Mark felt panicky and was sweating a great deal. Why the hell is she taking so long to come back? Everyone is waiting for her, he thought.

Silvana and her friend jumped into the cab. After giving the driver her address, she said, "Can you please drive faster? We're going to be late."

The driver increased his speed, passing the other cars. After forty minutes, the cab stopped in front of Silvana's building. Silvana quickly disembarking and climbed the stairs to her apartment. She opened the door, and was stupefied to see a house full of people.

Mark approached her. She was dismayed to see that his shirt was wet with perspiration. "Why did you take so long?" he asked, fanning himself with a newspaper. He looked relieved to see her.

"It took too long to style my hair. I have never visited the salon before. Consequently, I didn't know that it would take so long."

She gave him a quick peck on the cheek. "I'm going to go put on my wedding dress."

She rushed into her bedroom and put on the wedding dress. She put on her gold necklace, engagement ring, earrings, white shoes, and gloves. Then she glanced in the mirror.

Wow! I look so good in white, she thought proudly. For the first time in her life, she decided that she liked to wear white clothes. When she finished dressing, she came out of her bedroom.

Mark eyed her from head to toe. He stood motionless, looking at his bride. To him, she looked so striking in her white dress, which showed her perfect shoulders and slim figure.

"You look so gorgeous," he said in an awed voice. "I'm lucky to have a bride like you!" He beamed, his smile practically glowing.

She smiled and took his hand. "Don't lose your head because of my outer beauty. Love me for who I am and for my inner beauty."

"I love you for everything," answered Mark with pride.

They walked toward the front door. One of her relatives held a golden candle. Another family member carried a mirror, while Ulkar carried a beautifully-decorated basket with presents in it. The musicians went outside, playing an Azeri wedding song.

Silvana and Mark went out the door. After breaking a plate for good luck, they went downstairs. The couple stopped outside for a few minutes for photographs, danced, and then got into in a white limousine decorated with flowers and a big red bow. Other relatives got into other decorated vehicles. Esmira, her other children, and Ulkar also got into the limousine.

One person was missing from the happy company. Sadaget had refused to go to the wedding after seeing Ulkar carrying Silvana's basket. Not seeing her granny, Silvana climbed out of the limousine and went back to her apartment. She looked at her granny with sad eyes. "Granny, today is my big day. Why aren't you coming?"

"Why did you invite Ulkar and allow her to go with you in the same limousine? She will bring bad luck; her mother spoke detrimentally about your mom. Did you forget the day Ulkar didn't want to play with you?"

"I didn't invite her. She begged me to let her ride in the limousine."

"If she is going, I can't go."

Silvana held Granny's hands and looked directly into her eyes, feeling the urge to cry. "Please come. It is an important day for me. I want you to be there. You are like a mother to me," she begged.

Sadaget withdrew her hands. "Anyone who hurt you in childhood or mistreated you is my enemy. I don't want my enemies and such false friends at your wedding. As long as she will be in attendance, I won't go."

Granny, don't shoot arrows of poison, hate, and bitterness out of your mouth. God will not be pleased with you. Beware, otherwise, these arrows will shoot back at you, Silvana thought.

Her heart filled with frustration. "I can't tell her not to come, because she is already in the limousine."

"I asked you not to invite her, but you refused to hear me. Therefore, you will have to go without me."

"Granny, why don't you ever forgive anyone?" Silvana asked in a shaky voice.

When she got no answer, she left the apartment, feeling betrayed. She got back into the limousine, trying to look happy. Cars rushed by and horns blew all the way to the restaurant. Mark stared at his bride, feeling happy, and clearly in love because his bride was so elegant and pure. Out of happiness, he sang, "Baby, baby, I'm in love."

All the automobiles stopped in front of the Sabuhil Restaurant. The musicians got out of the car and played the wedding melody, while the happy couple entered the restaurant and sat in front of everyone at a big table.

Silvana's table had a magnificent crystal vase with roses, along with champagne, wine, soft drinks, and different types of national food, including black caviar with pickles. Silvana felt nervous sitting in front of everyone, knowing that they were all looking at her and Mark. She didn't like to be the center of attention at all.

She looked at her surroundings and saw that the place was packed with people. Many invitees came, but Silvana felt somewhat disheartened that many of her relatives were absent because of the death in the family. Most of the people in attendance were Esmira's friends; the ones that Silvana didn't like; neighbors, and her siblings' friends. Guests who knew that Sadaget was like a mother to Silvana questioned her absence.

A famous Azeri comedian welcomed everyone and congratulated the couple. A few guests laughed at his jokes. When he finished, a female singer started to sing a song, Wait and I Will Come. She wore a beautiful shiny purple dress that showed her curves. Her long black hair cascaded over her shoulders. She danced gracefully as she sang, which attracted the gaze of some male guests.

A few guests rose from their seats and performed the Azeri national dance. Some threw money at other dancing guests.

Narmin came up to Silvana. "Let's go dance."

"No, I'm shy dancing around people."

Narmin clutched Silvana's hand and pulled it. "It's your wedding. You have to dance."

Mark stared at both of them, trying to understand what Narmin wanted. Silvana got up from her seat.

"Mark, Narmin is inviting us to dance."

Mark rose and wiped his face with a handkerchief. He then walked toward the dance floor, followed by Silvana.

She was astonished to see how well Mark danced. He spread his hands and moved them like a slowly-moving branch. He smiled all the while, but was clearly nervous. Silvana could see it from his facial expressions. Suddenly anxiety consumed her, and she eyed him.

Am I making a mistake by marrying him? Is he the one I have been waiting for?

When they were ready to sit back at the table, slow music started playing. They were again invited to dance. Mark put his hands on Silvana's waist, and they slowly navigated the stage. Silvana looked at him, smiling, but inside she was uneasy. Her feelings were altering suddenly, from joy to sadness, as if she had an internal barometer signaling that she had made a mistake.

When the music stopped, they sat at the table and started eating. The dance group performed Michael Jackson's songs as the guests clapped. A young man wearing tight leather pants and a black vest danced. He gyrated and moved from side to side. Then a female dancer performed the Azerbaijani national dance while at the same time holding a large plate with rice in her hand. She wore a national dress with a long white skirt, white blouse, and a veil with a tiara. While dancing, she moved her free hand gracefully above her head. She came up to Silvana's table and put the plate on it. She then took Silvana's hand and pulled her to dance, at which time everyone surrounded her and Silvana and moved in circles.

The music stopped, the comedian asked the guests to sit and enjoy the food, then announced, "Anyone who wishes to say anything to the bride and the bridegroom, please come to the front."

Ulkar's father came up and said, "Today is a momentous day, because our good neighbor Silvana is getting married. Silvana kept her values and became a role model for many, even though she grew up fatherless. Her wonderful Granny Sadaget reared her. It is a pity that she couldn't make it to the wedding."

Hearing her neighbor's words about Silvana being fatherless annoyed Esmira. She wondered who had invited him to speak.

He turned toward the newlyweds. "Congratulations to a very special couple. I wish you a happy marriage and many children." He gave the microphone to the comedian and went back to his seat.

Esmira gazed at him for a time, frowning.

Why in the world did he have to mention that Silvana is fatherless?

Silvana's siblings approached her and Mark, congratulating them. Then most of the guests took photographs with the bride and groom. People started leaving the restaurant by 11 p.m. while Silvana and Mark stayed until most guests had left.

They then returned to Sadaget's apartment. After changing clothes, they went straight to the airport. From there, they flew to Dubai.

When they arrived at the hotel, they were exhausted but happy to be alone. The couple jumped into their pajamas and climbed into the bed. Mark kissed Silvana's lips and neck. At first, Silvana felt shy and tense.

"Are you okay? Mark asked.

"Yes, I'm fine. I'm just a little bit shy."

This was her first time making love to a man. Mark knew this, and made sure he was gentle with her.

He slowly took off her nightdress and then continued kissing her. Silvana's whole body became aroused. She liked the feeling from Mark's kisses and his caresses. After making love, both of them fell asleep.

They awoke at about 10 a.m. The couple took a shower and ate breakfast. Then they left the hotel. The duo held hands as they walked downtown and visited different shops. Silvana fell in love with Dubai. She found it to be a magnificent and modern city, with good shopping outlets.

They entered a jewelry shop. Silvana went over to a stall and looked at a necklace made with emeralds.

"Mark, it's so beautiful."

He leaned over the stall.

"Yes, it is. Can we look at it please?" he asked the salesperson.

The woman removed the necklace and gave it to Silvana, whose face beamed with admiration as she gazed at it. Seeing her interest in the jewelry, Mark decided to buy it.

"How much does it cost?" he asked.

"Five hundred us dollars," stated the shop girl.

Silvana's eyes enlarged upon hearing the price. "Oh God, it is so expensive."

She handed it back to the shop girl. Mark looked at Silvana's disappointed face and smiled. "We'll take it," he said.

He paid the salesperson, took the necklace, and put it in his bag. Silvana hugged him, overjoyed.

"Thank you, Mark! You are a wonderful husband!"

He smiled. "You deserve it."

After shopping, they walked back to the hotel and had dinner in the restaurant.

The next day, they booked a desert safari on which they rode camels across the wilderness. Everywhere Silvana looked, she saw yellow sand. The breeze blowing through her hair was warm but wonderful. Finally, they stopped at a camel farm. Silvana noticed a restaurant with cabins next to it. They were going to stay overnight in one of them. They entered the restaurant and she looked around in wonder. The walls were painted red, but the floor was covered with a fluffy red carpet. The restaurant had small round tables and floral arrangements. A few foreigners enjoyed their dinner at the tables. The belly dancers entertained the guests as they ate.

Mark ordered a steak with potatoes. Silvana sat next to him, resting her head on his shoulder and enjoying the belly dance with Arabic music in the background. She felt relaxed. Another dream had come true: she had seen deserts in films and had always wanted to visit one. Now she had crossed one. And on a camel, no less. She looked at the many stars shining brightly through the window.

"Mark, I love it here. I enjoyed my camel ride. Thank you very much for this experience."

"You're welcome," said Mark, rubbing her hand gently.

When dinner was over, they went to their cabin. The room had one queen-sized bed, a small table with two wooden chairs, and a tall standing lamp. Tired from the ride, they simply took a shower. Then they both fell asleep.

They stayed in Dubai for four days and then flew back to Baku. Silvana moved into Mark's apartment. After she had settled in, Mark put all of Silvana's papers together to get a visa for Kenya. He arranged an appointment at the embassy, and both of them went to the Kenyan embassy and got a visa for her.

After the paperwork had been taken care of, Mark bought tickets for both of them to depart on September 26th.

As the time approached for Silvana's trip, Esmira felt more and more anxious. She didn't want Silvana to leave, but couldn't change anything.

The day before Silvana left, Sadaget invited her sister Tamara and other relatives for dinner. Sadaget's apartment was full of people. Everyone was seated at the table drinking tea when Silvana and Mark entered the living room. They greeted everyone and sat on the sofa.

"Would you like some tea?" asked Esmira.

"Yes, please," answered Silvana.

"What is Mark going to drink?"

"Don't worry, Mother, he will choose whatever he wants to drink from the table."

She turned to her hubby. "Mark, don't be shy. Pour yourself whatever you want."

Mark poured a glass of Pepsi and drank it as the others spoke amongst themselves. After a short while, Sadaget put food on the table. In the middle of the table, the guests found soft drinks and bread cut into small pieces. Around this, Esmira's mother had placed dishes of Azeri cuisine, including salad and pickles.

Sadaget raised a glass of champagne and gave a toast.

"Mark, first I would like to welcome you to our family. I hope you will make my Silvana happy. You are very lucky to have a woman like her, because she is as pure as a diamond. Make certain that you treat her well."

Mark couldn't understand her, yet he listened intently to her with a smile on his face. After finishing her toast, she took a few sips of champagne and sat down.

Esmira got up with a glass of champagne and turned toward Silvana. "My dear, I'm very proud to have a daughter like you. I wish both of you a happy marriage and many children."

"Thank you, Mother." Silvana's face showed a hint of sadness, knowing that soon she would move away.

Mark got up and holding his glass of champagne, spoke, "Thank you very much for accepting me into your family. I'm happy to have Silvana as my wife. I will spend every day making her happy."

Drops of sweat rolled down his face. Mark looked lovingly at Silvana. "I know that you are troubled because she is moving away, but I promise we will be visiting you." He took a few sips of champagne and sat.

"Silvana, do you remember that, at age seven, you told me that you would marry a man from a distant country and away?" asked Narmin.

"Yes, I recall," replied Silvana.

"Indeed, you married a man from a far-off country. It looks as though you predicted your future."

Silvana smiled. "I didn't know my future. Only God knows it, but I knew who I was, where I wanted to be, and who I would like to become. This helped me to achieve my goals and dreams."

"You are very fortunate that you got what you wanted. Not everyone is lucky as you," remarked Narmin.

"This has to do, not with good luck, but with persistence, patience, focus, and embracing change," answered Silvana, as she gazed tenderly at Mark.

"I guess you are right, but not everyone is as persistent as you," commented Narmin.

Mark suddenly got up from his seat. "Silvana, we have to go back to our apartment. We need to ensure that we packed everything," he said anxiously.

Silvana got up also.

"Granny, we are leaving. We need to pack."

"Please, stay for a little bit longer and eat your food," implored Sadaget.

"Granny, we can't."

Sadaget got up, went over to Silvana, and hugged her.

"I'm not going to see you any longer. You are abandoning me. I wish that I could come with you," said Sadaget, with tears rolling down her pale, wrinkled face.

This is all Esmira's fault, since she could have certainly given her children a better life. Then Silvana would not be running away from here, Sadaget thought. The fact is that Esmira has made all of us unhappy.

"Granny, don't cry. I will be visiting you," said Silvana with a faint smile.

Sadaget wiped her tears, came up to Mark, and gave him a hug as well.

"Mark, I won't see you tomorrow. Have a safe flight. Don't forget to visit us," said Sadaget in Azerbaijani. Silvana translated, feeling depressed.

"Thank you, Granny," said Mark.

"I will come with Zaur and Narmin to pick you up at 5 a.m.," said Esmira.

"Okay, we are going now," said Silvana, her voice shaking.

Just as she was about to leave, she ran back to Granny and gave her another hug.

"Granny, please look after yourself." Silvana shed some tears.

"Bye, everyone," said Mark.

They left the apartment and took a cab from the bus stop. When they reached the apartment, they packed everything. The exhausted couple went to bed.

Esmira arrived exactly at 5 a.m. Zaur helped Mark to carry their bags downstairs.

At the airport, Mark went to the counter to get the boarding passes while Silvana stayed with her mother.

All too soon, he was back. "I got our boarding passes. It is time to say goodbye to your family."

"Mother, we are going to our gate." Silvana glanced at her mother with gloomy and tearful eyes.

Esmira began to sob.

"Why are you crying? You will see me. I'm not leaving you forever."

"You are going to a strange country. I'm not going to see you for a long while."

"We will, of course, call you," said Mark reassuringly.

Zaur approached Silvana and embraced her. "I feel the need to cry. My favorite sister is leaving us," he said, his eyes welling up.

"Do you remember two years ago that, when you met my friends, you lied to them? You said that I had moved away to

Germany. Looks like some of your untruths are coming true. I'm moving to a different country." Silvana trembled like a leaf.

"Are you cold?" asked Mark, noticing her agitation.

"No, I'm just nervous because I'm leaving my small family."

"You always dreamed of seeing different countries. It is coming true," said Zaur.

"You are right," said Silvana, trying to crack a smile.

"Silvana, it's time to go," stated Mark, impatiently looking at his watch.

"Mother, we are going now," Silvana said again.

The siblings hugged Mark and Silvana.

"Bye, my daughter."

Silvana and Mark walked away toward Gate 8, and Esmira chased after them.

"Please call me as soon as you arrive; otherwise, I will worry," Esmira shouted after them, tearing up.

"Don't worry. I will call you."

With tears dripping down her face, Esmira walked back to the cab.

As they sat on the cold rough seats in the waiting area, Silvana said, "I feel sorry for my granny. I was the only one to whom she liked talking about her worries, but now she won't have anyone at home to share her concerns."

"You will be able to speak to her over Paltalk, and even see her that way."

Silvana felt despondent about leaving her family, but at the same time was happy because she had married the man of her dreams and was starting a new life. Her emotions rolled around inside her as they waited for the next step to that new adventure.

They boarded the plane, and put their bags in the overhead compartment. Mark slept all the way to London, but Silvana couldn't fall asleep at all. She wasn't accustomed to sleeping in a seated position and spent a lot of time trying to get comfortable, crossing and uncrossing her legs.

After six hours, the plane landed at Heathrow International Airport. The newly wed couple got up, removed their bags from the overhead storage, and walked outside to the transit zone.

"I feel so sleepy and tired," said Silvana, barely keeping her eyes open.

"Why didn't you sleep on the plane?"

"I tried to, but just couldn't," answered Silvana, yawning.

"I hope that you will sleep on the next plane because the flight will be a lot longer than the last one."

Silvana glanced at her surroundings with amazement. "This airport is really huge. Pity that we are not staying for a few days in London. I would like to see your home country and capital," said Silvana, with a regretful tone in her voice.

"Don't worry, we will be back soon. I will show you London. It is truly a beautiful multicultural city."

When they reached their terminal, Mark left Silvana at the gate's waiting area and went to buy them some beverages. Silvana looked around, astounded to see so many black people. In her country, she was accustomed to seeing only Caucasians. She stared at them with curiosity and then began to read her book. Mark came back with a Pepsi, which he handed to her.

"Thank you," she said with a smile.

They spent two hours in Heathrow Airport. Then they boarded the British Airways plane going to Kenya. This flight was definitely the longer one. Silvana again felt uncomfortable from sitting all the time and for so long, because it made her feet hurt and her stomach upset.

The plane arrived in Kenya at 1 a.m., the next day. Silvana was so relieved that the long flight was over. After going through immigration, they proceeded outside, where a company representative greeted them. He drove the guests to a rented house provided by the company. Mark and Silvana were so tired from the long flight that they just unpacked what they needed to use and went to sleep.

Silvana woke up with an upset stomach, but it passed soon enough. She attributed it to the long, stressful trip. On Monday, Mark went to his new job, while Silvana stayed at home and unpacked all their clothes.

Chapter 11: Dirty Secrets Surfaced

Day after day, Mark went to his office, leaving Silvana alone within the four walls with nobody to talk to. Silvana was accustomed to being around people, but now she was alone all day. The only things she could do were to clean, iron, and cook. She wanted to leave the house, but was afraid to walk by herself in a strange country where she did not know anyone. At least Mark came home for one hour during his lunch break.

In general, Silvana disliked living in Kenya. She missed her family and life in Azerbaijan. She felt locked in a cage, unable to freely move around, because she did not know the place well and felt unsafe traveling by bus. From childhood, she had been independent and accustomed to going to the grocery store, moving around the city, and doing everything for herself. But now she was entirely dependent on Mark.

She tried watching television, but the channels were either in English or Swahili. No matter how thoroughly she looked to find Azeri or Russian channels, there weren't any. Once, while changing channels, Silvana accidentally pressed the wrong button and ended up unwittingly ordering paid movies. Finally, greatly frustrated, she turned off the television and put away the remote control.

Why does everything have to be in English or Swahili?

When Mark received the cable bill, he was surprised to find fees for films that he had never ordered. He entered the living room, where Silvana was sitting on the sofa reading a book, with the cable bill in his hand.

"Did you interfere with the remote control?" Mark asked, his voice high-pitched in anger.

She put the book aside and gaped at him. "I was changing channels, trying to find a Russian channel." Silvana nervously bit her nail.

He threw the bill on the sofa. It fell on her lap. "Look at it! Stupid, by changing channels, you have ordered films that I have to pay for!" shouted Mark, irate.

Silvana stared at his hands as he squeezed his fingers together. Her heartbeat sped up, and she tried not to move or say anything to anger him.

Mark is going to hit me.

Silvana mumbled, "I didn't do it on purpose."

Mark grabbed her wrist and squeezed it. "Listen to me! Don't touch anything that you don't know about. Now I have to pay money because of your stupidity!" he shouted.

"Let go of my hand!" she said, pulling it back.

He moved away from her. As she sank further into the cushions, she began to worry that he would hurt her. She sat silently, biting her lip and waiting for him to leave. When he finally did she went into the bedroom, feeling fearful and agitated. For the rest of the day, she remained quiet.

Six months passed, and unexpected changes started happening. Silvana continued to stay at home, but Mark frequented bars at least once a week with his new friends. It was their custom to socialize while drinking in the pubs, and he happily became a part of their group. Mark started coming home intoxicated. His eyes were usually red, and Silvana could smell alcohol on him.

However, his drinking habits had developed long before he met Silvana. While living in England, he was managing a hotel bar. He would often end up drinking with the customers, a ploy to get them to come back again as regulars. It was this habit that had contributed to his first wife leaving him.

Silvana wasn't happy, to say the least, when he started going out with friends. She blamed them for his drinking habits. Often, he would come home late and squeeze Silvana's wrists in perverse jest, causing her pain.

While he was living in the orphanage, a bitter and harsh woman (who used to babysit him and other children) would always pinch his hands if he disobeyed her or proved disruptive and made a mess. Perhaps this was the cause of his behavior toward Silvana.

Late one night, Silvana sat on the sofa, waiting for Mark to come home. She became so sleepy that her eyes started to shut, even though she strove to keep them open.

She glanced at her watch and yawned widely.

Why is he taking so long to come home? I do not like this whatsoever. In my home country, men come home straight from work. They do not leave their wives and children alone at home, nor do they drink.

The more she thought about it, the more distraught she became. I shouldn't have married him in the first place, but I did not know what I was getting into.

Tired of waiting, she dozed off right on the sofa. Mark arrived home at midnight. He tried to put the key in the lock, but because his hand was shaking, he kept missing the keyhole.

"Damn it," he muttered. Annoyed, he put away the key and turned the handle, but to no avail. He knocked on the door a few times.

Silvana jumped off the sofa, alarmed. Fear filled her heart as she glanced at the door.

"Open the door!" shouted Mark.

Hearing his voice, she felt relieved. She opened it, and Mark staggered inside.

"Look at the time. You shouldn't be drinking so late!" scolded Silvana.

He weaved over to her and grabbed her wrists, clutching them tightly.

"I didn't do anything wrong. I was just with friends drinking," he replied, slurring his words.

Silvana tried to pull her hands from his grip.

"Let go of my hands. You're hurting me!"

He spat in her face, and she turned away, startled.

"Stop spitting on me. I hate the smell of alcohol."

She pulled her hands toward herself. Mark smiled smugly and released them, then went into the bathroom. Silvana went into the bedroom and lay down on the bed, rubbing her painful wrists.

Mark leaned over the toilet bowl and mumbled to himself, I'm not doing anything wrong, just sitting in the bar drinking with friends. Why is she getting so upset?

Then he threw up. Damn it!

From the bedroom, Silvana could hear Mark vomiting yet again. She lay there despising him. She had never approved of drinking, and knew that those who tended to drink too much either became alcoholics, or destroyed their relationships with loved ones and God. Drinking tended to change a person's personality, and even affected their married life in a negative manner. Silvana tried to understand why non-Muslims wasted their time drinking in pubs, instead of spending precious time with their children and loved ones. Now Silvana was forced to face what she couldn't tolerate at all.

One day, eleven months into their marriage, Mark left his laptop at home. Feeling bored, Silvana decided to use it. She sat in front of the computer and started browsing through the pictures on it. But what she found on his computer left her thunderstruck and assaulted her senses.

Instead of seeing pictures of the two of them on his computer, Silvana discovered many pictures of other women, as well as porn videos. Silvana felt as if her strength had been flushed down the kitchen sink when she saw them. The very fact that a married man had many pictures of women on his computer was abominable. Infuriated, she erased all the pictures, her hands shaking.

Despite her shock, she decided to delve further. She checked his email and to her horror found emails to other women. Silvana opened one recent email to a woman called Penny and read it: 'When I sleep with another woman, I think about you.' She skimmed through his received emails, found her email to him, and opened the attachment. It was a photo of a beautiful woman with long black hair sitting on a bed. Tears of rage and disappointment dropped from her eyes.

So, when he slept with me, he thought about her.

Then she decided to teach him a lesson by emailing Penny. She typed, even though her hands shook.

"Dear Penny, I like you very much, and that's why I have decided to tell you the truth. A few years ago, I was in a car accident and was pinned by a car. As a result, I lost one of my testicles."

Silvana pressed the Send icon. Then, she decided to check the history of his Internet activities. Flabbergasted, she found out that he had a profile on an adult porn website. She felt dizzy, and powered down the computer before she could discover any more secrets that she didn't want to know.

"How could he be so foul in looking online at other women when he has a beautiful wife like me?" moaned Silvana as she trudged to her room.

The qualities that she disrespected in men, she suddenly discovered in Mark. Her image of him changed for good. She lost all trust and respect for him. She flung herself on the bed, crying, wishing she could go back to Azerbaijan. Why did I agree to come here with him? I should have stayed in my country! she thought. No, I know why; I did not want to be lonely any longer and needed to feel loved.

She called Esmira with tears flowing from her eyes. "Mother, I want to come back home."

"What happened?" asked Esmira, shocked at hearing her crying.

"I found out that Mark has been flirting with women online, and accesses adult porn websites. He has many vulgar photographs on his computer, and graphic videos also," said Silvana, sobbing.

"So, because of that you want to leave him," Esmira responded, surprised. "That's what most men do. You'll have to accept this sort of sexual misconduct as something normal."

Silvana shook her head. "No, married men shouldn't be flirting or be interested in other women. It is wrong and unacceptable. I'm coming home."

"Do you realize that if you come home, our neighbors will laugh at you, saying that Mark sent you back because you weren't good enough?"

Silvana wiped her tears with her sleeve. "But I'm not happy here. At times, he hurls vulgar words at me." Tears rolled down Silvana's face.

"You married him of your free will. So you're bound to stay now. In any event, many men tend to be rude to their wives. If you return, what Muslim man would want to marry a divorced woman? Our people would just talk behind your back."

"I am fed up worrying what people would say or think about me. Just let them go ahead and talk. They have despicable hearts and cesspool minds, full of only jealousy and spite! To Hell with them!" Silvana angrily shouted.

After talking to her mother, Silvana waited for Mark, biting her nails and feeling anxious. She realized that she had made a big mistake marrying a man who she did not know well. She sat at the table crying, whispering to herself, "I want to go home, but I would not be able to endure the gossip that would inevitably envelop me as a divorced woman. I've had enough of my mother's scolding.

They will just look at me as if I did something wrong, and I would be lonely again."

After pondering her mother's warnings, Silvana made up her mind. She didn't want to be alone, nor spoil her good name, which was more important to her than anything else. She had always been concerned about what others would think of her. Therefore, she chose to remain, unaware that she was making the biggest mistake of her life. As always, she allowed society to rule her decisions, therefore she did not live her life to its fullest or following her heart's desire.

When Mark came home at 6 p.m. she sat on the bed, waiting for him to change his clothes. As Mark changed, he glared at her face.

"Why do you look so overwrought?" he asked her. She kept silent.

"What happened?" Mark approached her.

"Move away from me," she said in a firm voice. She got up from the bed and opened the closet.

As she took her clothes out, she told him, "You are a nasty man who chases other women."

She turned to him, angrily forming her hand into a fist. "All this time, you have had our wedding picture next to your computer. Knowing that you were married, you still wrote to Penny that when you sleep with me you think about her. I just want to go back home," she finished.

"Those words you read don't mean anything," he insisted. "Stop removing your clothes from the cupboard."

He gazed at her with tear-filled eyes. From his downtrodden facial expression, Silvana knew that he wasn't happy with her discovery of his secret online life.

"Why did you write them?" Silvana shouted, trying not to cry.

"I had nothing else to do," said Mark, attempting to look earnest.

"Why did you save pictures of ugly women and their feet on your computer; for you to sit and look at them alone?"

"What pictures?"

"Stop playing the innocent lamb. You had many women's pictures saved on your computer, and I have erased them."

He came closer to her, trying to hug her. "Those pictures are not mine."

She pushed him away. "Just stay away from me. What about your profile on the porn website?"

"Don't be silly! I created that profile when I was single. I haven't used it since we've been married."

"I should have listened to my mother and never married you!" Feeling dizzy, Silvana left Mark in the bedroom.

As she paced from one side of the room to the other, she thought about what she should do next.

God, why was I so blind that I didn't see his true nature?

After discovering Mark's concealed side, she stopped trusting him. She would wake up at night to ensure that Mark wasn't looking at porn or writing to women as she slept. She caught him a few times watching porn late at night. He was looking at videos in which two women were having sex with one another and kissing each other's feet.

Mark had a penchant for female feet, and sometimes would watch videos where feet were displayed. As soon as he noticed Silvana, Mark would close the video. He could not understand why his wife was getting upset just because he looked at pornography.

After all, that is what many men do. This could not necessarily be viewed as cheating, he thought, not realizing that porn was causing him to sin by developing both lust and sinful thoughts within him.

Silvana was so fed up with Mark's misconduct that, as day after day passed, she regretted having ever married him more and more. Nonetheless, she admired his other qualities, since after all he was an intelligent, educated man and always made sure that Silvana had everything she wanted.

After living in Kenya for a year, Silvana became accustomed to watching television in English. However, staying at home all the time and putting up with Mark's drinking habits caused her despair. She wanted to work and to be around people. Only once a week would Mark take her out for the evening or on the weekends, and those days were her happiest.

One rainy day, Silvana got up and peeped outside as Mark sat at the table. A big truck was parked in front of their house.

"What is this truck doing in here?" she asked.

"Stupid asshole, how do you expect me to know what the truck is doing here?" shouted Mark.

Silvana scowled, feeling the blood pound in her temples. "I only asked a question. Why are you shouting like a mad man?"

Her anger got the best of her, and she shouted back, "Who are you trying to fool by wearing the mask of a loving husband and a friendly man whenever you are around others? One day your mask will fall off, and everyone will see your true self."

"Stop asking silly questions, and I will not shout. You are always causing problems with your stupidity and incessant questions!" yelled Mark, bursting into anger. "I just cannot handle your stupidity."

Without saying anything, Silvana went into her bedroom. Back in her country, when she was growing up, Silvana had been recognized for her good heart, and many other admirable qualities for which people respected her. She would never allow anyone to be rude to her, yet now she was facing what she disliked the most. Outraged, she lay down on the bed and covered her face with the sheet as she bawled.

Oh God, he is hurting my feelings. If I had known beforehand that he was a bully, I would never have married him. In Azerbaijan, he was different. Was he just pretending to love me?

Silvana soon realized that, in Mark's native country, going out drinking was a normal, traditional, and customary aspect of socializing. However, it was not normal for it to extend to the point where someone got drunk and started abusing one's partner, unable to control one's conduct, and not remembering anything from the previous day. The latter is a sign of addiction, which can lead to alcoholism and abusive, misdirected behavior.

Silvana noticed that Mark cherished and worshiped the control and manipulation of those around him, demanding that matters move forward and head in his direction only. He would get angered if she opposed him. Was that type of behavior a result of alcohol or just Mark's insecurities, fears, and a desire to feel the sensation of power? Silvana remained uncertain.

Instead of facing stigmatization from within Muslim society and leading a life of fear at being alone and abandoned, she chose to remain his wife.

Chapter 12: Cry Of The Soul

Silvana's English wasn't always adequate, so Mark enrolled her in advanced English classes. Going to these classes proved to be the best time for Silvana. She made a few Hispanic friends and in time decided to invite them over to her place. When Mark heard that Silvana had invited Hispanic people, he decided to retreat to the bedroom. This was all well and good, as far as Silvana was concerned.

One Sunday afternoon Silvana's doorbell rang. She peeped through the peephole and, seeing her friends, opened the door.

"Hello, my dear," said Marisa in broken English, a broad smile on her face. She was a typical Hispanic woman of average size, with curly black hair and a fair complexion. She entered, along with her two teenage children.

"Hello. Welcome to my house." The smile warmed Silvana's face.

She offered them seats on the sofa. "What would you like to drink?"

"Don't worry, we will drink whatever you have," said Marisa in a loud voice, looking around.

Silvana went into the kitchen. She came back with some soft drinks. She handed them to her guests and sat in an armchair.

"Was it easy to find my house?" Silvana asked.

"Not really. I made a few wrong turns, but after asking for directions, I was able to find it."

Marisa removed a fan from her handbag, feeling a little warm.

"Marisa, how long are you planning to stay in Kenya?" asked Silvana.

"We have three more weeks. Then we will go back to Venezuela."

Silvana nodded. "I will miss you."

"Is your husband at home?" Marisa asked, suddenly curious.

"No, he is not," Silvana lied, trying not to look into Marisa's eyes. She was uncomfortable.

"Oh. We wanted to meet him," said Marisa, disappointed.

"You might meet him before you leave Kenya." Silvana then changed the subject. "Your English has truly improved."

"You're right. This English class helped us a lot. I'm happy that we came to Kenya for a holiday."

Marisa got up from the sofa, her gaze roaming around the room. "Where is your bathroom?" she asked.

Silvana got up from her seat and asked Marisa to follow her. They stopped in front of two identical doors.

"It's right in here," said Silvana, pointing to the door.

Instead of opening the bathroom door, Marisa opened the bedroom door. Mark was lying on the bed in his underpants and white T-shirt, but upon seeing Marisa, jumped out of bed.

"Sorry," said Marisa, feeling awkward. She quickly closed the door.

Silvana felt embarrassed because her lie had been exposed.

"I didn't know that he was at home. He probably came through a different door," Silvana said, lying a second time to cover the first one.

Her guests stayed for about twenty minutes and then left. Silvana felt bad that she had had to lie, but what else could she do if Mark asked her to do it?

Two weeks after having had the Hispanic guests in her house, Silvana mustered the courage to go for a walk, to locate the local pharmacy. As she walked along, she passed through several streets lined by well-maintained two-story houses, most of which were surrounded by beautiful flowers and encircled by green grass.

As she approached a large cream-colored house, Silvana detected children's voices. She looked in the yard and saw a huge pool. Caucasian children played in the water. A woman and a man reclined in lawn chairs, enjoying their drinks.

"Where is the pharmacy?" Silvana asked herself.

Frustrated, she turned left at the end of the street, and to her surprise saw fewer houses. She suddenly found herself in an empty lot full of tall grass.

I'm lost, she thought, upset that she had not taken her cell phone with her. Otherwise, she would have called Mark to come get her. She kept walking straight, hoping to find a residential area.

Finally, she started hearing children's shouts. She came across old and short clay houses. Some of them had palm leaves on the tops of them, and old canvas in place of the windows.

She noticed a thin, underfed goat tied to a pole. A bare-chested boy sat near the goat, eating rice from an old aluminum bowl. His belly was bloated and his bone structure too thin. His eyes were sunken back in their sockets. Four thin children between ages 7 and 12, their heads shaved, ran toward her, playing tag. They then started running in circles around Silvana.

"Hey boys, run somewhere else," said Silvana.

One of them smiled. "I am not a boy, but a girl," said the girl.

"Leave her alone!" Silvana heard a woman's voice shouting.

She turned toward the voice and noticed an African woman standing with a stroller not far from a clay house that, instead of a door, had a piece of fabric hanging over the entrance. The children ran away, laughing.

The woman, a Kenyan native, pushed the stroller toward Silvana.

"Good morning," said the woman courteously, flashing her white teeth.

"Good morning," answered Silvana.

"Please forgive my children for disturbing you. Ever since their father left us for another woman they have been misbehaving," the African woman said.

"Oh, I am so sorry," said Silvana, looking at the children.

"There is no need to worry. He was beating me and absconding with my hard-earned money." The children came up to the woman and stood silently next to her.

While talking to her, Silvana found out that the woman was living in poverty, surviving on one dollar per day. Sometimes she was forced to beg online for monetary help. This did not help much; there were many who viewed her as merely a fraudulent African woman of some sort. The female glanced directly at Silvana with a quizzical look on her face. "Are you from around here?" She was obviously surprised that someone of Silvana's looks and apparent wealth would be in her neighborhood.

Silvana smiled and gestured at her surroundings. "I got lost. Do you know where I can find a pharmacy?" she asked, puzzled.

"Walk straight down two streets. On the third one, turn right, continue walking. Then turn right again. As soon as you turn right, you will see a pharmacy on the left side."

Silvana looked helplessly at the street in front of her. "So many turns, I may not remember all your directions and get lost," Silvana said sheepishly. She shrugged her shoulders.

"I will walk with you," offered the woman.

"Thank you. That's so sweet of you." Silvana beamed; here was an unexpected blessing. "What is your name?"

"Rehema," answered the African woman.

As they walked, Silvana glanced over at Rehema, and beheld a tall and thin African woman with short black curly hair, around 33 years old, her face bearing the imprints of a hard life.

Down the streets they walked, passing by some big houses where rich white people lived. Then they came across some more old houses of the Kenyan people.

"Where are you from?" asked Rehema.

"I'm from Azerbaijan," replied Silvana.

"How long have you been here?" her new friend asked.

"About two years."

"Do you like living in Kenya?" asked Rehema.

"Yes," lied Silvana.

They turned yet another corner.

"Here is a pharmacy," said Rehema, pointing at a small, old building.

"Thank you," said Silvana, with a grateful smile on her face.

"Will you be able to find your way back?" asked Rehema.

Silvana shook her head. "With a number of turns we made, I forgot the direction."

"Then I will wait for you. We will walk back," suggested Rehema.

"Thank you, Rehema. You are so kind."

"It's not a big deal, really."

Silvana entered the pharmacy and looked around. She saw a local man with torn clothing begging for money, so she gave him a few Kenyan shillings. After buying some Cataflam, she left the pharmacy.

They walked back together and approached Rehema's house. Silvana's acquaintance stopped. The female began to look for something in her old and peeling brown bag. She took out a piece of paper. Then she wrote down her name and a number.

"I mind other people's children and clean. If you need help, please call me," said Rehema, giving the piece of paper to Silvana. "I am desperate for a new job because the couple for whom I am working is moving back to the USA. I need a job so I can buy food for my kids and send them to school."

"I will call you if I need assistance. Thank you; from here I can find my way back." Silvana headed home.

***

Two years into their marriage, Silvana and Mark decided to have children. She stopped using birth control pills, hoping to get pregnant. Although they tried for a year to conceive, they were unsuccessful. Her inability to get pregnant disappointed Silvana.

On one Wednesday morning after Mark left, she knelt next to the bed and prayed to God: Why do those who give away or neglect children get pregnant easily? Although I love children, I cannot conceive. Jesus Christ, please give me a child.

Deep in her heart, she felt that God would answer her prayers. Silvana got up, filled with joy. Feeling hopeful Mark's wife sang as she cleaned the house.

After numerous failed attempts and resulting disappointments, Silvana finally noticed that her period was delayed. She told Mark about it. He suggested that she perform a pregnancy test.

On that day, he came back home early and gave Silvana a pregnancy test strip, which she took immediately. They waited for the lines to emerge. When both lines appeared, Silvana jumped for joy.

"Wow, God answered my prayers! I'm pregnant. We are going to have a baby!" she screamed gleefully.

"You need to see a gynecologist to ensure that you are eating correctly and taking all your vitamins," suggested Mark. Silvana could see the joy in his sparkling eyes.

"Oh, God, I can't believe I'm pregnant."

"Don't overdo it with your happiness. At an early stage, you can still lose it," warned Mark.

Silvana frowned and glared at him. "Why are you always negative?"

"I'm not negative, but I know how life works."

Silvana shook her head slowly. He'll never change.

She went back into the bedroom, sat on the bed, and picked up a book to read.

In the morning, Mark took Silvana for a check-up. The gynecologist performed an ultrasound to confirm the pregnancy and prescribed vitamins.

After a few days, Mark decided to stop by a children's shop to check prices for baby items. In looking over all the merchandise, he came upon some cute, white baby shoes, which he snapped up and purchased. Silvana was baffled by his purchase.

"Mark, you can't buy anything for the baby until I reach five months in my pregnancy. It is too early. Anything can happen to a fetus at this stage," said Silvana, glancing at the white shoes.

Mark handed them to her. "They are so beautiful and tiny that I couldn't resist." Mark beamed, radiating with joy.

Silvana put away the baby shoes. Mark's spouse decided not to buy anything until she reached Month Five of her pregnancy.

On the third month, Silvana developed cramps and slight bleeding. Concerned, Mark took her to see the gynecologist.

As Dr. Mbuki, the gynecologist, performed an ultrasound, Mark asked, "Is the baby well?"

The gynecologist stared at the ultrasound monitor. "I'm trying to locate a heartbeat, but can't."

She measured the size of the fetus. It was smaller than usual. She turned toward Mark.

"I'm sorry, but the embryo has started decomposing. Your wife needs to go to a medical clinic to clean her uterus as soon as possible before anything detrimental enters her bloodstream."

Mark was shocked at hearing the gynecologist's words. Silvana felt as if the whole world had fallen on her. She looked at the gynecologist with sadness in her eyes.

"Are you sure?" she asked, still hoping.

"Yes, I am. There is no heartbeat, and the fetus has shrunk. In checking through your uterus, I noticed fibroids that need to be removed. If you leave them, you may continue having miscarriages," Dr. Mbuki told them.

"When can you perform the D&C and remove the fibroids?" Mark asked, barely keeping his tears back.

The doctor looked at her calendar. "The procedure can be done on October 23rd at the Kenyan Wellness Clinic. Please arrive at 10 a.m. Don't eat or drink anything beforehand."

"Thank you, Dr. Mbuki," A wry smile twisted Silvana's lips as she gazed at the doctor.

After paying the doctor's fees, they went back home feeling dejected. Mark picked up the baby shoes and looked at them, crying. Silvana stared at Mark, keeping back her tears and feeling sorry for him. Overcome with sorrow and fury, she kept staring at him silently, feeling a constriction in her throat.

"Last week I saw a beautifully-carved crib. I was planning to buy it, but now the baby is gone." He kept sobbing, covering his face with the tiny shoes.

Silvana's heart filled with pity. She gave him a hug.

"Mark, don't cry. We will try again." She felt like crying herself, and wondered why everything in life came to her with such difficulty.

The doctor removed Silvana's fibroids and cleaned her uterus. After the procedure, Silvana felt weaker and depressed. She lay in bed without doing anything except stare at the ceiling.

Why me? Why do I always have to be disappointed in everything?

Seeing how depressed she was, Mark said, "We need to hire a helper for you. I will ask around for assistance."

"I know someone who I can call," said Silvana.

She got out of bed, picked up her handbag and looked for Rehema's phone number. After finding it, Silvana picked up the phone and sat on the bed. She dialed the female's number waiting for her to answer.

After they had greeted one another, Silvana reminded her that they had met when she was searching for a pharmacy. She then asked if Rehema was available to clean, iron, and cook. Rehema was indeed available, so Silvana supplied her address: Strausa Street, House 18, blue-coloured with a gray roof. After asking her new maid to arrive at 8 a.m. Silvana got off the phone.

On Monday, Rehema arrived exactly on time. She rang the doorbell. Silvana opened it.

"Good morning," said the housekeeper, happy that she had finally found a job.

"Hello," answered Silvana. "Please come in."

Rehema entered, gazing around. "You have a beautiful house."

"Oh, thank you."

Silvana showed her every room, including the kitchen. "I would like you to sweep, mop, tidy up the bathrooms. Sometimes you might clean the windows and iron. How does that sound?"

"Yes, no problem. Where can I change my clothes?" asked Rehema.

"You can change in the bathroom."

The maid went in and put on short pants and an old blouse. After that, she performed her duties.

Rehema came five times a week. She taught Silvana how to cook Kenyan food, cleaned for her, and even went with Silvana to the market. Silvana was delighted to have a housekeeper with whom she could go out and talk about things that worried her, including her conflicts with Mark, who sometimes swore at Silvana in front of Rehema. Seeing Mark's rudeness, the maid felt sorry for Silvana. She couldn't understand why Mark treated a good wife like Silvana in such a shameful manner. Sometimes, as she changed her clothes in the bathroom, Rehema cried, thinking of Silvana's plight. She herself feared him.

Five months passed by. Silvana unexpectedly found out that she was pregnant again. Although the couple was happy about it, at the same time Silvana remained worried that she would miscarry. During the early stages of pregnancy, Silvana felt nauseous. She would crave pickles but hated the smell of fish. As soon as she smelled fish, it made her vomit. At five months, her legs began to swell. By the time Silvana reached six months of her pregnancy, Mark had bought a crib, neutral clothes, and baby bottles. Mark was so excited; he couldn't wait until he could hold his child in his arms.

At about 10 p.m., one night during her seventh month of pregnancy, Silvana's water broke while she was sleeping. She woke up, feeling wet, and thought that she had accidentally wet the bed. Then she realized what had happened.

"Mark, get up!" she said, shaking him awake.

When she told him that her water had broken, Mark quickly jumped out of bed. He hurried to throw on some clothes.

"Change your clothes and get your bag with the baby stuff. We are going to the clinic."

Silvana quickly changed. She got the suitcase that she had packed a month earlier.

When they reached the hospital, the nurse directed them to a room. It had one bed, a television, and a chair. Silvana lay down on the bed. Mark sat on the chair.

After an hour, the nurse came with the wheelchair. "I'm taking you to the delivery room."

Silvana sat in the wheelchair.

"Can I come, too?" asked Mark.

"Yes, but put on this gown, please."

The nurse gave Mark a cap, blue gown, and big cotton socks to put on over his shoes. When he was ready, Silvana was taken to the delivery room.

She sat on the delivery bed as an anesthesiologist gave her an epidural injection.

Mark almost fainted at the size of the needle. Feeling weak, he sat down on the chair provided.

Silvana lay down on the bed. Then the doctor cut below her belly, and the baby was delivered. The nurse put the baby on Silvana's chest and she hugged her newborn.

"Why is her head so sticky?" she asked, touching her child's head.

"The baby was in a sac full of fluid," answered the pediatrician. He took the child from her and checked her vital organs as Mark silently watched them.

"The baby is fine," said the pediatrician. He handed the baby to a nurse.

Mark approached the doctor, concern on his face.

"What is her weight?" he asked.

"She is four pounds and sixteen ounces."

"Wow, she is so tiny. Can I hold her?"

The nurse gave the baby, a girl, to Mark. His eyes became wet as he smiled tenderly at his daughter. He held his child for a little while in his arms, filled with pride and joy. He then gave her back to the nurse. After dressing the baby and wrapping her in a blanket, the nurse took the baby to the nursery.

Silvana felt pain below her navel. The nurse rolled her back to the room on a gurney, where she helped Silvana into the bed. After that she left, but soon came back with the newborn child. She put the baby in Silvana's arms and withdrew again. Silvana was jubilant to hold her tiny daughter, who they named Marie, in her arms.

"Mark, I'm so glad that we were able to have her. At first, when I couldn't get pregnant, I thought I would never have children. All this time I was afraid of miscarrying."

Mark took Marie from Silvana and stared lovingly at her. "She is so pale and frail," he said, cradling her in his arms. His facial expression softened. "I'm happy that we bought everything beforehand. Now we don't have to worry about anything.

"You're right, but we did forget one item. Please get diapers for her."

"I will buy them as soon as I leave here."

Soon after, he left the clinic, promising to return in the evening. He went to the store and bought four big packs of diapers. He came back at 9 p.m., and settled down to sleep in a chair by the bed. Seeing him sitting uncomfortably in the chair, Silvana felt sorry for him. She told him to go home, that she would be fine.

Mark got up from the chair and kissed Silvana on her forehead.

"You did a good job," he said, and left.

Silvana tried to fall asleep but couldn't. She heard a baby crying and wondered if it was Marie. She wanted to get up and go to the nursery, but when she tried to move, the pain in her abdomen increased.

Oh, the pain is killing me. Why are the nurses not checking on the baby?

She again tried to sit up, but to no avail. Silvana decided to slide her legs off the bed and see if she could stand up that way. She slid down to where her feet could touch the floor and stood up, holding onto the bed. Slowly, she made small steps, the pain almost unbearable. Tears ran down her face as she slowly walked to the door, opened it. Then Silvana proceeded toward the nursery.

She entered the nursery and looked around, searching for her baby. Silvana found Marie in the back of the room in a small bassinet. Marie was sound asleep; it was another baby that was crying. She stood for a while, looking at her child, and then left the room. She slowly walked to the reception area, trying to find a nurse.

Upon seeing one, she said, "A baby in the nursery is crying." Then she walked back to her room.

Silvana stayed in the clinic for two days. Afterward she was sent home with her daughter. With Marie's arrival, Silvana's life turned into a whirlwind. She was getting up at nights feeding Marie, and during the day felt tired. In order to get a breath of fresh air when the sun went down, Silvana took Marie for a ride, walking with the stroller around the neighborhood.

Marie was an amazingly beautiful infant who slept most of the day. However, whenever she was hungry or had gas, she cried nonstop. Mark walked with Marie at nights, trying to burp her. He loved his child and made sure that she had everything.

Silvana liked this side of Mark. Slowly, she began to trust him again. She stopped getting up at nights to check on him. He continued to drink, but at least he had stopped looking at porn and writing to women.

However, one Saturday night, Mark went out to drink leaving Silvana alone with Marie. Silvana was sleepy, but tried to stay awake and wait for Mark. She looked at her watch and saw it was midnight. Mark's wife couldn't understand how he could leave her and the child alone at home.

Marie woke up and started crying. Silvana gently put Marie on her bed to feed her, and then went downstairs. Upset that Mark's drinking was more important than his family's security, Silvana emptied his bottle of Johnny Walker Black in the sink. Then she fixed milk for the child. She went upstairs and bottle-fed Marie.

As had become the norm, Mark came home drunk. He entered the bedroom.

"I'm back," he said, swaggering in.

"Why are you leaving us at home so late? Criminals could come and kill us," scolded Silvana.

"Leave me alone!"

"I emptied your Johnny Walker Black!"

Furious, Mark picked up Silvana's slipper from the ground. He pelted it at his wife, barely missing her.

Silvana picked Marie up from the pillow where she had been lying. "I'm feeding the baby. How can you throw a slipper at me? It could have hit her."

Mark made a step forward and fell on the floor. He got up slowly.

"If you hadn't chucked out my liquor, I wouldn't have thrown the slipper at you, idiot." Staggering, he went into the bathroom. He puked, as usual.

"I am only wasting money on her," she heard him mumble.

***

Marie grew into a happy toddler. She loved to walk around the house and open all the doors, especially the kitchen cupboards. She would walk into the kitchen and take out containers from the cupboard. Whenever Silvana saw her kitchen things on the floor, she would shake her head smiling, then put Marie into the playpen.

As Marie sat there, Silvana taught her the alphabet, numbers, shapes. The happy mother even played classical and nursery music for her child.

By two and half years, Marie was potty-trained. She could identify letters, shapes, and numbers. However, she was noisy. She would cry loudly, as if someone was hurting her, even if no one was near her.

On an unbearably hot day, Marie felt miserable. She was unusually hyperactive and noisy. When Mark came home from work, Marie was running around and shouting.

Mark looked at Silvana disapprovingly. "She is making too much noise. I'm expecting an important phone call. Take her upstairs now!"

"She is just playing. When you get the phone call, we will go upstairs," answered Silvana. She continued to allow Marie to play in the living room.

Mark sat at the table. He waited for the phone call, all the time looking crossly at Marie. When the phone rang, he answered, and gestured angrily toward his daughter. The child approached him, talking loudly. To her surprise, Mark kicked her. She fell on the ground and cried.

Silvana quickly ran to her, regretting that she hadn't taken her upstairs. She hugged Marie, trying to soothe her, and took her out of the living room. After crying for a while, Marie was feeling better. She seemed to have forgotten the incident. She was jumping on the bed and laughing when Mark came upstairs.

"Why are you letting her jump on the bed? If you can't control her now, what will she grow into? Trash?"

Silvana got up from the bed, enraged. "She is just a small child. Most children make noise, jump, and run. Why did you kick her? You could have hurt her." She scowled at him.

"It's your fault. If you had followed my instructions and had taken her upstairs, none of this would have happened."

"When I was bottle-feeding her, you pelted a slipper at me! Was that my fault as well?"

"Yes! You should keep your mouth shut and your hands off my alcohol!" retorted Mark.

"You are always trying to make me look as if I were wrong or stupid. I keep having to stand up for myself. I can't just stand by, keep my mouth shut, and let you put me down time after time."

"If you didn't do such stupid things, I wouldn't make you look as if you are dumb and foolish."

Silvana lifted Marie off the bed. "I don't do anything stupid. Your problem is you think that everyone is stupid and you are smarter than everyone else." Upset, Silvana bolted from the bedroom.

After a while, once things had settled down again between them, Mark and Silvana decided to have one more child. After two more miscarriages, Silvana got pregnant. She gave birth to Peter. While Silvana was in the clinic with Peter, Rehema stayed with Marie.

Mark again purchased many clothes for Peter. From the very time that the children entered his life, he loved shopping for them. He even bought a second crib and a new stroller for his son.

Silvana's children became her joys and miracles. She was extremely grateful to God for them. Later, Silvana gave birth to two more children; a daughter, Aygun, and a son, David.

When the children grew older, Silvana sent first Marie, and then later Peter, to kindergarten, but kept Aygun and David at home. Silvana's children were bright and talented compared to other children in the kindergarten. By the age of three, all of them could read well, because Silvana had spent a lot of time teaching them.

Mark enrolled Marie in the British International School. Later, Peter, Aygun, and David joined her. Silvana knew that the children's good future depended on a sound education. She made sure that they studied well, and she spent a great deal of time with them doing homework.

However, dealing with both the children and the house frustrated Silvana. She felt that she had too many responsibilities weighing on her shoulders, and wondered why Mark didn't help her at all. His only help was to pay the bills and to buy food. Every day when the children came home from school, Silvana checked their bags, went through each schoolbook with them, gave them their meals, went outside with them. Even when she was ill, she couldn't afford to stay in bed, because she knew that Mark wouldn't lift a finger to help her or to do homework with the children. Mark didn't even bother to so much as change light bulbs in his house; rather, he asked Silvana to change them. He shirked his responsibility of dealing with the laborers and the gardeners, shifting it onto her shoulders.

***

While Silvana stayed at home to look after the children and the house, Mark still went out with his friends, always coming back late. As the days passed, he continued to bully her. She disliked being terrorized or treated like a mere housekeeper by him. Instead she wanted to be able to tell him what she thought, or what would make her happy. However, because of his frigid personality as well as disapproval of her, she kept everything to herself and grew increasingly irritated by the day.

Silvana realized that she wasn't happy at all in her marriage. She couldn't forgive Mark for not acknowledging her abilities, and for not being there for her emotionally. How could she forgive him when he consistently hurt her feelings? She had had enough of her controlling husband. This woman yearned for the freedom to do what made her happy, the freedom to be herself, and not to have someone in her life who always made her feel guilty or worthless.

At the same time, Silvana was concerned that if the children continued to see her emotionally abused, they might grow up to become dysfunctional parents themselves. Therefore, she wanted to get out of her marriage and start a new life. Without a job, though, she couldn't make the steps to be financially independent or stable. How could she take care of her children or give them a good life as well as education without funds? Where would she go, in a foreign country with no true friends or relatives to rely on?

When the children started primary school, Silvana looked for a job and took driving lessons. Within two months, she learned how to drive an automobile and passed her driver's test. Mark bought a car for her. Before letting Silvana drive alone, he decided to go with her for a test drive. It was a windy day. The leaves flew all over the street. Mark sat in the passenger seat next to Silvana. She started the engine, trying not to be nervous. Next, she put her foot on the accelerator. The car moved smoothly, and she relaxed.

"So far, you are doing well," said Mark.

She smiled proudly. However, her happiness was short-lived. As she approached a traffic light, she started to slow down. What happened next was a shock to her.

"Why are you stopping in the middle of the road? Drive the stupid car, stupid idiot!" Mark shouted angrily, slapping her hand hard.

The pain in her hand made her tear up, but she tried to stay calm. "Why did you hit me?"

"I wasted enough money for you to learn how to drive. How can you stop in the middle of the road?" he snapped.

"I wasn't stopping. I was slowing down because of the traffic light," Silvana said meekly.

"You're always making stupid mistakes. If I had known you were like this, I would never have brought you here. I'd have abandoned you to your poor family."

Silvana continued driving silently, trying to hide her tears. She decided not to drive with him in the car ever again, and to find a job as soon as possible. Finding work was the ticket to her freedom and the hope for a new life. She was an ambitious woman who wanted to develop her career and become a motivational speaker. She knew that she could be that woman with God's help, along with her persistence and knowledge.

After a long search, Silvana got a job as an assistant in a construction company. She was happy to work and be around people. At first, her co-workers weren't friendly toward her, but after knowing Silvana for some time, they accepted her into their circles.

Silvana became good friends with her co-worker, Jabary. Sometimes during their lunch break, they went to the bank or to buy lunch together. He had a problem with his bossy and overbearing wife. She was always picking on him and making him look like a fool in front of others. Silvana started to encourage Jabary to stand up for himself.

Once while Jabary waited for a call from his wife, who was at the doctor's, he and Silvana had lunch.

Silvana asked, "Jabary, why are you allowing your wife to treat you with such disrespect? She always puts you down in public. You should put her in her place." Silvana took a sip of cola.

"My wife is extremely jealous, of everyone and everything. If I treat her the same way she treats me, I will bring myself down to her level."

"However, if you continue to keep quiet, she will continue embarrassing you in front of others. You are a man, and can't allow a woman to treat you like a mop. People will stop respecting you," said Silvana, picking at her noodles with a fork.

"I don't care what others think about me. I have a good job, children, and that's all I care about."

Silvana grimaced inwardly. I just cannot understand why he stays with a control freak. Is it because of material things or social status that he keeps her company?

"Did you know that my wife knows your spouse? I heard they both studied at the same university in the UK."

Silvana glanced up sharply at Jabary and almost choked on her food. She coughed, her eyes getting teary.

"Are you okay?"

"Yes, I am, but you surprised me with your news. I never knew they were acquainted. How did you find out?"

"I overheard her conversation with him about you," said Jabary.

Silvana looked at her watch. "You should hurry and pick her up from the doctor before she opens her big mouth."

"I'm not going to rush, since she will still find a reason to open her poisonous mouth," said Jabary, trying to finish his lunch.

Why can't the ground just swallow that witch? he thought to himself.

He swallowed his tension in an attempt to calm himself. Sometimes he was so fed up with his wife's behavior that he wanted to beat her. However, he was too awkward and uncertain to stand up for himself.

Jabary's phone rang, but he ignored it at first.

"Answer the phone. I'm sure she is calling you," suggested Silvana.

Jabary looked at his phone to see the number of the caller. Seeing his wife's number, he answered.

"Yes?"

"Where are you?" his wife Bapoto shouted. Silvana could hear her from where she was sitting.

"I'm on my lunch break," Jabary answered in an exasperated tone.

Jabary squeezed his hand in a fist to pool the tension mounting within his body. Like a fool, I allowed her money to lure me into her arms. Now I am paying for all of this. He shook his head, agitated, and started coughing.

"Worthless, why are you taking so long to come for me?" screamed Bapoto.

Jabary looked at his watch. "You told me to come at 2.20 p.m. It is only half past 1 p.m., so you will see me in fifty minutes."

Annoyed with Jabary, his wife hung up the phone.

Silvana grimaced disapprovingly, shaking her head. "Haven't you learned by now her true nature? She treats you as if you are her servant."

She shook her head at Bapoto's behavior. "Your wife works as a CEO for a multinational company. She has more money and a better job than you do. With those who have money or power, she speaks nicely, but with simple people like you, she is impatient, bossy and hangs up the phone whenever she feels like it."

"You're right, but she is my wife. I can't change her or quarrel with her," he said with a frown. She is a blood-sucking vampire, treating me as if I am her toy, he thought.

"Well, I feel sorry for you. How could you forget about your pride, dignity, liberty, and accept abuse from a female just so you wouldn't lose a comfortable life? If I did not have children, I would rather lose a comfortable life. I would struggle, raise my voice, stand up for my rights, and be treated with love and respect. However, I must consider my kids first."

She pointed her fork at her friend. "If you allow people to treat you like shit, you will always be dealing with shit, and allowing them to use or manipulate you. You have to be able to stand up for yourself, man!"

Without another word, Jabary got up from the table and threw away his leftovers. They left the eatery and, once outside, they stood between Silvana's Nissan and Jabary's Mazda.

"Why then do you tolerate your abusive husband's behavior? Is his money so important to you?" Jabary asked suddenly.

Surprised as well as angered by Jabary's question, she stared at him. "How can you suggest that I am staying with him because of his money? The money, the house; these do not make me happy. In any event, he doesn't give me any money at all."

Silvana's eyes narrowed. "Don't you know I hate that jail? To hell with his house and money! I stay with him because of my children. I don't have a place to go or money to look after them. I have to put my children's needs before my own."

"I didn't mean that you stay with him because of money. I just can't understand why you are not trying to get away from his abuse," said Jabary, regretting that he had mentioned Silvana's insulting husband.

Jabary looked at his watch. "My wife is waiting for me. I need to be at the clinic as soon as possible."

"But you were the one who didn't want to rush."

"I know, but today I'm getting a headache. I can't take any arguments. You know how she can be," stated Jabary, faking a smile.

Silvana frowned. "I can't understand people like your wife. She takes part in every church activity, and is so nice to her friends. Nevertheless, when it comes to simple people, she acts rudely. Unfortunately, I met many people like her in Mark's Anglican Church. That's why I stopped going there. They are just fooling themselves and others, thinking that going to church or praying will save them. First, they should show love, compassion, and respect toward poor and simple people. This will show that they are truly following God."

Jabary's eyes dropped. "I love her. I just can't live without her." He looked up again and gazed intently into Silvana's eyes. "However, you are not as helpless as you think. You can go to the shelter for abused women or to your church. They will help you."

"What church are you talking about? The one where the priest refused to help me in my worst times? He said that he has his burdens to carry, and I should not place my hardships on him. I don't want to even step into his church again. I don't trust such people. I can't stay with my children any other place as it stands. Did you not hear about the child abuse cases in those shelters?"

She recalled the night in a camp when she was a nine-year-old girl, when she felt someone's hand passing over her bottom. Feeling the touch, she got up right away, and saw a young man standing over her with his pants down. As soon as he saw her awake he ran away, leaving Silvana's heart fearful and with a profound distrust of men. Because of experiences like this, she made certain that her children, and every child in her care, were safe, secure, and never left any of them alone with a male or strangers. She shrugged her shoulders, trying to flush away her memories.

Jabary looked at his watch again, opened the door of his car, and got in. "I have to go now."

"Okay, see you tomorrow," said Silvana.

Arriving home, Silvana opened the door and went inside.

"Good afternoon, Rehema," she said when she saw her housekeeper.

"Good afternoon, Miss Jonson. Your husband called. He plans to go to the bank, and wants you to go along. He is on his way to pick you up."

"I was planning to relax before the children came home." Her irritated voice echoed in Rehema's ears.

Silvana heard Mark's car approaching.

"He is already here. I didn't even get a chance to change my work clothes." She raked her fingers through her hair in frustration.

"When the children come home, please give them something to eat and drink. Don't allow them to play outside alone," Silvana told Rehema.

"Okay. You'd better go before he starts quarreling," said the maid.

Silvana went back out and got into Mark's car.

"How was your day?" he asked.

"It was okay. What about you?"

"It wasn't so good. My stupid assistant is always absent, but we can't fire her. Today, as usual, she didn't come into the office. I ended up doing her work as well as my own."

He parked in front of the bank, and they went in together. Silvana's high-heeled shoes made a tapping noise on the tiled floor, which annoyed her husband. Mark glanced over at Silvana shaking his head in disapproval.

After paying the phone bill, Mark walked back to his car, followed by Silvana.

"Why can't you walk without making so much noise? You must be walking abnormally," said Mark, irritated, as they drove.

"I'm not walking abnormally."

"Yes, you are. Your shoes are making too much noise when you walk."

"Most women wearing high heels make noise when walking on tiles," remarked Silvana.

"Listen to me, weirdo. When I say you are walking abnormally, don't try to prove me wrong!" shouted Mark, shaking slightly.

"But you are wrong."

Mark suddenly stopped the car.

"You zero, I work with women. I can tell they are not making any noise. Get out of my damned car."

Seeing Mark shaking, Silvana feared he would hit her. She remained quietly seated in the car. Mark started the car and continued driving.

***

Mark loved Kenya so much that he decided to settle down permanently there. Thereby he bought a two-story house from an English couple. The house was located in the same area as their rental.

On the first floor, they had a kitchen with green walls and white cupboards, a living and television room with cream-colored walls, and a bathroom. On the second floor, they had four bedrooms with bathrooms and a study room for the children.

Before they moved to the house, Silvana spent some time selecting the colors for each room and bought lovely curtains. She adored living in the new house, but somehow she never considered it as hers, feeling like a stranger in the house. Mark always reminded her that the house wasn't hers. She knew that one day she would leave it behind. Silvana planned to work diligently, save money, and one day purchase her own. That way no one would be able to tell her that the house wasn't hers.

On a rainy morning, Silvana sent the children to school as usual, but instead of going to work she visited a heart specialist. She had always suffered from high blood pressure, but she was experiencing chest pain as well.

As soon as her children left, Silvana decided to clean the house before going to her appointment. Because it was Rehema's day off, Silvana washed the dishes and then cleaned the first floor. As she cleaned, she sang in her language. She loved singing. It made her feel happy. As soon as she finished cleaning downstairs, Silvana got ready to leave the house for her appointment.

In the clinic, the medic checked Silvana's heart and performed a stress test, but didn't find anything wrong.

After her appointment, as soon as she arrived home, Silvana continued cleaning the bedrooms and bathrooms. When she finished with the upstairs, she sat in front of the computer, making video slides of the children's photographs. She sang as she did so.

Mark arrived home early and unexpectedly. He entered the bedroom. "I didn't know that you didn't go to work," he said.

"I told you before that I had an appointment for today. That's why I stayed at home."

"What did the doctor say?"

"He said nothing is wrong with my heart."

"How much did you spend for your tests?"

"800 hundred shilling."

"So, you paid this money just to hear that nothing was wrong with you, again wasting my money! Dummy!"

Mark stormed out of the bedroom. Silvana, now disenchanted with her project, went downstairs and started ironing.

"Why is my bathroom soaking wet?" Mark yelled from upstairs.

"I was mopping," replied his wife.

"I can't use the bathroom this way. My socks will get wet. I need a towel to put on the floor. Stop ironing and bring a towel from the cupboard," Mark demanded in an irritated tone.

"I'm hanging a shirt on a hanger. Why can't you get a towel yourself?"

"No, you bring it! I can't walk on the wet floor."

Silvana climbed upstairs, took out two small towels from the cupboard. She gave them to him. He grabbed the towels from her and pushed her into the bathroom door.

"Why are you pushing me?" Silvana asked, distraught.

"Why did you bring small towels? They are too small and can't cover the floor," Mark snapped.

"Why don't you take one towel and dry the floor with it instead of spreading towels all over?" suggested Silvana.

"Don't mop my house, twit."

"If I didn't persist in cleaning my house regularly, it would indeed become and remain untidy," retorted Silvana.

"You don't have any house!"

He looked at the shelf in the bathroom and noticed Silvana's deodorant and perfume on it. He threw them in the garbage can.

"Why are you throwing my things away?"

"I told you, stupid. Don't put your things next to mine!" screamed Mark.

"But they are not taking a lot of space," said Silvana, on the verge of tears. She held back, though, so he wouldn't see her cry; instead, she left him alone and returned to ironing. He went to the cupboard and purposely removed a few towels and sheets. Mark spread them in the bathroom.

Before he had come home, Silvana had been in a good mood, but as soon as he opened his mouth, Silvana's heart filled with desperation and fury. She was so furious that she could barely keep herself from going to the kitchen and smashing windows with her bare hands, hoping that her wrists would get cut and that she would bleed to death. This way she wouldn't be taking abuse or his nagging any longer. However, she stopped herself when she thought about her children's future if she were to die. She knew that, without her, they would be lost and unhappy. If I were to die, he would treat all of them like animals, she thought.

She was emotionally tired and wished to get away from all of this, but she couldn't. She stood by the ironing board, praying silently, begging God for help.

Please help me escape. I can't take it any longer. Tears dropped on the shirt that she was ironing. Do you hear me, God? I can't live like this any longer! Why are you not helping me to find a way out? She felt so lonely and betrayed.

Silvana stopped crying and wiped her tears with her sleeve. Suddenly, she felt a compelling urge to end her life in order to escape from Mark and this unhappy, meaningless existence. She angrily looked up as if trying to see her Creator.

Is this what you want me to do? Why can't you hear my cry for help? Tell me why!

Then she recalled a friend's words, to the effect that if she died, her children would grow without love, wondering why she had left them. Tears dropped from her eyes once again.

I can't even end my worthless life. My children will suffer, but I will enter hell. That's what the devil expects. She chased away the urge to die, determined to live and struggle for her children and to exit her situation as a winner.

One day I will rise, and nobody will push me away or mistreat me again.

***

While working, Silvana applied to Samson University to obtain her degree, paying for it with the money she made at her job. Every Saturday she attended classes, while Mark stayed with the children. It was difficult for her to study, work, and mind both the children and house at the same time. Even though the idea of bettering herself was exciting, she was frustrated because of other responsibilities, so she didn't sleep well.

One Saturday morning, when she missed her classes, Silvana prepared breakfast for her children and ensured that they took showers. Afterward, she went to play with them outside until lunchtime. They played soccer, ran, and jumped, just being happy kids.

After the children had lunch, she decided that Peter, Aygun, and David needed a change of clothes, since they had karate lessons later. Silvana told Marie not to change her skirt, since it was still clean.

Meanwhile, Mark was in a pub drinking with his friends. At 3 p.m. he came back home to take the children to their karate lessons.

When Mark arrived, Silvana was ironing in the living room. The ironing board blocked the way to the steps leading downstairs. When Mark came in carrying cases of water, Silvana was in his way, and this angered him.

"Dummy! Move out of my way! As usual, doing everything at the wrong time!" Mark yelled.

Silvana didn't bother responding; however, she removed her ironing board and stopped ironing. She felt hurt by his words and the fact that she could never please him. Nothing she did was ever good enough for him.

After taking the water downstairs, he came back up. "Did you get the children ready for their lessons?" he asked.

"Yes, I did."

Mark stared at Marie, frowning. "Did Mommy give you other clothes to wear?" he asked Marie. She didn't answer.

Instead, her mother responded, "Although I told her to keep on the same skirt, I asked her to change her blouse."

"Sicko! Instead of sitting in front of the computer, ensure that the children are ready for their classes!" yelled Mark.

"I wasn't in front of the computer. While you were drinking, I was playing with them outside, cleaning the house, and ironing. Because her skirt was appropriate, I did not ask her to change into another one."

"Your mother does not know how to wear clothes properly," Mark said to Marie. "Where she came from, they didn't teach her how to dress in a suitable fashion."

Not knowing what to say, Marie kept quiet.

Silvana snapped, "Why are you always badmouthing me to the children? Just leave me alone!"

"Shut up, stupid!" said Mark. Enraged, he went downstairs.

Silvana's eyes welled up, but she tried to control her emotions in front of her children. She was so enraged that she wanted to yell, Get the hell out of my life! She wanted him to feel the same way she felt whenever he directed hurtful words at her. However, for the sake of God and the children, she kept her mouth shut.

With tears in her eyes and in an extremely low voice, Marie said, "Mother, why is Daddy so rude? He does not love us. He curses at us in public. I am embarrassed to have a father like him."

She began to sob. "He called me to the bedroom and hit me for no reason. When I tried to leave, he hit me again." Marie began to shiver. She grabbed her mother's hand. "I didn't do anything wrong. Why did he hurt me?!"

Her voice rose in anger. "He always picks on me, and treats me as if I'm nobody."

Silvana hugged her daughter.

"He loves you, and always makes sure that you have everything. Drinking has influenced his behavior," said Silvana with a sad smile, barely holding back her tears. "When you grow up, please don't drink alcohol. It will destroy your family."

Aygun embraced her. "Mother, if he loves us, why does he hit us and call us dummies, stupid?" she asked.

Silvana didn't know what to say at first, then she blurted out, "He does not have God in his life! People like him don't know better."

Marie hugged her mother and said, "Mommy, don't listen to him, okay? He is a bully, but you are not stupid. Just ignore him." She gently patted her mother's head.

"Thank you, Marie," said Silvana, filled with sadness and heaviness in her heart.

"We could leave him in this house and move to a separate house," Marie suggested.

Just then, Mark shouted from the kitchen, "What is a container with food doing on the counter? Why it is not in the fridge?"

His voice intimidated Silvana.

"I left it out because after ironing, I was going to eat my lunch," she answered. Along with feeling hurt, Silvana's heart now filled with anger.

"You are always wasting food, but can't even make a dollar!" shouted Mark.

"Am I not working and making money?"

"Do you spend it on something other than yourself?" asked Mark.

"How can I spend money when I must pay my tuition for university?" asked Silvana, shaking.

However, Mark ignored her last words. "Lazy jackass, if you can't take care of your house, I can get someone else."

Silvana came down downstairs. "Are you not always saying that the house is not mine?"

Silvana's words infuriated Mark. He threw the container of rice on the floor. Then he walked over to the dish rack, picked up Silvana's plate from the edge of the counter. He threw it in the sink, breaking the glass that was in there.

"You can't even make money to buy anything. You lazy woman! Did I not tell you not to put anything on the edge of the counter? Damn it, I also broke a glass last time because of you, stupid animal."

"You just broke a glass just now, for no reason! You are the stupid animal, not me!" shouted Silvana.

Then she looked at the floor, which she had already cleaned. Rice was scattered all over. Silvana was about to lose all control because she simply had enough of this ridiculous nonsense. However, thinking about God and how He expected her to live helped her to not get frustrated. Faith in God gave her hope that soon this would be over and she would start a new, happy life. She just needed to wait until she saved enough money, and then apply for a divorce.

"Get a broom and clean up this mess!" ordered Mark.

"I'm not going to clean up your mess," Silvana said. She raised her hand and angrily clenched it into a fist. Instead of striking him, however, she went back upstairs, leaving the rice on the ground. Mark didn't bother to clean it up either; instead he left the house with the children.

As he drove, he kept talking to his children in a raised voice. "Your mother is stupid. I do not want you to be like her at all." He looked in the rear-view mirror at the children huddled in the back seat. "Make sure that you win your karate competition tomorrow. You didn't even practice. I suppose, however, that you still expect to win."

"Why are you squawking at us? Mother said we must always be positive so that good things will happen. She believes that we can win," said Aygun.

"Dummy, if you do not practice, you will not win anything. I should not have listened to her stupid advice to enter you into that competition. You are just wasting your time with these classes and are going to lose a match."

Marie looked at him, teary-eyed. "Why are you calling my mother stupid? Leave her alone!"

Mark glared at her in the mirror. "You shut up! Otherwise, you will end up as dumb as your mother!" he shouted.

The girls started crying without end. Seeing their state, Mark decided to turn back home.

As soon as they had left, Silvana had gone into the bedroom. Standing in front of her religious icons and crucifix, she begged God for help. Silvana's heart filled with sadness, despair, and loneliness. She started to cry bitterly.

"God, please help me, I beg you!" She hungered for hugs, kind words, but she was alone as usual. Her soul and heart cried for help, yet no one heard her cry. She had an urge to yell out loud so the whole world could hear and feel her pain, and know how lonely and unhappy she was.

Silvana continued sitting in front of her icons. She cried for about forty minutes. As usual, her heart filled with anger as she wept. She was angry with herself for marrying Mark and not having enough strength to break off her marriage. Before, she was mad at God, thinking that He had assigned her this kind of life. After learning more about her religion, she realized that God loved His people. He didn't make them suffer. He gave humans free will to make choices and stepped aside. However, because of people's unwise choices and sinful nature, they put themselves in adverse situations. Of her own free will, Silvana had decided to marry Mark and didn't try hard enough to get out of the marriage. Therefore, she knew it was her own fault for allowing chains of fear to keep her shackled.

At the same time, she questioned why God didn't do anything to assist her. Her friend told her that God would answer her prayers, but in His own time. However, for Silvana, God was taking too long to answer. As she sobbed, her fury toward her husband grew. She was angry with people because nobody was there for her. Why can't they just be there for me, as I'm here for them? She tried to stop weeping, but couldn't.

"Please have mercy on me, a sinner!" she shouted with anger. "I beg you, God, save me. Please help me find a better job, so I can apply for a divorce. I do not want poisonous people like him in my company. He only spreads negativity and harm."

It had been a sunny day, but suddenly a strong wind blew and rain fell. To Silvana, it seemed as if God himself cried together with her. She knelt in front of her icons praying fervently.

"Heavenly Father, Jesus Christ, Mother Mary, St. Nektarios, please hear my prayers. Show me a way. Do you not see that I'm unhappy and can't take the abuse any longer?" She raised her hands toward the sky. "St. Nektarios, I beg you to please help me to get another job soon. Mother Mary, don't you have a heart? Why are you not answering my prayers? Why are you not helping me? I feel so heartsick and lonely. Lord of Lords, I beg you to show mercy upon me."

Suddenly Silvana grew madder. She stopped praying, and called her spouse.

As soon as he answered, she said, "I regret that I married you. One day God will punish you for my every tear dropped, and you will be alone."

She hung up the phone and tried to quell her fury. She wiped her eyes so that her husband would not see that she had been crying, and decided to write a letter to a lawyer.

Silvana had visited a lawyer a few months before to get information about a divorce. The attorney had asked her to write down everything that her partner did to her. Silvana decided that now was a good time to do that, and started typing on her computer. The more she typed, the more distraught she became.

"I have been emotionally abused for years by my husband Mark. I have decided to stand up for my rights to be treated with respect, understanding, and love by applying for a divorce. Today, I am raising my voice against abuse! For him, I have been zero, weirdo, sicko, a stupid maid, and someone who would be eating from a garbage can without him. He even said I would be fired from any job, and that my Azeri family was trash who ate from the garbage.

"Recently, he took a long time setting up a keyboard for the children. I pressed a button on the keyboard. It changed the keyboard's settings. My partner got mad as hell and used vulgar words. As he did, he sprayed me with fly spray. He even hit me once with a side table.

"He cursed at me for more than twenty minutes when the children were home. They heard every word. I ended up crying in front of my kids, and they wept with me. Once he left the house and asked me to check when an IT person could come to fix the Internet. The IT technician fixed the Internet, and once it was operational he left. Right after, the Internet suddenly stopped working again. On the night of my husband's return, I did not sleep and stayed up waiting for him. When he arrived, his first words were, "Did the IT technician fix the Internet?" When I said that he fixed it, but then the Internet stopped working, he started cursing at me, using words such as dummy, stupid, weirdo, sicko etc. It made me regret that I had stayed up for him instead of sleeping. After that, I stopped waiting up for him.

"Another time our son Peter was playing a game without permission, one that his father had planned to give him within two weeks. When Mark came home from the bar, he discovered that the child was using the game. He picked up a plastic stick, went to the child's bedroom, and started hitting him all over his body, calling him fat boy and stupid, and demanding why he had taken the game without permission. The child was scared, crying and saying that he was sorry. I became so scared that I just stood and watched Mark hitting Peter. He then dragged Peter from the bed and continued beating him. He pulled him into another room downstairs, dropped him on the bare floor, and ordered the child to sleep there. When Mark left the room, I spread a sleeping bag for Peter to sleep in. At first, Peter was too afraid that Mark would hit him if he were to see him in the sleeping bag, so he continued lying down on the bare floor. I was barely able to convince him to sleep in the sleeping bag. After the beating, the child ended up with all sorts of bruises and marks all over his body."

As she typed the letter, Silvana's heart filled with anger, because she remembered everything as if it had happened the day before. She wiped her tears and continued typing.

"I refuse to take abuse from anyone any longer. I would appreciate it if the divorce process could start as soon as possible. My children and I deserve to be treated with love, care, and respect. Regards, Silvana Jonson."

There were so many things she wanted to write but decided to keep it short. Silvana ended her letter and then cleaned up the mess that Mark had made.

For a few days, she was annoyed with him and didn't even want to talk to him, but as usual he behaved as if nothing had happened and he had not done anything wrong. With her anger, frustration, and anxiety dissipated and flushed, it dawned on her that, no matter how severely he hurt her, she could not find it in herself to hate him or retaliate by treating him equally as poorly. In fact, she felt sorry for him to such an extent that she continued to interact with him as if he had never done any harm whatsoever. As she realized that divorce would in fact be detrimental to both of them, she began to feel guilty, and continuously prayed that one day he would find peace and happiness. Yet, nonetheless, she made no plans to tolerate his emotional abuse any longer.

Chapter 13: Unexpected Changes

After working for a year at the construction company, Silvana left her job. Her supervisor, Erik, was a controlling womanizer who had been giving women employees a rough time by either nagging them, picking on them, or touching them improperly. His inappropriate misconduct frustrated employees, forcing some of them to leave. Silvana couldn't understand how a married man who had a beautiful wife and two children could behave like such a jerk.

Once during a lunch break, Silvana stayed at her desk trying to finish entering information into the system. All morning Silvana had felt lightheaded, but at lunchtime, she became weaker and her eyes got blurry. Unable to function, she decided to take her lunch break.

As she pushed back her chair from the desk, Erik approached her.

"Did you finish entering the information?" he asked.

"No, I will finish after my lunch break."

Erik grabbed her hand, but she pulled it away. "Mr. Erik, please keep your hands off me."

Erik got mad, and decided to punish Silvana for rejecting him. "You can't take a lunch break until you finish your work."

"But other employees have already taken a lunch break. I have to rest my eyes. I'm feeling dizzy, and my eyes are blurry," said Silvana, frustrated.

"If you are sick, stay at home. You are not doing anything important; therefore, anyone can do your work."

Then Erik removed his phone from his pocket. As he looked at something on the screen, he asked, "Why did you use that as your profile picture? Your enlarged belly betrays a pregnancy that you cannot cover with your hand."

Silvana's eyes bulged. She stood motionless, not knowing how best to respond. Is he blind? she thought.

She always heard compliments from others about her slim figure, so how could he think that she had a huge belly? She knew that, in the picture he was looking at, she had posed for the photograph with her muscular hand firmly on her belly. He had the nerve, cheek, and gall to think that she was concealing it! Silvana bit her lip, doing her best to keep her mouth shut, which she was barely able to do. She had the urge to exclaim, "Check your eyes, man!"

Silvana got up from her desk, agitated, and started walking away. Erik suddenly blurted out, "Why are you wearing big shoes? They look ridiculous on you."

Silvana made her hand into a fist, clenching it tightly, and opened the door with the other. She left for lunch without another word to Erik. Silvana knew if she opened her mouth, she would curse, and that would be unprofessional.

As soon as she came back from her lunch break, Silvana rushed to finish her work. At the end of the working day, to top things off, Silvana found out that Erik didn't need the information for another few days.

Not long after, Silvana stayed at her desk during her lunch break. Again, Erik approached her.

"What are you doing at your desk? You can't have a lunch break at your desk."

"Since I'm not having lunch, I stayed here."

"I'm unable to log into my email. Can you please help me?" Erik asked, with a glance at Silvana's huge breasts. Silvana saw how he looked at her, and felt awkward, but still got up and walked to his office.

Once there Erik asked her to sit at his desk. Silvana sat and looked at the screen. He leaned over her, putting his face next to hers, and moved the desktop mouse. He opened a Yahoo page, trying to log in, but a pop-up message appeared, indicating that the password was wrong.

Suddenly, he stroked Silvana's hair. Silvana shrugged him off and shot up from the chair. She gazed at him with disgust and slapped him. "Mr. Erik, you have gone too far this time. I will file a complaint to the police about your vulgar conduct."

Erik sneered, and crossed his arms across his chest. "You will lose your job, and with my connections, I will make certain no one hires you."

Hearing this made Silvana infuriated. She was bullied at home, and now at work as well. She barely kept herself from cursing him.

If other employees hadn't been there, Silvana would certainly have said, Bastard, keep your dirty hands off me!

Instead, she said, "I can work anywhere, but you can't manage employees, nor can you lead. Therefore, you need to learn not only how to manage properly and respect employees, but also to stop molesting women."

Silvana left his office and sat at her desk. Furious with Erik's behavior, she decided not to take any more bullshit from him. She packed all her things, then turned around to look at all of her co-workers.

"Girls, I'm leaving. I didn't come here so that a jerk like Erik could put his dirty hands on me or harass me."

She had realized that if she continued to be like a doormat and put up with nonsense, people would continue mistreating her, so she had finally decided to defend herself.

"You shouldn't leave. Just ignore him, like we do," suggested Toni.

"Why should I stay, and allow him to put his hands on me or abuse me just because he pays my salary? My well-being and decency are more important than money or a job."

Silvana collected her things from the table and got up. "Okay, girls, I'm going."

She left the office and drove home. When she reached home, Silvana called Rehema.

"What happened?" asked Rehema.

"This time Erik went too far. He purposely called me in his office and put his dirty hand on my hair."

"Oh, my God," exclaimed Rehema. "What did you do?"

"I slapped him, and then I left." Silvan felt the onset of an excruciating headache.

"You should have kicked him where it counts. That would teach him a lesson," remarked Rehema.

Silvana rubbed her temple. "My head is killing me. Sorry, but I have to go. I will talk to you later," she said, then she hung up the phone.

She lay down on the bed for a while and then got up to open the door when Mark brought the children home.

"Hello, guys. How was your school day?" she asked.

"It was good," answered Marie.

"Come here, my miracles," said Silvana. She started hugging them one by one. "Who do I love more than anything in this world?" she asked, beaming with love.

"Your miracles and God," said David.

Silvana patted David's head. "Who are my miracles?"

"We are," said Aygun, hugging her mother.

"Okay, now go upstairs and change your clothes. Then come back for your snacks," directed Silvana.

Mark looked at Silvana, and realized that something was wrong.

"What happened?" he asked.

"Erik touched my hair. I could see that that was not all he wanted to touch. So, I left," explained Silvana.

He sneered and shook his finger at her. "It is your fault. I asked you to stay home. I told you that if you got a job, men would harass you, but you didn't listen to me."

Mark's unsupportive words filled her heart with sadness. She gazed at him with weary eyes, feeling dizzy. She sighed heavily and her brow furrowed.

"I didn't do anything wrong. Why are you always blaming me, but supporting others?" She gave him a look of disgust. "I will never forgive you for that. I didn't flirt with him, nor did I give him a reason to flirt with me."

Overcome by weakness, Silvana sat on the sofa. From there, she could hear the children's voices coming from upstairs. Mark stood not far from her, an indifferent expression on his face. After a while, she got up and walked away, leaving Mark in the living room. Distraught because of Mark's offensive remarks, she decided to turn off the computer and go to sleep. However, a message from a thirty-two-year-old woman from Nairobi popped up.

"Hello, Mummy, how are you doing?" typed Hawa, a woman who Silvana had met through a social site.

"I'm fine, thank you. It sounds strange that we are almost the same age, yet you are calling me 'Mummy'," responded Silvana.

Silvana sighed as she sorted through her thoughts. I am convinced that she is going to ask for money. I do not know why she continues to think that I have plenty of money. If I had any, I would move back home with my kids.

"But you are like a Mummy, and a good friend to me. You comfort me and give me hope, more so than my mother," said Hawa kindly.

"Okay, you can keep calling me Mummy. How are your kids?"

"The kids are missing out on school because I can't pay for their books and clothes. They are hungry, Mummy. In addition, I got pregnant with another child. Can you please send money for my kids?" asked Hawa.

"I will try to send some money to you soon," typed Silvana, saddened by Hawa's poverty. "However, you cannot always ask people for money. Just get a job, or ask for help from the man who impregnated you."

"But, Mummy, he stopped helping me after he found out that I am carrying his child. In addition, he has a wife, and...I'm struggling. I don't want to live any longer." Hawa's words rang of desperation.

Do you think I want to live? I am struggling, as well, thought Silvana. Her eyes filled with tears, despondent because she didn't have any money for either of them.

"Hawa, keep going on. Once I get a better job, I will help you. Don't lose faith. God and I will help you."

"I have to go now, Mummy," typed Hawa, and she ended the conversation.

Silvana turned off the computer and prayed.

"God, I look at this fallen world and I am horrified. Children around the world are abused, and women are suffering. This world is a mess, and I do not know what might come next. I want to help people, even though my mom says that I should forget about helping others because they are unappreciative users. But I cannot change; I can't just close my eyes to the suffering of others. That is not who I am!"

With a heavy sigh, Silvana crawled into bed and covered herself with a blanket. She closed her eyes.

Why does everything have to depend on money?

Later, Silvana regretted that she had left her job. She spent a lot of time applying for many positions but to no avail. She was getting frustrated, and even angrier towards Erik, because she couldn't forgive him for forcing her to leave her position. Even though Erik had given her a hard time, Silvana had been happy around her co-workers, and had been able to earn money that she could use to buy books or other supplies online. Now she had ended up without any personal finances once again, wholly dependent on Mark.

***

Silvana's great-grandfather's father had been a well-known Orthodox priest in Russia, so she was curious about the difference between Orthodoxy and the Anglican religion. During a rainy day, while surfing the Internet for information, Silvana joined a Russian Orthodox group. People there could communicate with administrators while seeing and hearing them. Each administrator had his own chat group. Silvana ended up in a chat room hosted by a man named Vladimir.

Silvana's first impressions of him were that he had a beautiful smile and a kind face, but his eyes were sad. For a few days, Silvana entered his chat room and asked different questions about Orthodoxy. Vladimir was a priest's helper. He was a wise man, and had a wife and three children. Silvana decided to email him to find out how divorcing Mark might affect her and her children's lives. One afternoon, she sat at the table in front of her laptop typing an email.

"Dear Vladimir,

Others have told me that you have had multifaceted, vibrant, and abundant life experiences from which you have derived a depth of wisdom. Right now, I am mired down in a miserably unhappy marriage and shackled to an abusive man. I would like to get a divorce. However, I am reluctant, knowing that perhaps my children's lives as well as my own might take a turn for the worse. As far as I am aware, my own church does not condone or permit divorce. Will God forgive me if I seek a divorce? Would you kindly advise me about the best first step I might consider?"

Silvana smiled and clicked on the Send button, hoping to get answers soon. Every day, she anxiously checked her email, waiting to hear from him.

Vladimir took eight days to respond to her query. As soon as Silvana opened his message, she read it.

"Dear Silvana,

Based on information that you provided, I concluded that your entire life has been affected by your father's sinful behavior and mother's mistakes. Your father neglected you as if you never existed. Your mother did not give you the affection and love that you needed. Pray to God for Him to forgive them. Ask Him to bring positive changes into your life. Various churches view divorce as a sin, advising instead that couples ought to work on their relationships. However, because abuse can appear unbearable and ceaseless to the victim, it is cruel and unsupportable to expect victims to not only endure such physical and psychological misconduct over long periods of time, but also for children to grow up in such unhealthy atmospheres. God will forgive you if you decide to divorce. However, you must not leave your man before getting a job. When you divorce him, ensure that you stay friends with him. He is the father of your kids, and would always be there for them."

Silvana had more questions and decided to check if she could find Vladimir on Paltalk. She typed his name into Paltalk's contact search and came up with a hit. She sent him a friend request, and Vladimir accepted.

The next day, she took her laptop into the living room and called him.

"Good morning, Vladimir. I'm not sure if you remember me, but I'm the woman who emailed you asking questions about divorce."

"Good day, my lady. How can I assist you today?" asked Vladimir with a broad smile.

She looked at his peaceful face and gained confidence about what she was about to ask. "You said that God will forgive me, but am I ever going to have a happy marriage?"

"You have one already," stated Vladimir calmly.

"But my marriage is not happy because I'm getting emotionally abused," complained Silvana.

"What is your religion, my dear?" inquired Vladimir.

"Muslim, but I believe that Jesus is God's Son," Silvana answered.

Vladimir's eyebrows moved up. "I'm bewildered. Muslims view Jesus as a prophet, not God's Son."

A smile ran across Silvana's face. "My great-granny was an Orthodox Russian, so I grew up exposed to Christianity."

"Do you pray to God, my lady?" asked Vladimir.

"Yes, I pray but not often," replied Silvana, staring into his gray eyes.

"If you yearn for positive changes and a happy marriage, you need to pray to Him daily and get baptized in order to wash away your sins. Once you take these steps, your life will change dramatically, albeit incrementally. Meaning, don't expect big miracles right away. Okay, my dear?" he asked in a gentle voice.

"I tried to get baptized two years ago in the Anglican Church, but they refused me because I couldn't visit the church classes. It made me so upset because, in my heart, I felt closer to the Christian religion than to Islam. I felt as if the church had rejected me."

"You went to a man-made church. I'm glad that they refused to baptize you. You must get baptized only in an Orthodox church."

After talking for about twenty minutes, Vladimir said, "You know your direction now. Thus, you will be okay. My dear, do you have any other questions?"

"No," responded Silvana, feeling peaceful.

"See you soon, my dear. I have to leave now." He signed off of Paltalk.

***

Silvana wished to change her life and remove her children from Mark's negative influence. Therefore, she decided to be baptized as soon as possible, in order to bring positive changes into her life. After talking to Vladimir, she wondered if there was a way that she could be baptized without attending classes.

She picked up the phone and telephoned Rehema.

"Good morning, Rehema. I have news for you. I was told that if I get baptized, my life will change." Silvana's eyes shone with joy. She felt blissfully happy. "Can you believe it? I will start a new life soon!"

"Who told you this?" asked Rehema.

"A man who knows the future."

"I told you to stop going by what psychics say because they lie, and you will burn in Hell. Every time you go to them, you choose a demon over God."

Silvana crossed her legs. "He is not a psychic, but a man who serves God and has a gift given by Him. He can see things."

"Only God can see the future. Anyone who claims to see the future is demonic," contended Rehema.

"If his gift derives from a demon, why would the demon desire that I get baptized?"

"I don't know," acquiesced Rehema.

"I need to have hope that my life will change, and God is my last hope. If becoming Orthodox is a key to these changes, then I will get baptized," pronounced Silvana. Her heart filled with desperation as her eyes became wet.

"Getting baptized will bring you closer to God and put you on the right path. However, you must make every step to change your life. If you sit and wait, nothing will happen by itself," remarked Rehema.

"Would you please find a church for me where I don't need to attend classes? I want these changes to come as soon as possible."

"Okay, I will try," Rehema replied.

Hearing Rehema's promise relieved Silvana's worries.

"Rehema, are you still having problems with your mother?"

"Yes. As you know, she pressured me to get an abortion and to leave the man I loved. If it wasn't for her, I would have had my fifth child and a second husband. I wouldn't have to work as a maid," complained Rehema. "I just can't forgive her."

"If you want to enter Paradise, you have to forgive her. Try to start over and forget the past," advised Silvana.

"But she still nags me, and gets angry when she sees me with him," remarked Rehema.

"Just ignore her and marry him. Don't let people stand between the two of you. You deserve to be happy. Let's hope he will support your kids."

Silvana glanced at the time. "Oh, it's late! I need to start cooking. Talk to you later," said Silvana.

"Okay, bye," answered Rehema.

After talking to Rehema, Silvana felt so happy that she started singing loudly. "Glory to you, my Lord. I love you with all my heart. You are the one I worship and praise. You are my hope, redeemer, and joy." She was so overjoyed that she couldn't stop singing.

In the evening, she sent a message to Vladimir, asking him to call her on Paltalk. As soon as she had finished typing the message, he called her.

"Hello, my dear."

"Good evening," answered Silvana, with a joyful smile.

She could feel his glowing aura, which calmed her. Silvana looked at the screen and observed that the room he was in had green walls, and on one of them hung a painting of a young couple.

"Beautiful art," she remarked.

"Oh, yes. I bought the painting in Cuba," he answered, looking at it.

He turned back to her with a smile. "You typed that you have news for me. What is it?"

"I spoke to my friend. She said that she would organize the baptism for me soon," said Silvana.

"This is good news, my dear. I'm happy for you. Which church are you trying to get baptized in?"

"It's an Anglican Church."

Vladimir's facial expression changed at her answer. He seemed disappointed as his smile disappeared. "I told you before that it is better for you to get baptized only in the Orthodox Church."

Silvana frowned. "Why does it make a difference which church I get baptized in? The most important thing is simply to get baptized."

"It makes a substantial difference. The Orthodox Church is original, the one created by Jesus himself. In the Orthodox Church, you will find God's Grace, but in a false religion, there is no grace. Find out if there is an Orthodox Church in Kenya, and then come back to me," Vladimir told her.

He looked to the left. "I have to go now, because I have another call to attend," he said.

***

Later, after putting the children to sleep, Silvana turned the light off and tried to fall asleep, but couldn't for a long while. She thought about the idea of being baptized.

Why do I have to be baptized in the Orthodox Church? What is going to happen if I don't find an Orthodox Church?

Then she recalled that one of her friends mentioned going to an Orthodox Church that only local Kenyans frequented. She decided to find out their phone number in the morning and telephone them. She fell asleep, and rose at 4.00 a.m. to look for the Orthodox Church's phone number. She found only one, the Ethiopian Orthodox Church. Silvana wrote down the church's number and decided to call them as soon as the children went to school. She exercised, prepared breakfast, and woke her children up.

By 7.25 a.m., the children were ready for school. They then left the house with their father, leaving her alone. As soon as they departed, she dialed the number. A woman answered and gave Silvana directions to the Orthodox Church. When Rehema arrived at the house, they went to visit the church. Upon getting there, Silvana was stupefied to see that the church had only a few icons, and the picture of Jesus depicted him as a dark man.

A Kenyan native priest approached them. "Good morning. I'm Priest Emmanuel. How can I help you?" he asked, showing his white teeth in a welcoming smile.

"Good morning. I'm Muslim. I would like to become Orthodox. What is the procedure?"

"You need to attend three months of classes. Only then you can get baptized," instructed Priest Emmanuel.

"How many times per week do I have to come?"

"We have classes twice per week," replied the priest.

Silvana's heart started to beat faster because she didn't know if Mark would allow her to attend classes.

"I will think about it and then decide if I should go ahead with the classes."

"No problem. God's doors are always open for everyone," stated Priest Emmanuel kindly.

Silvana was radiant with joy, knowing that she could be baptized soon. But when she told Mark about the church, he wasn't happy at all, knowing that she had gone to a church where only black locals went.

"Don't embarrass me. You can't go to that church!" exclaimed Mark.

Agitated, Silvana asked, "Why?"

"Because, dummy, white people don't attend that church. If you go people would look strangely at you," chortled Mark.

"I'm not doing anything wrong. I just want to go to God's house. Why do people have to say something bad?"

"Here, there are certain things that local white people don't do. They don't walk around looking for a job, like you. They have money and work for themselves."

"I'm tired of all of this discrimination and divisions among people. Why do people only care about social status, skin color, and their pockets?"

"Silvana, you are not from here. You don't know anything about people here."

She bit her lip and scowled at Mark. "I have lived here long enough, and have met a few strange people. Some are full of themselves, walking around as if they own the world and ignoring others. They spend their lives worrying about making more money, building false images, or buying huge houses. Why should I care what ignorant hypocrites would say about my selection of a church of worship?"

Silvana left the bedroom, feeling anxious. The following morning, she typed a message to Vladimir.

"Good morning, Vladimir. Would you please call me? I would like to talk about the Orthodox Church."

After five minutes, he phoned.

"Hello, my dear. I got your message. Did you locate a church?" he asked, as he wiped his glasses with a wet napkin.

"Yes, I found a church, but it is an Ethiopian church. My husband said that I can't get baptized there, or attend church services."

"Did you check if there is a Greek Orthodox Church?"

"We have only Ethiopian Orthodox Churches," Silvana replied, frustrated. She wanted so much to change her life that she was rushing to be baptized as soon as possible.

"Then you need to go to your country and get baptized there."

Suddenly he said something very unexpected. "You have big, beautiful eyes. They are a mirror of the soul."

Before she could open her mouth to say anything, Vladimir left Paltalk again.

After talking to Vladimir, she decided to save money for a ticket and travel to her country to be baptized. In the evening, she let her husband know about her plans but, as usual, he didn't approve of them.

After a few days, Vladimir typed a message: "Hi, are you there? Oh, no, you are busy. I'm so sorry we can't talk."

As soon as she got his message, she typed back. "Hi, yes, I'm busy, but not so much that I can't talk to you."

Then he typed back, "Okay, you can call me."

She called him right away. They talked about Silvana's problems and directions that she might take. During their conversation, Silvana tried to find out information about his family, but when she asked questions, he said, "This is a personal question. You are only allowed to ask questions about your life or talk about your problems, not about me, or my family."

Hearing this, Silvana got irritated. "I'm tired of talking only about my problems and myself. When I talk about my problems, I dwell on them, creating negative energy around me. I would like to talk about other matters and have two-way communication, but when we chat, I'm the one who talks for the most part. However, friendship always involves two-way communication."

"We are not friends; I'm your guide. As soon as you are going in the right direction, I will take my leave. I don't believe in friendships. There are no good friends," said Vladimir with a serious facial expression.

"You are wrong. There is such a phenomenon as good friends, and I have them."

"You are so wrong. You don't have any friends. The ones that you think are your friends are only in your life for empty talk."

Even though Silvana knew that Vladimir was right, she didn't want to accept the truth. "I don't believe you. I have good friends," Silvana said, saddened.

"Show me a friend who helped you with anything or stood by your side during your most trying times," pronounced Vladimir, sternly.

Silvana gazed at him silently.

"If you can't accept the facts, it is your problem," he continued in a stern voice.

"Why does a man of God like you always think in negative terms when it comes to friendship?"

He didn't answer her question. "Goodbye, my lady," said Vladimir.

He signed off, leaving Silvana in distress.

However, after getting to know Silvana, Vladimir started talking about his family and even introduced her to his wife. After talking to her, Silvana sent a message to him. "Does your wife get jealous that we are talking?"

"No, she knows that I'm here only to help and guide you. I talk to many women to help them. My wife understands this aspect of my vocation and my calling in life. We trust each other. I'm just doing my job."

"I wanted to make certain that I'm not causing any problems in your life," Silvana typed back. "If it were me, I would never allow my husband to chat with women for any reason whatsoever."

"You need to learn to trust and not to be jealous. A happy marriage should be based on mutual trust," Vladimir typed back.

"When a woman and a man communicate with one another, often unexpected feelings can develop. Then flirting may start," remarked Silvana.

"If someone is committed to his or her marriage, they would stay away from wrongdoing," typed Vladimir.

"I agree with you," Silvana said, smiling as she left the chat room.

***

After a few weeks, Silvana suddenly came down with pneumonia and severe bronchitis. She developed whooping cough, which prevented her from sleeping at night.

"Are you going to the office today?" she asked Mark one morning.

He looked at her with a frown. "Yes, I'm going."

Silvana blew her nose. Mark gazed at her sternly, as if he hated her.

"Listen, I don't sit at home and scratch my ass doing nothing like you. I have plenty of work to do. Stay away from me with your flu. Last time you messed up my holiday with it."

"It wasn't my fault that I got the flu," retorted Silvana, hurt by her husband's unkindness and uncaring attitude. "I don't sit at home doing nothing. After all, who cleans, cooks, irons, and takes care of the children?"

"You have a maid."

"But she does not come most days," commented Silvana.

"Sort out your life and get another maid," said Mark, leaving the bedroom.

She sighed in resignation. It was like this every time she was sick; he would tell her to stay away from him, and wouldn't take care of her or ask her how she felt.

She left the bedroom and went into the living room.

Why does he look at me as if he hates me? Did I do something wrong? He is never there for me, even when I'm sick.

For two weeks, she stayed at home alone during the day. One day, Mark directed her to change the bedding, even though she could barely stand on her feet. He also asked her if she had ironed his white shirt. When she told him that she couldn't iron it, Mark said, "If you can't iron my shirts, I have money. I can pay for someone to iron them."

No matter how sick she was, Silvana would still get up to clean her house, iron, and take care of her children, because she knew that nobody would do it for her. Therefore, after hearing his complaints, she ironed his shirt.

During her illness, Silvana got depressed. When Mark was at work and the children in school, Silvana lay down in bed, feeling desperate. She started crying bitterly and praying.

"Father, I am so tired, carrying my burdens. Sometimes I wonder why I even came into this world. Life is a blessing if you not only live it to the fullest and have a fulfilling job and a loving partner, but also take part in activities that make you happy. However, I am chained down within these four walls. I cannot find peace. Please help me escape from this cage. I no longer have the strength to carry on."

She sat up and raised her hands in the air as tears rolled down her face. "Please hear me, my Lord. I don't want to suffer any longer. Father, please help me to get money for a ticket. I need to go to my country to be baptized."

Silvana started to wonder if God heard her prayers at all. "Father, are you hearing my prayers? What if my life does not change?"

Doubting herself and God, she again decided to look for answers from the psychics. She turned on the computer and entered the website of Life Readers. One of the readers was online talking to others.

Silvana typed to her: "Can you please do a reading for me?"

"No problem, just enter into private chat mode."

Silvana paid for a private reading and entered into a private chat. The psychic told her that her name was Mella.

"Good evening, Mella. Can you please tell me if my life will change?"

Mella closed her eyes, shaking slightly. "My guardian says that you are full of fears and always making rash decisions without thinking. You put yourself into problems. I see Mother Mary behind you, together with Mother Teresa. They want you to continue their work. I see a divorce coming, and after that you will find a new love. You will meet him in the church."

"Yes, fine, but I need to know when I will divorce."

"The divorce process will start in six months."

"When will I find a good job, though?"

"You will get it in four months," pronounced Mella.

Silvana's credits were depleted. She noticed a message asking her to pay more money to continue the reading. Suddenly, the chat window disappeared and the reader left.

Silvana sent a text to Vladimir the next day.

"Good morning, Vladimir. I'm feeling so happy. A psychic reader said not only that my life will change soon, but also that I will meet a new love after the divorce."

"My dear, you have disappointed me. I warned you before that those readings emanate and derive from evil, yet you again went to a psychic reader. Don't you realize that they are feeding your hopes and filling you with lies. They tell you what you want to hear?" Vladimir typed back.

"How can a simple tarot reading come from the devil?"asked Silvana.

"Nobody can predict the future other than God. The devil wants you to turn away from God and rely on such readers. Thus, he is pushing you to them. Every time you take a reading from them, you build a bond with a demon. Soon it will affect your life and children."

Vladimir's words put fear into her heart. She didn't want anything to affect her children's lives.

"But if they come from evil, why do they offer a positive outcome?"

"If you don't stop going to psychic readers, your end will be Hell. God gave you such tools as the Bible, spiritual guidance, and commandments. What else do you need to hear to recognize that He is the one you should follow, not mediums or psychic readers? Please confess, and stop betraying God before it is too late. Get baptized and pray. Your life will start changing. Remember, only He can change your life, not psychic readers."

"I know it, but sometimes when I get frustrated and faced with hard times, I wonder if God is here for me," stated Silvana bluntly.

"He is here for you, but you need to learn to be patient. Things will work out."

Silvana started coughing without stopping.

"Vladimir, I'm not feeling well. I will talk to you later."

Throughout her illness and depression, Vladimir continued chatting with her often. This was helping her avoid further depression. During one of their conversations, Silvana again complained to him.

"Vladimir, why God allows me to suffer instead of giving me what I need?"

"Maybe what you ask for is not good for you," said Vladimir.

Deep wrinkles crossed her forehead."How is having a happy marriage and peace of mind detrimental to me?"

"I don't know, but He does not bring suffering. He allowed you to suffer because He loves you and wants you to rely solely on Him, and to stay on a path leading to Paradise. If Jesus Christ didn't love you, he wouldn't remember you. He would leave you alone to let you follow the wrong path. He allows people to suffer because He hopes that they will develop a relationship with Him, and get rid of pride as well as become humble and compassionate. But when people have everything and don't suffer, they don't look for the Lord."

Silvana shook her head in disapproval. To her, God was a loving, kind, and merciful. Vladimir's speech about suffering made Silvana angry.

She said, "Why do people have to suffer to enter Paradise? If Jesus loves me, how could He let me suffer from childhood? Why did He let me be abused and hurt in my childhood? Why did He take away my father from me? I have prayed to Him for years to bring him back to me, but He hasn't answered my prayers. I have been close to Him since I was six years old.

"All these years, I have been praying and asking God to help me to get out of this unhappy marriage. Why didn't He help me?" Silvana asked angrily, crying. "Is this how He loves me?"

"My dear, crying won't help you. You need to blame your parents and yourself for the mistakes and choices you made. So stop blaming God! He loves you so much that when you cry, He cries with you. Remember, the Lord gave us free will to make either right or wrong decisions. He is helping you, but you can't see it. Why do you think I'm here? It is because He wanted you to follow true faith so that you would be able to enter Paradise."

Silvana continued crying as she recalled all of her childhood pain.

"You are crying like a little child. I gave you direction. You know what has to be done now. Remember that, after baptism, you have to continue receiving communion and going to confession."

Vladimir's phone rang. "I have to leave now, my dear. See you soon."

"Bye," Silvana said sadly.

***

As soon as Silvana felt better, something happened that caused her faith to come alive again. She couldn't believe that God had heard her prayers. Mark bought a ticket for her to fly to Azerbaijan!

Silvana was so happy that she prayed: "Lord, thank you very much for hearing my prayers."

The next day, Silvana packed her clothes. She arranged for Rehema to stay with the children for the three weeks that she would be away.

On the day of her departure, Silvana's children were sad. They couldn't understand why they couldn't go with her. This was the first time in their lives that their mother would be away from them for any length of time. They sat next to her on the sofa, trying to make her take them as well.

Aygun rested her head on Silvana's lap. "Mother, please take us too!" she pleaded.

"Aygun, I can't take you with me," said Silvana, patting her head.

"Why?" asked Peter.

"You can't miss school, and it is too costly to take you. You will stay with Papa, and Rehema will be staying with you until Papa comes home from work," she answered him. She felt sorry for them, knowing that they would not get the love they needed from their father.

"You are the kindest and most compassionate mother in the world. I'm going to miss you," said Marie, hugging Silvana.

"Who are my miracles and joys?" asked Silvana, with a heart full of love.

"We are," said David.

"Yes, you are. I love you so much!" Silvana hugged them.

Rehema entered the bedroom. "Your husband is ready to take you to the airport."

"Thanks, Rehema," Silvana said with a grateful smile. "Please don't allow my children to play outside alone."

"I love them like my own children. Don't worry, I won't let them out of my sight."

She came up to Silvana and embraced her. "Have a safe flight, and remember to enjoy your holiday. Don't let anything agitate you."

"Thank you, Rehema," said Silvana with a big smile.

Silvana turned to the little ones. "Okay, children, I'm leaving now. Please listen to Papa and Rehema." She hugged them again and left the bedroom, leaving the children with her maid.

Mark drove Silvana to the airport, and after spending twenty minutes with her, he gave her a good-bye hug. He pulled an envelope with money in it out of his pocket and gave it to her.

"This money is for you to spend there. However, it goes without saying that you don't have to spend all of it."

"Thank you," said Silvana. She hugged him one last time and then walked away.

***

Silvana was eager to go back home. From Kenya, she flew to England, and from there to Azerbaijan. When she arrived in Baku, she couldn't believe that she was finally in her own country again. She was so ecstatic to see her people and to hear her native language.

After finally passing immigration, she walked toward the exit, feeling light. Outside, she met her mother and sister. They hugged her, then carried her luggage to a waiting taxi. Silvana got into the back of the cab next to her mother, while Elnara sat in front.

Esmira wore a red jacket, red earrings, and black trousers with black shoes. Silvana remarked that she looked older and had lost weight, but had still kept her good taste.

"How was your flight?" asked Esmira.

"It wasn't bad, but I ended up sitting in Heathrow Airport for three hours, waiting to board the next plane."

"Why didn't you bring your children?" asked Esmira.

"Tickets are too expensive, and they can't miss school."

Esmira lit a cigarette gazing at Silvana. "You put on weight. Your face looks chubby."

Silvana rolled her eyes and gave her mother a sharp glance.

"How do you expect me not to put on weight in my situation? As soon as I become anxious or depressed, I start eating. I devote most of my time to my children and housework. I barely get time to exercise."

Silvana suddenly coughed and tried to wave away the cigarette smoke. "Mother, when will you stop smoking?"

She turned toward the window and looked outside. Even though it was dark, Silvana could see considerable changes in Baku. She saw many tall buildings. When they approached their street, Silvana noticed new houses that hadn't existed when she left. The taxi stopped in front of their building, and all of them got out.

Silvana stood in front of the building and gazed around. Nothing had changed at all. The buildings looked older, their paint worn, and the pine trees had grown taller, but that was about it. They climbed to the fifth floor and stopped in front of Sadaget's apartment.

Silvana noticed the new door, which was made of steel. Good, they have replaced the wooden door, she thought. She rang the doorbell. Sadaget opened the door.

"Hello, Granny!" exclaimed Silvana.

"Silvana, you came back!" said Sadaget in a joyful voice, moving to hug her granddaughter. "Come here for a hug. I can't see you. Since you left, my eyes have gotten worse."

Silvana came up to Granny and gave her a hug. She was happy to see her, and tears of joy rolled down her face. They walked into the living room. Silvana sat in a chair next to Sadaget.

"Your mother made me blind," complained Sadaget.

"How did she make you blind?"

"I had glaucoma and could see a little bit, but this stupid woman insisted that I should go for surgery. I went for the surgery, but after it I stopped seeing. Doctors messed up my eyes."

"Your eyes got messed up because you didn't follow the doctor's instructions. They gave you drops to use after the surgery, but you didn't bother to use them. So, stop complaining. Silvana is probably tired," said Esmira, trying to light a cigarette.

"Don't shut me up. I'm in my house and can speak as much as I want," said Sadaget, waving a fist in the air.

Silvana stared at her granny. Poor Sadaget was pale, and her face was full of wrinkles. For some reason, she was wearing sunglasses.

She edged closer to her mother and whispered in a low voice, so that Granny could not hear, "Why is Granny wearing sunglasses in the house?"

Esmira grimaced at the thought of dealing with her mother's childishness. "She is afraid that if people see her eyes, she will go blind."

"Granny always believed in this kind of thing. She just can't change."

Hearing their whispers, Sadaget frowned. "What are you talking about?" she asked loudly.

"Nothing, Mother," answered Esmira.

Silvana glanced at the living room. Before she left Baku, wallpaper had covered the walls of the apartment, but now it was gone. Instead, the walls were painted in ugly gray and light brown colors.

"Why did you replace the wallpaper with paint?" Silvana asked.

"I thought painting would look better. However, when I came back home, I realized the hired man had painted the house with the wrong colors. I didn't have enough money to change it," explained Esmira.

"But you are making enough money," said Silvana.

"The money that I make either goes for food, bills, or my debts. I don't have extra funds to fix the apartment."

Silvana got up and checked every room. Seeing the condition of her grandmother's apartment made her depressed.

"The apartment was in such good condition before I left. Your choice of ugly colors messed it up. Once I get a job, I will make sure those ugly colors are changed." She had always wanted to give Esmira a fulfilling life, but she hadn't been able to do it.

"You never told us about your friends. Did you make any friends in Kenya at all?" asked Esmira.

"Yes I have, but only a few. Most of my friends are online."

"You have always made many friends. I'm surprised that you have made only a few," said Esmira.

"In the time that has passed since I left Baku, I have met hypocrites from all over the world. They walk around full of themselves. Within, they are like rotten eggs, full of envy and jealousy. I love simple people who know the value of true friendship, understand goodness, and treat everyone with respect and equality. It is better to have a few real friends than to ally myself with hypocrites," Silvana explained.

"You shouldn't have left your country at all. At least here you had many good friends."

"Mother, for the first time in my life, I must agree with you. I made a big mistake leaving Baku, and now I'm paying for it. Can you believe that, in my kids' school, I even met some racist people? For them, skin color and inclusion, in both religion and social status, are vital. If you have the wrong skin color or religion, they won't even open their mouths to greet you."

That night, Silvana stayed up until 3 a.m. talking with her mother and sister. Her two brothers were absent because they had both married Iranian women and had moved to Iran. Sadaget had wandered out onto the porch at some point in the evening.

While talking to her mother, Silvana suddenly heard Granny thundering, "You stupid fools! For forty years, I have been without a man. Do you mean to call me a whore? Your daughters are whores!"

Confused, Silvana looked over at her mother. "Who is Granny swearing?"

"Every day, she curses at the neighbors. They hear her big mouth. I'm so embarrassed that I don't want to leave the house," commented Esmira.

"Why is she cursing at the neighbors?" Silvana asked, puzzled.

"She thinks that they are gossiping about her. Even the people on the radio-she thinks they are talking about us."

"That's horrible. You should take her to a psychiatrist and have her treated," said Silvana.

"It's a waste of time. She won't take any medication."

Granny started shouting, "You better shut your mouth! Oh God, make their houses drop on their heads. They want to come and kill all of us!"

Esmira leaped up from the chair and pulled her hair in fury. "Silvana, make her shut up before I smack her! She is like a vampire, sucking my life out of me."

"Mother, calm down. She is your mother and the one who looked after us," said Silvana.

"Stop smoking, Esmira. I can't breathe!" Granny shouted from the porch. "They are locking me in my house!"

"I think she has dementia, and because people talked about you and Samed, she remembers all of that gossip," stated Silvana.

Esmira stormed out of the living room. She rushed to the porch, squeezing her hands into fists.

"Come inside, old witch! People are sleeping."

"No, I'm staying here. I need some fresh air," Sadaget murmured.

Esmira grabbed Sadaget's hand and started pulling her up.

"Someone call the police! They are beating me!" screamed the old woman.

She took a knife from her bra and stabbed at Esmira. Silvana's mother fell to the porch floor, unharmed. Sadaget raised her hand again.

"Don't lock my door. Give me a key. I want to go outside!" shouted Sadaget, her lips covered with saliva.

"Silvana, help me! This witch is trying to kill me!" shouted Esmira, shielding herself with her hands.

Silvana rushed to the porch and stared at her Granny in shock. She quickly ran to her Grandma and grabbed her hand, trying to take away the knife. Sadaget held onto it with a death grip, and Silvana couldn't wrest it from her.

"Let go of my hand! I brought you up, not your mother! Now you are on her side, you ungrateful girl!"

"Granny, nobody is talking about you. Demons make you hear voices, which causes you to not be at peace with yourself. Please stop cursing at the neighbors," pleaded Silvana.

Sadaget tried to pull her hand away. "No, you don't know what you are saying. I heard them saying that you are a bastard child. I have to protect you!" she screamed.

With Silvana distracting her granny, Esmira was able to pull away the knife. She threw it to the other side of the porch, breathing heavily. Sadaget left the porch, mumbling to herself.

Esmira's arm was bleeding slightly. Silvana's heart was filled with pity for her granny and mother.

She stared at Esmira's bloodied arm. "Mother, are you okay?"

"Yes, I am. Just go to her room and keep that witch quiet."

"Mother, she has dementia and does not know what she is doing. I sincerely feel sorry for Granny. She can't find peace." She glanced at the wall that separated their apartment from the next one. "Yet our neighbors were jerks and always gossiped about us. They deserve to be cursed at," Silvana added.

"You should feel sorry for me, not her," Esmira said, leaving the porch.

She put a bandage on her wound and retired to her room to smoke. Then she took her medicine for her high blood pressure.

Silvana went into Sadaget's bedroom. She sat on her bed and hugged her.

"Who is my best granny? I love you, Granny. Please put your head down and try to sleep."

"I do not feel sleepy. Why do they still keep talking?" asked Sadaget, turning her head toward the window.

"Granny, try not to worry. You will feel sleepy soon," Silvana said, gently patting her granny's head. Sadaget took Silvana's hand and yawned.

"I feel calm and sleepy, holding your hand. You have something good within you."

"It is God's grace and love. Lay down now. I will sit next to you."

Sadaget lay down, but kept talking. To Silvana, Granny had become like a little child. She smiled, filled with love, thinking of her own children.

"Granny, don't speak. It is time to sleep."

After a long while, Granny fell asleep. Silvana left her bedroom and then checked on her mother. She was fine, so Silvana went to her own room. She rested her head on her pillow, yawning tiredly.

Silvana got up at 10 a.m. After having her breakfast, she told her mother about her plans to be baptized.

"You are a Muslim, and can't just become a Christian. It is a sin to betray your religion." Esmira warned her. "Besides, don't you know that soon everyone will become Muslim?"

"Mother, I never considered myself Muslim. I have always felt closer to the Christian religion."

"If you go ahead with a conversion, your life will get worse. I know friends who became Christians, and after that bad luck entered their lives."

"I don't believe in those things. I always believed that the Christian religion is the right one. I'm going to get baptized."

"You are making a big mistake," said Sadaget, jumping into the conversation.

"How can you betray your religion?" asked Esmira.

"Mother, being born in a Muslim family does not make me a Muslim. That which I believe and follow makes me who I am. Muslims believe that Jesus is only God's prophet. However, I believe, and always knew, that Jesus Christ is His beloved Son and our Saviour."

"God can't have a son," said Sadaget.

"Are you implying that God is not powerful enough? God can have whatever He wishes to have. We can be saved only by accepting Jesus as God's Son and our Saviour, He Who died for our sins," extolled Silvana.

Esmira looked at her daughter with disappointment. "Since you left Baku, it seems like you have changed. You've become angrier."

"Mother, I'm just trying to bring positive changes into my life."

Silvana decided to ignore them and to follow her mind. Before midday, she left the house with Elnara and went downtown. She was astonished to see so many tall buildings, small shops, and new automobiles on the road. Such vast changes in the city; Silvana couldn't believe that she had missed all of this development.

Together with Elnara, they visited the Russian Orthodox Church. Silvana spoke to Matushka about being baptized, who in turn asked her to come back to the church in the morning with two white sheets in order to be baptized. She returned to her apartment, feeling excited, and told Esmira about the arrangements.

However, her mother wasn't happy with the news. She didn't want her friends to say that her daughter had betrayed her religion. That evening, Esmira again tried to influence Silvana's decision. Hearing her mother's negative comments, Silvana wondered if she should change her mind and not get baptized after all.

Before going to sleep, Silvana prayed: "Jesus, I'm troubled. Vladimir told me that you want me to become Orthodox, but Mother said if I do, my life will get worse. I don't know what to do. Please, Father, give me a sign. Do you want me to become Orthodox?"

After praying, an anxious Silvana fell asleep for about five minutes. While sleeping, she dreamed that she was lying down on the ground with her hands crossed over her chest. A shiny, circular blue light was slowly approaching her. As Silvana stared at the light, she realized that it was coming from God to baptize her. At the same time, Silvana heard her mother's warnings about what would happen if she betrayed her religion, and this made her scared. However, the light approached Silvana and surrounded her.

Silvana woke up right away, and laughed because she knew it was a baptism in the form of a dream. God let her know that He indeed wanted Silvana to be baptized. She couldn't understand why the light had been blue, not yellow or white. Later she found out that the blue light represented God's wisdom.

She looked near the window where, in her dream, she had seen the light. It looked to her that that part of the room had a little bit of blue shading. Hearing Silvana's laugh, Esmira entered the bedroom.

"Silvana, why are you laughing?"

"Mother, look at the window. Do you see blue shading?"

"No, I don't," claimed Esmira.

"I prayed to God and asked Him to give me a sign to let me know if He wanted me to get baptized. In my dream, He answered by baptizing me with His light. Tomorrow I'm going to be baptized. My life will change soon!"

"Do as you wish." Esmira turned on her heel and left the bedroom.

Esmira wasn't happy with Silvana's decision but decided to support her. Even though Esmira was a Muslim, she would go to church to pray and light a candle. She herself had never planned to become a Christian, but she was starting to understand why Silvana would want to pursue being baptized.

In the morning, Silvana took two new white sheets from the cupboard and together with Elnara and Esmira, went to the church. When the three of them entered the church, they purchased three candles, lit them in front of Mary's icon, and prayed for a short time. Then Matushaka invited them into another room. The room was little, with a small pool of water and a few icons on the wall. Silvana was asked to take off her clothes and wrap herself in the sheet.

When she was ready, the priest came and prayed. He asked her to say the Lord's Prayer. Then she entered the pool. The water was cold, and Silvana drew back when her foot touched its surface.

Matushaka looked at Silvana. "Please go completely into the water," she said.

"But it's cold," answered Silvana, shaking.

Nonetheless, she slowly edged her whole body into the freezing water. Her teeth chattered. Then she was asked to put her head under the water three times, which she did. Silvana came out from the pool. Shaking, she walked around it, following the priest, with a burning candle in her hand. When the ceremony was finished, Silvana was happy to know that she had become an Orthodox Christian.

Suddenly, it came to her that it had been her destiny to be Orthodox. For many years, Silvana's granny had the Bible and an Orthodox teaching book in her apartment. Now Silvana realized that these books had been bought for her.

***

Silvana visited her relatives while she was in Baku. It felt so good to be appreciated by her peers again. Before she arrived for her visit, they asked her what food she would like to eat. Whatever she wanted, they cooked for her. She was so happy to be around people who cared about her that she didn't want to go back to Kenya.

However, on the fourth day after the baptism, she got very sick and stayed at home. She realized that going into the freezing water during the baptism had made her ill. Her mother gave her medicine, massaged her, and brought food to her bed. For the first time since she had left Baku, Silvana was relaxed and well cared for during her illness. She wasn't left alone at home, nor cursed at, but was allowed to rest and stay in bed.

When she got better, Silvana went downtown with her mother. Her eyes shone, and her face looked relaxed and happy. The sadness from her eyes was gone. She was glad to be away from her controlling spouse, and his house, which was more like a cage. She enjoyed the sense of freedom and felt the independence of being able to leave her house, travel on her own, visit friends, and go to the grocery store. She wished that this kind of life would last forever. However, at the same time, she felt depressed seeing her mother's problems with her granny.

Late in the evening they left the city and went back home. She fell asleep right away but awoke to the sound of Granny's screams. She quickly got up from the bed and ran out of her room. What she saw made her stop short. Sadaget was in the hallway, holding a knife in her hand and pelting shoes at Esmira. Silvana's mother stood by the door, trying to prevent Sadaget from leaving the house.

"Move from the door and let me go!" shouted Sadaget.

"No, you can't go outside!" exclaimed Esmira.

"Let me go or I will cut you to pieces!" Sadaget screamed out, wielding the knife above her in the air.

"What is going on?" Silvana choked out, shaking in fear.

"This wicked witch is fighting with me! Look what she did to my hands!" said Esmira. She showed Silvana her scratched hands, which were covered with small drops of blood.

"Granny, go to sleep, please," begged Silvana.

Sadaget lifted a shoe and pelted it at Silvana. "Don't tell me what to do!"

The shoe hurt Silvana's hand, and she rubbed it. At the same time, she kept a wary eye on Granny's knife.

"Mother, why does she want to go outside?"

"She thinks that the next-door neighbor was talking about her. She wants to quarrel with her," Esmira explained.

She stormed toward the phone. "I can't handle her. I'm going to call the police."

"No, you can't do this. Granny, please go to your room, or I will go back to Kenya right now!"

"Yes, go back. You are just like your mother!" shouted Granny.

Sadaget moved away from the door, spat on Esmira, and then went back into her room.

"Now you see what I'm going through," said Esmira.

"At least she is not emotionally abusing you like Mark, but only cursing at the neighbors. They know that her head is not functioning. So, there is nothing to be embarrassed about. In fact, who cares what they think?"

***

Soon Silvana grew homesick, even though she was so happy being back in her own country. Part of the reason was because of seeing the problems between her mother and grandmother. It increased, however, after talking to her children, and seeing them crying for her over Paltalk. She wanted to go back to her children, and waited impatiently for the day of her flight.

At the end of April, Esmira and Elnara dropped her off at the airport.

"I hope you won't take so long to come back here. Next time, make certain you bring my grandchildren."

"I will try to visit you in the next two years," said Silvana, feeling happy to go back to her children, but not to the prison within her home.

"Whenever Mark curses at you, don't give it any attention."

"It's hard, but I will try."

Silvana let out a long sigh.

I just do not like living in that country. I endured a great deal of pain. I am not at liberty to move around at will. I hate spending most of my days at home.

Esmira hugged Silvana, and strode away feeling miserable.

Silvana spent two hours sitting in the airport on the cold steel chairs, chatting with a Turkish woman. Both of them boarded a Turkish airline. Silvana liked the Turkish plane. It was huge and had comfortable chairs. She was given a small purse with socks, a small toothbrush, toothpaste, and delicious food.

As she flew to the United Kingdom, Silvana thought about her good time in Baku.

She loved the attention and care that she had received. I could move to Azerbaijan with my children, she thought.

In Kenya, her children didn't have a life. Their existence revolved around going to school, doing homework, and sometimes going to the cinema. In Azerbaijan, Silvana could take them for boat or carousel rides, and for walks in the park.

Even though Silvana wanted to stay in Baku, she was happily going back to her only joys and purpose in life, her children. God had given her these miracles, and it was her duty to make certain that they were loved, that they followed God, and were brought up with good values and morals. Silvana knew that without these, she and her children would be unable to enter Paradise.

When Silvana returned home, her children were happy not only to see her, but also to get the gifts she had brought. Silvana had bought two pink teddy bears for her daughters, and electronic cars for her sons. She unpacked her bags and returned to her regular daily routine.

However, after two weeks, Silvana regretted that she had come back. One day, Mark went to drink, as usual, while Silvana stayed at home reviewing schoolwork with the children and preparing them for exams.

Late in the evening, Mark came home from a pub in a good mood. He entered the bedroom to find Silvana already in bed.

"I bought ice cream for the children. Where are they?"

"They are sleeping," answered Silvana.

Mark went downstairs. "Silvana, put some water in the fridge," he thundered.

Silvana got up and went downstairs. She removed a few bottles from a box and put them in the refrigerator.

"Why are you telling people what is happening at home? What you tell your friends makes the rounds."

Silvana gazed at him without blinking. "What did I do this time?"

"You piece of trash. Why did you tell your friend that I'm an abuser and a bully?" exclaimed Mark.

Silvana felt as if her strength had been drained from her. "Who told you that I spoke about you?"

"You told your friend, and she passed it on to someone else, and that person told me. Don't talk about me or I will hire people to have you killed," warned Mark.

"Go ahead and have me killed." Silvana stared straight into his eyes, unwavering, but inside she wondered which of her friends had betrayed her trust.

"I didn't say anything wrong. All I did was tell what is happening to me. Why should I be called trash for that? You can kill me if you want, but I'm not going to keep my mouth shut like other abused women do. They are so afraid to lose their status and their husband's money that they don't say anything and act as if nothing is wrong. For them, wearing jewelry and driving a Prado is more important than self-esteem."

"Normal people don't talk about their problems. You should keep your mouth shut!" shouted Mark.

"I do not care what normal people do. I just abhor those miserable souls who have nothing better to do than spread gossip about what I have said."

She left the kitchen and went to her bedroom. As she lay down in the bed, she felt hurt and saddened by the fact that one of her friends had betrayed her. Tears of frustration soon followed.

Looking at Mary's icon, she prayed. "Mother Mary, other people pray to you and you answer, but when I pray, you are playing a heartless woman. I don't see any love from you. Lord, I feel you have abandoned me. You see my suffering, but don't do anything to help me."

The next day, Silvana picked up her phone and texted her mother.

"Mark came home drunk and threatened to kill me if I continue talking about him."

"Silvana, you know when Mark drinks he says rubbish that he does not mean. You shouldn't take his words seriously. I have told you this on prior occasions. Don't talk about him."

"I'm not talking about him because I want to gossip. I'm hurt, and I feel better when I speak about my pain and what he does to me. However, that ugly-hearted woman didn't have the right to tell him my words. Seeing the wicked behavior of these people, I have lost all desire to be kind to any of them. One of them even said it was my fault because I chose to stay with my abuser. They don't understand that I'm staying to ensure that my children don't go hungry, homeless, or without education. I don't have money to give them all of this, nor shelter to take them to."

"Put your trust in God. He will help you," implored Esmira.

"Yesterday I had trust in Him, and look what happened."

"He cares for you and will help you. Keep faith in Him and pray," typed Esmira.

Silvana put her phone away and looked at her Jesus icon, dismayed at the gossiper's behavior. Because of this "friend", Mark had cursed at her and threatened her with murder.

"Father, I always try to help everyone. Why do people have to be so wicked and ugly? Why did this woman tell him what I said? What did she try to gain? I'm just tired of being around this kind of people."

She closed her eyes, trying to fall asleep, but out of the blue she started to feel nauseous. She got up and stumbled into the bathroom, feeling as if someone had squeezed her brain and then she blacked out.

When Silvana opened her eyes, she found herself sprawled on the floor, her head in agony. She slowly rose and, feeling weak, walked back to her bedroom. She lay in bed silently until she fell asleep.

Chapter 14: Enduring Abuse

As each day passed, Silvana felt more and more as if heavy chains shackled her, and she wanted to break free. Mark's hostility toward her had caused incalculable harm and damage. She felt incredibly betrayed. If he had been a stranger mistreating her, Silvana wouldn't have felt as emotionally hurt and injured. The fact that her husband not only was bullying her, but also didn't support her in any of her activities and undertakings, saddened her beyond belief and expression. She had expected Mark to be not only loving and gentle, but also to be her best friend.

She began volunteering at a local charitable organization, where she managed their website; a job that she enjoyed immensely. But she was afraid to tell Mark, because she knew he would disapprove. Eventually, she told him, since she didn't like the idea of concealing aspects of her life from her spouse.

She approached him one day as he was sitting at his desk in front of his computer.

"Mark," she started.

"What do you want? Can't you see that I'm working?"

She is always disturbing me, incessantly and ceaselessly. Just hearing her voice irritates me.

"I'm working as a web designer for a charitable organization," said Silvana calmly.

He looked at her indifferently. "How much are they paying you?"

"It's just volunteer work; I don't get paid."

Mark shook his head in disapproval. "You are dumb, working for free. As usual, wasting your time. You should devote your time to a job search instead."

"But God expects us to help others," she answered, frowning slightly.

"You can't even help yourself, but want to help others? I'm busy. Leave me alone!"

Silvana's shoulders drooped. She trudged out of the bedroom, regretting that she had told him about her volunteer job.

After a few hours, she heard the doorbell ring. It was an African beggar who Silvana always tried to help. She saw who it was and walked toward the door. Because she took too long to answer, he kept ringing the bell.

"Idiot!" Mark shouted from the bedroom. "Don't you know that I am trying to work? Go and see who is at the door!"

Silvana went outside to the beggar, who was now standing by the gate.

"Miss, my house burned down. I am staying with kind people. Would you please give me something to eat? "

Silvana frowned, but her eyes were kind. "I know that your house didn't burn down, but I am willing to help you."

She quickly ran inside and cautiously filled her shopping bag with some food items: juice, crackers, chips, and a tin of corn. While doing so, she looked up to the top of the steps, fearing that Mark would see her. He disliked beggars and usually chased them away.

She quickly ran back outside and gave the bag of food to the beggar.

"Thank you, Miss! God bless you!"

As she watched him leave, she thought to herself, Life is so unfair. After the divorce, I may not even have a place to live, ending up like this beggar. However, I would rather be free than have a house where I am imprisoned.

Silvana worked diligently towards gaining her independence and to find a satisfying and rewarding job.

One day, she chatted with her friend Jane via Messenger sharing her worries and concerns.

With a unique perspective on life, Jane helped Silvana to look at her own circumstances within a prism, offering various angles of possibility. She taught her how to achieve liberty, and not to worry about who might approve of or accept her. She advised Silvana to do what made her happy, live life to the fullest, and follow her heart's desire.

"I feel like my life is being wasted by staying at home. I studied so hard and got my degree so that I could get a good job, apply my knowledge to work, and continue to learn more in life. Instead, I'm an unpaid maid in my own house."

"Don't give up hope. Keep applying for jobs. Whatever is meant for you, you will get it," typed Jane.

"I want to lead, motivate employees, attend seminars, and take part in different projects," Silvana replied.

"I sincerely understand, but you are refusing to make the necessary and required steps to leave him. The simple fact is that if you continue staying with Mark, you won't be able to achieve your dreams."

Silvana blew out a frustrated breath. "Yes, but the equally simple fact is that I can't leave him without a job. When Mark finds out that I'm leaving him, he will take away my phone, the Internet, and my credit card, leaving me helpless. Where would I take my children? I would be depriving them of the comfortable life that they are accustomed to." Silvana's heart filled with hopelessness and helplessness.

"Have faith, but demonstrate more perseverance and commitment to simply get away from him. One day you will get what you need and wish," typed Jane She felt sorry for Silvana.

"But you have been humiliated by Steve as well," Silvana responded.

"Yes, he mistreated me too many times, and I have asked him to leave. In your case, Silvana, it seems that you cherish being abused. If you didn't, you would leave Mark instead of making excuses."

"It's easy for you to dispense advice, because you are not in my shoes. I don't make brash decisions or take abrupt steps without considering the pros and cons."

Jane suddenly changed the topic. "Are you still going to the prayer group?"

"No, I stopped going there because of the insipid advice I got from a spiritual leader," moaned Silvana.

"What advice?" wrote Jane, somewhat impatiently.

"When I told the spiritual leader the unfortunate nature of my situation, she told me that I ought not only to ask God's permission to file for divorce but also to pray and wait for Mark to alter his misguided ways. In addition, she believes that because women always expect their men to uphold their standards when the men do not do so, they want to leave the marriage, which is not the Christian way. I couldn't take that mentality. It filled my heart with anger and confusion because I do not expect anything besides a cessation of bullying and a demonstration of love and respect."

"That woman has never experienced abuse. Consequently, she has misjudged your predicament in trying to advise you," typed Jane sympathetically.

"I would never expect an abused woman to stay in such a broken marriage-unless, of course, her partner changes. I would tell her to find an escape hatch and forget him forever. As you know, Mark's abuse depresses me and I feel lonely. Only my faith in God helps me to deal with it. Many times during my depression I cry, asking Him to help me find a route out of depression, anger, and my unhappy marriage. Since I started praying and entrusting my problems, hopes, and even my anger to the Lord, I have felt better. One day He will deliver me from my suffering. "

"God is great! He will indeed deliver you. Frequent the Orthodox Church, and you will find God's Grace within, and peace."

A moment later, she typed, "I'm sorry, but I have to go. Some buyers are coming to see my house. I will talk to you later."

"Good luck with the house," Silvana typed back.

***

Once she realized that her existence wouldn't change if she wasn't proactive, Silvana wondered if she would ever be happy, and what kind of life she and her children might have after the divorce. Therefore, she hesitated to apply for one because of her fears regarding the future. The fact remained that Silvana needed answers to her questions, and instead of searching for answers from God, Silvana kept looking for them in the wrong places. She continued to turn to psychics, even though she knew that God didn't approve of anything associated with the occult.

Silvana found a website where she was able to get free readings from mediums. Silvana believed in predictions, not realizing that such readings were just peddling false hope. Therefore, she became so addicted to them that every other day she tried to get a free reading, repeatedly asking the same questions.

When will I get a job?

When will my life change?

What kind of life will my children and I have after the divorce?

Every false reading promised her a better job, a better life, and genuine love. They told her what she needed to hear. However, Silvana was disappointed time and again when their predictions didn't come true.

Finally, at the same time that she was drowning in the sin of turning to the occult instead of steadfastly believing in Almighty God, Silvana experienced a spiritual breakthrough. She finally understood that only God could see into the future. However, although she tried to stop, she was drawn like a magnet back to the company of psychics.

At one point, while lying in bed, she prayed, "Father, I have betrayed you by frequenting psychics. Although I keep trying to break this habit, whenever I get frustrated I go back to them. Please help me to stop."

She shifted to her left side, closed her eyes, and fell asleep, confident that her prayers had been heard. Soon after that night, she was freed of the urge to seek out readings once and for all. Silvana was still full of fear and worry, which prevented her from taking steps to end her marriage. However, most of her fears and worries disappeared because of God and her good friend Jane.

Even though they had never met in real life, they became good online friends. However, Jane couldn't understand how a loving woman like Silvana could stay with an abuser like her husband. As they chatted online one day, she typed, "It seems as if you love being treated like a slave."

They'd gone over this ground before, but neither minded. They both knew that, someday, there would be a breakthrough.

"No, I don't," Silvana typed, frowning.

"If you didn't like it, you wouldn't have stayed in your marriage for so many years," said Jane.

"I'm not a slave, but I can't leave as yet. I have to think about my children first. I need to get a job and have shelter or accommodation."

"You are always offering excuses. It sounds like you don't even wish to make the first step to leave. However, if you decide to leave, half of his property would be yours, and after the divorce, you would have a great deal of money, as well."

Silvana heaved a long sigh. "I neither need nor want any of his property. I just want to leave and take the children away with me."

"Don't be silly. You can't just leave without asking for anything. You have children. Do you want another woman to come and seize what belongs to your kids?"

Silvana shook her head in disapproval. Talking about material items annoyed her.

"Why does everything have to be about money? I don't give a damn about his belongings."

Jane became frustrated with Silvana's stubbornness and left the chat without saying goodbye. She didn't like the fact that Silvana always complained without trying to solve her problems. Jane herself had endured a difficult and arduous life, but she had never let anyone abuse her. After the painful separation from Steve, she couldn't start a new relationship but was quite happy on her own.

***

A few days before Christmas, Silvana and Mark decided to go to a fundraising Christmas dinner, which was scheduled to be at 7 p.m. When Rehema found out about the Christmas dinner, she offered to mind the children for the entire day, in order to give Silvana free time to prepare for it.

Silvana had been involved in some charitable work for the Kenyan Life Center, where abused women and their children found asylum. Sometimes Silvana, together with Rehema, went to the Kenyan Life Center and spent a few hours with the children, reading and playing games with them. Silvana loved being around the children, who were happy to have her companionship. Being around them filled Silvana's heart with joy, because she was able to give them the love that she had never received as a child. At the same time, she felt sorry for the abused women and tried to help them. She listened to their concerns and gave them advice.

The dinner was for the Kenyan Life Center, and Silvana was eager to go. Long before the dinner date, she had bought a beautiful long purple dress, with shiny silver high-heeled shoes. She looked forward to putting them on.

After Rehema picked up Silvana's children, she was alone with Mark in their roomy two-story house. During lunchtime, standing in the kitchen, they talked about the children's outstanding grades, their promising future, and their many opportunities.

Then Mark began to talk about things that they couldn't achieve in life. His blue eyes clouded over. Silvana knew that he regretted the many opportunities he had missed out on.

Silvana looked at him thoughtfully. Maybe that is why he always tries to tear down my self-esteem and control me.

Mark's mouth curved down as his eyes darkened. His voice was grim when he spoke. It sounded to Silvana as if he blamed her. "It's already too late for us. We can't do anything about missed opportunities."

Silvana disagreed. She believed that it was never too late to make changes in their lives or to pursue their dreams. She knew that people could do so at any time or age. However, she blamed Mark for her missed opportunities. Fear of him, as well as not having self-confidence or faith in God, stopped her from making the necessary steps to become something more.

I have to stop being around negative people because they impede me. I need to surround myself with positive people, those who not only believe in a positive outcome and fight for their dreams and happiness but who also encourage others to do the same thing. Negative people only drag others down with them.

"If I had not married you, I would never have missed out on opportunities and would have achieved more in my life!" Silvana blurted out suddenly. "This marriage has kept me back!"

In her heart, Silvana knew that if Mark's pessimistic thinking, controlling behavior, and emotional abuse hadn't affected her, she could have developed her career path and achieved her goals. However, instead she had spent most of her married years at home as a house cleaner, listening to her husband's negative remarks and pessimistic predictions about her future and her achievements. At the same time, she blamed herself as well, for allowing him to bully her and not taking the steps to bring about positive changes. The first time he had started bullying her, she should have put an end to it right away.

The lines on Mark's forehead grew deeper as his brows knitted.

"You are blaming me for being a failure? I made your life worse, nasty woman?" Mark suddenly burst out with anger. "You can't even get a job. You are nothing, and that's what you'll always be!"

Seeing his anger, Silvana moved away from him.

"Without me, you'd be eating food from the garbage, you stupid Azeri woman! What is the matter with you? You can't even speak English correctly. Who will hire you with your poor English?"

Silvana's eyes grew watery. "Why are you always negative? I'm not uneducated. I have my degree and many diplomas, so someone will hire me eventually."

"You can do nothing right, so if you were to be lucky enough to get hired, you'd get fired immediately for incompetence," Mark sneered out of spite.

Silvana's heart was on fire with anger. She stood silently, fearing to say anything, but looked at him with saddened eyes. It hurt her to hear these words from her partner, a man who should love her.

"You are saying that it was me who spoiled your life? You are indeed an ungrateful woman!" shouted Mark in anger.

Poor Silvana stood in the middle of the kitchen, trying hard not to cry. She had heard this broken-record refrain for years, and it tore down her self-confidence and any belief she had in her abilities.

She glared daggers into Mark's eyes. "If it weren't for your pessimistic thinking, discouraging me all the time, I could have achieved more in my life, but this marriage has held me back!"

Mark's face turned purple. "You are an ungrateful dummy. I have messed up your life? Who paid for your studies? When you came here, you didn't have anything! Who gave you clothes and took you to different countries? Ungrateful trash! I want you out of my house and my life!" he shouted, pointing at the door.

His words felt like a knife piercing her heart. Her feelings were a mixture of anger, loneliness, and frustration. She was concerned that the neighbors might hear him, and would think that she really was trash. As he cussed at her, she cowed by the stove and looked into his furious face. His shaking body movements showed his fury. She feared that he would hit her with something. She knew from experience what his anger made him capable of, so she kept silent.

Her eyes narrowed as she stared at him, lost in thought. I shouldn't have said anything to him in the first place. It is true-if not for his money, I wouldn't have been able to enroll in school or see other countries. But I paid for my degree myself. She shook her head. I don't need his money or his house. I need a husband who will be there emotionally for me, not just financially.

She wanted him to call her "my love", "darling", "babe", and "sweetheart", but those were never the names she heard. She felt lonely and saddened as she watched him. Silvana knew that it took two to make a relationship work, and she was willing to make it work. It seemed, however, that he was not.

"Mark, why are you so hateful? What did I do to you?"

"I'm not hateful. I just don't like stupid people around me," snapped Mark.

Silvana shook her head, tears falling from her eyes.

"Do you not see that, with your beastly behavior you have been killing my feelings for you? At home, when you look at me, your facial expression always seems to be like I have done something wrong or that you dislike me. However, with others, you talk nicely, smile, and make jokes. You smile and speak to me nicely only when we are with other people. Why do you pretend?"

Mark replied, "Listen, other people are not stupid or deaf like you. In order for you to understand, you have to be treated like an animal. Then you listen and follow instructions. How many times do I ask you to turn off the lights, but you forget? You take things from the fridge without asking me. You allow our children to waste food and water. You dry clothes in the dryer when it is sunny. You have lived here for so long, but your English is still poor. I just don't like your stupidity."

The muscles in Silvana's lower lip spasmed. The pain passed through her heart. Her eyes narrowed.

"Yes, you are right. I'm stupid because I married you. I was a young, home-loving girl who had never dated anyone. Any man would have married me. But no, I let my senseless romantic nature guide me to you."

She shook her head again. "I just want to go back to Azerbaijan."

"Pack your damned clothes and go back to your country. Nobody wants you here or likes you!"

Mark continued to curse at Silvana until he seemed to run out of hateful words to say. He stomped out of the house, leaving her with a last look of anger. The door slammed shut behind him. She knew he was headed for the bar, and wondered if they would still be going to the Christmas party. Despite being distraught, she still wanted to go. She wanted to put on her beautiful dress, surround herself with people, and get compliments.

Silvana cleaned the house as she cried silently, and then took a shower. She put silver polish on her toenails. When her nail polish dried, she worked on a project hand-stitching curtains for her children's bedroom and waited for Mark to come home.

As soon as Mark staggered in at 7 p.m. he sloshed into the small TV room and cursed at her.

"Your worthless life just got worse! Get the hell out of my life. You understand, right?" He spat on her at every word.

Silvana didn't move from the sofa where she sat stitching the last curtain. She glared at him.

"What are you doing? Stop spitting on me! Why are you coming home drunk and cursing at me?"

"If you don't like it, then get the hell out of here. No one wants you here."

Silvana had the courage to retaliate if he hit her, but she didn't like to fight. Instead, she secretly turned on a recorder. She wanted evidence to take to the court for future divorce hearings.

She knew that, most times when women were abused, people didn't believe their accusations, especially when a man was a recognized charmer. Rather, they blamed the woman. To everyone else, Mark was a charming and loving man, the perfect husband. Silvana knew that this was true of other abusive men from her friends who were experiencing the same thing.

"I didn't say that you are my problem. Stop spitting on me. I said that your negative thinking affected me," Silvana retorted. She didn't like seeing Mark drunk. He was offensive without alcohol, but drinking made his behavior even worse.

"I don't feel sorry for rubbish like you, given what you have told me, you stupid woman," Mark said, spitting on her again.

Silvana told herself to calm down. Aloud, she said, "What I meant was that by saying over and over that I'm stupid, that I'm a zero, and that I would be unable to do or achieve anything in my life, you took away my self-confidence. When I applied for my studies, you told me that I would fail because of my poor English and that I was wasting your money. Do you know how frustrated I became at hearing your negative predictions?"

Her hands had stopped shaking, and now she was enraged. "I was afraid that I would fail, and that you would get mad at me for wasting money. Because of your negative remarks, I was going to quit, but thanks be to God I didn't."

"Leave me alone, zero. You are nasty trash!" snarled Mark.

"It is you who is nasty. I told you before, stop spitting on me!" Silvana shouted.

Mark suddenly noticed Silvana's computer, which was lying on the couch.

"Don't use my Internet!" He picked up her laptop from the sofa and tried to smash it. "I will break your computer if you do!"

Silvana quickly lunged toward him and grabbed it away.

"Hey, don't break my computer! You have already broken two. It has my project and other important files."

Silvana snapped it up and put it away. Next, she knew, he would threaten to tear up her passport. That was the pattern.

"I'm telling you, if you have a problem with me, get another man," growled Mark, hitting Silvana's hand.

Allowing Mark to curse at her was one thing, but she would never allow anyone to raise a hand to her without hitting back. She gave him a smack on the hand that had hit her.

"Get away, idiot! You are an abuser. Do you think I need a man after being abused by you? I don't need another one."

"If I'm an abuser, then leave my house. Stupid piece of trash!" yelled Mark.

"Don't call me trash! Trash is the woman who sleeps with different men. I never let any man touch me, nor have I slept with any man other than you!"

Silvana tried to hold back her tears and indignation. All my life I did what is right but not suitable for me. I'm a beautiful woman, and men always wanted to date me, but I refused to date anyone because I was keeping my virginity for the one who I would marry. How could he call me trash?

"You are worse than trash, like your entire family!"

"My family is not trash."

"Your family eats food from the garbage. You will join them soon."

"Leave my family alone! They don't eat food from the garbage. God will punish you," growled Silvana.

"I'm not like you, with no money. I have money and can pay people to look after me."

He picked up a fan from the floor and struck Silvana's left hand. The pain made her flinch. When Mark tried to hit her again, Silvana grabbed the fan and shoved him with it. Mark fell and ended up lying flat on the tile, with the fan on top of his chest.

Silvana kept him pinned to the floor with the fan and shouted at him, "I'm fed up with your abuse! You have been treating me inhumanely for years, and have not acknowledged anything good in me. For all these years, you have called me zero, stupid, and dummy. You told me that if I were to get another job, men might want to harass me because of my skin color or even rape me. I hate the day I moved to Kenya! I'm not going to let you bully me any longer or put me down regarding everything I do!"

Silvana's heart was full of fury. She couldn't stop shouting. "People like you don't deserve to have a woman like me in your life. Do you know what you deserve? A woman who is genuine trash!" She wanted to cry and scream but restrained herself.

"Stop yelling! The neighbors will hear you. Let go of the fan!" Mark pleaded.

Silvana obeyed and moved away from Mark so that he could get up.

"Nasty trash, you said that I'm wasting your time, but you only need my money," he snarled.

"What money?" Silvana laughed. "Do you give me any money? Most of the time, I leave the house with only one dollar in my bag. I stay with you only because of the kids. I don't want them to have a hard life."

"Take the stupid kids and leave my house by tomorrow. Go back to your beloved Azerbaijan. If you don't go, I will hire someone and have all of you killed."

"I'm not afraid to die. Do you think I wish to live? What is the point in living if I'm not happy? So, go ahead and hire somebody."

Silvana was fatigued and irritated. Thoughts of committing suicide still plagued her. At the same time, she didn't want her children to live without a mother and was afraid she would burn in eternal fire for killing herself.

Silvana knew that she was the only source of love for her little ones. Without her, they wouldn't be happy. Mark loved them, but didn't know how to show real love. His way of showing love was to ensure that the children had material things and a comfortable life.

"I'm not going to Azerbaijan! I will stay in Kenya for as long as I want to stay," Silvana firmly assured him.

"I'll call immigration. They'll deport you and the children."

"Go ahead and call them. I didn't do anything wrong, nor am I residing here illegally. Therefore, they can't deport me."

Mark left the TV room and went into the bedroom. From where she stood, Silvana could hear him cursing her. Retching soon followed.

Silvana sighed and went to see where he was puking. She found him lying down on the floor, throwing up. She pitied him, but not enough to clean up his vomit. Her mother used to puke a great deal when she was drunk. Silvana never liked seeing her mother drunk either, and disliked the behavior even more when it was her husband.

She left him alone to lie in his bile. Silvana went back to the other bedroom and sobbed bitterly. If my mother had not slept with my father, I wouldn't have been born. It's their fault that I'm a bastard, and my life has been unhappy. I shouldn't have ever married Mark. I should have listened to my mother. Oh-h-h!

Silvana's left hand, which Mark had struck with the fan, throbbed painfully. Frustrated with the fight and her unhappy marriage, Silvana decided to take steps to leave him.

Right now, she was financially dependent on Mark. Ever since she had gotten married, Silvana had worked only for a short time, unable to save any money. She was in a foreign country, without family and money. Where could she go with her children, without finances and without a place to live? If she didn't have the kids, Silvana could leave easily, because she wasn't afraid to stay alone without any help. However, with children, she had to think of how it would affect them before making any rash decisions or taking any steps.

Silvana loved her children more than anything else in this world. They were her blessings, sent to her by God. They filled her heart with love and joy. Without them, her life would be empty and pointless. She wanted to keep them safe from abusers, and to give them a better life than what she'd, along with a good education. Growing up, she had seen how her mother had difficulty supporting them and had barely spent time with her and her siblings owing to her work. Silvana was protective of her children and would never let them out of her sight or send them anywhere alone. She knew that after her divorce, she would end up working and would have to leave her children with someone else. She didn't want to leave them with anyone other than Rehema or her mother. "How can I work if I don't have anyone to look after my children?" Silvana used to ask Rehema.

Silvana always thought about the pros and cons before making any decisions. She also knew that she wouldn't be able to stay in an unhappy marriage for much longer. It annihilated everything good in her, changed her personality, and affected her children emotionally. She didn't want to spend her days worrying about whether Mark might disapprove of something she had done.

After the fight and vomiting, Mark fell asleep.

Silvana called Rehema. "Would you please bring the children back," she asked in a depressed tone of voice.

"What happened? Why are you still at home?" asked Rehema, puzzled.

"We had a fight, so we didn't go anywhere."

"What was wrong this time?"

"He got angry because I told him that marrying him had hindered my development."

Rehema blew out a breath. "You know his character. Why do you bother saying anything to him? Just adapt yourself to him. Make certain everything is in order when he comes home and that the children don't make any noise or clutter things up. Make certain that the lights are off and that the cell phone is unplugged. This will keep him from getting angry."

Silvana couldn't believe what she was hearing. "Why do I have to change myself to suit him? Am I a slave? Yes, sometimes I may fail to turn off a light or unplug the phone, but that doesn't give him the right to go on like an insane man."

"I agree with the opinion that he shouldn't react this way. However, many things could be prevented if you would attempt to adapt to his wants and his way of doing things. For instance, he calls you a thief and gets irritated if you have a soft drink, eat his chocolate without asking him, or cook. Why can't you ask him first?" countered Rehema.

Silvana's eyes widened at her friend's naiveté. "I'm not a child. Neither am I a stranger or a servant working in his house. I'm his wife. This gives me equal rights. So why, as a wife living in the same house, should I have to ask for permission to cook something or drink in the house?"

"The fact is that it will prevent an argument."

Silvana's heart filled with anger.

"Rehema, you are not in my shoes. Thus, it is easy for you to judge and dispense advice for me. However, I believe that, when people get married, they must share everything. On the one hand, if I want to go into his wallet and take some money or use something of his that is personal, I have to ask for permission. But as his wife, when I use things from the fridge, I shouldn't have to ask for approval. I didn't get married in order to lead my life in fear or to have to be mindful of what I can say or use. This is not how marriage works. It's not what I signed up for."

"Don't get upset. I'm just trying to help you. He gives you food, clothing and supports the children. What else do you need?" Rehema asked.

Silvana couldn't believe that her friend would support Mark and be so senseless. To her, Rehema sounded just like her brother, who used to hurl out the same lines.

"Rehema, you don't understand anything. Do you think material things without emotional support make me happy? No, they don't." Silvana's voice became unsteady.

"But he loves you. He ensures that you and the children have everything."

"How can I feel loved while being constantly put down and bullied by him? My mom bought food and clothes but never hugged me or spent time with me. Without the basic needs of love and closeness taken care of, do you think that my mother's food and clothing made me happy? No, I was a lonely child who needed Mother's hugs and affection. For my mom, giving us material things was a way of demonstrating love. Mark does the same thing, but it is wrong. If you truly love someone, you spend time with that person, listen, share thoughts, do things together, and try to understand one another. You support them emotionally, respect them, and encourage them. I don't see this from Mark, and this is what would make me happy."

"I hear you, but for now please be patient for your children's sake. On your own, you can't support them, so you have to stay with him."

"No, I'm not going to do that. I'm going to leave when the time is appropriate." She was growing weary of this lengthy exchange with Rehema.

"I believe that, with God's help, I will survive on my own. I'm educated and ambitious, so I can get a job and start my life anew. I'm just tired of being manipulated, exploited, and controlled."

"Well, only you know what is best for you and your children," Rehema agreed.

"As human beings, we don't know what is best for us. Only God knows. We can only ask and try to get what we want the most," Silvana replied.

Silvana was developing a headache. Her legs were hurting from standing for so long.

"Please bring my children back home. We will talk tomorrow." She hung up the phone, exhausted.

Twenty minutes later, Rehema dropped off Silvana's children and left right away.

"Did you have a good time at Rehema's?" Silvana asked as she hugged Aygun.

"Yes, Mommy. We played with her pups. They are so cute! Can you buy one for us, please?" Aygun asked.

"I will ask Papa to buy it. Wash your hands so you can eat," instructed Silvana.

She gave the children something to eat, and then put them to bed. After praying with her kids, she hugged them and turned off the light in their bedrooms.

Once the children were asleep, Silvana lay down in bed next to Mark, saddened both by his vulgar words and by her unhappy marriage. She tossed and turned, trying to understand how she had ended up in this situation. Thoughts about her miserable existence in a foreign country with nobody to turn to or to understand her caused Silvana's eyes to tear up.

"Father, people are so unsupportive of abused women, and do not understand the effects of abuse on them. Did you put me in this situation so that I can support them in their predicament and raise my voice against violence? It is too much for me. I do not want to carry this cross anymore."

As she let out a sigh of despair, she sang a song under her breath. It poured out of her overflowing soul.

O Lord, my soul is lonely
Crying for help but no one listens
It's locked in a cage
Open the door!
O Lord, heal my desperate soul
Dry my tears
Help me break free of the chains
So, that I can fly free like a bird!
O Lord, I'm tired of struggling
Just wishing to be released
Yet something keeps me back
Heal me and let me go!
O Lord, I cry to you every day
I do not have the strength to endure
Hear my prayers and crying voice
Test me no more, no more, no more!
O Lord, I walk in the darkness
Brighten my path
I need you and your light in my life,
I can't survive without you.

Break the chains, I beg you! I can't fight any longer!
O Lord, I am lost in emptiness and mired in a rut
Just trying to run far away
But these chains are keeping me down
O Lord, don't let me drown
Release all my pain
Break now the chains and
Let me go far away!

"What are you mumbling?" asked Mark, half asleep.

"I am singing," answered Silvana, trying to sound calm. She did not like to let others know of her emotions or pain.

"Shut up! I do not want to hear any noise."

Silvana got up, enraged. "If you don't want to hear my voice, close your ears. Every time I speak or sing, you tell me to shut up. As long as I am alive, I will not shut up."

She left Mark and settled down in the living room on the sofa. The events of earlier in the day still bugged her. During her silent internal prayers, Silvana started to cry.

"My Heavenly Father, I beg you to please hear my prayers. Why are you testing me, my Father? Why can't you accept me with all my faults and give me what I need? Do you not see he is hurting me?"

Silvana wiped her tears with a tissue. "I'm so lonely and hurt. You know I never felt loved-always abandoned. My parents never hugged me or said they loved me. My dad left me, and people were unkind toward me. This left my heart empty. My Lord, surround me with your love. I wish you'd hug me like a father hugs a daughter. I wish you could pat my head like a father pats a child's head."

Silvana's tears continued streaming down her face. She tried not to sob loudly so that her children and husband wouldn't hear her. "Father, I'm happy and grateful for my four miracles, but I'm unhappy in this relationship. Why did you chain me down in a marriage that affects me negatively? I'm full of anger and miserable, but you see this as a sin. How can I get rid of this state if he keeps upsetting me?

"Father, he always cusses me, badgers me, makes me feel guilty, never spends time with me. He does not support me emotionally. Every day I become increasingly afraid to anger him, wondering if I was just plain stupid, downright no good, or just doing everything incorrectly. Other people see my talents and goodness, but not him. As far as he is concerned, everything I do is meaningless, even my religion and prayers. When I catch the flu, he tells me to stay away from him so he won't get it. Do you remember when I got very dizzy and couldn't walk, but he left me alone with the children and went to the office? I could barely get up and get the children ready for school. How could he leave me alone in this condition? He only cared about his job, not me. However, I feel sorry for him, because in many respects he is evidently unhappy. Please forgive him and allow him to find true happiness in my absence."

She tried to fall asleep, but the memories of her past injuries, her childhood, and the stories of her parents' lives prevented it. She recalled everything that had happened when she was a child. Silvana's heart filled with wretchedness and regret, especially when she thought about her father, Samed. She couldn't understand how he could look after his other children and forget about her existence. She was also upset with her mother, Esmira, for not being emotionally there for her. However, at the same time, she knew that Esmira tried her best to support her children. Esmira never felt loved either, so she didn't know how to show her feelings to Silvana and her other children.

"Father, I thank you very much for my children. Please don't take them away from me, but keep them safe from all evil, and from people who are just abusers. Give them a happy future and help me to bring them up in a right way. I love you, my Father, with all my heart."

Every time Silvana would say to God, "I love you", her heart would fill with love for God and humanity. She would feel a warm energy emanating from her heart and spreading through her whole body, and this time was no exception.

After praying for a while, Silvana felt relieved and stopped crying. "I know that one day you will change my life by giving me everything I need. Forgive me for my negativity," Silvana said with hope in her heart.

She believed that with God in her life, anything would be possible. Silvana knew that in His own time, He would answer her prayers. He was loving and never forgot His children. He gave them what he knew was best for them. Therefore, Silvana decided to be patient and continue praying, putting all her hopes into His hands.

Chapter 15: Broken Chains

The following autumn, Silvana fell ill, the worst illness of her life. Her whole body hurt, and she burned with fever. She went for a blood test because of the great pain she was in. It confirmed that she had yellow fever. Despite being sick, Silvana was unable to stay in bed for very long. To her disappointment and dismay, her house cleaner Rehema became ill as well, which meant that Silvana had the responsibilities of the entire house around her neck. The children had exams going on. They didn't have anyone to review the term's work with them other than their mother. Therefore, lying on the sofa and hot from the fever, Silvana struggled to review six subjects with them.

At one point during this time, she raised her head and gazed at twelve-year-old Marie. Her eyebrows pinched together. Tears built up in her eyes.

"Please go get your social studies book."

Marie got up and brought it as Silvana stretched her legs. "Oh my God, I can't take the pain. I'm feeling so hot," she said, grimacing.

Marie looked at her worriedly. "Mother, are you okay? What would you like me to do for you?"

"I want you to do well in your schoolwork and get good grades," Silvana said, smiling slightly.

She took the textbook from Marie and read for her. As she read, her eyes closed. She stopped, forgetting that she was reading.

Suddenly, Silvana asked, "Did you buy flowers?"

Seven-year-old Aygun glanced at Marie and shrugged her shoulders, not understanding why her mother was talking about flowers.

Silvana opened her eyes again. "Oh, I forgot I was reading."

She closed them. "Marie, tell me when do we celebrate Labour Day?" she asked.

Immediately after, she said, "Somebody, please turn on the fan. I can't bear the heat." Big beads of sweat cascaded from her face.

Nine-year-old Peter, who was sitting at the table, turned on the fan.

"I'm waiting. When do we celebrate tea day...sorry...Labour Day?"

"May first," the girls answered.

Silvana dozed off and dropped the book on the floor. Seeing her sleeping, Marie decided to help her siblings with their schoolwork.

As they were reviewing their homework, they heard Silvana talking to herself: "Mother, I want to come back home. I'm not happy here."

After a while, Silvana sat up and gasped, "I can't take the pain!" She cried and shook uncontrollably.

Six-year-old David ran to her. "Are you okay?" he asked, holding her hand.

"I'm sick," replied Silvana. "But we need to continue reviewing your schoolwork."

"Don't worry. We will review it ourselves," Marie assured her. "Lie down and relax." She gently patted her mother's head.

Silvana lay down again, thirsty and still shaking. Seeing his mother shivering, Peter ran upstairs, brought a blanket, and covered her.

"Marie, please help your siblings study," Silvana told her daughter. "Then focus on your social studies. Call me when you are ready for the questions."

The children went into the study room while Silvana stayed alone in the living room. As she dozed off for a few seconds, Silvana muttered, "Granny, what did you cook?"

Being ill, but unable to stay in bed because of her responsibilities, frustrated Silvana. Mark wasn't helping her at all. He didn't even bother to ask her how she was feeling or if she needed anything.

The fact that she was married to a selfish man who didn't pay any attention to her irked Silvana. She couldn't forgive him for leaving her sick and all alone at home.

On Monday night, Silvana's joint pain intensified. The pain was so intense that she couldn't get up from bed or move her legs. Poor Aygun, seeing her mother in pain, massaged her legs.

"Mother, are you feeling better?" asked Aygun in a soft tone, looking at Silvana with concern.

"Yes, I feel a little bit better, but my legs still hurt badly." Tears from the pain fell from her eyes.

Aygun put her hands over her mother. "In the name of God, pain leave my mommy's body."

"Mother, don't cry," said David. He also gave Silvana a massage, trying to reduce her pain.

Silvana hugged them and, with love in her heart, uttered, "Thanks for your care. Your actions show that you truly love me."

She pulled back and gazed into their eyes intently. "Saying "I love you" to someone is not enough. What we do to make someone happy demonstrates what we feel toward another person."

Aygun looked toward the front door and frowned.

"What is it?" asked Silvana.

"Why is Papa taking so long to come home from the bar?"

"He does not care for you at all. How could he leave you alone, ill, and instead spend time drinking with his friends?" added Marie, looking serious. At her age she understood many things, and did not like her father's behavior toward her mother.

"As you grow up, make certain that you show your love toward others, not with empty words, but through your actions toward them," Silvana told her.

She grimaced in pain as she tried to move her leg. Her joint pain was so bad that she could barely move. It took a lot of effort to even speak.

"Do we make you feel loved?" asked Aygun.

"You always tell me you love me. At the same time you are trying to help me just to make me happy." She smiled gratefully.

"But Papa loves you as well. He always buys everything for you and for us," said Peter.

"Yes, he gives us a comfortable life, but at the same time he is not here emotionally for us and says derogatory words to me. Love shouldn't be shown with material things but with care, love, understanding, gentleness, patience, closeness, and emotional support," said Silvana.

As she spoke, her physical pain increased. Silvana wanted to take a painkiller but could not get up from the bed. Finally, she asked the children to go to bed, sad that she couldn't tuck them in.

At 9 p.m. with the children fast asleep, Mark came back home.

Hearing his steps, Silvana shouted, "Mark!"

"What happened?" asked Mark, entering the bedroom. He was, as usual, drunk.

"I'm in intense pain and can't move. Can you please give me one of your painkillers?" Silvana asked.

Mark smiled. "You see, God is punishing you for eating my chocolates without permission."

"According to my Orthodox religion, illness is not a punishment, but a blessing, because it cleanses the person's soul and builds a strong bond between God and the person," answered Silvana, writhing in pain.

"Oh!" she groaned, "Get me the painkiller, please. I can't take this any longer."

"Since God is cleansing you, let him heal you as well," Mark sneered. He turned and left the room without giving Silvana the painkiller.

Frustrated, Silvana texted her mother, trying to find comfort and to distract herself from the pain.

"Mother, how is Granny doing?"

"She is growing worse and refusing to eat. Most days, she sits on the porch cussing our neighbor Safar and me. She thinks that he plans to kill her. I didn't eat at all today. I just sat on the porch, ensuring that she didn't curse him.

"She said that she hoped I would die," Esmira moaned. "I'm fed up with this life. I don't have money and am deeply in debt. It is better to die instead of living in poverty."

It was plain that she was feeling hopeless.

Silvana was filled with worry, and tried to type something to soothe her: "Mother, please don't commit suicide, because that will take you into an eternal burning fire. I will help you one day, but don't wait for help from Mark. He does not care about you."

"My life is a sort of living Hell. My mother hates me and throws away the food I prepare for her. She is constantly embarrassing me in public. At night, she curses loudly at people and tosses things at me," Esmira complained.

Silvana knew that Sadaget blamed Esmira for her grandchildren's unhappy lives.

"Be strong and ensure that she eats. If she dies, I don't know what I will do. Plus, you have no money to bury her."

"I can't force her to eat. My blood pressure is very high. I will talk to you later," typed Esmira.

Silvana stayed in bed, crying from both the unbearable pain and the worry that her Granny would die soon. She wanted to spend some time with her granny before Sadaget died. She also wanted to help her mother, but she was helpless herself. With all of her worries about her Granny and still in pain, Silvana barely managed to fall asleep. However, when she did, she saw her Granny's funeral in a dream.

Seeing her Granny's death made her cry so much that her sobs echoed throughout the bedroom. Fortunately, because of his drunkenness, Mark slept soundly without hearing anything.

Silvana got up once that night and sent her mother a voice message: "Mother, be patient and stay strong. God will help you, and as soon as I land a job I will help you." She then went back to sleep.

After another four days, her fever was gone. However, the joint pain remained. Plus, the anger trapped inside her felt like a weight on her chest. Silvana could barely keep herself from shouting at the children. Anger made her irritated every time they didn't listen to her.

***

Another month went slowly by, and December eventually came. Silvana prepared for Christmas as she waited for Rehema to return to work.

Unfortunately, Rehema's mother got sick, and she had to stay at home with her. Silvana found herself getting up early in the morning, cleaning windows and wiping down the walls and doors. The task of getting the painting done outside also fell to her.

After cleaning her house, she bought beautiful golden curtains and hung them up in the living room. Then she called a painter, who came and painted the walls of the house on the outside. A few times Silvana went outside to check the painter's work. As the laborer was leaving, Silvana checked his work again and noticed that he hadn't painted the back wall of the house properly. She went back inside the house and said to Mark, "Before paying the painter, come and check the wall."

"What is wrong with it?" snapped Mark.

"He didn't paint it correctly."

Mark went outside and looked at the wall. Seeing the sloppy work, he complained to Silvana, "All this time you have been at home. Why didn't you check his work before he finished?"

"I was checking it, but because the paint was damp I didn't notice it. Should I pay the full amount for his work?" Silvana's voice was shaky.

"Yes, pay the meathead and tell him that I don't want him to come back here anymore. Let him leave my house," Mark snarled, his voice raised.

He stomped over to the painter, enraged. "You messed up that wall, instead of making it look better, you jerk. Take your money and leave."

He gestured toward Silvana. "Give him his money!"

Silvana gave the painter the money, and he left.

Soon after, Mark's friend came and they decided to go out to the pub. However, as they were leaving, Mark noticed that the painter had left thinners and paint cans outside.

"Why didn't you tell the worker to put them away?" he growled at Silvana. "Go and put them away yourself now!" he ordered in a commanding voice.

"I will do it later on," Silvana replied.

Mark gave her a sharp look, and left with his friend. Silvana decided not to move anything. She was angered by the fact that, while she worked hard at home, Mark just went out to have a good time with his friend.

In the evening, Mark came home drunk as usual. Silvana was sitting on the sofa, stitching a dress. When he saw the thinners and the paint cans still outside, he became infuriated.

"Why didn't you remove them? I don't want rubbish in front of my house where people can see. You don't know anything about taking care of the house. Go and remove them now!" he said in a firm voice.

"No. You remove them." Silvana fixed him with a cold glare.

Mark went outside, picked up the cans, and threw them inside the house. Thinners spilled on the floor. "Get the mop and clean up the mess!" he ordered.

Silvana remained on the sofa. "You made the mess, so mop it up yourself."

Mark proceeded to clean it up. However, when he picked up the stepladder that was standing in his way, he purposely dropped it on Silvana's foot and walked away.

Pain shot through her. She clutched her foot, and saw blood oozing from an abrasion. Furious, she got up from the sofa and shouted, "Stupid man, you hurt my foot!"

The pain increased, making Silvana even angrier. She picked up a nearby empty bucket and hurled it at him, but it missed.

"I've had enough of your abuse," she yelled. "This entire week you have been harassing me. While I was working diligently, fixing your house for Christmas, you were relaxing and drinking with your friends. The next time you abuse me, I will open my mouth and curse you back!" She squeezed her hands into fists, barely keeping herself from hitting him.

Silvana went into the bathroom, turned on the tap in the bathtub, and rinsed her wound. She grimaced from the burning pain.

Father, how many times has he hurt me? she whispered.

After she turned off the water, she could hear the kids whispering in the bedroom next door. She limped into the bedroom to send them to sleep in an attempt to return things to normal. She always made sure that the children were in bed by 8:30 p.m. in order for them to get enough sleep for school.

When she saw the wound on her mother's foot, Marie ran toward her. "What happened? Did Papa do this to you?"

Silvana couldn't lie to her children. "Yes, Papa dropped a stepladder on me and hurt my foot."

"Why did he do that?" asked David, his eyes on Silvana's foot.

"He got infuriated because I didn't remove the paint thinners and other things from outside."

"Why didn't you remove them?" asked Marie.

"Because I'm tired of doing everything around here, while he goes off to drink in some bar," Silvana nearly shouted in frustration.

She put her arms around Marie. "When you grow up, if any man disrespects you, leave him right away," she said in warning.

Aygun approached her mother, staring at the gash on her foot. "I heard him shouting at you, but I was afraid to stand up for you. I'm sorry for staying in my room," said Aygun, looking guilty.

"Don't worry. I'm okay," said Silvana. She sighed deeply, trying to keep back her tears.

After talking for a while, all of them prayed to God.

"Mother, what sins can send people to Hell?" asked David.

"Treating people miserably, loving material things, lying, pride, boasting.

"Papa drinks, abuses you, and does not go to confession. Will he go to Hell?" asked David.

Aygun looked pleadingly at Silvana. "I don't want Papa to end up in Hell. I hope he will confess."

"Pray for Papa. Jesus will help him to find the right way," said Silvana reassuringly.

But without me in his life, she thought at the same time.

"Mother, will God punish him for hurting you?" asked Peter.

"As is customary in life, how people behave toward others may come back to haunt them. Unless he repents and changes his ways, God may choose to punish him. However, at times humans might tend to harm themselves with poor decisions and choices that can be viewed as evil in God's eyes. Nonetheless, such punishment does not always prove to transform them because often people do not consider God's actions as punishment and see no reason for change."

She smiled lovingly at them and stood up. "It's getting late. Go to your bedroom, boys. It's bedtime."

After Silvana turned off the light, she headed back to her bedroom. Mark went in a while later and apologized.

"Silvana, I didn't mean to hurt you. It was an accident."

She scowled at him. "No, you purposely dropped it on my foot. Leave me alone!"

Mark returned the scowl and left the bedroom, leaving Silvana nursing her bruised foot. She lay on the bed, her tears dampening the pillow. As she sighed with despair, she felt a strong impulse to cry out loudly from within her heart: Jesus, Son of God, I am so weary of my life. I feel like a bird locked in a cage. I wish I could fly away to my freedom. At the same time, I pity him because he appears unable to find happiness, and thus a path to You.

Christmas Day arrived a week later. Silvana was so exhausted that she wanted to stay in bed, but her children woke her up so that they could open their gifts.

All of them went downstairs to the Christmas tree. The children unwrapped their gifts as Mark and Silvana took pictures. Mark gave Silvana a beautiful gold chain, but Silvana didn't feel any joy from it. She gave it back to him immediately. She still remembered the stepladder he had dropped on her foot a week before. However, the children were overjoyed with their gifts, and spent the rest of the day using whatever they got for Christmas.

The day passed peacefully. However, as Mark slept peacefully that night, Silvana spent it fuming and thinking about applying for a divorce. She decided to leave him, not only to put an end to her abuse, but also to be able to lead her life peacefully.

As she lay in bed, she texted Vladimir. "I have not only been putting up with garbage from some people for the sake of God, but also trying not to hurt their feelings. I decided not to take nonsense from anybody anymore," typed Silvana.

"What do you plan to do?" responded Vladimir.

"I decided to be just like them. I have realized that if you are gentle, friendly, or kind, there are those who will mistreat you."

Vladimir typed, "Jesus Christ said to his disciples, 'Blessed are you who are poor, for yours is the kingdom of God. Blessed are you who hunger now, for you will be satisfied. Blessed are you who weep now, for you will laugh. Blessed are you when people hate you, exclude you, insult you, and reject your name as evil because of the Son of Man' (Luke 6:20-22). When these people mistreat you, they are helping you to enter Paradise. So, you should be happy for that."

"I don't need that way of entering into Paradise. I can enter heaven by leading a righteous life and following God's will, and by treating people with love while remaining humble. However, if I don't stand up for myself, I will allow negativity to affect me, and folks will be more than willing to take advantage of me. I'm a simple woman who loves everyone, but if I'm mistreated, I get mad and open my bitter mouth," responded Silvana.

Vladimir continued, "Matthew 5.39 says, 'But I tell you not to resist an evildoer. On the contrary, whoever slaps you on the right cheek, turn the other to him, as well.' This means when someone hurts you, don't fight back. When your mate is cursing at you, don't curse back."

Silvana shook her head in disapproval. "Vladimir, you do not understand anything. The fact is that there must be an end to all of this foul behavior. In our world, you must simply say 'no' or 'enough', thus removing yourself from the company of abusive people and from the situations they create. Otherwise, people will continue to take advantage of you, assuming that you are either naive or too ignorant to notice. To survive, you must stand up and speak up for yourself, but without resorting to violence or inflicting harm to others."

Silvana started yawning. "We will chat another time. Thank you very much for being a good friend. If this world had more people like you, our society would thrive. However, as long as it's full of envy, pride, selfishness, and racism, we will never see positive changes. We will continue seeing abuse, lies, innocent death, and hunger."

***

Silvana continued looking for a job at the beginning of the new year, and to her surprise she received two offers. The first job offer was from Metromax for a position of manager's assistant, and the other one was for a real estate manager. At first, Silvana didn't know which position to accept, but because of the flexibility that the second job allowed her, she decided to take the real estate manager position. Overjoyed, she called Rehema to pass on the good news.

"Rehema, I found a good job. They have offered me a good salary and flexible hours."

"I'm happy for you. Now you can be independent and have your own money," said Rehema, relieved for her.

"Yes, you're right. I can also start the divorce process as well," Silvana said gleefully.

"Are you sure you want to divorce?"

Silvana rolled her eyes. "Why everyone asks me the same question. Of course, I want to divorce and get away from this abuse. Am I getting anything from this marriage?"

"He can change," Rehema suggested in a low voice, trying not to irritate Silvana.

"I have been waiting too long for him to change, and he never has. Anyway, can he remove the pain he has caused? Can he erase the memories of being abused by him?"

"No, he can't," answered Rehema, regretting that she had gotten into yet another discussion about the divorce.

"Therefore, there is no going back. Even if God Himself asks me to stay with him, I won't," Silvana said with rage in her voice. "However, I will try to forgive him after the divorce."

"Don't get distressed. I was trying to keep your family together for the sake of your children."

"Keeping my family together in an unhealthy environment with a bully won't bring anything positive into my children's lives. You have not walked in my shoes, so you do not understand anything about my situation," stated Silvana in a firm voice. "I will work for two months and then file for divorce."

"Do as you please."

"I have to go now. Talk to you later," said Silvana, and she hung up the phone.

Silvana took a week to sort out her work clothes. She was excited and joyful about the new job, and looked forward eagerly to her first day at work.

On the first Monday in March, she put on a black suit with black shoes and went to the office. As soon as she entered, the director introduced her to the rest of the staff.

"This is Silvana, and she is your new manager."

"Hello, everyone," said Silvana with a warm smile.

"Good morning," answered her co-workers.

Silvana accompanied the director into her new office, and was flabbergasted by its size. There was a big black desk, computer, printer, phone, and a comfortable chair. Overjoyed with the excellent setting, Silvana gratefully sank into her soft chair. She sat for a while and acquainted herself with her duties, tasks, and responsibilities.

**

It was a windy Saturday in the spring, and Silvana had planned to stay home and relax. However, she ended up having to go with the children to their karate classes. Mark dropped all of them off and went to drink. Silvana sat outside of the room on a bench with another mother, and waited for the classes to finish.

After two hours, Mark arrived. Seeing Silvana chatting to a parent, he shook his head and glared at her furiously. However, when he approached her and the other woman noticed him, he was all smiles. As soon as the mom departed, he started in on Silvana.

"You trash, what was that you were saying?"

"Nothing. We were just talking about our children."

"You don't know what to say and when to say it. You better shut your mouth. You always end up talking to low-class poor people!"

Silvana's lip twitched. "She is not a lower-class woman. Anyway, God wants us to be humble and to treat everyone equally."

"You don't have a religion. What do you know about God?"

"I have my religion, and I prefer to talk to poor, simple people instead of being around fake, rich ones with rotten hearts." She felt hurt, and tried not to cry or curse him back.

"You don't want to talk to well-heeled people because you came from penury. That is the reason you feel uncomfortable around wealthy people," responded Mark.

"I didn't come from poverty."

Mark strode toward the garbage bin and pointed at it. "You will be eating from this garbage bin, while I will always have money," he taunted her.

Silvana moved away from him and stood at a distance until the children came out. When they got back home, Silvana was in such a state that she didn't want to talk to anyone or do anything whatsoever. Mark's unkind words had pushed her back into a depressed state.

Later that week, Silvana visited her attorney and asked her to start the divorce process.

"Are you sure that you are ready for a divorce? It's going to be an uphill battle since you plan to ask for his house," her attorney advised her.

"Yes, I'm ready. He has been abusing me emotionally for years. I've put up with it because of the children. However, when a man raises a hand to me, enough is enough," stated Silvana. The incident with the stepladder was foremost in her mind.

"I worry about your mental stability. You are suffering from depression and anger. Will you be able to handle this battle emotionally too?"

Silvana leaned forward, keeping her back rigid. "Do you think a woman who has withstood unbearable levels of abuse for so long is not strong enough? Lulu, I would like to start a new life free of abuse. For that, I'm ready to accept any challenges and battles."

"I understand you perfectly. Therefore, we are going to initiate the process as soon as possible. I will need both your children's birth papers and your marriage certificate. Once you get them to me, I will submit the divorce petition application, along with your letter delineating your abuse. Meanwhile, get copies of both his bank statements and the deeds to his properties," Lulu told her. She leaned back comfortably in her office chair and smiled confidently at her client.

"Thank you, Lulu. I will try to get all the papers by next week." Silvana was all smiles too.

"Be careful, and I will see you soon," Lulu replied.

Silvana left Lulu's office feeling relieved.

During the week, she copied the necessary papers while Mark was at work, concealing all of her activities from his view. When she got all her papers ready, Silvana dropped them off at Lulu's office and waited to hear from her.

***

Summer came, and Silvana received a call from her attorney as she worked on a project in her office.

"Hello," said Silvana.

"Good morning, Silvana. This is Lulu. I have good news for you. I have filed your petition for a divorce, so you had better talk to Mark before the petition is served on him by the court," her attorney advised.

"What is going to happen after the divorce petition is served on him?" asked Silvana.

"He will have thirty days to respond to the petition and to hire an attorney to represent his interests. During the divorce process, the court may issue a temporary order for child custody and spousal and child support. Both of you will have an obligation to supply personal information, such as bank and income statements. You might have to take part in divorce mediation to resolve outstanding conflicts. However, if there is no mutual agreement, then a trial date will be set, and both of you will argue your case before a judge."

Silvana listened quietly to Lulu, and grew nervous hearing all of the steps that had to be taken. "How long will the divorce take?"

"It may take six months to one year, depending on what sort of agreement you forge with Mark. If he does not accept your stipulations, then the divorce will be delayed."

Silvana's lips pursed. "I hope it won't take so long. I would like to move into a new life as soon as possible."

"I will try to speed up the process, but it does not depend on me. Right now, I have to meet with my next client, so we will talk later."

"No problem. Goodbye," said Silvana.

After talking to her attorney, Silvana anticipated Mark's reaction when he discovered her petition for a divorce.

He may get drunk and then try to hurt me. Maybe I should leave the house with the children before he finds out. Then she changed her mind. No, I'm going to stay and stand up for myself. Whatever might transpire, I will deal with it. No more living trapped in fear.

After reflecting for a while about the divorce, Silvana kept herself occupied with her new work.

***

In the middle of the summer, Silvana's employer hired a new attorney, one who had newly arrived from Canada.

As Silvana sat at her desk, her boss entered her office, accompanied by another man. He was tall, and she could tell that he was a foreigner right away.

"Good morning, Silvana," said the supervisor.

"Good morning, Mr. Smith," answered Silvana with a broad smile.

"How are you today?"

"I'm okay. Just trying to complete the report that you have requested."

"I just dropped by to introduce our new employee," Mr. Smith said. He gestured toward the man who was with him. "This is

290

Andrew Constantine, from Canada. He is going to be our company's new attorney."

Silvana was flabbergasted to see a man with long hair and a mustache in her office, which was a rare sight anywhere in Kenya. Something in his appearance reminded her of Azeri men. His black eyes seemed to burn with passion and boldness, a trait that she had seen so often in Baku. He seemed to be around 45 years old.

Silvana got up and shook his hand. "Nice to see you here, Andrew."

John Smith's cell phone rang, and he held it to his ear. "Yes, tell them to wait, please. I'm coming now."

He smiled at Silvana. "I have to leave, but feel free to go on with your conversation without me." Then he left.

"Andrew, please sit down," offered Silvana, smiling broadly.

"Thanks." Andrew took the chair on the opposite side of Silvana's desk.

"How long have you been in Kenya?"

"About two weeks," said Andrew.

"How long do you plan to work in Kenya?"

"I'm not sure, as yet. It looks like you want to get rid of me soon," Andrew said with a small smile. He had a pleasant and soft voice.

"Not at all." She worried that he had misunderstood her.

He shook his head and grinned. "My apologies. I was kidding. Silvana, where are you from?"

"I am from Azerbaijan." Her rosy cheeks ignited.

"Oh, your parents lived in the USSR!?" he responded, slack-jawed with surprise. "My parents also lived in the Soviet Union. However, they moved to Canada from Romania. I was born in Ottawa."

He gazed into her hazel eyes. "Why did you leave Azerbaijan?" he asked.

"I married a British man who decided to relocate here. However, I'm going through the divorce process, so I don't know how long I will remain here."

Andrew's eyes bulged as he gazed at her without blinking. Silvana sank into her chair as if trying to hide in it.

"I'm so sorry to hear about your divorce. It is indeed a painful process."

"Yes it is, but it's all for the best." Her eyes sparked with the pain of disappointment and she changed the subject. "What about you? Are you married?"

"I'm single," said Andrew.

Suddenly he got up from his seat. "I just remembered, I'm supposed to go to a meeting. I have to leave, but we will talk again. It was nice meeting you."

As he shook Silvana's hand, she felt something pass through her body, a sensation not unlike an electrical shock. He left Silvana's office, leaving her to wonder.

Two weeks had gone by since Silvana had spoken to the attorney. Finally, she mustered the courage to approach Mark to tell him about the divorce petition. She found him sitting on the sofa and watching the TV.

"Mark, I need to speak with you."

"Not now, I'm watching a film," snapped Mark irritably.

"But I need to discuss something with you."

Mark turned around and looked at Silvana. "I told you, not now. You always disturb people. You need to know when you can do things and when you can't."

"I have applied for a divorce," Silvana blurted out, looking directly into his eyes.

"What?" Mark felt a tightness in his throat.

"I have decided that I'm not going to take abuse from you any longer. Therefore, I have started the divorce process," she said emphatically.

Mark got up from the sofa and dropped the remote control.

"Why did you do it?" he asked in a very low tone.

"I'm fed up with being treated like a maid, devoid of respect and appreciation. Don't you see that we don't have a loving relationship? We don't communicate or spend time together. We live in this house like two strangers. You find time to speak with your drinking partners for hours in bars. However, when I want to say something, you either say, 'I'm busy,' 'Leave me alone,' 'I don't have time to hear your rubbish,' or 'You don't speak properly.'"

Mark moved closer to Silvana, thunderstruck. He hadn't expected this. He knew that his image as a family man would be jeopardized if she went through with her plans. He knew that the divorce would expose his abusive personality and ruin his reputation.

He grabbed her hands gripping them tightly. "Listen to me you jackass. You always do stupid things. You think your life will be better without me? You will be begging for money on the streets. If you decide to leave me, I will not give you a cent. I will erase you and the kids from my life."

Silvana tried to pull her hands away. "Again you are abusing me. That's why I'm ending this marriage. I'm not going to spend the rest of my life being cussed at, disrespected, and controlled by a jerk like you. The court will make you support the kids."

"If you didn't act like such an idiot, I wouldn't treat you in this way. You don't know when to shut up and what to say," Mark said.

Silvana was so angry at his words that she did not want to even look at him.

"Yes, keep blaming me as usual. According to you, everything negative that happens is my fault. You have always tried to make me feel as if I'm stupid and can't do anything properly. I can't even open up my heart to you to say what I feel or what worries me. I know that you will say something negative to make me feel bad. Everything I do, I have to wonder if it will anger you. Why do I always have to worry about that? I want to live my life peacefully without this nerve-racking tension."

Mark slowly sat back down on the sofa. "If you hadn't spoiled my computer, things wouldn't have gotten this way."

"Your computer got destroyed because you had all those photos of women on it. I was shocked by my discovery. When I erased the pictures I accidentally damaged the computer. That does not give you an excuse to bully me."

"What about when you forget to turn off the lights at night? I pay for the electricity. How do you expect me not to get mad? Then you take food from the fridge, cook without asking me, and eat my chocolates."

"Yes, I shouldn't forget it, but it does not give you the right to bully me. I live in this house, too. I'm not a maid, I'm your wife. So why should I ask permission to cook meat in my own house? What about the times when you cussed me for nothing while at the same time you treated your friends in a pleasant manner? Everyone now thinks that you are a charming man. However, at home you are a miserable and controlling one."

She was tired of living a lie, pretending as if nothing was wrong in her life. She abhorred seeing how he pretended to be nice and loving among others but rude to her. Silvana's heart filled with rage and disappointment. When she had been single and had dreamed of marriage, she had planned to have a happy, long-lasting one. Unfortunately, this dream did not happen, and now, after this conversation, she was even more convinced that divorcing would put an end to abuse. She would finally gain her freedom.

"I do not need anything from you," she hissed. "Just give me a divorce. I will move far away from here."

"No, please. I'll...I'll change. Really! You can believe me. Besides, the children need both of their parents. Please change your mind," said Mark, his eyes wide and pleading.

Silvana threw her hands up in the air and paced agitatedly. "How many times have you promised to change? You never change, and most times you don't even apologize for your abhorrent behavior."

She put her hand up and shook her head as Mark tried to say more. "No, the children will be perfectly fine with me, because they are not going to see me abused any longer. You hurt me so badly that I can't forget every rotten word you ever said to me and the things you failed to do."

Tears started rolling down Silvana's face. "I shed many tears, but I hid them from you and the kids. Why did you treat me in such way? What did I do to you?

Mark approached her and took her hand, desperate to get her to change her mind. He started to pour on the charm that others always saw, and what had attracted Silvana to him in the first place.

"I knew that you were an intelligent woman and capable of more. I tried to be rough so that you would become someone more."

Silvana pulled her hand back and moved away from him. "Just leave me alone, you and your excuses."

"I hope you know that with no money and without me, you won't survive. You don't have a place to live. Where will you go? You will ruin the children's future," said Mark, trying to put fear into Silvana.

Silvana turned toward him. "Don't worry about what I have. I don't fear difficulties and struggles. It is better to struggle than withstand abuse."

She left Mark alone in the room and went to her bedroom. If he thinks that he can affect my decision, he had better think twice.

Days passed, and Silvana continued staying in the same house with Mark, waiting for the divorce petition to arrive. Mark stopped his abusive behavior. He kept trying to halt the divorce by making Silvana think that she wouldn't survive without him. However, his tricks were not working. This time nothing could change Silvana's decision to leave.

While waiting for the divorce process, Silvana found herself becoming attracted to Andrew. They would eat lunch together, chatting merrily. However, being married to Mark stopped her from starting a relationship with him.

At the same time, Andrew also enjoyed Silvana's company. He made jokes to hear Silvana's laugh, which he loved. He also loved gazing into her eyes and admiring both her simplicity and her wisdom. Knowing what she was going through, he waited patiently for Silvana's divorce so that he could invite her out on a date.

At the end of summer, Silvana decided to tell the children about the upcoming divorce. She gathered them in the living room and had them sit down next to each other.

"Your father and I are going to divorce soon," she began.

"Why? Don't you love him anymore?" Marie asked, troubled.

"Marie, people don't divorce because they stop loving each other. They divorce because the marriage does not work anymore."

"Why are you getting a divorce then?" asked Aygun.

"I'm tired of being abused by Papa. No one should stay with an abuser," stated Silvana.

"After the divorce, where are you going to stay?" Peter asked, blinking back tears.

"I'll move to a rented apartment."

"What about us?" David asked, biting his lower lip.

"All of you will come with me."

"I don't want to go with you. You don't have money. You won't be able to buy things that I want," Peter said.

"Are material things more important than our kind and loving Mommy?" asked a flabbergasted Marie, looking sternly at her brother.

"No. But Papa knows math, and Mother is not good at it. If I leave Papa, who will help me with math?" Peter asked.

"You always think about yourself," said Marie, crossing her arms in front of herself.

"Mother's English is not good and she is uneducated. If she loses her current job, who will hire her with poor English?" said Peter.

Marie got up from the sofa and stared at her brother. "Why are you repeating Father's words? Mother's English is not poor. She has a university degree as well as many diplomas."

"Leave him alone," said Silvana.

She offered him one of her warm smiles and looked into his eyes. "Peter, I'm not going to allow you to stay with your father. If you stay with him, you will become just like him."

Silvana sat back and looked at them. "For now, all of you just concentrate on your schoolwork, and you will be okay. Remember, I love you and God loves you too."

She hugged them and went into the kitchen to cook dinner.

***

In the middle of autumn, Mark received the divorce papers, notifying him that he had thirty days to file his response. He sat on the sofa and slowly read their content. Then he waited for Silvana to come home from work.

When she came in, Mark told her about receiving the papers.

"Silvana, please stop the divorce process. I love you and I don't want to lose you," he begged in a shaky voice.

Silvana stared into his watery eyes without blinking. "When I needed to feel your love, you weren't there for me. I needed your hugs, to hear tender words from you, and to feel appreciated, but I didn't get any of that. I don't need your love any longer."

She left Mark in the living room and went upstairs to change out of her work clothes. After reading the divorce petition again, Mark finally decided to surrender and give Silvana whatever she might ask for. Later on, he hired an attorney and submitted his financial information to the court to determine what Silvana would receive.

The court hearing was set. During the proceedings, Silvana was asked to produce proof of the abuse. She gave her attorney a memory key/thumb drive with the recording of her abuse. The lawyer put the memory key in his computer and allowed the judge to listen to it through a headpiece. Standing by, Mark became curious about the contents of the recording.

As the judge listened, Silvana looked at his face. From his expression, Silvana guessed that he didn't like what he heard. Finally, the judge took off the headphones and said, "I have listened to this recording for ten minutes. I must say it has saddened me. No one should have to go through this. However, I will be unable to use this recording as evidence in court.

"I will require additional time to review all of the petitioner's documents, as well as the respondent's documents, along with the divorce petition with the petitioner's statements of chronological events. If Mark Jonson continues abusing Ms. Jonson, then she can apply for a restraining order against him."

The judge adjourned the hearing to a later date. Subsequently, Silvana and Mark attended a number of court hearings. Finally, at the last one, the judge dissolved their marriage. They were granted joint custody of their children, who were permitted to stay with their mother. However, Mark was granted visitation rights. In addition, the judge ordered him to pay child support and to leave the house to Silvana.

As he stated this last stipulation, the judge turned toward Mark. His face turned blank as he stared at him.

Mark's lawyer approached Mark and whispered, "Do you agree to these terms?"

He nodded sadly. "Yes. I don't have a choice, really, because the children need a safe place to live. My house is the best place for them."

He glanced toward Silvana. "She has to keep the children. With my work, I won't be able to look after them."

"Mark, do you understand these terms?" asked the judge.

"Yes, I do."

"Since both sides consented to the terms, after signing the papers you will be officially divorced."

Silvana's lawyer gave Mark and Silvana papers to sign. After signing, they went back home. Silvana had never been so happy, but Mark felt rejected. He spent the rest of the day in the bedroom, while Silvana played with her children.

After getting over the shock of the divorce, Mark searched for a place to rent. Finally, he found a two-bedroom apartment and decided to move there.

On a Sunday morning, Mark packed his clothes in boxes while the children watched his every move.

"Father, why are you packing?" asked David.

"I'm moving to a different place."

"Are you taking Mama and us with you?"

"No. We are not married anymore. You have to stay with her," Mark stated.

"But I don't want you to move away. Please stay," begged Aygun. She hugged Mark and cried.

"I can't stay. But I will be visiting you. Now, go to play or do something, but don't disturb me as I pack."

The children left the bedroom, leaving Mark alone. After putting his clothes in the boxes, he loaded them in his car. When he finished, Mark went into the living room where the children were watching TV.

He came up to them. "I'm going now. Come and give me a hug."

They got up and hugged him.

"When we will see you?" asked Peter.

"You will see me next weekend," he reassured him.

"Why do we have to wait so long?" asked Aygun, twisting her lips.

"That's what happens when people divorce," Mark said sadly.

He turned his head toward the kitchen. "Silvana, I'm leaving," he called. He wiped his watery eyes with his sleeve.

"Okay. Don't forget to lock the door," Silvana called back from the kitchen.

Feeling empty, but knowing that his insulting behavior had caused all of it, Mark left the house, leaving his children and ex-wife behind. He deeply regretted that he hadn't done anything to change his abusive behavior.

The week passed peacefully; however, the children asked for their father almost every day. They felt gloomy not having him around, but Silvana felt joyful and finally free.

After the divorce, feeling deserted, Mark went to bars often, spending hours drinking.

One night his friend Stephen, who hadn't seen him for a while, came to the bar. He was startled at Mark's appearance. His eyes were red-rimmed and sunken. He also noticed that in the two months since the divorce, Mark looked older and had lost weight.

"Mark, when are you going to stop drinking? Weren't your drinking habits a contributing factor to the breakup of your marriage?" asked his friend.

"I try to stop, but I can't because, without the children, I feel lonely," Mark slurred in a drunken lament. He squeezed his plastic cup tightly, almost spilling his drink.

"I understand, but you need to do something about this habit. You can end up on the streets as a vagrant," advised his friend as he sipped his beer.

"After losing my family, I don't care any longer," complained Mark hopelessly.

"You should care. You still have the children, and they need a father. You had better start attending a group for alcoholics. There you will get help."

Stephen put a hand on Mark's shoulder. "I will take you there myself, but now please go home. You have been here for three hours already."

Mark got up, so drunk that he could barely stand. "Waiter, please bring my bill!" he called out.

Seeing him swaying from side to side, Stephen decided to drop him home. The waiter brought the bill, and after paying, both of them left the bar. Stephen drove Mark to his apartment, leaving Mark's car parked at the bar.

Mark staggered up the few steps and, with shaking hands, opened the door. Stephen left after seeing him go inside and close the door.

After a few days, Stephen took Mark to an anonymous group for alcoholics. The members sat in chairs arranged in a circle. One by one, they introduced themselves and related the problem they were having and why they were there. When it was Mark's turn, he wanted to get up and leave, but seeing everyone staring at him, he didn't.

Feeling ashamed, he said, "My name is Mark, and I'm here because my friend asked me to come here to get help."

"What kind help do you need?" The facilitator, a thin brunette, was all attention as she eyed him.

Mark didn't know what to say at first. His eyes roamed around in panic. He didn't know what to say. Inside, he asked himself, Why am I here? Is anything wrong with me?

"Mark, we are waiting for your answer. Why are you here?" continued the facilitator.

"I'm here because my friend thinks I'm an alcoholic."

"Do you agree with your friend?" she asked.

"No. I don't drink every day. I only drink about three times a week."

"That is quite a bit," said a man in black. He looked at Mark with sunken red eyes.

"Where do you drink?" questioned the facilitator.

"In the bars, as most of us do." Mark smiled, but he felt a touch of shame.

"How long do you spend in the bars?" the facilitator asked.

"Four to five hours."

Another woman gazed wordlessly at Mark with narrowed eyes and then hit her leg softly. "I can't believe you spend about five hours drinking, and you say you don't have a problem," she said, grinning.

"Mark, I won't be able to help you unless you acknowledge that you have a problem with drinking," demanded the facilitator.

Mark chuckled. "But I don't have a problem."

"Mark, can I ask you a personal question?" said a fat-looking man by the name of Michael.

Mark nodded warily.

"Are you married?"

"I got divorced recently."

"What is the reason for your divorce?" asked the facilitator.

Mark looked away. "I don't want to discuss my personal life in here."

"Every member of our group is here to discuss their private life," insisted the facilitator. "Only once I know what is going on in your life can I assess your situation and help you deal with your addiction. With that said, what was the reason for your divorce?"

Mark's eyes ran across the members of the group and then stopped on the facilitator. His whole body took on a shrunken appearance.

"My wife accused me of emotionally abusing her," said Mark, trying not to look at anyone. "But I don't think I abused her. I tried to make her a better person, and to prevent her from making mistakes."

"How did you correct her?" asked Michael.

"I have been cursing at her and making her feel that she can't do anything properly, so that she would listen to me," Mark finally admitted.

"What? How can you make someone a better person by cursing? Are you nuts?" asked Michael, horrified. He started to get up.

Mark stared silently at Michael's red, puffy face.

"Please refrain from name-calling. We are not here to judge, but to help each other," said the facilitator.

"Sometimes we must use force to get people to listen to us," said Mark, showing a fist.

Another participant shook her head in disbelief. "Mark, you can't earn people's loyalty and respect by force or by treating them like animals. If you want respect, then earn it, and show respect to others as well."

"Mark, give us an example of a situation where you 'tried to teach her', and how," asked the facilitator.

"A few times, my wife forgot to turn off the light or unplug the phone. The first time, I asked her to try to not make the same mistakes. She continued ignoring my request. So, I ended up shouting at her and calling her a damned asshole. After that, she never forgot to turn off the light or unplug the phone."

"Man, you are sick," said another member, whose nametag read 'Alex.' "That is not teaching or making someone better. That is a sign of you being a manipulative abuser, trying to control your wife." He looked at Mark disparagingly.

"I must agree with Alex. This is a pattern of abuse. Sometimes abusive behavior is caused by drinking habits," said the facilitator. "Have you been more offensive before drinking or after?"

Mark paused to think. He started squeezing his fingers nervously. His left leg trembled and his back hurt. "I was more abusive after drinking. I couldn't control my anger at that time."

"Mark, today we clearly see that you have a problem with drinking. You need to think about it, accept it, and then try to change. Continue coming here, and we will help you with your addiction. If you don't deal with your drinking habit, it will continue to affect your conduct and mind," said the facilitator.

She then moved on to the next member.

Mark stayed until the end, then left with his mind full of what he had heard during the meeting.

Days passed, and Mark continued going to the meetings. They helped him to realize that his behavior toward his wife was unacceptable, and he had indeed turned into a ruthless man. Little by little he stopped going to the pubs, and tried very hard not to drink.

**

After divorcing Mark, Silvana felt as if the chains that had kept her shackled had finally broken apart, allowing her to be as free as a dove in flight. She decided not to depend on anyone. With that, she also realized that she needed to relocate to a different country, or even back to Azerbaijan.

At first, it was difficult for her to adjust to a new life without Mark. Even though he had hurt her feelings, he had done good things as well. He had been the one who paid the bills, shopped for groceries, and went to the market. Now she was forced to undertake these tasks herself without any sort of assistance. Mark did continue to help Silvana financially; however, he refused to pay Rehema, which forced Silvana to let her go.

Long after the divorce, Silvana detected positive changes in Mark's behavior. Because he had taken a positive step and had begun attending support groups, he had stopped drinking.

Surprisingly, he looked happier whenever he met Silvana. She pitied him, but could not get over how he had treated her during their marriage. To her credit, she decided to forgive him and remain friends instead of totally erasing him from her life. The forgiving aspect was difficult for her, because she couldn't forget all of the painful words that Mark had hurled at her like salvos.

She still combated inner turmoil and emotional pain within herself, caused by the wounds and scars of Mark's abuse. As she battled with her anger, she finally decided to take steps to heal and stop dwelling on the past. She knew if she couldn't forgive, she wouldn't enter Paradise.

Silvana permitted Mark to visit the children whenever he wanted. However, it was hard for them to adjust to an absent father. They would ask when he would next come to see them. However, albeit slowly, the children acclimatized to not having him home on a daily basis, and seemed happy to be free of his badgering and nagging.

Meanwhile, Mark's former wife, who was a lawyer, got a short-term contract in Kenya to represent an English company's interest in a workplace discrimination lawsuit. She contacted Mark when she moved there with his two sons.

He helped her to look after his fourteen- and sixteen-year-old boys. Once she witnessed positive changes in Mark's conduct toward her, including renewed and genuine attention, her heart warmed to him and they started dating again.

While Mark was seeing his English ex-wife, Silvana started going out with Andrew, who took her to see films or out for lunch. It wasn't long before they fell deeply in love with one another.

Every day after putting the children to bed, Silvana received a call from Andrew through Paltalk. She was overjoyed by his devotion, and would not fall asleep at night until she had heard his voice.

***

One Friday, Silvana lay down on her bed waiting for Andrew's video call. She rested her laptop near the bed and kept gazing at it. Her eyes closed and she opened her mouth widely, yawning.

Why is he not calling?

Paltalk rang, and she quickly answered, pressing on Video call.

"Good evening, my hazel-eyed girl. Did I wake you, babe?" asked Andrew. From his face, he fingered his wet and brown hair aside.

Silvana smiled blissfully and turned on her side. "You didn't. I can't fall asleep until I hear your voice."

He stared at Silvana lovingly. "Wow, every day you look more beautiful. What did you do to look so beautiful?"

Silvana jokingly winked at him. "God made me beautiful, and you are making me happy."

He picked up his guitar and started playing. Silvana rested her head on her pillow and stared at her laptop, watching his every move.

"You are not only beautiful on the outside, but also on the inside. I can see your beauty in your eyes, heart, and mind."

Silvana raised her head, enjoying the compliments. Her cheeks flushed and her heart melted.

"You are so intelligent," Andrew continued. "I've met many women throughout the world, but none can be compared to you. I do really love you. You are deep in my heart."

Silvana felt so happy that streams of tears flowed from her sparkling eyes. "I love you too."

"I hope you didn't get upset with our canceled lunch. I didn't expect that meeting to take so long."

"Andrew, I don't care about lunch. Just seeing you and hearing your voice every day makes me happy. After being abused for so many years, I never thought that God would bless me with a good, loving man like you."

He moved his chair closer to the computer and played another melody. The song ended, and he smiled at her. "Silvana, I feel the same way about you. With you, I can be myself and talk about anything. You have a kind, caring heart, and a good soul. That's why my heart fell for you," he said tenderly.

Silvana blushed at his words.

She was blissful, but at the same time afraid that the happiness wouldn't last.

Does he love me or is he playing games with me? What if he finds someone else and leaves me?

She chased the negative thoughts away and focused on positive ones.

"I want to make up for the missed lunch. Why don't we take the children to a movie tomorrow?" Andrew suggested.

"We can't. Mark is going to keep them tomorrow. Maybe we can do something during the week after Valentine's Day." Silvana yawned, unable to stifle it.

"Oh, next Thursday is a holiday. We can take them to a safari," suggested Andrew.

"They would be delighted to see the animals, especially the giraffes," said Silvana.

"Babe, I need to read some reports before I go to sleep, and you need to get your sleep. I'm leaving you for now. Good night," said Andrew.

"Can you please sing one more song?"

Andrew turned from side to side in his swivel chair, holding his guitar in his hands. Then he started singing as he played a new tune:

"One twinkling star shone brightly in the sky,
And many tiny stars surrounded it.
The star shone brightly trying to be visible.
It needed someone's love and care.
You are that shiny star, Silvana.
My feelings grow for you day by day."

As he sang, Silvana fell asleep.

Seeing her sleeping, Andrew sat silently for some time, his eyes fixed on her.

"Good night, babe." He turned off his computer.

On Valentine's Day, Silvana went to her office earlier than usual. When she got there, she was astonished to see an enormous bouquet of roses on her desk. She looked at them with slightly furrowed brows. Who were they from?

She walked over to them and looked for a clue. She found a card between the flowers, which read:

"My lovely Silvana, would you agree to be my Valentine today?

Yours, Andrew."

She put the card down on the desk and smiled happily as she smelled the roses.

Lord, I'm so happy with the positive changes in my life. It's time to leave the past where it belongs and move on.

She looked at the roses again.

Father, just when I thought that I would never feel happy again, you have blessed me with my Andrew.

She sat at the desk and went through some papers left by her secretary.

Early in the morning Andrew entered the office in a red long-sleeved shirt, black pants, and a tie. He came up closer to her and gave her a kiss on her forehead.

"Happy Valentine's Day, darling," he said.

A shy smile sparkled on her lips. "Happy Valentine's Day to you too, and thank you for the beautiful flowers. I love them."

"You're welcome, my love. Will you be able to come to dinner at my home this evening? Say, about 6:00 p.m.?"

Silvana paused and pondered if she should go to his house. She didn't want to cause gossip by going into a man's house. Also she wanted to avoid temptation. However, after weighing the pros and cons, she decided to go.

"Yes. I can come if you pick me up. I don't want to drive today."

He rubbed his hands together with glee. "I'll pick you up before six."

He looked at his watch. "I have a meeting with the boss. I'll see you later." He left the office in a hurry.

Silvana decided to call Rehema to see if she could leave the children with her. She dialed her number, and Rehema picked up on the second ring.

"Hi, Rehema."

"Good morning, Silvana! How are you? Since I stopped working for you, I don't see you or hear from you."

"I should have been calling you, but since the divorce, I have more responsibilities on my shoulders. I don't have time to do anything at all. Did you find a new job?"

"Yes, I'm working for another white couple. How is your life going after the divorce?"

Thinking of Andrew brought a smile to her lips, and she leaned back in her chair. "It's not easy to be a single mother. But I prefer to be a struggling single mother instead of a controlled and bullied married mother."

"Yes, I agree with you. No one deserves to be abused. You should have left him a long time ago."

"It's better late than never. However, I'm content with my life. I became independent, I'm working at a job I love. I started dating Andrew," Silvana replied.

"Oh, yes, I remember him. He is from your office. But I didn't expect that you would date him."

"Why not?" Silvana leaned forward.

"I thought that, after the abuse, you wouldn't trust men or rush into a relationship," replied Rehema.

"Sometimes I catch myself thinking about it, but I try not to allow past negative experiences to control my life. Meeting an abuser does not indicate that the next man will be a bully as well. Yes, since I'm vulnerable, there is a chance of attracting predators who hunt after vulnerable women. However, I'm strong and I have the ability to recognize predators."

She decided to change the subject.

"How are things going between you and Zuberi?" Silvana picked up a pen and started drawing small hearts on a piece of paper while she listened to Rehema's reply.

"It is going well. He has invited me to his house to meet his parents," said Rehema.

"It looks like he is into you."

The two women shared a laugh, and then Silvana said, "Tonight, I'm going to go have dinner at Andrew's house. Can you please stay with the children for a few hours?" She drew a huge heart and wrote "love" inside of it.

Rehema couldn't believe her ears. "Oh, my gosh! You never dated a man other than Mark. Aren't you afraid to go to his house? There will be so much temptation when the two of you are alone. Many things can happen between you."

Silvana shook her head in disbelief. "Rehema, you have known me for a long while now. You should realize that I don't allow temptations to push me into doing anything wrong."

"True," Rehema conceded. "What time do you want me to come?"

"Can you please come at 5 p.m?" Silvana wrote "Andrew" inside the heart.

"Okay, no problem."

They said their good-byes, and Silvana hung up the phone. The rest of the day she kept herself busy with work. She left the office at 4 p.m., and picked up the children from school.

As she drove, she talked to her children. "Tonight, I'm going out with my friend, but you will stay with Rehema. Please listen to her and do all your schoolwork."

"Who is your friend?" Peter asked, curious.

"His name is Andrew and he works with me." A smile made its way across her face.

"Is he your boyfriend?" asked Aygun.

Silvana glanced at Aygun in the rear-view mirror. "Yes, he is my boyfriend. You are asking too many questions, nosy."

"Are you going to marry him?" asked Peter.

"I don't know."

"Can we meet him?" asked Marie.

"Okay, you will see him today," Silvana said, getting annoyed at all of the questions.

Rehema arrived at 5 p.m. The two women hugged each other.

After a little small talk, Silvana gave Rehema instructions for the evening.

"Would you please take out the children's dinner from the fridge and give it to them? Please make sure that they are doing their homework. I'm going to go take a shower and get ready to go."

After her shower, she put on a blue dress with white shoes and applied her makeup. By the time Andrew appeared at her door, Silvana was ready.

He rang the bell. Silvana rushed to the door and opened it.

"Hello," he said, giving her a smile.

"Hi, Andrew. Can you please come inside? My children want to meet you."

He entered and she led him into the living room.

"Good afternoon, everyone," he said, smiling at Silvana's children.

"Hi," answered Marie, looking at him with curiosity.

"Please sit down," said Silvana.

He sat in the armchair. Silvana walked behind him and put her hands on his shoulders. The smile on her face broadened.

"Guys, this is my friend, Andrew Constantine."

She came around, sat next to her children, and introduced them to him.

Andrew gazed at them. "You have beautiful kids."

Silvana proudly looked at her miracles. "They are not only beautiful but are excellent students in school."

"I'm impressed," said Andrew.

He looked at Marie. "Marie, what is your favorite subject in school?" he asked.

"Math and social studies," she answered, avoiding his eyes.

"I never liked math. Peter, do you like playing football?" Andrew asked with a smile.

"Yes, I play every week in school."

"Maybe if your mommy doesn't mind, one day I will come and play soccer with you." Andrew gave a wink to Silvana.

Aygun came up closer to her mother's boyfriend. "Are you going to be our stepfather?"

Andrew was startled by the unexpected question and looked blankly at Silvana. She decided to come to his aid.

She got up and smoothed her dress. "Andrew, it's time for us to go. I would like to leave early so I can come back before they fall asleep."

Andrew got up as well. "Children, it was nice meeting you. See you later."

Rehema entered the living room.

"Rehema, make sure they eat all of their dinner. And please make sure their schoolwork is complete."

"Don't worry about them. Go and have a good time. You deserve it." Rehema smiled at her and Andrew cheerfully.

Silvana was all smiles as she hugged her children. "Don't give Rehema any trouble, please. I will be back soon."

She took Andrew's hand. "Let's go, Andrew."

As they sat in his vehicle, Andrew remarked, "Silvana, God blessed you with sweet children. You are very lucky."

Silvana radiated with pride. "Yes, I'm the lucky one."

In about thirty minutes, Andrew stopped in front of his apartment. He got out of the car and opened the door for Silvana. He unlocked his front door and led her into the living room.

"Please sit, and I will be right back."

Silvana sat on the sofa and inspected the surroundings. She looked over at a small round table and smiled when she saw a white tablecloth, candles, wine glasses, and roses in a vase. Her boyfriend came back with matches and lit the tall red candles.

"Silvana, please sit at the table." He turned on the CD player, and Silvana heard her favorite song.

"When I look into your eyes, I'm sinking in them.

I'm not lonely anymore because I found you, my love.

Your smile melted away my heart."

He left and went into the kitchen, where he removed plates of food from the oven and put them on a big tray. He then carried the tray to the living room. Silvana helped him put the dishes on the table. Once they were seated, he poured some wine in both their glasses.

"Babe, please pass your plate," he said. He dished out some rice, potato salad, spinach, and broccoli for her. He gave her the plate and then served dinner for himself.

"I'm so happy to be alone with you, sweetheart. I feel as if I have known you my whole life," said Andrew.

Silvana's cheeks blushed. She looked at him somewhat bashfully. "I feel the same way. I felt so hurt and lonely before meeting you. But now, I'm truly happy."

He got up from the chair and removed a red gift box from his pocket, which he gently opened it as he approached Silvana. He knelt down, holding the box close to her. Silvana looked at it and was astonished to see a beautiful diamond ring.

"My shining star, will you marry me?"

Silvana sat dumbfounded for a while, not believing her ears. Her eyes wandered from the ring to Andrew.

Oh, my God, he is asking me to marry him! Am I dreaming?

Andrew looked at her startled face and, not hearing an answer from her, asked, "Are you okay?"

Tears appeared at the corner of her eyes. She trembled like a leaf.

She finally spoke, her voice shaking. "Yes, I am." Her eyes sparkled. "I didn't expect this was coming so soon. Yes, I will marry you."

Her heart raced as she kept back her urge to cry. She could not stop smiling. He removed the ring and put it on her finger. She lifted her hand admiring the ring.

"It is so beautiful. Thank you very much."

She hugged him tightly and then let him go. Andrew walked toward the CD player and put on some slow music.

He returned to Silvana and reached out his hand. "Will you dance with your future spouse?"

Silvana smiled. "Sure."

She took his hand and stood up. He put his arms gently around her waist and she put her hands around his neck. They moved slowly, swaying to the music.

Silvana felt peaceful and loved for the first time in many years. Suddenly, a few doubtful thoughts entered her mind. As she leaned her head on his shoulder, she pondered, What if he is just like Mark, pretending to be nice, but on the inside an abuser? She tried to chase away her worries. No. Don't be silly. Don't allow one negative experience to affect your current relationship.

They continued dancing. She looked at him, wanting him to kiss her. Should I ask him to kiss me? Go ahead; cowards are losers, she encouraged herself.

"Andrew, kiss me."

He gave her a gentle look and sealed her lips with his. His tongue entered her mouth as his hands caressed her back. She tightened her arms around his neck and continued to kiss him passionately.

At that point, the music stopped.

"Darling, please sit down on the sofa. I will right be back."

Silvana sat on the couch as he removed the dishes from the table. Then he brought a glass of wine for her and for himself.

"This is for you," he said.

"Thank you, but no more wine for me tonight," stated Silvana.

He put the glass on the side table. "When do you think we should have our wedding?" he asked.

"Whenever is convenient for you. Just pick a day."

Silvana took his hand gently and gazed into his hazel eyes. "Before we get married, I need to make a few things clear. I have children and they come first. I need to make sure that you will be able to love them as your own. Are you prepared to take care of children that are not yours?"

Andrew smiled. "Silvana, I love children. I won't have a problem taking care of yours. A man who loves you should also accept your children and love them."

"Thank you, sweetie pie."

He took his cell phone from his pocket and looked at the calendar. "What about May 2nd?" he asked.

"That's a good day, but remember, we need to visit an Orthodox Church first," Silvana insisted.

He kissed her forehead. "Babe, don't worry. I will take care of everything."

She moved closer to him and leaned her head on his shoulder. He hugged her and she sat silently, enjoying his closeness. She had always dreamed of sitting next to someone she loved and being hugged by him. Her eyes became wet; however, these were tears of happiness. He caressed her head, gently playing with her hair. She felt so safe and secure in his arms that she could have stayed sitting next to him for hours.

However, that was not to be. She looked at her watch and was startled to see that it was 8:30 p.m.

She moved away from him. "It's late. Can you please drop me home?"

"Oh, the time! Of course!"

On the drive back to Silvana's house, her boyfriend said, "Silvana, please decide if you want a big wedding celebration or just a small one with a few friends."

"I don't care about a big celebration. The most important thing is to get married in the Orthodox Church. Without the church, God wouldn't bless our marriage," explained Silvana, as he held her hand in his.

"We must at least invite a few friends and celebrate with them," said Andrew, caressing her hand.

"Okay. I don't have a problem with that," said Silvana.

He stopped in front of her house, and they got out of the car.

Taking her hand, he said, "Thank you for coming for dinner. Don't have any doubts, please. I'm not like Mark. I will devote my life to making you and your children happy."

Silvana gently touched his face. "I know, and I will make you happy, too. Bye for now."

She raced toward the door, then waved as he got back into his car. Once inside, she closed the door and stood for a while, leaning on it and smiling happily.

After a few days, Andrew entered Silvana's office. He came up to her and kissed Silvana's forehead.

"Good morning, shining star. I have spoken to the priest. He can marry us on May 2nd."

"Oh, that's good news. It's only three months away, though, and so much has to be done."

Silvana got up and walked around the room. "We need to invite friends, decide where we are going to have a celebration. I need to get a wedding dress."

Seeing her pace, Andrew could not stop smiling. He approached his girlfriend, put his hands on her shoulders, and directed her toward her seat. "Darling, sit down, please. Don't worry. I will sort out everything."

"I just want everything to be perfect for our wedding," said Silvana.

"It will be perfect. You get your dress and invite your friends to celebrate with us. Leave the rest to me."

Silvana smiled and squeezed his chin gently with her hand. "Oh, you are so sweet."

"I'm sweet because of you."

He kissed her again. "Anyway, we will talk later. A client is waiting for me," he said and left the office.

On Saturday, Silvana decided to tell her children about her marriage plans and take them shopping.

While sitting in the car with them, she announced, "I'm marrying Andrew in May."

The children became quiet for a while. Then, "Is he going to come to live with us?" asked a puzzled Aygun.

"Yes, he is."

"But you always used to say that strangers can be abusers. Now you are bringing one home," said Peter.

"Andrew is not a stranger. He is a good man and will never hurt you."

"Should we call him Father or by his name?" asked Marie, biting her nails.

"You can call him whatever you think is right. Today, we are going to buy a wedding dress for me and beautiful clothes for you."

"Oh, yes! Can I choose my dress?" asked Marie.

"Yes, baby, you can."

She stopped in front of the bridal shop. They got out of the car and went inside.

"Wow, so many beautiful dresses," said Marie, looking at a rack of silky dresses.

"Can I help you?" asked a saleslady.

"Yes, please. I'm looking for a wedding dress, dresses for my girls, and suits for my boys," answered Silvana.

"Please follow me," said the salesperson. She walked over to a section of the store that displayed many white bridal gowns.

Silvana's eyes widened as she gazed at them. "Do you have dresses in different colors?"

"Yes, we have many. I have a beautiful pink one that you may like," replied the salesperson.

She stepped over to a nearby rack and came back with a long pink dress.

"Wow, it's gorgeous!" exclaimed Silvana. "Can I try it on, please?"

"Sure." The salesperson gave the dress to Silvana.

"Children, stay inside and wait for me right here."

She went into the dressing room and put on the dress. When she came out, Marie stared at her mother, speechless. Her face showed her surprise. The pink silk gown draped along her bare skin. The soft fabric graced her feminine body and the purple lacing at the top sat across her breast. The sleeves hung gently around her elbows.

"Wow, Mother, you look like a princess!" said Marie, touching the fabric.

"Thank you, Marie!"

"You are going to be the most beautiful bride in the world," said Peter.

Silvana grinned, and she decided right then and there. She changed back into her old clothes and gave the dress to the salesperson. "I'm taking this one."

Then she walked around searching for suitable clothes for her children. She bought two beautiful pink dresses for the girls and white suits for her sons. They left the shop, feeling happy.

Weeks passed, and Andrew arranged the wedding day with the priest. He bought a white suit for himself and jewelry for his bride. He also managed to invite a few of his friends to the wedding and made a reservation in a very nice restaurant. Silvana also asked a few of her co-workers, as well as friends. She had planned to invite Mark but decided not to. However, she called Mark and notified him about her marriage plans.

Mark wasn't pleased with all. "You can't bring a man to live in the same house with the children!"

"I'm not your wife anymore. You don't have the right to tell me what I can do."

Mark got irritated. "Don't you read in the newspapers about how men sexually abuse children?"

"Mark, you should know me by now. I don't trust men and yes, a lot of them are abusers. I have considered all of that, and Andrew is a good guy. He would never hurt them."

"Okay, I'm just warning you," said Mark.

Silvana sighed inwardly. He always has to spoil something.

"I have to go, Mark." She hung up the phone, regretting that she had called him.

That night as she lay in bed, she felt overjoyed thinking about her upcoming wedding. She imagined herself walking down the aisle in her pink dress. She saw herself approaching Andrew as Aygun and Marie walked behind her.

Oh, my God, finally I'm going to get married in a church.

Shortly after, she fell asleep, grateful for the positive changes in her life.

Soon enough, it was May 2nd, the wedding day. Silvana got up early in the morning and happily sang "Glory to God in the Highest." She was so overjoyed that she couldn't stop singing.

"Mother, you are disturbing my sleep," called Peter from his bedroom. Silvana entered his bedroom, still singing.

"Peter, wake up. We need to prepare for the wedding."

"I'm tired. Please wake up David first."

Aygun and Marie got up and came into Peter's bedroom.

"Don't be lazy. Get up," said Marie, as she pulled his hand.

"Leave me alone."

Nonetheless, he slowly got out of bed. Hearing their voices, David got up as well.

"Mother, what is going to happen today?" asked Marie, yawning.

"We are going to eat first. Then we will take showers, put on our new clothes, and wait for a few of my friends. They will take us to the church. After the priest marries Andrew and me, we will go to the restaurant," instructed Silvana.

"But what are we going to do in church?" asked Aygun.

"You will walk behind me and carry our rings. After that, you will sit next to Rehema."

She shooed them out the bedroom door. "Go and have your breakfast. Then take your showers. Make sure you brush your teeth properly. You're going to smile a lot today."

"Mother, are you going to have a honeymoon?" Marie asked.

"No more questions. Go and have your breakfast. It's on the table."

Aygun left the bedroom, followed by her siblings.

Silvana was about to take a shower when the phone rang. She ran to it and picked it up.

"Good morning, my love."

Silvana's heart raced as she heard her groom's voice. "Good morning, Andrew."

"I didn't sleep all night, thinking of you. I may come to see you for a short while," said Andrew.

"No, you can't come. It's bad luck to see a bride before the wedding ceremony. You will see me in the church."

She closed her eyes, imagining him kissing her neck.

"You are so sexy and beautiful. I can't wait until I make love to you. I crave your touch," Andrew told her.

"Sweetie pie, you know I can't lust. Please don't tempt me to sin. You will get all of that tonight."

"Okay, darling. I'm sorry," Andrew said with a sigh.

"I'm going to go take a shower. I'm sure you don't want me to be late." She laughed.

"Okay, you go. See you at the church."

Silvana hung up the phone and rushed into the shower. Then she put on her pink dress and applied her makeup. By the time she was ready, Rehema had arrived, along with Jabary and his wife.

"Wow, you look so beautiful. Mark does not know what he lost," said Jabary.

"Can you please not talk about him on my wedding day?"

Jabary blushed. "Sorry."

"Do you need any help?" asked Rehema.

"Not really. We're ready."

The bride looked at her watch. It was 10.30 a.m. "Everyone, let's go; the limousine is waiting for us outside," she said.

Silvana walked toward the door, followed by her children and her friends. Outside, Aygun stood motionless for a second, viewing the limousine with her mouth opened wide. "Wow! It's so huge!"

Andrew anxiously waited for Silvana outside the church. Upon seeing the limousine approaching, he felt relieved. It drew to a halt in front of the church, and everyone got out.

Andrew rushed toward the limousine but stopped short when he saw Silvana.

"You are gorgeous!" he gushed. Silvana smiled widely, and he offered his arm to escort her.

Rehema gave Marie a small tray. On it were the wedding rings.

"The bride has arrived!" bellowed someone from inside the church.

Silvana walked side by side with Andrew, her arm entwined with his. They were followed by her children. They entered the church and gradually walked down the aisle to the altar.

Silvana saw that the church was filled with many people, and glanced up at the large icons of Mary and Jesus Christ. She smiled gratefully.

They approached the priest, who took the rings from Marie. He gave lit candles to the couple, and blessed them three times.

"Silvana, do you agree to take this man as your husband?" asked the priest.

Silvana smiled through her tears. For many years, she had dreamed of getting married in a church, and now her dream was finally coming true!

"Yes, I do," she uttered in a soft and hushed voice, gazing at her husband.

"Andrew, do you agree to take this woman as your lawful wife?" queried the priest

"Yes, I do," said Andrew.

The priest blessed the bridegroom three times, holding the ring and pronouncing, "The servant of God, Andrew, is betrothed to the handmaid of God, Silvana, in the name of the Father, the Son, and the Holy Spirit. Amen." Then he put the ring on the groom's finger.

Next, he proceeded to bless the bride, holding her ring in his hand and repeating three times, "The handmaid of God, Silvana, is betrothed to the servant of God, Andrew, in the name of the Father, the Son, and the Holy Spirit. Amen." The priest then put the ring on the bride's finger.

The priest's helper brought sacramental wine. The priest made the sign of the cross over it three times and offered the couple a sip. He joined the couple's hands and continued with the rest of the ritual. When the ceremony was over, friends and well-wishers approached them, their faces wreathed in smiles. Then the limousine took them to the restaurant.

Silvana walked around and talked to the guests as Andrew watched her. He couldn't take his eyes off her. When she finally had a chance to sit next to him, he said, "Tonight, you are going to be mine. I will pass my lips over every inch of your body."

Silvana grasped his hand, smiled shyly, and whispered, "My whole body wants to be kissed and touched by you. But please, let's not talk about it now. Someone may hear."

The photographer took pictures of the guests with the newly-wed couple. At this point, Silvana's children left Rehema and came up to her. She hugged them, faced the photographer, and pulled Andrew closer.

After about three hours, the guests started leaving. After everyone left, Silvana, her husband, and her children got into the limousine and went back to her house.

She put the children to bed, and then went into the bathroom to change into a nightgown. When she entered the bedroom, Andrew was lying in bed naked. She smiled, then climbed in with him. He got up slowly, pulled her closer, and kissed her lips. Then he started pulling up her red nightdress. They made love, sealing their promises to each other.

Andrew kept gently kissing her shoulders and neck as he hugged her. They talked about the future as they lay in each other's arms.

"Silvana, as you know I'm here only temporarily. I would like to go back to Canada as soon as I can. Would you agree to move Canada?" Andrew asked.

Silvana rose up and kissed him. "Yes! I have always wanted to get away from here. But I need to sell the house and make sure that Mark allows me to take the children with me."

"We can deal with all of that after the honeymoon," said Andrew.

Silvana put her head on his chest and soon fell asleep.

* * *

Days passed, and Silvana's children grew accustomed to Andrew. He played soccer with them and told them funny jokes.

A month after the wedding, she decided to talk to Mark about her plans to move to Canada.

When he came to pick up the children, she said, "Mark, please come in. We need to talk."

Mark frowned. "What happened?"

"Nothing. I just want to discuss something with you."

Mark entered and settled down on the sofa. Silvana sat opposite him.

"Andrew and I decided to take the children and move to Canada."

Mark got up from the sofa. "You can't take my kids with you."

"Yes, I'm taking them with me."

Mark glared at Silvana. "I'm not going to allow you to take them away from me."

Silvana got up and looked sternly at him. "Do you remember when you hit Peter with a plastic stick, leaving marks on his body? I still have those pictures. If you won't allow me to take the children with me, I will use those images and apply for full custody. After that, you won't see them at all."

Hearing Silvana's threat, Mark sat back down, defeated. "Okay, you can take them, but make sure they are safe."

"Father, let's go," Peter shouted from outside.

Mark shot a glance at Silvana. Her ex-husband got up and left with the children.

Soon after, Silvana put her house up for sale with an advertisement in the newspaper. Within four months, she had a deal on it.

The day after selling her house, she sat with the children in the living room and tried to explain the situation.

"I never told you before, but we will be moving away."

"Where?" asked Marie.

"Canada."

"What about Papa? Is he coming with us?" asked Peter in a shaky voice.

"Papa now lives with his other family, and I have a new husband. Your father can't come with us," explained Silvana.

"But I'm going to miss him," said Peter.

Silvana gave him a kiss. "Don't worry. You will be seeing him through Skype, or he will visit you."

She got up. "Now go and do your homework."

The children left the living room, feeling disappointed. Two weeks later, Andrew and Silvana packed everything in containers and shipped them to Vancouver. Then Andrew bought plane tickets for everyone.

The day before the trip, they invited Mark to spend time with the children. All of them sat in the living room. The children surrounded Mark.

"Father, when will you come to visit us?" asked Aygun.

"I don't know," he said, feeling disappointed.

"We will miss you a lot," said Marie, holding his hand.

He gave Marie a kiss. "Remember, Papa is not as bad as you think. I just tried to make sure you learned everything and didn't make mistakes. I love you and am proud of you. All of you are very smart children."

His eyes got teary. "I promise I will visit you."

Marie, hearing the sadness in his voice, said, "Father, don't be sad. We're not leaving you forever."

He turned away, trying to hide his tears.

Mark spent a few hours with them and then left, promising to take them to the airport.

Silvana felt sorry for him. She had truly wanted her first marriage to work, and had waited for him to change, but he hadn't. She was happy that Andrew was the kind husband she had always wanted to have.

In the morning, all of them got up early and rushed to get ready. Andrew helped Silvana pack the last items.

Mark arrived at 7 a.m., and all of them got in his car.

He didn't say a word the entire time that they were in the car.

"Mark, did you bring Peter's ID card?" asked Silvana.

Mark didn't answer.

"Mark, I'm talking to you!"

"What happened?" Mark asked.

"Did you get Peter's ID card?" asked Silvana again.

"Yes, I put it in his bag."

Finally, they reached the airport. All of them got out of the car.

Mark hugged the children and then shook Andrew's hand. Silvana pitied her ex-husband. She hugged him, and he trembled.

"Mark, I sincerely hope that you will find your peace, as I have found mine."

Mark felt like crying; he realized now, too late, that he still loved his ex-wife. Now he was losing her and the children.

"Have a safe trip," he said and strode away, not wanting to see them leave. He sat in his car, leaned his head over the steering wheel, and cried bitterly. He regretted not being a loving husband, but it was too late to change that.

Silvana and her family boarded a plane to Canada. She sat next to her husband and leaned her head on his shoulder. Her children sat in the seats in front of her. She felt so happy and relieved as they left Kenya.

"Goodbye, jail," she pronounced, peering down at the small airport as the plane flew over it. Finally, she was able to leave the country where she had spent so many long and miserable years.

***

Two years had passed since Silvana had moved to Andrew's native country. They had settled down in a huge, cozy house. Many unexpected changes had occurred since then.

Silvana's negative life experiences had propelled her to become a voice against abuse, a motivational speaker, and a mentor. She had started attending conferences around the world, promoting awareness of abuse and the plight of victims. She had been invited for TV and radio interviews.

In September 2014 Silvana went to San Francisco, where she gave an interview to the local newspaper. She also took part in a conference for abused women and children. Earlier, she had been invited by the International Association of the Abused to give a motivational speech to support battered women and men. Her speech was very successful, and it attracted local journalists' interest. After her speech, many women approached Silvana, asking for advice. She was pleased with the response to her speech, and enjoyed giving advice to people, knowing that her guidance helped them.

In San Francisco, she stayed at the Diamond San Francisco Hotel. She loved the fact that the hotel was located close to many sightseeing attractions, such as Union Square, City Hall, and AT&T Park. Fortunately, it was also close to the Henderson Conference Center, where she was scheduled to speak.

Her speech was scheduled for Monday at 11 a.m. Silvana got up early in the morning and wrote some notes for her speech. Once finished, she selected a black dress suit to wear and then took a shower.

She went downstairs to the breakfast room, where she had some fruit and an omelet. Then Silvana headed back to her room and put on her red jacket and shoes. She left the Diamond Hotel and walked to the Henderson Conference Center.

At the conference, she saw many people of all ages. Silvana became a little nervous. She started trembling at the sight. She sat in the first row and repeated to herself: "Silvana, don't worry. You can do it. Just go on stage and talk without panicking." She stopped shaking and tried to relax.

The first speaker walked to the stage. The noisy audience went silent.

"Dear guests, I would like to thank you for attending our conference. As you know, our association always supports the victims of abuse. We are traveling around the world to raise awareness of abuse, as well as to help those who are trying to get away from it and start a new life. We have invited a very special and strong woman to give us an inspirational speech today. This woman has experienced emotional abuse, as well as many hardships, but she came out of it a winner.

"Before inviting her on the stage, I would like to mention a quote from the Bible: 'Blessed is the man who remains steadfast under trial, for when he has stood the test he will receive the crown of life, which God has promised to those who love him' (James 1.12).'

"Silvana is a living example of success and hope. Her experience indicates that humans can turn their lives around and have positive changes. After going through all of her trials patiently, she has been blessed by God for her faith in Him. Indeed, God has crowned her with a happy marriage, love, a successful business, and healthy children."

The speaker paused and looked at the audience. Then he continued.

"However, not all of these blessings came to her easily. She has made every step to break her chains and find freedom. She never gave up, and never lost faith in God, but continued to be persistent—praying, believing in a good outcome, trying hard to bring positive changes. Please, allow me to invite to the stage Mrs. Silvana Babaeva."

Hearing her name, Silvana again felt nervous. She had never liked being the center of attention. Now she was going to stand in front of many people.

She slowly got up from her seat and moved toward the stage, trembling.

Calm down, Silvana, she muttered to herself.

She climbed onto the stage and approached the microphone. The audience applauded at the sight of the beautiful, confident woman before them.

"Good morning, dear guests. While some of us are overeating, buying expensive clothes, traveling, going to clubs, and enjoying our lives, many are being abused and rejected, crying for help. Too many of us ignore this cry for help and purposely close our eyes. Consequently, many children die from physical abuse. Some teenagers commit suicide because of bullying in the schools."

Silvana paused for a minute and peered at the audience. Their curious eyes stared at her as they listened to her speech.

"These people suffer because of the negligence of our society, as well as social distrust and ignorance. How long will we continue to be selfish and pretend that we don't see the suffering of others? We, as one big caring family, must unite and say 'no more' to abuse, 'no' to bullying.

"You deserve to be happy, respected, loved, and to live in a healthy environment. You didn't come into this world to be abused or treated as a slave. Your purpose on this earth is to be a good mother, a leader, and a loving wife. Therefore, stop exposing your children to any form of abuse by allowing them to witness it. Instead, get the hell out of the abuse now! You have to show a good example to your children by being a strong, loving, caring, kind human being, who can say no to abuse!"

She paused, took in a deep, calming breath, and continued talking.

"Do you know that when someone gets emotionally abused, it affects the person's whole personality? The victims lose self-confidence, suffer from low- esteem, and even develop depression, anger, and anxiety. Their depression makes them see everything on the dark side. This affects their thoughts, behavior, and even eating and sleeping habits. Because people misunderstand these warning signs, they reject the abuse or refuse to believe.

"Some wonder why these women stay with abusive partners and blame them for taking the abuse. Actually, it is because the victims of abuse live in fear, afraid to struggle alone. They are financially dependent on their partners or have no place to go. They also don't want to leave their children without basic needs. Abuse affects these souls so much that they believe that they don't deserve anything good. They lose all faith in their abilities. They also wonder why God deserted them.

"I am a living testimony of God's love towards us; I myself an abuse survivor. Today I'm here to testify that God did not abandon you. He has delivered me from my suffering and will deliver you.

"Some abuse victims still love their partners and don't wish to break up their marriage. If that is you, talk to your partner about his or her behavior, and visit a counselor together. Tell them how it affects you and your children's lives, and ask the partner to change. If he or she changes his or her behavior in a positive direction, then you can stay and work on your marriage. However, if there are no changes, do not submit yourself to his or her sinful actions by staying with an abuser. In this case, get educated, find a job, and start saving money. Then get out of the abuse."

Silvana paused and looked at the audience with a smile on her face. She felt joy in her heart, knowing that she was doing something positive.

"If you desire to change your life," she continued, "then you need to get rid of your fears and become an active change agent, because inaction is your worst enemy. Don't let your fears keep you from a better life. Face them by accepting the challenges with a smile on your face. Stand up for yourself, not by fighting back, but by leaving negativity behind. Don't be afraid to remain alone, to make mistakes, or to ask for a help. Everyone makes mistakes and learns from them. You are not alone; God is with you, and there are good people ready and willing to help. Just reach out to them.

"After considering the pros and cons of your situation, go ahead and move forward with your life by removing yourself and your children from abuse! However, I must warn you, it won't be easy. But you will survive on your own. Your children will be fine once you are a loving and protective parent.

"We live this life only once, so let it not be wasted. Live your lives meaningfully and keep good morals and values. How can you live your life in a meaningful fashion if you are abused, hurt, depressed, and angry?"

"That's right!" shouted someone from the audience.

"So, get out of the abuse and lead your life to the fullest, doing what makes you and your children happy. If you enjoy singing, dancing, painting, or traveling, then do it. Remember, everything is achievable with God in your life. Once you have faith, keep praying and put every effort into achieving your goals."

As Silvana spoke, more people entered the conference room. She paused to drink some water.

"Parents, protect your children," she continued. "Know where they go and who they talk to. Learn how to recognize the signs of abuse or bullying. If the bullying in their school does not stop, transfer your child to another school.

"This world is full of child molesters. Don't leave your kids unattended, and monitor their Internet activities. Make sure you can trust the people you leave your children with—even relatives. Most important, give them all of your love, along with a good education. If a child grows up feeling unloved, as a needy adult they will select a partner who may be an abuser. Remember, your child will be a product of the efforts that you yourself have put into their life, along with the lifestyle you have lived. In addition, a good education will help them to be productive and to have a better future.

"It is time for you to make some changes in how you think, act, and see or accept things around you. Don't allow anyone to put you down, push you around, delay your development, or take advantage of you. You are not a bad person. You deserve the best. Think positively, and believe in your abilities and strength. Most importantly, put all your hopes, worries, and pain in God's hands while making steps to bring good changes into your life. Your faith in God and in the possibility of everything, as well as positive thoughts, will attract positive experiences. You will be more motivated to make the needed steps. Your faith will lessen your frustration and depression.

"Now, please stand up and repeat after me: 'In the name of the Lord, I declare that I can do everything that is right and good. I'm not alone or rejected anymore. With God's blessing, I'm going to make every step to change my life. I will achieve my goals, be who I would like to be, and have a happy life'."

Silvana again paused and looked at the audience. She suddenly realized that, if it hadn't been for her negative life experiences, she wouldn't be able to understand their pain, and wouldn't be standing on the stage that day.

"Now repeat these words, please," she said.

"I'm beautiful, healthy, and intelligent. I deserve to be happy, respected, loved, and understood. I'm a good mother, leader, wife, friend, husband, or father. I forgive those who hurt me. I allow God to enter into my life, heal all my wounds, and lead me on the right path. If any negative thoughts, frustration, or anger enters my mind or heart, I will chase it away and replace it with positive thoughts. I won't dwell on my past hurts anymore. I will move forward and take with me only good memories. Moreover, if bad memories return to me, they won't affect me anymore, in the name of the Lord."

Once the audience had finished repeating her words, Silvana continued, "Thank you very much for following my instructions. You can sit down."

Silvana felt content and hoped that her listeners could share in her happiness.

"Now please try to relax. Close your eyes. Imagine that you are in a beautiful garden surrounded by beautiful flowers and angels. Listen to the soothing song of angels praising the Lord. Repent and ask God for forgiveness and healing. Let go of all of your worries, anxieties, addiction, fears, and pain. See how they all leave you. Now imagine that God sends you healing, and fills you with love, peace, joy, grace, and forgiveness. He loves you. He is here for you. Visualize your future, and believe that you will receive it from God. Thank the Lord for every little blessing."

She gazed at the audience and smiled, thankful to God for all of her negative experiences, because they had made her who she was now. They taught her to love and understand people.

Silvana paused and took a sip of water. She wiped sweat from her face and continued talking.

"Now you can open your eyes." She looked out onto the faces turned up toward her. "You must also learn to love yourself, but not in a selfish or ignorant way. Loving yourself means that you do what is good for your health and wellbeing while staying humble and kind towards others. Make sure that you have built a good relationship with God, and live a righteous life by following God's Commandments. Without believing in God, you will not reach Paradise, either in this life or in the future. The Kingdom of God lies within you! Search for it, and everything in your present life will fall into place like pieces of a jigsaw puzzle."

She took a deep breath and finished her speech: "It was my pleasure to speak here before you. Thank you very much for your attention and patience."

Silvana walked away from the stage as the audience clapped loudly.

When the conference was finished, a reporter from Women's Power magazine approached Silvana and asked her to give an interview. Silvana arranged a meeting for Tuesday morning. Before walking back to her hotel, she decided to use the bathroom. On the way, a short, slim woman approached her.

"Miss Babaeva, can I ask you a question, please?" she asked, looking shyly at the ground.

Silvana stopped and moved to the side. "Yes," she said.

"I listened to your speech. It was very motivational. I came to this conference hoping to find a solution for my brother," stated the stranger.

"What happened to him?"

"My brother is married to a ruthless woman. He has been taking abuse for a long while. We have been trying to help him to get out. He is unemployed, so he continues taking the abuse. He has put on weight and now sees himself as a fat, useless loser. I don't know what to do to help him." She rubbed her face and gave a long sigh.

"I understand your frustration. First, he needs to know that he is not a loser or a useless man. He has to stop finding comfort in food. Instead, he must find it in God and in prayer. Once he builds a good relationship with God and develops the habit of continual prayer, he will be filled with God's grace, which will help him to deal with his situation.

"However, he should make steps to fight the adverse effects of abuse, and to bring positive changes into his life. For example, when he gets stressed out, he should go for a walk. This will reduce his stress right away and help him lose weight. Once he loses weight, he will feel good about himself. While he is getting thinner, he should continue applying for jobs and enrolling in courses to acquire new skills."

"But he does not believe in himself. He thinks nobody will even want him," said the woman with a faint smile.

"He has God by his side. He does not need anybody else in order to be happy. He must learn to love and respect himself, with all of his faults. He needs to know that he can survive on his own without his wife's material things. Once he makes small changes, looks after himself, and has healthy eating habits, his image about himself will change. I'm sure women will love him for who he is.

"However, he needs to make those steps to get out of the abuse and get a job. Please tell him to stop holding onto material things, but fight for peace of mind and freedom from abuse instead. 'Fighting' means getting a job and changing his life, with positive steps.

"Most importantly, he must first address his partner. One never knows, but perhaps after mediation and counseling, both of them might change in such a way that the marriage could work once again, as it had in the beginning."

The lady smiled gratefully. "Thank you very much for your valuable advice."

"You're welcome," answered Silvana.

The woman walked on, and Silvana strolled toward the bathroom.

As she was washing her hands in the bathroom, she heard sobbing.

She went over to the stall door where the crying was coming from. "Are you okay?" she asked.

The sobbing increased.

"Do you need any help?"

"No, thank you," came the tear-filled answer.

"You are still crying. You will feel better if you talk to someone," insisted Silvana.

A young woman opened the door and came out. She looked too skinny, and had sunken eyes.

"Thank you for your concern," said the woman with a faint smile.

"You're welcome."

The young woman splashed her eyes with water, and then glanced at Silvana again. She recognized her as a guest speaker for the seminar.

"Are you Silvana, who spoke today about abuse?" she asked with curiosity.

"Yes, I am."

"My name is Yasmin. I'm originally from Iran, but my husband is an American Muslim. We live here. I attended this seminar to find a solution to my problems. Hearing your speech brought back all my pain."

Silvana felt sorry for Yasmin and wanted to help her, with good advice at the very least.

"The bathroom is not a good place to speak. If you would like to talk about what worries you, let's go to the lobby," she suggested.

They left the bathroom and strode toward the lobby area. As soon as they sat down in the armchairs there, Silvana said, "Please tell me what worries you."

"I'm going through the divorce process. It is affecting me," explained Yasmin.

"Why are you divorcing?" asked Silvana.

"My husband was always hitting me."

"Why?" Silvana asked, sitting up taller.

"He is a man who likes everything his way. If I didn't suit myself to his likes, he would hit me. He also was angry with me because I couldn't get pregnant, and wouldn't wear the hijab. The last time he hit me, it was because I left the house without asking his permission. He used a piece of iron that time."

As Yasmin was talking, Silvana could see her pain and fear.

Yasmin continued, "I got a few stitches on my head and reported it to the police. After that, I applied for a divorce."

"Hmm. Did he ever go for a check-up to determine if a medical condition on his part kept you from getting pregnant?"

"No, he never went for a check-up. He and his mother blamed me and mocked me for being childless." Yasmin removed a tissue from her purse and wiped her eyes.

"This divorce process is affecting me. I don't have anyone to support me. He has been threatening me ever since I applied for a divorce. However, my parents keep asking me to stay and pray for him to change because in our Muslim culture, people look down on divorced women. I started getting more depressed and my heart filled with anger. A few days ago, after his last visit, I was so desperate that I almost took my life," continued Yasmin with a sigh.

Silvana was moved by the tears that ran down Yasmin's face.

"In your situation, you shouldn't care what people think. Do what is good for your well-being. You will never please everyone. Some people will always talk behind your back. This is their nature, and that can't be changed."

Silvana shook her head. "You can't commit suicide. Your whole life is ahead of you."

"I don't want to die, but I can't control my thoughts when I'm depressed. During that time, I feel disheartened and don't have the will to live. Nobody is even there to comfort me." Yasmin started crying, and rubbed her face with her hands. Some people in the lobby stared at her.

Her story reminded Silvana of her own suffering. She sighed as she sorted through her memories.

"I know how it feels to be hurt, to be without supportive people around. However, I must tell you that there are some good people out there. You will meet them, as I did."

She grasped Yasmin's hand. "Please stop crying. Everything will be fine," she pleaded, feeling Yasmin's pain. She had felt the same way when she was married to Mark.

"Depression is a serious condition that needs to be dealt with before it pushes you to commit suicide. It is sometimes caused by imbalances in the brain, but your depression is situational. It may go away once you leave the situation, but in both cases, it needs medical attention. You need to talk to your doctor. He or she may prescribe medication, advise a change to your lifestyle and diet, or ask you to get involved in activities that make you happy and relaxed. Daily exercising will lessen your depression and stress level," Silvana told her.

"Thank you for your advice. I will make an appointment next week," said Yasmin with a faint smile.

She covered her face with her hands. "My heart is so full of anger that I don't know how to get rid of it."

"You must learn to forgive as you heal. Without forgiveness, anger won't go away. Most important, don't dwell on past hurts, but think about your bright future. As soon as anger comes, chase it away by replacing it with love or happy thoughts. At the same time, ask God to help you forgive and heal. Also surround yourself only with good, encouraging people."

Yasmin listened to every word. Speaking to Silvana helped her to see things in a different way. It seemed to her that Silvana clearly understood her situation. She, in the past, had been full of anger as well. It had taken a long while for her to forgive those who had misunderstood her, lied, hurt her, or tried to take advantage of her kindness.

Silvana looked at her watch. She got up and said, "Yasmin, please accept my apology, but I have to leave. Don't worry, your life will change. Just keep staying positive and strong. Have faith in God."

Yasmin got up too. "I'm happy that I was able to talk to you. Now I know for sure that I'm on the right path. Thank you very much," she said with a smile.

"You're welcome," replied Silvana.

After talking to Yasmin, Silvana felt tired, and walked back to the hotel. She spent the rest of the day in her room, reading and watching a show.

Early on Tuesday morning she took a shower, and got dressed. At 9:50 a.m., the phone in her room rang.

"Mrs. Babaeva, the reporter from Women's Power Magazine is waiting for you in the lobby," said a male voice over the phone.

"Please tell her I will be downstairs shortly. Thank you."

She hung up the phone and left the room.

When Silvana entered the lobby, a tall blond reporter approached her.

"Good morning, Silvana. My name is Angelina. I hope you don't mind answering a few questions."

"Good morning. I will gladly answer all of your questions." Silvana smiled.

They walked toward the sitting area and sat in the armchairs. The reporter took out a recorder from her bag.

"Is it okay if I record our conversation?" asked Angelina.

"Yes, go ahead."

The reporter turned on the recorder and asked her first question.

"Silvana, where are you from originally?"

"I'm from Azerbaijan."

"Is it true that you have been married to an abusive man and you left him?"

"Yes, it is."

"How long were you married?"

"I was married for about 15 years."

"Wow, that is a long time! How did you dispel your fears and break the chains that shackled you?"

"Several factors led me to the gates of my freedom after cycles of abuse. Above all, my journey has made me appreciate that, although I have been a sinner like everyone else, I have repented by loving myself in a fashion that has propelled me beyond the cage of selfishness. The fact is that I do not need anyone's love to be happy. When you love yourself, you don't let anyone hurt you and maintain control over you. You make choices that are good for you and your children. When you dislike yourself, people denigrate and disrespect you, which only serves to attract negativity into your life.

"I also realized that dwelling on my ongoing pain and on my painful past was only sending negative energy into the universe, thereby producing more negativity. I focused on what I wanted in life by controlling my thoughts and by keeping them positive by believing in an advantageous outcome. I began visualizing my future career and its relationship to my life, as if such a career was already a component of my life.

"The most enlightening aspects of my success were not only the strength of my faith in God, but also the reinforcement of God's command over all my worries, and praying daily. God is the root of our lives that nurtures us; therefore, all of our intentions must be directed toward Him. Only under God's grace was I able to rid myself of frustration and fury, and to forgive. Instead of allowing my fears to control me, I have accepted them by deciding to face whatever comes my way. Moreover, seeing how abuse affected my life and future, I decided to put an end to it."

"What are your future plans?"

"I'm hoping to continue empowering women, to help them escape from abuse and become independent. To achieve this goal, I'm planning to open The Garden of Hope and Faith, an NGO Foundation."

The reporter made a few more notes, then smiled at Silvana. "Thank you for answering all my questions."

"You're welcome," replied Silvana with a big smile on her own face.

The reporter turned off the recorder.

"Silvana, I have enjoyed speaking with you. Thank you for making this interview interesting. I wish you success in everything you do," said Angelina as she got up from her seat.

"It was my pleasure talking to you."

"Bye," said Angelina.

"Bye-bye," answered Silvana, relieved that the interview was over.

Silvana went back to her room and started packing her clothes. In the evening, she boarded a plane for home, and landed in Canada the next morning.

After leaving the airport, she took a taxi. She was supposed to have arrived home a day later, but Silvana had decided to change her flight. However, she hadn't told Andrew, hoping to surprise him and the children. She was very exhausted, but at the same time felt happy, thinking that soon she would see her husband and her children.

As she rode toward home in the taxi, Silvana thought about her life, failures and achievements. She was happy with the latest surprising changes in her life. After suffering for so long, she had finally gained everything she needed for a happy and peaceful existence. She had married the loving gentleman of her dreams, and along with everything else, had been able to open a restaurant, which she had named Exotica.

The events of her whole life showed that there was indeed a light at the end of the dark tunnel. With God's presence in her life, she was able to leave the darkness and find the light.

After forty minutes, the taxi entered her gated community. It passed a lake and many trees before it approached a tall gate.

"Madame, would you like me to drive in or stop here?" asked the taxi driver, interrupting Silvana's thoughts.

"Please stop right here." She didn't want Andrew to hear the sound of an approaching car, so she had decided to get off in front of the gate.

Silvana opened it with a remote control. The driver removed her bags and put them in her yard. She paid the driver and strolled toward her house, leaving her luggage on the ground. While walking, she gazed around and smelled the scent of the beautiful red, yellow and pink roses growing in the yard.

Silvana stopped by a small fountain. She looked at the statue of the angel, and took a deep breath of the fresh air. There was peace and joy in her heart.

Jesus Son of God , it is so good to be home, to have a roof to live under and to be surrounded by beautiful nature.

She looked at her house. It was as big as a mansion, with large windows. Painted a gorgeous blue color, it had a huge porch where Silvana entertained her guests. The house had one big kitchen, nine huge bedrooms with bathrooms, a huge living room, a gym, and a study hall. Even though material things didn't motivate her, she was happy to have this house. She had enough space for her mother, stepfather, and granny to live in.

As Silvana approached her front door, she heard Andrew and the children giggling. Instead of going to the front door, Silvana walked around the house and peeped through the windows inside.

Andrew was sitting on the big sofa surrounded by the children. All of them were looking at the TV and giggling. Seeing them chuckling, Silvana smiled. Andrew always made Silvana laugh.

"Father, can you do something funny like that man on TV?" Marie asked happily, chuckling.

Andrew walked around the room and made sounds like a monkey. The children laughed again.

Silvana looked at her old granny, Sadaget, who sat by herself in an armchair, complaining. As usual, she was wearing her old sunglasses. She was now completely blind.

"Why are you making so much noise? I'm getting a headache," she said in Russian, her wrinkled hands shaking. When she was angry, she preferred to speak in Russian, instead of Azeri.

Andrew came up to her and made her get up. "Come on, Granny, have fun with us and stop grumbling."

"Esmira, where are you? Please take me back to my room," Sadaget called out.

Seeing her resistance, Andrew stopped bothering her.

"Father, Granny does not like noise. Please leave her alone before she starts cussing," said Aygun.

Andrew came up to Sadaget again and gave her a kiss on her forehead.

"Who kissed me?" Sadaget asked with annoyance in her voice.

"Babushka ya tebya lublyu," said Andrew in Russian.

"I love you too," she answered in broken English, with a broad smile. She got up and moved her hands in the air, trying to hug Andrew.

"Where is my Andrew?" she asked in Russian.

Seeing her hands moving in the air, Silvana's husband approached her again. Sadaget hugged him.

"Andrew, you are like the son that I never had. Thank you for making these children and my Silvana happy."

Peter got up from his seat. "Guys, let's play a game. I will show you some movements and you tell me who am I."

"Okay," answered Aygun.

Peter lay down on the floor, which had a beautiful cream-colored carpet with a leopard pattern. He slithered on the floor like a snake.

"You are a caterpillar," guessed Aygun.

"No," answered Peter.

"Snake," said David.

"Yes, you got it," Peter said joyfully.

Silvana walked to the kitchen window, smelling food. She peered inside and saw Esmira standing by the stove, stirring something. As usual, her mother looked fashionable; today she was wearing a black skirt and red top.

Silvana recalled the days when she regretted that Esmira was her mother. Thinking about those regrets, Silvana felt ashamed. She realized that her whole view of Esmira had been wrong. She may not have spent enough time with Silvana, but she had devoted most of her time to work in order to give her children food and clothes. Silvana was happy to know that she was in her life.

Esmira's young husband, Vusal, approached her from behind and kissed her on the neck. She pushed him gently away.

"Not now. I'm cooking."

Silvana walked back to the TV room's window and gazed at those whom she loved the most. Seeing all her family brought tears of joy to her eyes. She felt so happy and peaceful.

Father, I have been hurt, and felt so lonely in a strange country. However, you have given me everything that I need. Look at my children and my husband. They are in my life, and happy. I'm so pleased to have my mom and Granny living in my house. Thank you for giving me all these blessings.

After finishing her prayer, Silvana dried her tears and went to the front of the house. She opened the door.

"Hello, guys. I'm back," she said, all in smiles.

Everyone froze, surprised to see her home a day early.

"Who came? Silvana, is that you?" asked Sadaget.

Andrew came up to Silvana and hugged her as he smiled. "Baby, I didn't expect to see you today."

The children rushed towards their mother.

"I decided to surprise you by coming home a day earlier."

"Silvana, is that you?" Sadaget asked again, turning to her side.

"Yes, Granny, it is me."

Silvana hugged the children and then Granny.

"Silvana, your kids are not letting me rest. They are so noisy that I'm getting a headache," said Sadaget, trying to sound like a little child who needed attention. Granny's complaint made Silvana smile, because she knew Sadaget's intent.

Silvana kissed Granny on her forehead lovingly. "Granny, just ignore them please."

Then she sat on the sofa. Andrew and the children joined her.

"Baby, how was your speech?"

"It was successful. Can you believe that, after the speech, many women approached me! I was interviewed too," Silvana said, with excitement in her voice.

"Wow, that's magnificent. I'm so sorry that I wasn't there to hear your speech."

"How could you be there if you stayed here to look after the children?" Silvana asked in a gentle voice. She wanted to kiss him, but didn't want to do so in front of the children.

She leaned back against the sofa. "I feel so tired from the trip. I could close my eyes and fall asleep right now."

"Sweetheart, put your head on my shoulder and close your eyes. Guys, Mother is tired. Let's all close our eyes for a few minutes and sit quietly," suggested Andrew.

Silvana followed his instructions. She felt so loved and peaceful with her head on his shoulder, surrounded by her family. Her husband was so caring and loving that he made her happy every day. Whenever she was sick, he made sure that she was well taken care of, and would never leave her alone at home.

As she sat next to him and dwelled on her happiness, Silvana caught herself thinking about Mark. She wondered if Mark had finally found joy and peace in his heart. After all, he worked hard to give us a comfortable life. He deserves forgiveness, Silvana thought.

She got up from the sofa and asked Andrew to go get the luggage that she had left by the gate. He brought her two suitcases in and put them in the bedroom.

Even though she was tired from her flight, Silvana unpacked her luggage and took out the gifts she had bought. Esmira got a nice black top with a bracelet, Sadaget was given pajamas. Each of the children got new clothes. However, for Andrew, Silvana had bought a beautiful gold chain with an Orthodox Crucifix.

He hugged Silvana with a grateful smile. "Darling, you know I don't need expensive gifts. You and the children are my precious gifts."

"I know, but I was reminded that you had lost your crucifix when I saw this one, so I knew it was for you."

"Thank you, honey," said Andrew, kissing Silvana on her lips.

His kissing aroused Silvana. She kissed him passionately.

He pulled back and smiled. "Wait. You're tired, remember? Lay down for a little while," he said.

Silvana put on her nightdress and lay down on the bed. After a while, she fell asleep.

Andrew made sure that no one disturbed Silvana while she slept.

The next day, Silvana and her husband went to their Exotica restaurant.

She greeted the manager with a smile. "Good morning, Afag. How is everything going here?"

"Good morning, Mrs. Babaeva. Everything is fine. We have received a few orders, and our chef is working to fill them," said Afag.

The manager removed a white envelope from her pocket. "This is for you."

Silvana glanced at the envelope and took it from Afag. Then she took a piece of paper out of her bag.

"Afag, please send this recipe to the kitchen. I would like this cake baked tonight and offered to our customers as a sample. Starting next week, we are going to have it on our menu."

Afag gave a short nod, and handed over the paper to a member of the wait staff, who carried it to the kitchen.

"Please let the chef know that tonight we are having an Arabic night," Silvana continued. "I expect a mixed variety of food, such as Greek, Turkish, and Arabic. Please don't forget to call the belly dancer. I would like to hire her for two hours for tonight."

"At what time do you want the belly dancer to be here?" asked Afag.

"Seven p.m. is fine."

Afag nodded once more and went to the kitchen.

Tarhana, the cleaner, approached Silvana. "Good morning, Mrs. Babaeva. What would you like me to do today?" she asked with a faint smile.

Silvana gazed around. "As you know, I'm a perfectionist, so my restaurant has to shine. Please walk around and make sure that the floor, walls, doors, and windows are spotless." She gave Tarhana a firm but friendly smile. "I would appreciate it if, in the future, you wouldn't ask me what to do. You know your duties and what is expected from you. Just follow them and keep the restaurant perfectly clean, please."

The cleaner left to follow Silvana's instructions. From her previous experience, she knew that even a little dirty spot couldn't escape Silvana's eyes.

"Darling, what would you like me to do?" asked Andrew with a smile, looking at the envelope in Silvana's hand.

"Thanks for asking, but I will manage on my own. You need to rush to your office," said Silvana in a gentle voice.

He looked at his watch. "You're right. Bye, honey." He kissed Silvana on the lips and left.

After allocating tasks to everyone, Silvana went into her office.

This private space had cream-colored walls. On the large dark-brown desk were her wedding picture and her children's photos. On one wall hung icons of Mary, St. Nektarios, and Jesus.

She sat in her soft, dark-brown armchair and looked at the icons with a warm smile. Then her attention turned to the envelope.

Silvana opened it slowly and removed a folded piece of paper from it. While she unfolded it, a cheque fell out on the table.

Silvana lifted the cheque and, upon seeing the amount paid to her name, dropped it on the desk in shock.

One million dollars!!

With trembling hands, she opened the letter and read it.

"Dear Silvana, I have read the article about your plans to open The Garden of Hope and Faith, a charitable organization that would help the victims of abuse. In order to help you with your purpose, I am donating this amount. I hope your organization will grow and become a voice against abuse.

Regards,

Abuse Survivor B.J."

With her hands shaking, Silvana placed both the cheque and the letter back in the envelope. She was not only astounded but also excited that her dream of transforming the lives of those who find themselves in helpless and forlorn states was coming true.

Tears of joy fell on her desk, at the same time that her heart raced like a speeding jet preparing to take flight.

After all, tomorrow will be a new and better day for both me and those I am rescuing! Silvana whispered to herself.

She got up and left the room in a rush. Lying ahead of her was more to do than she could grasp or fathom.

***

Thank you for taking the time to read *Broken Chains*. If you enjoyed reading it, I would appreciate it if you could leave a review on Amazon and Goodreads. Your reviews make a difference!

Acknowledgement

I would like to thank all those who have shared, not only their positive, but also their negative life experiences with me, including emotional and sexual abuse, domestic violence, bullying, stigmatization, and other problems that trouble many families. My dear friends, your lives have inspired me to write this novel entitled Broken Chains. I would like to express my heartfelt gratitude to my freelance and independent editors: Kathy Ree, and Brian Harvey for helping to shape my manuscript. Brian sincerely believed in my talent and supported me in my career, not only as a fiction and nonfiction writer but also as a motivational speaker and blogger. Finally, thank you, Lord, for guiding and supporting me, and transforming my existence into life!

Autobiography

Emiliya Ahmadova was born in the city of Baku, the capital of Azerbaijan. Emiliya is a loving, and spiritual person, devoted to the well-being of other people. She developed a passion for reading, literature, poetry, and foreign languages.

Emiliya has diplomas in business management, as well as a Bachelor of Arts (B.A.) in human resources management. She also has International diplomas in the advanced study of the theory and practice of management, administration and business management, communications, hotel operations management, office management and administration, and Professional English from the Cambridge International College, in addition to a certificate in novel-writing.

Emiliya likes being around people, adores travel, enjoys playing soccer, and relishes helping other people. She has written A Hell For All Seasons (mystery) and My Twin Sister and Me (children's book).

During her lifetime, she has encountered a variety of female friends who have been physically and verbally abused as children or adults. Some of them had been neglected, had childhood traumas, or ended up in relationships with abusive, controlling men. Knowing that these people were unconsciously crying for help but that no one was there to help them or hear their voices, she felt and understood their pain and witnessed their hopelessness, frustration, fears, disappointment, and isolation.

In writing Broken Chains, Emiliya seeks not only to depict other people's struggles and dilemmas but also to give a voice to those who are in the same situation. She also wants to show that there is always hope and light even in the loneliness of darkness. Emiliya sincerely hopes that this novel will assist other people to get their lives on a positive track, the way that her protagonist Silvana did.

Thus, beyond the fictional world, she emerges as a global voice and motivational speaker for combating abuse in all its incarnations.

Glossary

1. Khanum means Miss or Mrs. and is a respectful form of address for women in Azerbaijan.

2. Nard is a table-style board game for two players only in which the playing pieces are moved by rolls of the dice.

3. Tasbeeh-Beads.

4. Kishi is an Azeri word referring to a man.

5. Chayhana refers to a small restaurant where people can drop in to order a spot of tea or a nibble of food or a snack.

6. Muallim is used when one addresses a person who is a teacher by his or her first name. It is viewed as an honorific or considerate form of addressing anyone in Azerbaijan.

7. Kaaba is a building at the center of the Al-Masjid Al-Haram mosque in Mecca.

8. Babushka- granny.

9. Bey-Mister is used with the first name of any male in Azerbaijan and elsewhere throughout Central Asia as a sign of respect.

10. Matushka is an Orthodox priest's wife.

Books by Emiliya

A Hell For All Seasons features seven bone-chilling short stories that span the globe, inviting you to partake in a spine-tingling supernatural adventure that you'll not soon forget.
Inside you'll discover what happens when unsuspecting schoolgirls, strait-laced physicians, a swash-buckling cowboy, selfish hypocrites, a drunkard, female medium, and ordinary university students encounter their worst nightmares.

What have they done to spark supernatural phenomena?
Bad choices and bad timing come to haunt them in earth-shattering ways to teach them a much-needed, if not ill-guided lesson, filled with moments of terror, hours of chaos, and years of regret.

'This is a worthy collection of great stories for horror aficionados with an imaginative and clever title that accurately reflects the book's content, and I would highly recommend horror lovers go looking for it.'
Brian O'Hare, author of *Fallen Men*

'Ms. Ahmadova has done a terrific job of relating small but very meaningful stories. Every one of them is a frightening world unto itself, and all of them are very worth reading. Highly recommended for aficionados of short horror stories.'
K.R. Morrison, author of Be Not Afraid and UnHoly Trinity
***

My Twin Sister and Me, written by an ex-Scout leader, is a story that introduces children to Scouting in Venezuela.
 Glue on the windowsill and toothpaste in the shoes. Who did the deed?
Twelve-year-old Cub Scout twins Julieta and Rafaela have to deal with their older sister's ugly tricks, which get them into trouble.
At school, Julieta is being mocked for the freckles on her face and her crooked teeth. Forgetting her own plight, however, she stands up to a bully, Claudius, in order to protect her friend Montano from being persecuted. Out of kindness she agrees to go to the movie with

Montano. Due to situations beyond her control, it ends up being an embarrassment in more ways than one. However, once again, she stands up for Montano.

Another time, their Uncle David surprises the family by flying from his home in the US to Caracas for a visit. His visit causes worry; something is wrong. Julieta faces her fears in order to save her ill uncle in the middle of the night. After saving him, she becomes a hero in the uncle's eyes.

The Scouts plan to attend a Jamboree in Russia, and the girls get caught up in the planning and carrying out of various schemes to pay for the adventure.

This book not only introduces children to Scouting, but also teaches them values, morals, kindness, and faith. My Twin Sister and Me shows how to manage anger, face one's fears, the importance of self-respect, and how to deal with bullying. Above all, it helps kids learn how to show kindness to others.

Oh--and very importantly: how to have fun.

***

Caribbean Tears: Sheila is kidnapped and shipped to Venezuela, where she is sold to a brothel owned by a woman by the name of Bernadette. There her nightmare begins, as she is forced into prostitution. She is tormented nightly by the brutal Victor, who is Bernadette's lover and the brothel's supervisor. Despite her daily tortures, Sheila keeps hoping for escape. She befriends the other women at the brothel, including a teenage girl, who benefit from her positive outlook.

Will Sheila be able to escape her nightmare and get her life back?

Printed in Great Britain
by Amazon